Solomon's Gold

Also by Leonard Tourney

Elizabethan murder mysteries
The Players' Boy is Dead
Low Treason
Familiar Spirits
The Bartholomew Fair Murders
Old Saxon Blood
Knaves Templar
Witness of Bones
Frobisher's Savage
Time's Fool
Catesby's Ghost
The Conjurer's Daughter
Falstaff's Murder

Doctor William Gilbert mysteries
The Kindness of Witches
The Cuckold's Bride
Solomon's Gold

A DOCTOR WILLIAM GILBERT MYSTERY

SOLOMON'S
Gold

LEONARD TOURNEY

LUME BOOKS
A JOFFE BOOKS COMPANY

LUME BOOKS
A JOFFE BOOKS COMPANY

Lume Books, London
A Joffe Books Company
www.lumebooks.co.uk

Copyright © Leonard Tourney 2023

The right of Leonard Tourney to be identified as author of this work has been asserted in accordance with the Copyright, Designs and Patents Act 1988.

This book is a work of fiction. Names, characters, businesses, organisations, places and events are either the product of the author's imagination or are used fictitiously. Any resemblance to actual persons, living or dead, events or locales is entirely coincidental. The spelling used is British English except where fidelity to the author's rendering of accent or dialect supersedes this.

We love to hear from our readers!
Please email any feedback you have to: feedback@joffebooks.com

Cover images © Shutterstock

ISBN: 978-1-83901-561-8

To the Coggeshalls of Halstead, Essex; forebears.

Men of acute intelligence, without actual knowledge of facts, and in the absence of experiment, easily slip and err.

William Gilbert, *De Magnete, 1600*

Prologue

Thames Estuary, 1290 A.D.

It is Year of Grace, 1290. Edward, the first of that name, is England's king. He orders the Jews expelled from the land, both to please the Pope but even more himself, for he hungers after their wealth that he may pay his debts and get the nobility off his back; for them, the Jews are a loathsome plague upon the land. Besides, he believes Jews undermine the virtue of a Christian nation, even those who say they have converted to the true faith.

Or so the king claims, and his word must not be doubted or controverted.

There are also stories about the Jews, terrifying stories. How they sacrifice Christian children, how they perform satanic rituals, how they conspire to take over the world.

And it is for that reason that the boy—Jacob Silva, aged eleven—along with his mother and father, his younger sister, and seventy others of his tribe, have boarded a vessel to go to France where they hope to resettle and worship the Lord God of Israel without impediment. They have taken with them all their worldly goods, and these have been stowed in the hold of the ship; securely, according to the shipmaster, a gaunt-faced man who looks like a fasting cleric, or perhaps a retired pirate. That long, livid scar on his right cheek looks like a battle scar and is a warning to his crew: *disobey me at your peril.*

Now the tide is out, far out, and the ship rests in the mud and sand of the estuary, awaiting refloating, which the captain says will occur before dawn. In the meantime, while it is still light, he invites his passengers,

Israelites all, to disembark and walk with him on the drying sand. The shipmaster says exercise is good for the body and the mind. Best go now, while the opportunity presents itself, he says cheerfully. He beckons them to follow him.

No one objects. He is, after all, the master of the vessel and for now their commander-in-chief. They climb down the ship's ladder and follow him. He walks forward confidently toward the sea, which is visible as a thin, blue line in the distance.

Jacob Silva is not the only child among them. There are dozens of others. They race ahead of their parents, fascinated by the lure of the distant water, something most of them have never seen; the sea. Their excitement is understandable, their energy infectious.

Parents call them back, bid them *be careful, don't slip or fall*. But there's no restraining them. They are children, already weary of the three day's confinement below deck in the dark, the cramped, poorly lit space, odoriferous, rat infested, a floating sepulchre. At least here in the open, the air is clear, the stink of rotting seaweed at least natural, the air invigorating with its freshness.

Parents scurry after the children to rein them in, looking toward the sea. They do not notice the captain has turned away, run back to the ship, climbed aboard, and watches them from the bow, bent forward like a second figurehead. They hardly notice that the tide has turned, that the sea is returning, rushing back to its place. It will presently lift the ship off the sand, that it may proceed to its destination; a port in France, a port in Holland or in Spain. History does not record which.

The tide's return is not slow and measured but rapid and voracious, as though it had a mind to regain ground at any cost. Before they know it, the passengers are knee-deep in water, struggling now to return to the ship. They are alarmed, beginning to realize their peril. They scream, the men as well as the women, dragging their children behind them and then hoisting them on their shoulders. Before they know it, the water is waist high.

All this has transpired in less than an hour. They call out to the shipmaster, who looks down on them from the deck like a gargoyle, or malevolent deity of some different, even more brutal world.

The rope ladder by which they descended has been drawn up. Shipmaster's orders.

Some of the men and a few of the women appeal to the shipmaster to give aid, to let them come aboard. *Have mercy*, they cry. *In God's holy name, have mercy. We shall drown, we and our children with us.*

But he mocks their misery, laughs cruelly. He calls down to them that they should remember Moses and his command that the Red Sea be parted so that the Israelites might cross on dry land. Perhaps God will perform the miracle a second time and save this small group of pilgrims. This is what the shipmaster says.

His words are like a sermon, the ship's bow his pulpit.

But Satan is the author of it, this perverse homily. He has written every word.

"Pray to your Hebrew god," the shipmaster cries, and behind him members of the crew stand looking down as well and snickering. Great fun, this. And don't the Jews deserve it for crucifying Christ?

The ship's hold is full of chests containing the Jews' wealth. Gold and silver cups and plate, jewels to wear upon one's fingers or hang around a neck, coins of a dozen nations, all discreetly tucked among cloaks and gowns and bed and table linen. The crew is mindful of that, as well.

There is no laughter among those struggling in the water. This is no laughing matter. There is crying rather, appealing not to the shipmaster now but to heaven. The ship rises with the tide as though lifted by divine decree. The sails are set. Overboard, the water is up to shoulders and necks. The tide rushes in even faster. It is diabolical. There is no miracle to be had on this terrible day.

The boy, Jacob, watches his parents struggle, moving their arms frantically, their faces struck with horror. He sees heads disappearing beneath the water, he sees his family drowning, his father, his mother, his little sister. The ship now moves toward the open sea, fully sailed, driven with what captain and crew consider a good wind.

Jacob is a thin, pale boy of eleven. Once, when he was eight, he fell into a pond. His feet could not touch the bottom. There was no one around to help. The water was cold and foul tasting. His heart seized with fear of drowning; he flailed his arms and kicked his feet, more in frustration and terror than intent to keep afloat or move toward the bank. In those desperate moments, he learned to swim. What else could he do, since the alternative was unthinkable to his young mind?

It was what he does now.

The ship, when aground, lay but a quarter of a mile from the shore. That is what he swims for, ignoring the cold of the water, waving his arms, kicking with his feet. He feels himself not only afloat but propelled forward, and the more he does it, the faster he moves. Success empowers him, as success will. He keeps his eyes fixed on the shore, which is distant at first, less so as the minutes pass.

He is numb from the cold, his strength failing, when he feels his feet touch the sandy bottom. Then he struggles forward, knee-deep, then ankle deep, exhausted, trying not to think about his mother and father, his young sister, or the others; strangers to him but fellows in faith and blood.

Of the company of exiles, Jacob Silva was the sole survivor, the sole witness. In years to come, he would remain in England, conceal his Jewish identity, and live to write the account of the experience that it might be recorded, that the angels might read it if no earthly man or woman did.

That God might punish those who committed the enormity.

It is the least he owes to his dead mother, his dead father, his dead sister, and the others, all so ruthlessly betrayed.

Years after, the esteemed Raphael Holinshed will mention the atrocity in his *Chronicles*, the magisterial history of early England. He will not mention the name of the captain, or that of his ship, or any of the passengers save to remark that they were Jews, rich Jews, sent into exile. He will not write that there was a survivor of the incident, a witness to bear testimony of it. He will not write what happened to the treasure of those wretched souls. He did not know.

One can imagine such things, make it the stuff of stories and dreams, plots and counterplots. Perhaps the ship sank and took crew and goods down with it, a parable of justice. Perhaps the treasure was taken up and hidden away, a lesson in avarice. Perhaps it was never touched for fear it was cursed, a cautionary tale. One can well imagine such a thing, in so wicked a world. We tell such stories to make sense of chaos.

In any case, it is no story for children. It might make them think less of mankind and despair at the triumph of evil.

The learned and much revered Holinshed will resolve none of these mysteries. But, of course, there are answers. Something happened to the

Jews' wealth, their coffers of silver and gold plate, their jewels and the sacred emblems of the faith.

They exist somewhere, as does the truth of what happened then and thereafter.

One

London, 1576

The message received by the young doctor was plain on its face, without dissimulation or sentiment, written in an awkward hand of one unaccustomed to writing and not anxious to improve his skill.

Your old Jew is dead. Hanged himself. Come, Doctor, see for yourself.

William knew the writer better than he wanted to. The warden of the *Domus Conversorum*, a residence for converted Jews in Chancery Lane. His dealings with the man had been unpleasant.

The note was brought to him at his house shortly after nine in the morning while he was in the midst of treating a patient. Because of the note, the doctor canceled his next appointment of the day, even though the patient was a wealthy silk merchant who had contributed generously to the Royal College of Physicians, of which the doctor was a member and an officer. He told his manservant where he was going and set out to walk the several streets to the Domus, where the man referred to as "the old Jew" resided or had resided, if the message received was true, and not some jest practiced upon him. It would not have been beyond the warden to do such a thing; he was a meanspirited fellow with a cruel streak and the breath of an East Cheap sewer.

The doctor's name was William Gilbert, and he was a young man in his early thirties, a graduate of Cambridge, and the son of a prominent lawyer and judge in Colchester, a town in Essex. He had been practicing in London for the past several years, where he quickly made a name for himself in medical circles and had become attending physician to several members of the queen's court.

His rise in that regard had been meteoric but not unaccompanied by tribulation and dangers, some of which had threatened his life and driven him at times into a near despair. His salvation in each case was his profound commitment to his profession and his work as a natural scientist. He was not only a physician but an investigator of the natural world and its operations, and most especially the physical properties and powers of magnets, which he held to be not only critical to the compass, that invaluable device of navigation, but also to an understanding of the structure of the Earth. He experimented constantly with his magnets, communicated with other learned men of like interests both in England and abroad, read widely and deeply, and aspired one day to collect his observations and the results of his experiments in a book, a book that would be written in Latin so that it could be universally read and approved.

He had already decided upon a title: *De Magnete*. It was not a title to attract common readers, but then it would be written for other scholars, a species that had a great tolerance for such things.

That worthy ambition, the writing of his book, he would indeed accomplish, but he could not know that then, as a young practitioner living in London in 1576. No one sees the future with such clarity or certainty. Not even the astrologers who believed, foolishly in William's mind, that the stars dictated the fortune of even the humblest of God's creatures.

It was a cold, gray morning, the air filled with the smoke of coal fires and the stench of sewage that ran down the gutters and poured from the windows and caused any number of diseases of which the inhabitants knew not the names, although they suffered from them. At such an hour the narrow London streets were busy as usual, crowded with wagons and carts, clattering over cobbles and potholes, as well as the usual troop of pedestrians and horsemen; no one, it seemed, was content to stay at home. William navigated the streets with skill and speed. He was a tall, thin man, dressed plainly in gray or dark doublet and hose and a modest white collar no wider than three or four inches. Smooth-faced and fair, he disdained the fancy dress of many of his class that made them look like peacocks on parade, aping the garb of the French or Italians, bejeweled as though they wore their whole income on their backs, perfumed as though they were above decent English sweat.

As the son of a well-to-do lawyer and judge, he was by birth a gentleman, a status he had strengthened by his Cambridge education and his professional attainments. He had no wife, nor children by mistresses or casual encounters, although he enjoyed the company of women and had once been so besotted with one that he would happily have died for her. She had married another and then died in childbirth. It was the tragedy of his young life, a lesson in the depth and duration of grief that he put to good use when he consoled the dying and their survivors. It was also a lesson in love—its frailty, its tentativeness—when he considered loving again.

He complied with current regulations regarding church attendance but was neither pious nor puritanical in his views. He held God, the Great Maker, as the author of the visible world as well as the invisible. He venerated Christ as a teacher of good morals and the author of salvation. He kept the holy days and feast days, obeyed the law, and honored the queen. In none of these practices was he extraordinary or exceptional.

He had a great many friends in the city and several significant connections at court. He was respected among his professional colleagues, trusted by his patients, beloved of his servants, and a good son to his father and stepmother.

William lived in a handsome house on Fleet Street with a fruitful orchard, garden, and stables. He was healthy and strong of limb, blessed with a loving and affluent father of whom he was eldest son and therefore heir. He had every reason to be content with his life, positive about his future, secure in his place in his world.

This was the state of his life on the morning he received word of the death of him whom the writer of the message had disdainfully called "the old Jew."

Two

Within minutes, he had arrived at his destination; a single building resembling more a church than a house, with a stubby crenelated tower at one end and clerestory windows on the single-story extension. This was the place in which Isaac Silva had resided ever since William had come to London and become his physician. It was a refuge set aside for converted Jews who—having had all their property confiscated—now were wards of the crown, given a modest stipend, and provided with simple lodging. The Domus, as it was commonly called, was presided over by a warden. In this case, a man named Simon Meredith, a paunchy, moon-faced man in his forties who had secured his position because he was somebody's brother-in-law. As William saw it, the man had little else to recommend him. It was Meredith, the impudent fellow, who had written the message about Isaac, about his hanging himself, and bidding William to come and see for himself, as though William might contest the fact otherwise.

As well William might. That Isaac should have taken his own life seemed most improbable to him. To William's mind, Isaac's conversion to Christianity was genuine, not just a fraud to achieve free food and lodging. Besides which, suicide was a cardinal sin, its punishment damnation. It was likewise condemned in the Jewish faith. He had not read the Talmud, the revered commentary on Jewish law, but Isaac had often spoken of it, sometimes cited it. Isaac Silva had converted to Christianity, but his conversion had not erased his memory of the faith of his youth, or caused him to discard the wisdom of the rabbis that did not contradict the words of Christ.

Besides, William had known men and women who had taken their own lives—because of mortal illness, despair, or sometimes just loneliness or boredom. Isaac Silva was not that kind. He was a sanguine man, good humored, not given to melancholy or self-loathing, a thinker, a scholar. Was he really dead? And by his own hand? It seemed impossible.

A porter answered the door and showed William into the warden's quarters, where he found Simon Meredith sitting by a fire warming his hands. Meredith looked up, recognized William, and then smiled. The man was missing several teeth, but so were most men of his age in England, a testimony to their fondness for sugar or reluctance to clean their teeth.

"Doctor, you've come. Good, sir. You shall presently discover that you've lost another patient, though not by your hands."

"I would think not," William said, trying to ignore the insult to his profession. "If as you have written, Master Silva has taken his own life. I assumed the note was from you and not some other person."

On William's earlier visits, Meredith had done little to hide his dislike of doctors. William supposed the warden had had some bad experience, or merely feared disease and death, twin evils that doctors would inevitably remind him of.

"Master Silva hanged himself?"

"Come see for yourself, Doctor."

"You didn't take the body down?"

"No, Doctor. I thought best to leave it where it hanged…that the cause of death might not be disputed."

"Very considerate of you, Master Meredith," William said with a heavy irony he didn't expect the warden to catch.

A corpulent man, the warden struggled to his feet and pointed to William the way, although Willian knew it well enough himself, having visited Isaac on a variety of occasions during the past year and become not only his physician but his friend. Isaac had studied medicine himself, although somewhere in Spain before returning to England to avoid the inquisition. He had been suffering heart palpitations for some time and because of his age, had been at risk of dying in his sleep.

"Did he leave a note, a letter, some writing explaining himself?"

"He left nothing, Doctor. His manner of death speaks for itself."

"Death rarely speaks for itself, Master Warden. And I warrant you, suicide never does."

10

* * *

It was a small, windowless room with white-washed walls, a high beamed ceiling, a single bed with a straw mattress, a modest fireplace and a box the size of a seaman's chest. On the wall above the bed was a crucifix; a standard adornment of all the living quarters in the Domus to remind its residents that although they might be Jews by birth, they were now Christians by baptism, saved by Christ's blood and the mercy of the queen.

From a rope secured to a hook in one of the beams hung Isaac Silva, age sixty or sixty-five by William's reckoning, his neck broken, his face covered with a dark bruise as though it had been dipped in malmsey. His eyes were open, his jaw dropped, his tongue extended. William shuddered, looked once and then turned away. As a physician, William was inured to the pale, ghastliness of death, the mockery of the living, the indignity of it. But this was something more, something worse. It wasn't only that he had known the man as a patient. Isaac had been a friend.

Behind him, Meredith said, "I told you, did I not?"

"You told me he was dead."

"I guess the old man renounced his new faith at last."

"How so?" William asked, although he knew what Meredith would say.

"Why, taking one's life is a mortal sin, is it not, Doctor? No decent Christian could do it."

"Nor Jew," William said. "Suicide is also against Jewish law, the Talmud forbids it."

The warden looked at him suspiciously. "Who is this Talmud?"

"It's a sacred book, a collection of writings of the rabbis, the Jewish law."

The warden considered this. "Then he was no Christian if he believed such things, read such a book, which I have no doubt is condemned as heretical by our learned clergy."

"It may be, but he read it before he converted."

"That makes little difference, if you ask me."

William would not think of asking him. William and Isaac Silva had discussed the teachings of the Talmud on numerous occasions. Its precepts were, after all, part of Isaac's history, a history that he conveyed to William more than once. William was curious about all things, and although Isaac rarely spoke of his personal life, he was comfortable speaking about ideas, as was William.

William looked up again at the body, this time not with horror or grief but a cool detachment. This time looking for signs. Then, he took in the room for the same reason. For him, medicine was a kind of reading—not letters of an alphabet, but the signatures of disease, malformation, dysfunction. There was something like that here, something out of place, something wrong with the scene of this crime, this self-slaughter. How was he to read it?

"How did Silva get himself up there?"

The warden's eyes followed William's up to the ceiling. William judged it to be a good ten or twelve feet high. "Why, he must have stood upon the bed, Doctor," the warden said. "There is no stool or chair here."

William turned toward the warden. "He hangs high, then, higher than he should if he stood upon the bed. He was not a tall man, a little over five feet, I think. Tell me, sir, how could he get up to secure the rope, to make the noose? How could he have secured the rope whereby he hangs? Where might he have found the rope?"

The warden laughed a little. "Why, these be good questions, Doctor, to which I must admit I have no certain answer. A desperate man is a resourceful man, don't you think? He might find a rope on any street in London, borrow it for some purpose. After all, he was no prisoner here. He got out and about from time to time. And as for the height of him, I grant he was no tall man, yet as I say, he might still have gotten up by some means."

"By ladder, perhaps?" William suggested.

"Why, yes, Doctor, a ladder would have fit his purpose well enough. He might have placed the top rung against that roof beam."

"Then where would such a ladder be? You did not find it here, did you?"

The warden shrugged.

"Perhaps the ladder mysteriously vanished, like a magician's trick," William said.

"Stranger things have happened, Doctor. Here in the Domus, I mean. I could tell you stories."

"I imagine you could, Master Warden, and I suspect they would be strange stories, as strange as this. Get him down now. I've seen enough."

"Then you will affirm he died by his own hands, Doctor?" Meredith asked.

"I will affirm no such thing, Master Warden. Get him down and do it now."

Meredith looked startled by the command. Meredith glowered under his heavy brows. His hands fell by his side and made a fist. "I can't do it myself alone, Doctor, I must have help."

"Then get help," William said. "I remind you that Master Silva, your charge, had no help to get himself up. Yet you can't get him down by yourself, sir?"

"I will get help. I'm warden here, not a gravedigger. There's those who make a living taking care of corpses. I would not deprive them of their trade; would you, Doctor Gilbert?"

"Just get him down, damn you, Warden," William said. "Secure whatever help you need to do it."

The warden called for no gravedigger, that was an idle threat. The man who came, William had seen more than once about the Domus. He brought with him another fellow William hadn't seen before, no more than a youth. William watched as the young man climbed on the older man's shoulders and cut the rope. Isaac's body fell to the stone floor with a thud, ending up in a heap like a rag doll. The warden and the boy carried Isaac Silva out the door, leaving the rope around the dead man's neck.

"What will you do with him?" William asked.

"Bury him, like any other dead man," the warden said.

"Make sure he's buried decently. In a Christian churchyard. He is a Christian. He's a ward of the queen."

"You needn't worry, Doctor. He will be given what's due him, given what he is…was."

Three

The Domus was in the neighborhood of the parish of St. Michael of the Angels. The church itself was a venerable structure of gray stone with an adjacent churchyard whose monuments declared it to be several hundred years old. William was given to understand that this is where residents of the Domus had traditionally been buried and where Isaac Silva's body would therefore rest.

In the afternoon, William went there himself to make sure his friend's body was appropriately handled. He did not trust Meredith's assurances that Isaac would be *given his due*, as the warden had put it, especially in light of the man's insistence that Isaac had hanged himself.

He spoke first to the sexton, a cadaverous person who looked on death's door himself and talked with some manner of accent; Welsh, William thought. London was full of persons from all over the land. One heard every manner of speech, some unintelligible to him. The great number of foreigners added to the stew with their incomprehensible babble and wild gestures, as though they were ready to take flight.

He had spoken to the man but a few words before he realized that he was already apprised of the circumstances of Isaac's death. The dead man was a suicide, the sexton declared. The warden of the Domus had so stated. He had indeed a document declaring that fact, which he waved in front of William's face as though it were a royal edict that it was treason to dispute. The Jew, the sexton declared, could not therefore be buried in the churchyard itself, but perhaps in some roadside beyond the city walls.

William asked to see the vicar.

"I cannot say he is in, sir."

"Why can you not say? Can you go and seek him out?" William did not bother to hide his irritation.

"I suppose I might, sir."

"Then I pray you do it, Sexton."

William waited, looking over the churchyard. Some of the headstones were newly erected but most were moss-covered with names no longer legible. It was a sad scene. To think mortality came to this, obscuring individual personalities, merit, achievements. He felt himself falling into a state of melancholy when the sexton returned with a pudgy cleric who identified himself as John Spencer, vicar. William explained the purpose of his visit, although he suspected the sexton had already informed the cleric. This gentleman in sonorous tones, rendered the same verdict. The church did not permit the burial of suicides in holy ground.

"Why not?" William asked, although he knew very well. Suicides, like bastard children and witches, weren't welcome in the churchyard but were buried by the roadside or thrown into ditches. Stakes were sometimes driven into their bodies to confirm their damnation. Suicides weren't permitted to keep company with the righteous, not even in death.

"Because he took his own life," the priest answered.

"That's debatable, sir," William said.

"That's what Master Meredith conveyed to us, Doctor."

"I don't doubt that's what Master Meredith conveyed. He and I have discussed the issue at length and have not agreed on the cause of death."

"He is the warden, formally appointed."

William shot back, "And I am the dead man's physician, and an officer of the Royal College of Physicians. The dead man was also a friend of Lord Burghley. They corresponded, exchanged letters. This Jew you despise has been a guest in his lordship's country house. His lordship will take a special interest in how Isaac Silva met his end—and how his body is disposed of. Mark my words."

"Do you mean, Doctor, *the* Lord Burghley?" The Reverend Spencer was wide-eyed at the mention of Burghley's name. William was not surprised.

"I have the honor of being one of his lordship's physicians," William said. He did not like name-dropping, but sometimes he found it useful, at times necessary. "Surely there's no canon law forbidding the burying of those slain by another's hand?"

The priest hesitated, exchanged glances with the sexton. "You mean, Doctor, you believe he was murdered?"

"I do."

"But the warden is of another opinion?"

"That's what I said, Master Spencer. Since there are two opinions of his death, Vicar, I wonder if you might judge between those views yourself, being as you are obviously a man of… discernment. After all, the church daily buries scoundrels, whores, thieves, and worse, but it will not an old man hanged by the neck from a beam he could not reach were he twice his height; a Christian convert who had no cause to take his life, left no note to explain his action, and could not have ascended to the beam that secured the rope save he had wings."

The priest looked down, hesitated. William had dealt with contentious priests before. After all, physicians and the clergy often worked in tandem as ministers to the sick and dying, but they did not always agree as to diagnosis or treatment. William took the cleric's hesitation as a good sign. He could see the uncertainty in the man's eyes. He had seen the man pale at Burghley's name.

"I wonder if a contribution to the church might help you in resolving your dilemma, Vicar, since the cause of this poor man's death is disputed."

"I hope you are not suggesting a bribe, Doctor?" The cleric gave William a look of dismay. William dismissed it as disingenuous.

"A contribution to the church, I said. No bribe. Something to help the poor and the needy. Lord Burghley would call it a good cause and certainly approve. Wouldn't you agree, Vicar?"

For a few moments there was silence between them. The vicar looked beyond William, over his shoulder, as though he were communicating with one of the buried, standing there eavesdropping on the dispute.

"Find a place for Master Silva," the priest said to the sexton. The sexton muttered something beneath his breath. The cleric gave him a sharp look of reproof.

"I will arrange for a stone to mark the grave," William said. "I am sure Lord Burghley will be pleased with your cooperation in honoring his friend. Tell me, Vicar, your name again so his lordship may convey his thanks."

The priest beamed. "John Spencer."

"Very well, Master Spencer," William said, extending his hand. The priest told the sexton to be about finding a place in the churchyard.

"Why, the churchyard's near full, sir, what with the plague and sweating sickness," the sexton responded.

"I said, find a place," the priest said. "A proper place for Lord Burghley's friend."

"If you say so, Master Spencer," the sexton replied.

Four

William endured a restless night of tossing and turning. He knew that the investigation of Isaac Silva's murder was not his business. He was a doctor, not an officer of the law, but the warden's obdurate insistence that the death was suicide would not likely invite the attention of the constabulary or sheriff. Isaac Silva, in the warden's estimation, was just an old Jew, a member of a detested race and a man near death in any case, while the city was full of more serious crime that needed to be suppressed. William had shown he had the power to achieve for his friend a decent burial and appropriate Christian rites, but what sway would he have with the officials of the city, whose views doubtless would be the same as the warden's?

In sum, he concluded, the investigation would fall to him. He could not leave Isaac unavenged, his death a mystery to haunt him forever.

Usually an early riser, he awoke with the light already streaming in at his window and could hear the familiar noises of the street outside at midmorning. The rumble of heavy laden carts and wagons, the cries of vendors, rowdy apprentices, masters shouting orders or railing at their servants. Since moving to London he had gotten used to the clamor. Most nights and early mornings he hardly heard it. This morning he heard every cry, squeak, and rumble as though it came from the next room.

Had he slept at all? He felt he was in a fog, bleary eyed, with a pain in his neck. Was he sick? He felt his forehead and was relieved to feel it cool to his touch. He had not dreamed of the hanged man, not dreamed at all that he could remember, but he saw him now in his mind's eye, not dead, but staring at him, appealingly, as though asking for help. His manservant knocked and looked in, saw his master sitting on the bed in his nightshirt, and asked if he needed help dressing.

"When did I need help?" William snapped. "Do I look like I need help?"

The manservant, Thomas, who was younger than William by a dozen years and had just come up to London from the country, blushed furiously and closed the door quietly behind him.

William was worse with his cook, who prevailed upon him to eat and was surprised when he stormed from the kitchen complaining about the fare. "What, is it Lent, that we should have so little variety?"

His snappishness was not like him. He was well known as a kind and generous master, beloved of his household, envied by less well-tempered friends who could not keep servants contented enough to stay beyond a few months or a year before they stole away to some other gentleman's house or nobleman's manor.

But Isaac's murder, and William's sleepless night, had put him on edge. He would ask forgiveness of his cook and manservant, but later. For now, he canceled several appointments he had for that morning, not with patients, but with colleagues at the College who wanted his opinion on several new applicants with what he considered dubious qualifications for admission. These discussions, he knew, could wait, as could the applicants who were practicing medicine already except without sanction of the College. They might find the delay annoying, but they would not go hungry for want of patients.

His pursuit of justice for his friend could not wait. He was confident he could find what happened to Isaac Silva, but he knew he must act now, if he was to act at all.

By noon he was back at St. Michael's. He wanted to give the vicar his contribution to the poor of the parish, a bribe as the vicar had called it, and perhaps it was. William knew how things worked in London. Half its denizens walked about with their hands out. The other half were digging into their pockets to grease the wheels. He could not have saved his friend's life, but he did have power over how his body was honored.

He found the sexton in the churchyard, supervising the digging of a grave he presumed was Isaac Silva's. The site was at a little distance from other graves but still within hallowed precinct of the faithful dead, as William had insisted upon. A sweating gravedigger had just raised the last shovelful of earth, exposing the rectangular cavity and creating a pile of earth, rocks, and a few disarticulated bones of some earlier occupant by its side. William was not shocked or surprised by this. Everyone knew that burial places were increasingly scarce in the city, especially in the older cemeteries. Every Christian deserved a decent resting place, but that didn't mean that sooner or later his body would not be displaced by another. It was, after all, only a body; the dust of the earth. In the resurrection it would be raised, made whole and perfect, though it be dust.

William watched as sexton and gravedigger stood by, waiting to do their duty. The coffin was a plain wooden box, but any honest man, come to his mortal end, might fit within it without shame. He had no expectations it would be otherwise.

The vicar came up from somewhere behind them. He was dressed in his cassock and chasuble that magnified his paunchiness, and wore a stern, disapproving expression as though he had been called to preside over an orgy. He nodded once to William and then proceeded, reading the service for the dead in a practiced, sonorous voice, but quickly—as though someone were clocking him or he had some appointment he feared to miss.

It was clear to William that neither vicar nor sexton approved of the burial. William didn't care. Their hostility to the Jews, even if converts, was no business of his, who was of a different mind. He had known Isaac primarily as a man, not as a sectarian. When they had conversed together they had not talked of religion, at least not in any contentious way. Had William been Catholic, he would have made the sign of the cross over the grave. As he was not, he merely bowed his head for a few moments and wished his friend well in the life to come. His valediction was in Latin, for although he was no Papist he was a scholar, and Latin seemed more decorous for such a solemn occasion. *Requiescat in pace.*

When the grave was covered over, William pulled from his purse what he had promised and handed the sum to the vicar. "For the poor of the parish and whatever other good works you deem fit, sir."

He also gave something, much less, to the sexton. Neither thanked him.

When he was alone, William looked down at the new grave and felt a wave of sadness for his friend and patient. It was a sad and ignominious ending for Isaac Silva to die so. Sad and ignominious for any man. Isaac had left his old faith for a new one, but had been poorly treated by his fellow Christians, even before his death. Isaac had told him stories, not self-serving fictions, William was sure. For his conversion he had been berated and scorned. But worse, Isaac said, his conversion had been doubted. His strong assertion of faith had not been sufficient to overcome the deep-seated enmity, suspicion, and cultivated hatred of the Jews. It wasn't only Isaac who had experienced such enmity. The queen's own physician, Doctor Lopez, like Isaac a converted Jew, suffered equal disparagement, at least by his enemies at court.

On the way out of the churchyard, William met the sexton again.

"I'll arrange a monument for Master Silva," William said. "I trust you will see that it is placed properly."

"I will, Doctor."

"And will you likewise see to it that Master Silva's resting place is not disturbed? I would hate to learn that the grave has in any manner been desecrated by malicious persons. Lord Burghley would be even more displeased."

"Lord Burghley, Doctor? Is he some great lord of the realm that I should know of him?"

"A very great lord, Master Sexton," William said. "A lord who has the ear of her majesty on a daily basis. A lord who can command a small army against his enemies. Master Silva was a friend to Lord Burghley."

"Though he were a Jew?" the sexton asked, skeptically.

"Though he were a Jew, Master Sexton," William said.

Leaving the churchyard, he went directly to the warden's quarters at the Domus, where he found Simon Meredith sitting in the exact same place as the day before, warming his hands before the fire and contemplating, William imagined, the pleasure of having one less resident to look after. He glanced up as William entered, and raised an eyebrow.

"Doctor Gilbert, here again? I supposed your business with us was done."

"Not done, Master Warden. Not by half."

Meredith frowned and got to his feet. "What do you mean, Doctor?"

"I have questions."

"What questions? Ask them and be on your way. I'm sure you have patients to cure of their ailments. Do you not?"

"I do have patients, sir. But as I say, I am also curious about a number of things."

"Then speak, Doctor. I have much to do this morning and must be about it."

"Did Master Silva have any visitors of late?"

"Only yourself, Doctor; yourself and a young woman who said she was his granddaughter."

"Granddaughter?"

"So she said. I think she visited him twice this month."

"But no one else?"

Meredith shook his head. "None that I know of."

"What's her name, this granddaughter?"

Meredith shrugged again. He took out a much-worn ledger book and paged through it. As warden, one of his few duties was to keep account of who came and who went at the Domus. There was always a chance that these supposed converts were in fact spies and would be visited by those of the same inclination. If you were a Jew in England you could recite the Creed from morn until eve, but still not get the average Englishman to believe your conversion was anything but a self-serving fraud.

"She gave the name of Johane."

"Johane what?"

Meredith struggled to read his own writing. "I think the same name as Silva."

"And where does she live?" William wanted to know.

"She did not say, only that the old man was her grandfather. Since they bore the same family name, I reckoned it likely that it was true what she said about being related to him. When she left, she said she would return soon, by which I suppose she meant she lived nearby, and it was convenient to her."

"Can you describe her?"

"About eighteen or twenty, I would say. Thin, brown, no chest to speak of, hair long, black and oily, eyes of the same color if I remember rightly. Oh, yes, full lips, like a negress."

He was surprised that the warden remembered the girl in such detail, but then he had heard the man was somewhat of a lecher, despite his unprepossessing appearance. Isaac had told him that, among many other things, about the warden of the Domus.

"What was the day of her visit?"

The warden looked at his book again, squinted, and said, "Friday, but three days past."

"It's unlikely that she has heard of her grandfather's death. She may return."

"And so she may, Doctor."

"I must know if she does."

"Well, Doctor, should she return, I will let you know. You have my word."

"Do you know where to find me? Give me paper and pen."

William wrote down where he lived. "If you tell me of her next visit and give her my name and where I live, there's money in it."

The warden looked up sharply, wide-eyed and grinning. "Money, Doctor? How much?"

William named a sum. Too little, he saw by the warden's expression. William doubled it.

The warden thought it over and nodded yes. "Half now."

William agreed.

Five

It was not much to go on, this granddaughter the warden had spoken of. He wasn't even sure she existed. It would not be beyond the warden to make it all up just to get rid of him or fatten his own purse. Isaac had never spoken of a granddaughter, never spoken of any living relative. But it might be true, and if it was, William wanted to find her. Assuming she was indeed Isaac's granddaughter, she deserved to know that her grandfather had died and how.

William imagined she would agree that it was unthinkable that Isaac should have taken his own life, and in that way. Isaac had been old and not well, but his mind had been lucid, and he bore his afflictions with stoic equanimity. In his conversations with William, he had admitted he was not long for this world, but as a convert he had faith in Christ, in the resurrection, in all those doctrines that gave hope and consolation in the face of death. No, with all other evidence that Isaac did not die by his own hands; such a death was contrary to everything William knew about the man.

He hoped Isaac's granddaughter would agree. But should she not, it made no difference to him. His judgment did not depend on hers, whoever she might be, whatever she might know.

When he returned home, he immediately instructed two of his household servants to begin a search of the neighborhood around the Domus. "Begin at the doorstep of the Domus, then expand your search outward. You are looking for a young woman named Johane. Her last name is uncertain, but Johane is not that common a name. She is a girl of eighteen or twenty, probably unmarried, possibly a servant in some house or perhaps the daughter of some merchant, more likely the former."

He gave them the description the warden had given him.

"No beauty, then?" his manservant Thomas said, smirking.

"Not according to the warden, but then I wouldn't trust his judgment, nor his ability to tell a fair maid from a drab. He's cunning, but no scholar. Look for a girl of that name, Johane, Johane Silva, but if it's Johane something else, ask her if she has a grandfather living at the Domus."

"If we find her, Doctor, should we say her grandfather has died and that is why we seek her."

"No, leave that to me. It's a sad duty I am practiced in. Tell her I am her grandfather's friend and have a message from him."

The servants went off readily. At least it was a duty different from their usual duties; not exactly a holiday, but a chance to be out and about in the city.

Meanwhile, William returned to his desk and recalled his first meeting with Isaac Silva. It had occurred upon the recommendation of Lord Burghley, the queen's chief minister, whom William had attended more than once and whom he counted a friend as well as a patient. Lord Burghley knew Isaac. They had a mutual interest in the nurture of rare species of plants, especially those found in Asia, where Isaac had traveled as a young man, arriving in England in his later years as a refugee from the Spanish inquisition. Somewhere in those years, he had converted to Christianity.

Isaac had a weak heart, and sometimes trouble breathing. Burghley was concerned. But William had soon realized the condition was easier to diagnose than to remedy. Isaac was dying. He had been dying for the last three years, growing weaker with each one. William's attendance consisted largely of consolation, and the recommendation of diet and moderate exercise that doctor and patient both knew would merely delay the inevitable. But a friendship had developed between them as well. Isaac had studied at no university, but he had learned much himself, and while William was more interested in geology and chemistry than plant life, he found Isaac's informal lectures fascinating. He also enjoyed hearing stories of Isaac's travels, which were full of adventures, exotic locales, and meetings with strange peoples whom William had only read of in books.

But, in all this flood of memory, overriding all was the awareness that his friend had been murdered. The evidence, if plain to him, should be plain to any man, even the warden, were the latter not so stupid and corrupt. The question, then, was not the fact of murder but the cause.

Who would have wanted Isaac dead, and why?

Late in the afternoon, the first of his servants returned to report he had found no young woman named Johane Silva within a half mile of the Domus. He had asked at every house and shop, asked every passing serving man or serving woman. None knew of a girl of that name, or anything close to it.

"She may be from farther off, Winchester or East Cheap," the one servant said, whose name was Rolf and was Thomas's cousin. "Or maybe there's no such woman in the first place."

William was disappointed but not surprised. He knew it was an uncertain enterprise even when he ordered it. But then he was surprised, when Thomas returned an hour later to report not only that he had found the girl, but that she awaited him in the entryway.

"She came willingly, Doctor, when I told her who summoned her. She says her grandfather often speaks of you."

"Are you sure it is she, Johane Silva?"

"Her name is Johane Sheldon, Doctor. She said she used the name Silva to gain easier entrance to the Domus, thinking the warden would not believe who she claimed to be, otherwise."

"Well, let her come, then."

William saw that the girl was not exactly as the warden described. For one, she was tall and slender, hardly scrawny, and she had fine eyes, dark and lustrous, and sensuous lips, not thick like any African he had ever seen—and there was more than one in London. He would not himself have called her hair oily, but he assumed the warden had said so because of a dislike of her. Isaac once told him that he suspected the warden disliked Jews, and he found his appointment as a caretaker of those converts-in-residence curiously ironic. Indeed, Isaac said he believed Meredith thought of himself more as a jailer than a caretaker, and it pleased him to think of himself as such. *Keep the Jews locked up, those that aren't send back to where they came from. It's where they belong, else they contaminate good Christians.*

"I am William Gilbert. I was your grandfather's doctor, and also his good friend."

He realized that he had said *was*. Did it suggest her grandfather was dead, or merely that he once was his doctor but no longer? He pointed to a chair on the other side of his desk; it was where his patients sat when he conferred with them.

She made a little dip with her head to acknowledge him and smiled. She looked around at the room, taking in the books, the manuscripts, the medical instruments and especially the terrella, a replica of the Earth that he used for his magnetic experiments and demonstrations. She stood, walked toward it and examined it. "What is that, sir, may I ask?"

"It's a terrella," he said. "It means 'little Earth'. A model of our world reflecting the magnetic poles."

She looked puzzled, but not uninterested. She turned away from the terrella and looked at him with her dark eyes.

"Poles?" she asked.

It was a question he was often asked, even by those of his countrymen pretending to be learned, and he had a ready answer. A concise explanation deliverable in just a few sentences. He said this to her now, even though satisfying the girl's curiosity was beside the point of their meeting. It might be idle curiosity on her part, it probably was, but William was so devoted to the subject he could not fail to shine light upon it for Isaac's granddaughter.

He pointed to the north and south pole of the terrella, explained magnetic force, demonstrating the principle of it with magnets he had at hand. She listened, genuinely interested he thought, then suddenly looked away.

"My grandfather says you are his good friend," she said.

And by the tense of her verb he realized she was unaware of Isaac's death.

He sighed heavily, never having gotten used to announcing the death of someone's loved one, despite what he but an hour before told Rolf.

"I regret to say, Johane, that your grandfather is dead."

For a moment, she looked as if he had said something in a language she did not understand. Then her dark eyes welled with tears.

"Was it his heart, sir? I know it was bad."

"It wasn't his heart," William said.

She paused, then asked, a fearful look in her dark eyes. "What was it, Doctor Gilbert?"

He was not prepared to tell her the truth, and looked quickly for a softer phrase, something between a lie and the truth. But there was nothing there, nothing that could soften the blow and not violate any future trust between them.

"The warden found him dead…he was hanged."

She gasped, looked at him unbelieving. "What do you mean, hanged?"

"By a rope, from a beam in the ceiling, the ceiling of his room."

"No, no, no," she cried, in disbelief. "He couldn't have done that, he wouldn't have done such a thing! He was a religious man, a good Christian. He would not have taken his own life."

"I agree," William said, somewhat relieved that she shared his view of Isaac's death. "I think I knew your grandfather well enough. It wasn't suicide."

"Then what?" she asked, more as a demand than a question.

"I believe someone murdered him, perhaps more than one; two or three."

He told her about the height of the bed, the position of the body, and why he was convinced Isaac had not hanged himself. How he could not have done so, because he would have lacked the strength, the height, and most important, the motive. He described the evidence as he might have described one of his experiments, with hard facts, numbers; and he listened to himself talk, his own voice. Even to his own ears, he sounded cold; detached from his own grief and insensitive to hers. It was not how he wanted to come across to this girl. Isaac had been his friend, not the subject of an autopsy or anatomy lesson, his body stretched out before gawking students.

"Who would have done this? And why?" she asked when he paused for a moment.

"I don't know. Your grandfather never told me that he had enemies, that he feared for his life. Jews—even those converted to Christian faith—are disliked, but selecting one to kill, and to misrepresent his death as was clearly done…why, this is horrible to think of."

She agreed, her face fallen and, momentarily, her eyes shut as though saying a prayer for the dead. He wondered if she prayed as a Jew or a Christian. Perhaps it made no difference.

They talked for another hour. She told him about her life. She was born in a town whose name he did not recognize. It was north of London, but more village than town. Her parents were dead, she said. She had no siblings. She had recently come to London to find work. She could read and write and thereby found work as governess in a merchant's house. He was no Jew but was friendly toward them, having Jewish friends abroad with whom he did business. Her grandfather had been her closest living relative. She visited him regularly, she said. She was not a Christian herself, not even religious, she said, but she respected her grandfather's conversion and loved his stories of his travels.

"He was born on a little island off the coast, an island called Livesey, by the narrow sea separating us from Europe. He ran away as a boy and from there began his travels. He was in Egypt and Africa. He had a great lord for a friend."

"Lord Burghley?"

"Yes."

Then he asked her the question he had wanted to ask her even before she entered. "Did your grandfather have any enemies, say among Jews who might have hated him because he renounced his Jewish faith?"

She shook her head. "None," she said. "I don't know if he conversed with any Jews in the city. To tell truth, there are not many to converse with."

"The warden, Master Meredith, said you were his only visitor, aside from myself."

"He said that, did he?"

"He swore you were the only one."

"Then he lies about that, too."

"You know he had other visitors?"

"Not at my last visit, which was but a month past, but the time before that, when I went to his room two men came out as I entered. They said nothing to me, hardly looked my way, and then stole off before I could inquire who they were."

"Did you ask your grandfather who visited him?"

"I did. He said they were old friends from where he used to live, near the sea at Livesey. A dot in the water, so my grandfather described it. During those years our family retained our Jewish faith but kept it hidden. We attended Mass when England bowed the knee to Rome, observed the new religion of King Henry and continued under the queen that now is. My grandfather's conversion broke the chain of a thousand years and more."

"Does your employer know you are a Jew?"

"Yes; as I have said, by blood, not by practice."

"Tell me of these two men. What manner of men were they?'

"As any others, Doctor. Men of middle years, perhaps thirty-five or forty. One was taller than the other and stouter, with a black beard cut short to his chin and close-cropped hair like a soldier's. The other was thin. He wore a hat or maybe a cap. He smiled at me as I passed him, but it was no friendly smile, more of a smirk, I think. It made me shiver."

"And their dress? How were they dressed? Like gentlemen?"

The girl thought for moment, said she had not regarded their dress as much as their faces. But then she said, "No, Doctor, more like townsmen, tradesmen."

"Not carpenters, smiths, grocers?"

"No, more like secretaries, higher servants, people who care about how they look."

He nodded. "Your grandfather said they were old friends, but not what they talked of?"

"Old times, he said. Things that had happened long ago."

"Then these were men from the village you spoke of, the one on the island."

"They must have been," she said.

"Would you recognize them if you saw them again?" William asked.

"I think so. Yes, I would recognize the both of them."

"These men may have been your grandfather's murderers."

"But why…why would they kill him?" She held her head in her hands.

He thought for a moment. Then he said, "Revenge is sometimes a cause for murder, but more often he who kills wants something his victim has."

"My grandfather had nothing," she said bleakly, looking up at him. "He had forfeited his worldly goods to the queen as a condition of occupying the Domus."

William thought about this. The girl was right. Isaac had nothing, at least nothing material. But what *had* he had? He thought, then said, without even knowing if it were true: "He had knowledge."

"Knowledge of what?"

William had no answer. At least not then.

"We shall find out the why of this," William said. "I promise you."

"But why, Doctor, are you willing to help me? He was my grandfather. I must find out why he died and who caused it."

"He was my friend," William said.

"And will you seek justice for him, Doctor, if no one else will?"

He told her he would.

She prepared to leave. Then she turned to him and said, "His books and things. His little library at the Domus. I'm sure he would want me to have them."

"I'm sure he would. You are his only heir."

"Will you go with me?" she asked, hesitantly.

"Of course," he said. "We should go now. I don't trust the warden. He's the kind of man who would gladly throw all your grandfather's belongings into the street without a thought, or sell them off if there's money to be made from them."

"You think little of him," she said.

"Very little," William said. "He's both incompetent and corrupt. His type is legion at court and in the city."

"Can we go now?" she asked.

William said they could. He would only have to give a few instructions to his manservant. William rang a bell for him.

Johane walked over to the terrella and examined it.

"Magnets," she said. "I have heard they can be used to find things that are gold, is that not true, Doctor?"

"Some have believed it," William said. "Magnets are thought to do a great many things. Surely, if the gold thing has an alloy of iron or copper, the magnet will attract it. As far as discovering things buried beneath the earth, that's another story. Some have said it's possible. Some deny it."

"But what say you, Doctor?"

William shrugged. "I've never put my magnets to the test. At least, not for gold hunting."

Six

It was now early evening, and when William and Johane arrived at the Domus the door was fast shut. It took a series of sharp knocks to have the porter answer and let them in.

The porter was a little old man with a bent back and a weather-beaten face that gave the impression he had spent his life in some southern climate or perhaps at sea, battered by wind and wave. He seemed confused at first at seeing the both of them, not understanding what was wanted of him, although William had come there dozens of times—Johane as well, by the warden's account. Perhaps seeing them together put him off. William told him they wanted to see the warden, but the porter misunderstood that, too.

"Master Silva is dead," the porter said. "It's too late to visit him. You must wait until the next life, that is if visiting is allowed there."

"We don't want to visit him," William said, annoyed by the old man's feeble attempt at wit. "We know he's dead. We have come for his effects."

"Effects, sir? In faith, sir, I don't know what those might be."

"His belongings, what he may have had upon his person or in a chest or in safekeeping by Master Warden."

Finally, the porter said he understood. He said, "You must have the warden's permission for that, sir. And he's not here to give it." He said this with look of satisfaction, as if all his duty was to prevent entry, not facilitate it.

"I was Master Silva's physician," William reminded him. "I already have the warden's permission to collect his personal effects, his belongings. You may ask him when he returns if you will, but I doubt he will be pleased to know you've countermanded his orders."

"Countermanded, Doctor?"

"Disobeyed."

This evidently frightened the old man into a reluctant cooperation. He opened the door wide and bid them enter.

He led them down the passage toward Isaac's room and then beyond to a kind of disorderly and cluttered closet full of casks and boxes.

He pointed to a box sitting in the corner. In it, William could see a stack of books, papers, and a small chest he recognized as Isaac's. He picked it up, gave the porter a few coins for his service, and waited until the porter left.

"You gave him too much, Doctor," the girl said.

"I wanted to be rid of him," William answered. "I didn't want him looking over my shoulder."

It was a pitiable cache of effects for so long and rich a life, William thought sadly, looking at the box's contents. But it was all Isaac's worldly goods. He remembered the long conversations he had had with the old man, extending beyond medical issues into philosophy, politics, and natural history. William had many acquaintances in London, but few real friends. Isaac Silva had been one of those friends.

He knelt on the stone floor with Johane as she looked through the books, William translating the Latin and Greek titles for her, describing the contents, simplifying the science where needed. He could tell she valued them, unlearned as she was. She held them in her hands carefully, seeming to appreciate their value.

"Though I cannot read a word of them, still they are precious to me—as memories of my grandfather."

"Then you shall have them," William said.

He took another look at the small collection.

"There is one thing missing, here," William said. "Your grandfather had a copy of an old book, written by one of your ancestors. It had been in his family for years. I remember him showing it to me. It was a prized possession, since it was your family's history. I don't see it here."

"I remember the book well. He showed it to me when first I came to find him at the Domus. Perhaps he hid it in his room," she suggested. "Given it was of such value to him."

They carefully put the books back in the box, and William picked it up. Then they went to Isaac's room.

The sheets and bedclothes had been stripped from the bed, and the small chest of drawers in the corner was now empty. William imagined Isaac's clothing had been bundled and given to the poor, there being no thought that they would be wanted or needed by the family of the deceased. Both William and the girl looked around the room carefully, but it was a plain box of a room, without any place where something might be hidden. Indeed, it was as though Isaac Silva had never resided there, had perhaps never even existed but in William's imagination.

"Maybe the two men took it," Johane said.

"An old book? They'd be unusual thieves that would prize that," William said. "If they thought any book of value they would have taken them all in hopes some bookseller would give them sixpence for the lot."

The girl made no response to this.

"These things are yours now," he said, nodding toward the box. You are his heiress."

"His only heiress," she said.

William took another look at the ceiling beam from which Isaac had hung like some terrible medallion on a chain. What had his murderers wanted of him? Were they seeking revenge for some earlier offense of his against them, or was his hanging a threat, to be interrupted should he agree to disclose some secret? If it were that, evidently he had kept silent, even in the face of death.

"Tell me more about this book, the one you said had been in your family for generations," he said.

"It's a family history, nothing more. Of interest to us who descended from the first of our faith in England, but hardly of interest to any other not of the family. It relates how the Jews were expelled ages ago, and how some returned later."

"Well, a historian might take some interest in that, but hardly miscreants who would hang an old man. Was there anything about the book, its cover, binding, gold illuminations, that would make it worth stealing?"

"The pages were parchment, very thick," she said. "Its covers two slabs of wood, like shingles rough-hewn, bound with cord. My grandfather kept it in a silk bag, also gone, evidently."

"Wrapped in silk. A sign your grandfather valued it."

"He did, Doctor. Oh, he did very much. Toward the end, he talked of it constantly. Stories. Family stories. From centuries ago."

* * *

He walked with her back to the house where she said she served as a governess, carrying the box of books for her as though he were her servant. He did not mind. William thought she was a pleasant young woman, intelligent, bearing her grief with Christian fortitude, though she had declared herself neither Christian nor Jew, except the latter by blood. She had lived in London for two years, she said, but wished to return to the village where she was born and reared. She missed the smells and views of the countryside and hated the crowds and stench of the city. She had no young man courting her. She had made that plain from the beginning, and it surprised William, given the qualities he had observed in her.

Now it was near dark, faint lights could be seen within the houses and shops. He asked her if her absence would be noted by her master and mistress. She said it was unlikely. Both were in the country at the time and her pupils as well, a boy and girl aged ten and eight. The butler was in charge of the house, and when his employers were gone, he did what pleased him and had little interest in the comings and goings of the other servants. "He is given to drink and dice," she said in almost a whisper. "Even if he should be sober, he will hardly know I'm gone."

When they came to the house, she showed him where the servants entered. He offered to carry the box in for her, but she declined, took it from his hands and bid him goodbye.

"If I can help in any way, Mistress Silva, let me know. You know now where I live."

"Will you let me know if you discover anything as to who killed my grandfather and why?"

"I will indeed," William said. "And I hope if you remember anything else—any detail your grandfather might have mentioned, especially if it is the name of someone he knew here in London, or someone he might have quarreled with."

"You shall know it, Doctor" she said. "I promise."

The girl gave him a little curtsy and closed the door.

That evening, William wrote to Lord Burghley, informing him of Isaac's death, which in his letter he called murder. He knew Burghley would want to know. As for the warden of the Domus, William knew he would do nothing to investigate William's suspicions. Murder in the Domus would look bad, and would reflect on the warden. Indeed, he suspected Meredith was complicit in the murder. Why otherwise should he not have recorded the visit of the two strangers, or denied there were any other visitors to Isaac at all except for the granddaughter?

Knowing the man, William would put no offense past him. He was like so many other minor functionaries in the city; looking out for himself, inviting and taking bribes gladly, and the devil take the hindmost.

He sent the letter by messenger, and by late the next day he had a response. It was brief and written in Burghley's own hand. He commanded William to come at once to Theobalds, Burghley's country house. Burghley said he was most grieved at the news and wanted to hear more.

It was a command William could hardly refuse, even were he inclined to. He might himself feel helpless in bringing Isaac Silva's murderers to justice, but Burghley was not.

Seven

Since coming to London, William had visited Theobalds many times, yet he never approached the Burghley's magnificent country house, but it amazed him that so large and imposing a structure could be the habitation of anyone other than a prince or even a king. It encompassed a great tract of land not a dozen miles from London, rose upwards to towers and battlements and chimneys like something conceived in heaven, was composed of the finest materials brought from Italy and France, the masterpiece of dozens of stonemasons, glaziers, bricklayers, carpenters. It was a testimony not only to Burghley's wealth, but to his power in the kingdom. That year, he was the queen's Lord of the Treasury and Principal Secretary, admired for his political acumen and influence even by those who disliked and envied him—of whom, as in the case of any powerful man, there were many.

He was also William's good friend and patron, so that when Burghley summoned him, the doctor made no delay in obeying. Their shared history had been brief, only a few years, but intense. They not only shared an interest in things scientific, but also Burghley had saved William from a cruel death when he was falsely imprisoned for murder and malpractice. Since that time, William had prospered and Burghley had played a part in that; a large part, since the powerful lord had opened doors that otherwise might have been closed to him. Burghley had encouraged William too in his magnetical experiments; shared rare volumes in his library; and trusted his son, Robert Cecil, to William's special ministrations, though young Robert, dwarfed and hunchbacked as he was, was near beyond help—at least by any science William knew or could imagine.

William rode on horseback to Theobalds, leaving London not an hour after receiving his summons, and arriving before six o'clock, in time to be welcomed by manservants who knew him by sight and name. These escorted him through a half dozen impressively furnished rooms to Burghley's library, which he used also as an office when he wasn't at court, where he was often besieged by secretaries, clerks, petitioners, bishops and lesser clergy, as well as noblemen and their wives, their siblings, and their cousins.

William Cecil, Lord Burghley, was a man in his sixties with great flowing white beard and wizened face. He had a piercing eye, a calm demeanor, and a head for facts and figures. He was a man of some piety, learned in the law, and a shrewd politician. He was sitting at his desk in a chair, propped up with velvet cushions. He had a bad back that he often complained of. There was no remedy for it, William told him, at least not in their time, perhaps not ever until the world's end.

"You wasted no time in coming here, Doctor," Burghley said with an approving nod. He pointed to a chair opposite him.

A large fire burned on the hearth, making the room uncomfortably hot, but not for Burghley. William sat down and prepared himself to endure it without complaint. He was, after all, only a physician in the city. There were almost a hundred of his kind. But he was in the presence of man who was arguably the most powerful in England, next to the queen of course, who was no man but greater, since she wore the crown.

"Tell me the facts of Isaac Silva's death."

Burghley was not one to beat around any bush.

William told him what he had seen in Isaac's room. "I estimated the height of the beam from which the rope was tied, the height of the bed from which he supposedly reached the noose. Isaac was a short man, as you know, my lord; a small man and old. He could not have reached that height. At least not unattended."

"Unattended?"

"Hoisted by his murder or murderers, for I think it might have been two men who did this. It would have taken two. One to lift him up, the other to place his neck within the noose."

"Do you not think he would have struggled?" Burghley asked. "He was old, much older than I, yet not without strength."

"He might have struggled, my lord, but to no avail. Perhaps he was disabled in some manner before he was raised up. Perhaps even poisoned."

"Was there any sign of poison?"

"None that I could see, my lord, and yet there are poisons that can kill within a minute and show no sign but he that is poisoned seems only to fall asleep."

Burghley knew about poisons. He was himself an excellent botanist and had often shown William the exotic plants in his garden, explaining which were beneficial to man and which injurious or even deadly. The Italians were reputed to be great poisoners in their statecraft and in their private broils. But the truth was that the English were equally proficient. Burghley knew this, as did William. Poison or some sleep-inducing drug therefore was a possibility.

William told Burghley about Johane, Isaac's granddaughter, of what she had told William and what she could not.

Burghley fell silent and stared into the fire. As for William, he felt he was being slowly roasted, but he would not complain of it. For a moment, William thought Burghley might have fallen asleep; he had not, and turned to look at William. "Who were these men, these men the girl, the granddaughter, reported having seen going from Isaac's room?"

"By his granddaughter's account two men whom Isaac had known earlier, men from a village where he once lived."

"I know it, a forlorn place by the sea, an island when the tide is in, not far from the mouth of the Thames. It is called Livesey, and is a desolate place. This girl was named Johane?"

"Yes, my lord, Johane Sheldon. One of my servants found her, brought her to my house. I told her of her grandfather's death, which greatly grieved her. He was her only living relative."

"He never mentioned her to me. Still, he was a man most used to secrecy. He concealed the fact he was a Jew for years, until his conversion to Christianity. I don't remember him talking about his family. If he had a wife, children, or grandchildren, I never knew of it."

"He told me once he had been married. He said he had a son who died. He never told me more than that."

"More than he told me, at least about his family. Was this wife an Englishwoman?"

"I think so, my lord. I remember her name was Elizabeth."

"Her family name?"

"I don't recall, if he ever said. He was the same in our dealings. He never asked me about my family. I never asked about his."

"Did the granddaughter know these two men?"

"She saw them leave as she entered her father's room at the Domus. She asked Isaac who the men were. He told her they were old acquaintances from his native place."

"Acquaintances, not friends?"

"Acquaintances."

"Isaac told her they spoke of old times, but would say nothing more about them than that."

"You told her that he was murdered, or so you suspect."

"I did, my lord, and she agreed with me that the facts make that interpretation almost certain."

"And I agree as well," Burghley said. "But the great question—"

"*Why*, my lord. Why kill a harmless old man?"

"I think yes," Burghley said. "Why was he murdered? What did these men, if there were two, what did they want from him?"

"I have no thought, my lord."

Burghley sighed heavily, then said, "The motives for murder, Doctor, are more than a few. There's revenge for a wrong real or imagined, a desire for illicit gain, a concern to suppress the truth or to discover it. Jealousy is as old as Adam's sons. I could go on. But come, Doctor, I want to show you something."

Adjoining Burghley's library was another room of almost equal size. It contained his cabinets of curiosities. These cabinets, glass cases, displayed hundreds of objects collected from travelers who knew Burghley delighted in exotica—jewelry, weaponry, coins, and objects of art and craft from a dozen nations and several continents. William had been shown this display before, had been given a guided tour of it during his first visit to Theobalds several years previously. He was happy to see it again. He knew Burghley would have added to it, for his host was a zealous collector.

Burghley, using a crutch to walk because of a bad knee, showed him to a cabinet in a far corner. Within it were objects that had the appearance of gold. Burghley reached down, opened the cabinet door, and removed one from its place. He held up to the light.

It was a rectangular plate, about the size of a ledger book and an inch thick, and it looked very much like gold. On it were engraved figures, and a kind of writing, but not a script he recognized, at least not at first.

"Do you know what this is, Doctor?" Burghley held the plate carefully, almost reverently. Was it because it was made of gold, or because it had some other value? Burghley was a rich man. William suspected the latter.

"The writing is Hebrew, my lord, or so it seems."

"Can you read it?"

"No, my lord, it is not one of my languages. I can recognize the script, having seen it often in books."

"Isaac *could* read it, and he knew what the writing was. Hebrew, he told me. Hebrew writing. The Commandments given to Moses on the mountain, or at least the first five. Each character there represents one commandment. Engraved on a gold tablet."

William looked at it again. The lettering, incomprehensible to him, was exquisite. The tablet had every appearance of being ancient and of incalculable value.

"Isaac said something else," Burghley continued. "He said King Solomon of old had it made from gold come from Africa. He said that according to legend it had been in the temple in Jerusalem. When Jerusalem was taken, the remnant of the Jews in the city hid it away. Then, centuries later, it was found again, by a Jew living in France. This same Jew came at length to England. But then, Isaac said, the plates—for there are two— were lost again."

"How did you come by it, my lord?'

"Some six years since, it was given me in exchange for a debt. A nobleman in the north, whom I shall not name, gave it to me. One of his tenant farmers had discovered it buried in a field, plowed it up, took it to his master, and thereby won his lord's affection and set himself up well in his esteem. The nobleman didn't know what to make of the writing. He could hardly read English, I suspect, for as you know, our nobility often disdain learning of any sort, except for Machiavellian stratagems to secure and maintain their place in the kingdom. But he did know it was gold. He had it assayed—gold, but mixed with an alloy. He thought the writing thereon was mere decoration, all curious figures without meaning, to avoid the uncomeliness of a featureless surface. He gave it

41

to me for the value of the metal, thinking that was the worth of it. But when I saw it, I knew it was something more."

"I noticed, my lord, there are holes in the end of it. What make you of them?"

"It's too large to hang about a neck, too small to hang upon a wall. I suspect the holes connect it to another tablet, one containing the last five of the Commandments."

Burghley placed the tablet carefully back into cabinet from which he had taken it, as though it might break if handled without reverence. "Isaac said that the tablets are called Solomon's gold, because Solomon himself had it made for himself, with gold he had from Sheba's queen. Made them that he should never forget the Commandments Moses had received. He said the legend was that Solomon kept it at his bedside and every night recited it, for although he was the wisest of men, he was also the most abject because of the weight of his sins."

"Then it is indeed a priceless relic," William said.

"Priceless, yes. And it would be of even greater value were the second tablet to be found."

"You said, my lord, that Isaac knew what it was when he saw it. Had he seen it before?"

"No, he read of it, read of it in his family history."

"I wonder that it should have been mentioned there, in the history of a single family."

"Doctor, how much do you know of your country's history, especially as it pertains to the Jews?"

"I know a little, my lord. I know that a long time ago there were Jews in England and then they were expelled. The Edict of Expulsion, I believe it was called."

"Yes, during the reign of the first Edward. It was in the year 1290, almost three hundred years before our time. That edict is still in force, as you know, although you also know we have among us Jews who have converted to Christianity, as Isaac, housed in the Domus."

"I know that well, my lord. One such is Doctor Roderigo Lopez, although he lives in his own fine house in London and ministers to the queen."

Burghley paused. There was a bottle upon the table and two glasses." He poured claret into one of the glasses and pushed it toward William. Then he poured one for himself and sipped it. "I will share with you a story our friend Isaac Silva shared with me when he had seen the gold tablet in my collection. Isaac swore it was true, that his ancestors made a record of it."

Burghley paused to take another sip from his glass. He motioned to William to do likewise. "I'll tell you a tale, Doctor, that will chill your blood. In the year of the great expulsion, there was a certain shipmaster who took aboard his ship several dozen Jews, who having been expelled under the king's edict, forsook their homes, their lands, their property. They were not poor, these Jews, wealthy sons and daughters of Abraham rather, and they boarded the ship believing that the shipmaster was an honorable man who would convey them and their goods safely. They hoped for a new life in Holland or in France, I know not which."

Burghley paused, took another drink, and motioned to William to join him. William had not, as yet, touched the wine.

"So to continue the tale, the passengers boarded the vessel, arrived at the mouth of the Thames, when the tide was out. The ship grounded itself in the sand, and they waited. In the meantime, the shipmaster, a wily old fellow who hated every Jew that ever lived, invited all the Jews to walk upon the sand. He told them it would be their last opportunity to 'stretch their legs', as he put it. The Jews were glad of the chance, especially the children. You see there were children among them, not just rich old men and their wives."

"I fear the end of the story is already in view, my lord," William said.

"Ah, Doctor, a wise man always sees the end coming. That is why he is wise."

"I beg pardon, my lord, I did not mean to interrupt."

"You are forgiven, Doctor, this time at least. But I will proceed. The Jews walked upon the mud and sand, the tide came in with a vengeance, and the shipmaster, well, he wisely ran back to his ship, pulled up the ladder by which they had descended, and mocked the Jews who cried out for help but were lost in the flood."

"Horrible, my lord, that any man should have been so treacherous and unfeeling."

"I agree, Doctor. But there was one of his victims survived, swam to shore, and lived to tell the tale."

"Was anyone ever punished for that enormity, the shipmaster, a plain murderer, and of dozens of the innocent, for I do not believe that any Jew is worthy of death merely that he is a Jew. Indeed, that any man should suffer for his religion's sake is wrong to me, an offense against good order in the commonwealth, an offense against God."

"Not all Christians are so open-minded, Doctor.'

"So it may be, my lord, I speak only for myself. I cannot give account of others, care not what they believe or no. But you said, my lord, that one among them did not drown."

"True. A boy who knew how to swim."

"May I ask where you learned all this, it being a story I never before heard."

"Because Isaac Silva was my friend, and he was descended directly from the survivor of the outrage. The story had been handed down in his family for generations. The survivor was a mere boy, a boy with the will to live and to conceal the faith that condemned him. He wrote of the enormity, every detail he remembered, seeing his parents and a younger sister drown before his eyes. He said that for weeks bodies floated up on the shore. The stink of their corpses was awful. The people of the village supposed the ship had sunk somewhere just off the coast, that all hands and passengers were lost. That's what the people of the village believed. But the truth was otherwise. There were no Christian bodies among the dead, only dead Jews."

"Otherwise, my lord?"

"The truth, according to Isaac, was that the ship sailed on, and when it returned it landed elsewhere and the shipmaster and his friends aboard shared in the spoils."

"How did the boy survive once ashore?"

"Ah, the record tells that tale. He was a good swimmer and a clever lad. He found work as a cobbler's apprentice. Lived to marry, have sons. When Isaac became a Christian, he took again his true family name. He lived under the nose of the people who had cursed him and his tribe. No one knew. Within the family he practiced his religion secretly, like the Spanish Jews did more recently to avoid the horrors of the Inquisition. They were Christians, but in name only. The account he wrote was passed down through the generations. Isaac read of it as a boy. Surely, his grand-daughter must know of it, too."

"She said nothing of the story," William said.

"Well, she wouldn't, would she? You are a gentile, naturally she is suspicious of you, or at least careful about what she says."

"I wonder, my lord, why you have disclosed it to me."

"Because, Doctor, that story and the tablet I showed you, the page of gold, are not disconnected. They are part of a larger story. Isaac told me that plate was once aboard that ill-fated ship, that it was part of the goods the Jews carried with them, secured in the hold of the ship. That the book was divided among the conspirators as booty. There's even more; before the ship left England, the Jews' goods were unloaded and hidden. The shipmaster and his crew intended to return after the voyage, but the ship was lost in the Channel. Fate dealt them a hand they deserved. One of their victims survived, but none of the victimizers."

"Then how did the page you have make its way to the north of England?"

"God only knows, Doctor. After so many years, the pages might have gone anywhere along with those who benefited from the murders. I mean the shipmaster and their descendants. Speaking of larceny, was anything taken from Isaac's room?"

"A book, a record, even the one of which we are now speaking." William remembered the old book he had noticed was missing. "Yes, my lord, a book he had, perhaps even the book in which his ancestor's life was recorded. It was not among his things."

"The very record I spoke of, the record he showed me," Burghley said, his voice rising with excitement. "Obtaining it might have been a motive for his murder."

William agreed. "It is hard to know why the two men might otherwise have wanted Isaac dead. He had no money, no objects of obvious value."

"But he had a record of an old and unresolved crime that involved theft as well as murder," Burghley said. "He also knew where the Jews' goods were buried. Well, he knew the island upon which the treasure was concealed, although not the exact place. An island called Livesey. The manuscript spoke of it. So Isaac told me."

William could read the human body. He knew its parts and its operations. He could not read minds, what man could? And yet in this instance, he looked at his host and seemed to see clearly the port for which Burghley sailed.

"My lord, is it your thought to find this treasure, this hoard, even after all these years?"

"It is," Burghley said. "I have had it on my mind ever since Isaac told me the story, told me of hoards buried by the Romans, the Saxon, the Danes. They are found in fields, on hillocks, buried in ruins and even sunken in the depths of lakes and ponds. How else might those ancient folk have concealed their treasures but beneath the earth or water? There are those who spend their idle hours digging up mounds of earth and disrupting the soil in fields in hope of finding Roman coins or Viking swords."

William thought about this, remembering the Roman coin he had found himself in Colchester as a boy, the town having been in its earliest days a Roman fortress. He also knew of a neighbor there who believed devoutly that a store of gold and silver was buried in the foundation of the castle that overlooked the town.

"If Isaac's family history, his book, was taken, my lord, then those who took it now also know of the treasure, the island on which it is buried."

"Which makes the need to find the treasure before the murderers do all the greater," Burghley said.

"Will you send men then to this island, Livesey, my lord, to search the treasure out?"

"It was my thought so to do,"

"And you have hope of finding it?"

Burghley laughed. He drained his glass. "I do, Doctor. Hope is one of the cardinal virtues, Doctor. Without it, all is gloom and doom. I want to know if the missing half of the tablet can be found. If the rest of the Jews' treasure is found at the same time, that's more the better. The queen will be pleased—and enriched the more. But tell me, this granddaughter, I've never met her. Is she a good girl, I mean a virtuous young woman who might be trusted?"

"I do believe so, my lord. Her name is Johane, as I have said, Johane Sheldon. She is twenty and a maidservant, a faultless young woman if I read her aright."

"Only a maidservant."

"Nothing more, my lord."

"Is she bright, can she read, can she keep secrets?"

"I have no doubt of any of what you ask of. She is governess for her master's family."

"Does she know the village, the place where her family is from?"

"I don't know, my lord. She tells me she is from a town north of London. An orphan, both parents being dead."

Burghley stopped talking. For a while he sat looking into the fire, his mind seemingly elsewhere. William knew Burghley well enough to respect his silence. You didn't interrupt a man of Burghley's intellect when he was thinking. That was the rule. Then Burghley spoke again.

"I could send a troop to Livesey and do more harm than good. Where would they be housed and how would their presence be explained? The inhabitants of the isle would be panic-stricken by the presence of armed men, or if informed of their true purpose, they might undertake themselves to discover the treasure, digging here and there until the island is full of holes and trenches, every cellar examined, every grave disinterred, every tree uprooted. Some diligent seeker may find the hoard before my men do and abscond with all. No, Doctor, I think a more subtle and discerning approach is needed. To discover the location of the hoard without alarming or exciting the citizenry and then securing it for the queen, to whom it now belongs, since there are none alive to claim it."

"And what might that approach be, my lord?"

"To send someone there to make discreet inquiries, someone whose reason for being there has nothing to do with treasure hunting, or at least not seem so. It would need to be someone I trust to undertake the task without thought of personal gain, someone who answers to me alone and none other. Someone I believe I could trust implicitly—to follow my orders but also to use his own brain."

Burghley had a hundred or more servants to see to his administrative needs; a dozen or more secretaries, stewards, assistants, and servants. He also had a private army of several hundred men, commanded by a captain William knew personally. As Burghley talked of this agent who would go to the isle, William considered which of these men Burghley might mean. A wily soldier, his armor put off to hide his identity? An upper servant with a natural amicability to make careful inquiries? All this passed through William's mind in a few seconds.

"You sound, my lord, as if you already have someone in mind."

"I do, and first, it should not be a troop, but rather a single person and perhaps a second."

William waited.

Burghley smiled. "Actually, Doctor Gilbert, I was thinking of you."

"Me, my lord?"

Burghley laughed. "I amaze you, Doctor, do I not? It is plainly written on your face."

"My lord, you do indeed. I am bewildered by your choice of me. I have no gift for treasure hunting. I know no more of this island of Livesey than you have told me of."

Burghley held up his hand. "But I choose you, Doctor, and, for good and sufficient reasons I will presently explain."

William had not expected this, but he could have but one answer. He owed Burghley too much to deny him. Besides, his previous service to the queen's minister had not gone unrewarded. Absent his patients' fees, he would suffer no ill; Burghley would see to that. His reputation was that of a generous master, and Burghley had often proved it in William's case.

"I am always at your disposal, my lord. I do remember how you once saved my life, and for that I must be grateful for the longest of seasons."

"Then hear me out, Doctor, and tell me if you can do what I need done."

"You know I will do anything, my lord, as long as it is within my means and brings no dishonor on me or on you."

"You need not do anything, Doctor, but something in particular for which I think you uniquely qualified. And as for honor, you need not fear. I assure you, neither yours nor mine will be in jeopardy."

Eight

William stayed for supper, always a delight at Theobalds, for Burghley employed excellent cooks in his kitchens and although William ate sparingly from long habit, he enjoyed the savor of lamb and the rich sauces of French cuisine, not to mention the desserts, for which Theobalds was famous. Afterwards, Burghley brought him back to the library, where William and his patron occupied the same chairs as before. The cluster of servants who typically surrounded Burghley, awaiting his next command, were dismissed so they could speak in private.

"Doctor, I said I had a mission for you, one for which you were uniquely qualified. I waited until now to disclose details for at the time of the conception it was—how shall I say?—half-baked. Now it is fully done and ready to serve."

"I am ready to hear it, my lord."

"Before you do, let me tell you this, when I showed Isaac the gold tablet and the writings, he was able to read the text. But more, he told me that his ancestors had an identical tablet, one that was among the goods of the drowned Jews. The precious tablet was listed in his family history by name and was much revered by the Jews of England who knew of it. Presumably, it went down with the ship, or was secreted in some hiding place on Livesey."

"May I ask, my lord, how more particularly I might be of service in this?"

"You may, and I shall tell you forthwith. Doctor, as I said earlier I might send men to Livesey isle to dig up every piece of earth upon the island, explore every attic and barn, sea cave and cottage. All that is within my power, but it would do more than inflame the curiosity and avarice of every treasure hunter in England of whom, as you know, there are not a few. They would be stumbling over each other with their picks and shovels. Moreover, my men would be readily identified, questions would be raised at court about my purpose. My enemies would find a way to slander me for some offense against my high office, that it was beneath the dignity of her majesty's chief minister to go hunting treasure rather than pay attention to affairs of state. And should nothing be found, I might end up a laughingstock, the object of ridicule and scorn both in this country and abroad. No, Doctor, what is needed is someone to go to Livesey as my agent, under a false but plausible pretense, say a doctor to see to a patient for whom local doctors have given neither help nor hope."

Burghley paused and looked at William, waiting for him to speak.

"You are thinking of me, as you said before, my lord?"

"Look, Doctor, I know the occupant of the manor house on Livesey, a Sir Arthur Challoner. He is lord of the island, a magistrate. The Challoners have governed for a hundred years or more. My plan is that you go there, sent by me as a courtesy to Sir Arthur. He is afflicted with a number of ailments, or so he claims. You are to doctor him, give him what aid you can, but also seek out the two old friends of Isaac who visited him."

"And if I find them?"

"Report to me. The scriptures say that vengeance is the Lord's, yet He does often use men's arms to achieve it. I will see these men hanged for their murder of a just man."

"But I know them only through Johane Sheldon's description."

"Ah, I have a plan for that as well."

"And that is, my lord?"

"Persuade the girl to go with you."

"The girl?"

"Johane Sheldon."

"With me? Under what guise? Surely not as a companion, a partner?"

Burghley laughed. "Well, Doctor, not as your *inamorata*, if that's what you're afraid of."

"I suspect it would be what she fears, my lord. She is a virtuous young woman. She may find my company distasteful to her and her reputation in jeopardy."

Burghley laughed again. "Then swear to her that you will preserve her chastity and that I said I will have your head, or even some more privy part if you break your oath. That will reassure the maiden."

They both laughed at this. Burghley was a solemn man in most of his moments, but he was capable on occasion of a pleasant humor, sometimes even bawdiness.

"Mistress Sheldon shall go as your assistant," Burghley said.

"A *woman* as my assistant? I know doctors who have men in such a place, but no women."

"Well, perhaps it's time to innovate, Doctor," Burghley said. "You have ever been the first to question the dictates of tradition in your science. Look forward, not backward. I see no reason a woman cannot attend you. Say this to those who question her role: she is a nurse to Sir Arthur's lady wife, who by his accounts at least suffers her own set of maladies. If this woman goes with you, there's two pair of eyes and ears on the ground."

"What must our eyes see, my lord? Or ears hear?"

"You mean, what exactly do you want you and this woman to do?" Burghley leaned forward in his chair and looked at William directly. "Neither of you will draw untoward attention to yourselves and can associate freely with the people there, which I understand has diminished mightily in the last hundred years until only a few families still reside there. A village so small has no secrets. It can have none. The girl may spot the two men who visited her grandfather. Either she or you may hear rumors about Jewish treasure hidden somewhere, or about Jewish gold, or about a certain gold tablet, possessed or sought. As I said, you will be my eyes and ears, you and the girl. You will report to me, directly, and to no other."

"I understand, my lord," William said.

There was a silence between them, a solemn silence as though they were in church and William pledging his faith before the altar. Burghley read it as William's hesitancy—William could see that. But he did not want his patron to think he was afraid, although he suspected spying for Burghley would not be without its dangers. "I worry about leaving my patients," William said.

"And undoubtedly your income therefrom," Burghley said, laughing and looking relieved.

"Well, yes, my lord. I am not independently wealthy."

"Upon my oath, you will suffer no loss from serving me in this enterprise, Doctor. Neither you nor the girl. Isaac's book makes it clear that the false captain and his crew never returned to collect their ill-gotten treasure but were lost at sea before they could. It's buried somewhere on the island, I suspect. That was also Isaac's view."

"I wonder that he did not search for it himself?"

"Ah, well, he ever proclaimed to me that he cared little for earthly goods. Even before his conversion he lived like a monk. I myself don't have the luxury of being indifferent to money. I am an officer of the crown and committed to enriching her majesty's treasury as I can. Common people assume that because she is queen she must be without financial needs. I tell you, the opposite is the case. More than once she has gone abegging to the lords for a greater allowance. I could tell you stories about her royal penury that her extravagance sometimes belies, but I will spare you."

"Your wish is my command, my lord."

"I did not expect any less from you, Doctor. Go see Johane Sheldon where she lives and propose to her my plan. If she is willing, move forward with dispatch. If not, then we will pursue another course. I would not force the girl against her will, it would serve no useful purpose, but make ready yourself to depart within a fortnight, accompanied or unaccompanied."

William was invited to stay the night at Theobalds, which he had done often when attending on Burghley's family, especially Burghley's young son, Robert Cecil, who had numerous afflictions incidental to his crooked back and stunted growth.

Before sleep, William reflected on what he had undertaken. He realized that in one way it was a treasure hunting expedition, a more sophisticated and more complicated version of what he and his friends had played at as children. He remembered himself digging for Roman coins in the pasture of his father's house in Colchester. And he had found them, along with other objects he was sure were what the Roman legionaries had left behind them when they returned to their own country, after occupying his for near four hundred years. Indeed, he knew the ground of all of England was sowed with evidence of earlier peoples. What had they done with their treasures, their precious gems, their idols of stone, the broken swords and knives, their bows and arrows? Surely not all had turned to dust, but lay beneath tilled fields, wooded glens, fens, and forests. Beneath all, slept the detritus of antiquity. That it should be awakened and recovered seemed not unreasonable to him.

The riches the false captain and crew had taken were not the same. By ancient account, they had been concealed to await the robbers' return. But they had not returned. They were still there, the worldly goods of wealthy Jews, undoubtedly gold and silver and even the golden tablet that was the companion piece in Burghley's cabinet of curiosities. Somewhere concealed on this remote island, Livesey, Isaac's birthplace.

William was not so naïve as to believe he could find the specific artifact Burghley coveted, but his heart raced at the thought of the pursuit.

That it might prove a dangerous pursuit did not deter him.

Nine

He was offered breakfast but begged off, conveying his thanks to his host by one of the servants he had come to know, since he was given to understand that Burghley still lay abed. This was unusual for Burghley, who was notorious as an early riser.

By mid-morning he was back at his own house in London, allaying the anxiety of servants who had worried when he did not return home the night before. He changed his garments and soon arrived at the house of Johane Sheldon's employer, introduced himself to her master and then asked if he might speak to her, concocting beforehand some tale as to why he wanted her, that he was a cousin of hers and he had come to tell her of an inheritance. But he had no sooner identified himself and said her name than the employer explained that Johane was no longer in his employ. She had been his children's' governess and was much beloved by the whole household, but had left abruptly without explanation. She had left behind her clothes, books, and other personal things.

Johane's master sighed heavily. Then he said, "I tell you, Doctor, we are worried for her safety. Such a departure is quite against her nature as we have come to know it."

"She said nothing to the children in her charge?" William asked.

The gentleman shook his head sadly. "I pray she has not fallen afoul of some malicious person, which happens to many a young woman. Especially now that she is an heiress. Is it a great amount of money she is now possessed of?"

"No great amount, but sufficient to improve her condition," William said, realizing as he did that this was not far from the truth. If Burghley would compensate him for his service on the isle, surely he would do likewise for Johane Sheldon, and thus indeed improve her fortunes. She might even end up in Burghley's household as governess to any number of his lordship's wards, of whom there were at least twelve by his count.

"Has she friends outside the family?" William asked.

The gentleman thought for a moment. "Yes, a woman in the next street. Also a servant. I do not know her name, but she resides at the house of a silversmith. His name, I believe is Putney…yes, Putney."

William thanked the gentleman and was being shown out when he paused and turned. "You said she left behind her things?"

"Yes, as though she were returning, but she did not."

"Was there a box? A box of books, and papers among them?"

"There was," the master said. "A box with scholar's books, in several languages none here reads, nor I suppose did she. She is but a woman. What woman knows Latin or Greek? I have no idea where she got them."

"Her majesty is conversant in both tongues, sir. Don't belittle women so. If they learn not in our universities, they may yet teach themselves with good profit. The books were an inheritance, from her grandfather, a worthy and a learned man. May I take them with me?"

"You may, sir. They are no use to me or of any value otherwise that I can determine."

The master of the house beckoned to a servant, gave orders, and within a very short time returned with the box of books William had helped Johane carry from the Domus. William examined them briefly, thanked the master, and said he would see that Johane got them.

"Tell her if she wishes to return to us, she may. The children miss her terribly. She has quite won their hearts."

"I think that unlikely, but I will tell her."

William left, more deeply concerned than he had let on to Johane's former master. If she had left her grandfather's books behind, surely this was a sign she was deeply in trouble, perhaps even threatened by the two men who he believed murdered her grandfather. She was a witness to their presence at the Domus and might therefore bear testimony against them if the case ever proceeded to trial.

He returned to his own house, deposited the box of books in his study, then set out again to find Johane's friend.

Ten

Finding the silversmith's house was not difficult, for as one passerby informed him, Gabriel Putney was the only one of that trade in the immediate neighborhood of merchants and lesser gentry. William approached the house and knocked; a servant answered, and upon being told William's name and profession, assumed his master had called for a doctor and beckoned him to enter. Then, before William could explain the purpose of his visit, the servant insisted on conducting William upstairs, where he was led into a large and comfortably furnished bedchamber where a sallow-faced gentleman with bristly white hair lay in his nightclothes, looking very poorly.

"Master Putney, the doctor has come," the servant announced in hushed tones and quickly departed, so quickly that William wondered if the affliction suffered by the man upon the bed was some contagion the servant feared to come close to.

"Thank God, Doctor, I am sick unto death." The voice was weak, shaky, whiney. The man's expression evinced the desperation of the dying: the eyelids half closed, the mouth gaping to show yellowed teeth–that is, what teeth were left to him.

William did not bother to disabuse the sick man of the belief that he was the doctor expected, but went at once to the bedside, and taking the man's wrist, felt his pulse. Rapid, like a fluttering bird. He could tell by his hand on the man's flesh—William pressed his hand to the man's forehead—that he was suffering from no fever, but the man's pulse was hardly a testimony to his body's soundness, either because of some illness or mere excitement at thinking of himself on the cusp of death. He had

had patients who were capable of inducing symptoms in their own bodies just by fearing the worst. Perhaps, he thought, this man was one. He looked into the man's eyes, which were clear and steady, and then had him stick out his tongue.

The tongue was coated, but so it was in many of his patients who were perfectly healthy otherwise.

"What are your specific complaints, sir?"

The man replied in a barely audible voice. "I ache in all joints and sinews of my body, Doctor. There is no part that does not cause me pain and suffering. I pray daily that the Lord will take me."

"You might better pray for health, sir." William said. "The Lord will take you in His own good time, I trust. Yet better later than sooner, don't you think?"

The sick man thought about this, mumbled something under his breath, and shut his eyes, as though William's next probing would inflict pain.

William asked the man how long he had suffered so and the man began to say he had done so for a good many years, to the detriment of his peace of mind and his occupation. He said that his wife would no longer sleep in the same room with him because she could no longer abide his groans and heavy sighs at night or his more articulate complaints in the daytime. "That she still lives with me I take on trust, having not seen her face for more than a month."

William remembered seeing an older, well-dressed woman at the foot of the stairs. He assumed this was the wife alluded to. She had seemed anxious and stood wringing her hands, looking after him when William climbed the stairs.

William was in the act of expressing sympathy for the man's plight and commencing a physical examination of his arms and limbs, when after a soft rap at the door two maidservants entered the room. One carried a tray, presumably a late breakfast for their bed-ridden master.

One of the maidservants was a young woman William judged to be about twenty or twenty-one, pretty, with a slender body, yellow hair, and a pretty oval face. The other was Johane Sheldon. She seemed different, somehow. She had done something to her hair, perhaps cut it. And she was in disguise. Why?

Johane looked shocked to recognize William, but managed to regain her proper composure after a few seconds. She shook her head almost imperceptibly to signal that he should say nothing about knowing her. The other girl, seeing her master was about to be examined, blushed, put the tray of food on a small table by the bed and, with Johane, bowed, and stood back.

William continued his examination and quickly deduced that the man suffered from arthritis. He recommended some remedies he believed worked to lessen pain, but could give the man no hope for a cure. He also told him to occupy himself with distractions. "Don't let the pain dominate your imagination," he said. "Music helps, a good book, the conversation of friends and family."

"The latter causes me pain in and of themselves," the silversmith grumbled.

William wrote down the medication that would ease the man's pain, or at least make his life more endurable. During this time, he glanced at Johane from time to time. After her initial look of surprise at seeing him, she had stood expressionless, awaiting instructions from her new master. There was no sign that she knew William at all. He thought, *she will make a most discreet spy on Livesey island*. That is, should she consent to come with him.

William received a modest sum for the visit, paid to him by the servant who had admitted him. He pocketed it cheerfully. He had come to the house to see a serving girl who knew Johane and might know where she was. He had accomplished his purpose without ever revealing it, aided the sick by chance, and managed to do all of this without incurring any risk to himself or the person he sought. Johane had simply appeared. He took it as a good sign. But now he needed to talk to her. She obviously had not wanted to be recognized. Why? Why was she here? Why had she left the place she enjoyed, children she loved to teach, a kind employer who thought well of her?

He had taken his fee and was walking out of the door when he noticed Johane on the other side of the narrow street. She was standing in front of a grocer's, watching him, having waited for him to leave. She made a slight motion beckoning him to follow her. He did. She stopped on the next street, at the gate of a church porch. He had walked by the church many times but could not remember its name. Saint somebody. She turned, and waited for him to catch up. Then she went inside.

The church was empty at this hour, dark and cold. It smelled old, and indeed if it was the church William thought it was, the building had been old for the past hundred years or more. The empty nave was long and narrow, the air within stale, smelling slightly of incense, or perhaps the dead. Disease had been rampant in the neighborhood, especially the sweating sickness, a mysterious affliction that often took its victim's life within hours and for which no remedy was known.

On a bench she sat still, almost prayerful. As soon as he was seated by her, she whispered.

"How did you find me?"

"I asked your employer if you had a friend. He told me about the silversmith. It was only by chance that I was mistaken for the doctor sent for, brought up, and then saw you."

"Why were you looking for me?" she whispered. "Have you discovered something about my grandfather's murder?"

"Perhaps something as to the motive."

It was not the time or place to disclose what he had learned from Burghley about the Jews' treasure, it would only confuse her with the numerous facts, although perhaps, as Isaac Silva's granddaughter, she already knew.

"The motive?"

"I'll tell you later. For now, I have more pressing news which I hope will appeal to you. Lord Burghley wants to employ you."

Surprise caused her to raise her voice, although William detected as much fear as curiosity. "What? Lord Burghley? What would he want of me?"

"You will learn that presently," William said, lowering his voice in hope that she would do likewise. "But first, tell me why you disappeared from your previous employer's house, left no word as to where you were going or why."

She paused for a moment, then said, "The two men who I saw at the Domus, the men who visited at my grandfather's…"

"Yes, I remember them."

"I saw them again. I was returning to my employer's house. I turned and caught them following me. I recognized them at once. It helped to have the two of them together, which is how I remember them. They knew where I lived. I was frightened. I feared for myself and the household, the children. I believe, as do you, the men are murderers."

"So you simply disappeared?"

"My friend told me the silversmith was looking for another servant. I went there, thinking it would be safer. I altered my appearance somewhat, as you can see."

"You acted wisely," he said. "You are right to fear them. I don't know what they want of you but if they are following, they want something, perhaps something they think you know or have."

"I have nothing they should want," she said. "I fear they mean to hurt me since I saw them at the Domus. But you spoke of Lord Burghley wanting me to serve him. What manner of service might that be?"

"Well, it is service that would have you out of London before month's end."

"To where?"

"The isle of Livesey, where you grandfather was born. But come with me now to my house where I will tell you what his lordship has in mind—for the two of us."

He told her what Burghley had related to him; the story of the treacherous shipmaster and the drowned Jews and their treasure, the gold tablet containing the five Commandments. He told her this was part of her family's history, a history recorded by the single survivor of the enormity from whom she was directly descended. The story horrified her. She could hardly believe that anyone could be so cruel. To drown innocent exiles, including their children.

"I knew none of this."

"Your grandfather never told you?"

She shook her head. "He told me little of his youth, but was ever more interested in mine. I don't think he knew I existed until I came to him at the Domus. He asked me a hundred questions about my late father, his only son, with whom he had lost touch over the years—to his great regret."

William laid out Burghley's plan for the both of them. At first she found it all confusing, the mission to Livesey, its purpose, her role in it. She said she had no training as a caretaker of the sick. She had no inclination to spy, or search for buried treasure. It was a fool's errand, she thought. What he described to her was all a different world than what she knew. She was a domestic laborer; she had no greater aspirations. She supposed some day she would wed, have children, but there was no young man in her life at the moment. Her parents had died years before, she was an orphan and learning of her grandfather's existence had been a stroke of luck. She had learned of it from a clergyman in her native place. An elderly man, who knew her family's history far better than she, who somehow knew of her grandfather, his conversion, and where he lived in London. She had moved to London to find him, only to lose him again by a murderer's cruel hand. Tears came to her eyes as she recounted her own history.

He thought there was a quiet beauty in her sadness, that she thought too little of herself or what she might achieve.

"I will school you," William said. "I will teach you what you need to know, to make you fit for the work. Are you quick to learn?"

"I think of myself as such. I taught myself to read and cipher, and to speak French."

"To speak French? That's a difficult language for an English mouth."

"A girl with whom I once worked was French, she could hardly speak English, so to help I learned her tongue to teach her mine."

True and honest accomplishments, then," he said. "I have no doubt you can quickly learn what you will need to aid the sick—or at least, appear to have that skill."

"But what of the men?"

"Men?"

"The two who murdered my grandfather, who followed me here."

"They may continue to search for you here, in London. The island may prove a refuge for you in that respect."

But even as he said this, he knew it might be otherwise. No refuge for her, nor even for him. Isaac had told Johane the two men were from his native place. They were in London now. He prayed to God they would stay here, lost in the multitude of villains and cutthroats that comprised a good number of the city's denizens. Burghley had said he wanted her grandfather's murderers discovered, but William had seen he wanted Solomon's gold even more.

He reached over and placed a comforting hand on hers. She didn't flinch or look offended by his touch.

"Trust me," he said.

Eleven

On the day following, Johane left the silversmith's house for William's, ostensibly as a maid but in fact as his pupil.

She had fooled none of his other servants, who quickly surmised that she was something other than a serving girl. For one, she did no work, either in the bedchambers upstairs or the kitchens. For another, she was far too pretty in their estimation. She had smooth clear skin, a lustrous eye, and most important, she had hands not made raw by the hard work of housekeeping. They imagined she was William's mistress and were pleased that the master, whom they respected and admired, had a bedmate at last, someone to distract him from his work, possibly provide him with children. William discovered all this from his manservant Thomas, who regularly conveyed to him what was spoken of below stairs.

"I'm not sure I like knowing that I am pitied by you all for having no mistress till now," William said, after resolutely denying that Johane *was* his mistress, but stopping short of explaining just what purpose she did serve. Thomas was a young man of twenty-two whom William trusted implicitly, since he had been brought up at Theobalds, Lord Burghley's house, and his lordship had recommended him to William.

"Not pitied, Doctor. No, not pity, but only out of loving concern for your…health, your mental health."

"A condition improved by a bedmate?" William said, laughing.

"Well, sir, a companionable one, at the very least, no mere drab pawned off on you for a modest dowry, or some demanding scold who will not let you sleep."

"I will accept that, then," William told Thomas, who was a married man with a cantankerous wife but nonetheless seemed to appreciate the benefits of the marital state. He had heard the two wrangling, a contention that partly amused and partly horrified him. His father's house had been a place of peace and contentment, his father having chosen his wives wisely and being a man predisposed to conciliation and domestic tranquility.

William had himself contemplated marriage once, several years before, when he was enamored with the Dutch girl, the daughter of a lecturer at Cambridge. He believed she loved him as well, but her father had steered her toward a Dutch suitor, a wealthy burgess of Amsterdam. She had married him, not William. Had a child by him, not by William. And by report had died in childbirth—to William's inconsolable loss.

Since then there had been other women in his life, but nothing intimate or lasting that led him to conceive of any as a wife. He was not like other men, fixed on a prospective bride's money or title, but sought a confidante, someone with whom he could share his varied interests—or at least someone who could comprehend his passion for knowledge, for discovery, for science. He had yet to find her, or she to find him, whichever fate determined or God provided.

But none of this he could think of now. William had a talent for focusing on the business at hand. He thought it the key to his success at Cambridge and now in his medical practice. And the business at hand precluded a role as suitor, to Johane Sheldon, or any other women he knew of his own social rank.

For his pupil, William put together a course of study in anatomy and physiology, in practical treatments for a variety of ills and complaints. This included herbal brews, medicines, dietary supplements, and a store of skills such as the cleaning, binding, and healing of wounds. Creating the course excited him, gave him pleasure. He had never thought of himself as a teacher, but he wondered now if he might be good at it. Meanwhile, he continued his own practice, taking Johane with him as though she were an apprentice and indeed representing her as such, often to the wonder of his patients, who might be accustomed to the ministrations of so-called wise women but were unused to seeing a woman, and especially a young and pretty one, by the side of the estimable Doctor William Gilbert.

That their association would cause tongues to wag among servants, friends, colleagues, and patients, William knew was inevitable. He knew tongues would wag if he did no more than lie abed or stand still. He was a successful young man without a wife, not bad looking and in good health, a pleasant companion, and not without personal qualities a woman might find appealing. He had a good income from his medical practice and lived in a fine house. He knew he enjoyed these assets without feeling prideful or vain in knowing it.

Besides that, he was under orders. Burghley's orders. If Johane was to learn, she must be taught. Not just from books, but from practice. For William, that was the sum of it.

Quick to learn, so she had described herself. And truly, William thought, Johane was not only quick but hungry for knowledge, as though she had fasted before and was now filling herself. She had professed no interest in medicine before; she now grew intensely interested.

He reserved the early mornings for his tutoring of her. He put her behind his desk, a strong-legged trestle table that held dozens of books as well as his papers and manuscripts, and now a work space for her own writing, in a notebook with an Italian leather cover which he had provided her. There she wrote, keeping her head down while he instructed her. He used a human skeleton that he had secured from a Colchester hangman to explain the parts of the body, naming the bones and musculature. He used a cadaver he had at hand to explain the mysterious inner workings and plumbing of the body, male and female.

She was an able pupil. Learning that his interests went beyond the healing art, she asked him about his study of magnets and magnetism, and professed to him that, should she be able, she would serve as his assistant in that effort too, as soon as their service to Lord Burghley was accomplished.

"You have no other plans, no plans to marry, no young man suing for your favors?"

"No, Doctor, at least not at this moment."

"Moments change. We say, 'moment to moment' to express that," William said.

"I would like, Doctor, to assist you in your magnetical studies," she said again.

He remembered the interest in his experiments she had expressed before. He thought then it was merely something she said, to flatter him or to be respectful to someone above her in station; the learned doctor, a gentleman. But now he saw she was sincere. He could see it in her face, in the intensity of her gaze. He was more than flattered.

"About that, we shall see, Johane. But first we must do what Lord Burghley commands."

"I am not without fear in this," she admitted.

"I would think less of you, were you without fear," William said. "Were you fearless, then you would be lacking in imagination. What we hope to do will not be gladly received, at least by some at Livesey and we may not know who these are before they are upon us. But I believe just as you have the wit to learn quickly, you have the courage to face what we must to see your grandfather receive justice."

"I pray I do have such courage," she said. "Will we face it together, Doctor?"

Her question startled him, with its implication of an intimacy he had not considered and certainly not intended. He felt his face grow hot, and he quickly turned back to the skeleton that stood propped on its stand like a taciturn houseguest.

"And this part here, is called the tibia."

She repeated the name of the bone and wrote it down in her notebook like the dedicated pupil she was. She wielded the plumed pen slowly and deliberately, with a quiet intensity. He could not see her face, but he imagined its expression was like that when she told him of her interest in his magnets.

"It is Lord Burghley's desire that we travel together, that once on the isle we separate; I will go to Sir Arthur Challoner, you to his lady. Her name is Mildred Challoner, and she suffers from some ailment Lord Burghley was unaware of. You shall find out soon enough when you attend her. But our real mission is this. We will find out what each knows about the Jewish treasure, for though they be man and wife and thus one flesh, at least according to Holy Writ, one half of the marriage bed may keep secrets from the other half."

She looked up at him thoughtfully. "Are the two of them so impoverished that they must search for treasure?"

"Oh, I do think they are well enough off. They live in a manor house, the only one on the island. But some, as you may observe in your rich patients, never have enough."

"But what if Lady Challoner doesn't like me, prefers another to assist her?"

"She will like you well enough," William said. "Why shouldn't she?"

"I am from away, another part of England, and although my grandfather was born on Livesey as were my ancestors, I cannot reveal that to her or anyone there. I would immediately be suspected of having some hidden purpose—which I do, yet would not let it be known."

"Don't worry. Lord Burghley has commended you to them and whom Lord Burghley commends, none dares refuse. I guarantee you that we will be well received, the both of us. Besides, Lord Burghley has placed you in my charge. He has been most direct in telling me how I am responsible for your safety… in every respect."

She asked about magnets again, and again, about their power to attract gold.

"There are many things said about magnets and their powers," William said. "Often by persons who have not put their supposed knowledge to any test, but have simply passed on old wives' tales or invented facts to deceive the gullible. Sometimes by persons who would not know a magnet from a cobblestone."

"Are you saying then, Doctor, that magnets have no such power?"

"In their pure form, gold, silver, copper brass are not magnetic or are only slightly so, but if iron is added, that is, if the thing to be attracted is what is called an alloy…"

"Alloy, Doctor?"

He explained what it was, the process, the miracle of it, like the alchemists' transformation but no myth or magician's trick.

"If gold or silver is smelted with another metal, say iron or steel or silver or copper, then the magnet attracts these. Most of those precious objects we label as gold or silver are not purely so. Gold in its pure form is soft, flexible. Time will not harden it. Were you to wish to bend it, you might do so easily. It would make a poor ring, a worse bracelet or plate, for which solidity is required."

"Why should I wish to bend it?" she asked.

William laughed. "I have no idea. I offer it only as a hypothetical."

"A what, Doctor?"

"A hypothetical. An example, something stated as though it were a fact."

"So, not true?"

"Well, no, but offered for argument's sake. True or false is not the issue."

"I think you have lost me, Doctor."

He explained again.

Then she said, "But were the magnet large enough, if the force it exerted were strong enough, could it lift gold?"

"Alloyed gold, as I have said."

"Rings, plates, bracelets? All these?"

"Well, yes. It has been done—not by me, but by others."

"I imagine bringing these and other precious treasures up from the depths of the earth and from the seas." She said this dreamily, her eyes fixed in the middle distance, where perhaps she saw the very things she spoke of shining before her.

"It would take, as I have said, a very large magnet to do what you imagine, or perhaps a whole set of them, bound together to enhance their strength. You are conceiving of not merely a magnet, but a veritable machine."

He was pleased with her curiosity about magnets, which he thought gave promise for her successful spying when they should come to the island. All knowledge, to his thinking, began with a curious mind. What other motive was there to seek beyond what was obvious in the world but unexplained? Curiosity was a gift of God, the Maker of all things. His greatest gift to man.

That night, the night before their leave-taking, William had a dream. It was provoked, he recognized upon waking, by Johane's questions, her curiosity. In the dream, he saw the great magnetic machine he had envisioned, an intricate device of wheels and hoists, erected upon solid ground but lowering down, down into some pit dug into the earth where it might clasp treasure like a great claw. In the dream, it was not the prospect of treasure that interested him, any more than it would have been were he awake. It was the mechanical contrivance itself, the machine of his imagination. It was a thing of beauty, not just utility. In the dream he built it, with his own hands and tools, according to his design.

And, most wondrous of all, it worked.

Twelve

Their first night of the journey they spent as guests at Theobalds, with Lord Burghley as their host. Johane said to William, taking him aside, that she had never seen such a palace. Since her wonder at the splendor of Theobalds matched his own at his first visit, he laughed and assured her that her amazement was not unusual or unwarranted. "Even the queen in her visits has proclaimed my Lord Burghley's house a wonder of England, finer than any of her palaces."

"It has a forest of chimneys, Doctor. It is the size of a city. And enough liveried servants to make an army."

A servant came to show them to their rooms.

"I will not be sleeping with the maidservants?" Johane whispered to him as they climbed the stairs.

"You are no longer a servant," he whispered back. "You are a guest of the house, a guest of the lord treasurer. You shall have your own chamber."

She nodded her head.

"Does that bother you?" he asked.

"I will grow used to it," she said, smiling.

"I know you shall," he replied.

Burghley's suppers were impressive affairs, filling the great hall not only with a table the length of a field, but a half dozen of them of equal length and all the room not only full of Burghley's family and its guests, but it would seem his entire household.

"The great lord has his servants drink and break bread with him?" Johane asked.

"It is an old practice, observed by his lordship and honored by many others. He considers even the scullions and the cooks, the grooms and the gardeners as part of his family. He's father to them all."

William and Johane sat together, huddled with other members of the household—by their dress secretaries or upper servants, visiting merchants, and minor officials of the court William did not recognize. At his table, William could hear various languages spoken; French, German, Dutch, and others he did not know. The common tongue was not English but Latin, a tongue William spoke readily, prompting Johane to pluck at his sleeve often and ask him what he said and what was said by others at table.

"Merchants' talk," he said, "and some political intrigue and gossip far beyond my own understanding. I am a poor translator for you."

After supper, William and Johane were escorted, not into the library of the house where William had usually conversed with Burghley, but into a gallery which during the day would have looked out on the vast gardens of the house. Braces of candles illuminated the long room, splendidly furnished in the center of which was yet another hearth, ornately decorated, with a furious fire. Servants were everywhere. Burghley was well known to be a scrupulous governor of his household, prizing loyalty above all, but not forgetting competence and steadfastness.

As they settled, Burghley had directed Johane to the chair nearest to him, looked her over carefully, and for the first hour or so seemed to forget that William was present. This surprised William and abashed him somewhat, for he thought as leader of the assigned expedition he would receive the lion's share of his lordship's attention while Johane would sit quietly by, listening. But he was in no position to protest nor to intrude. Besides, he remembered that to Burghley he was a known quantity. The nervous, overawed young woman sitting next to him was someone to be discovered, weighed in the balance, before his lordship was prepared to put his trust in her.

And overawed Johane seemed to be. Had she been bound to her chair, she would not have sat so still, her eyes lowered as though at prayer, her face aglow in the firelight—not from the heat but from the intensity of blood rushing into her head. William imagined her thoughts, she who had but days before been but a maid in a silversmith's house, before one she recognized as supremely powerful, living in a palace, and with dozens of armed guards and watchful attendants at his command. He sensed her fear. A gallery furnished as she had never seen before, with tapestries and carpeting and stuffed chairs, not the simple wooden stools with which she would have been familiar. Had she been in the presence of the queen herself, she undoubtedly would not have felt more cowed, more threatened, more undone. He knew she would be conscious of her dress, which was a simple homespun skirt in an even more modest pattern, no brocade or other frills, with no jewelry, and her long black hair about her shoulders. She looked more like a barmaid or a country wench than one suited for such a place. William felt the impulse to comfort her in some way, but he did not dare interrupt their host, and she avoided his eyes even as she avoided Burghley's.

"Your name is Johane Sheldon, or so Doctor Gilbert gives me to understand?"

It was a simple enough question, but she hesitated before answering. Burghley seemed to sense her terror. He smiled, leaned toward her, and reached out to touch her hand which was resting in the folds of her skirt. She recoiled at his touch, as though she thought he might harm her, call his armed attendants, have her carried off or thrown from the house, unworthy in dress and demeanor or birth.

"Not Silva?"

"No, my lord." Her voice trembled as she admitted this.

"Don't be afraid, child," Burghley said in a fatherly tone.

"Sheldon, my lord. My real name is Johane Sheldon. I used the name Silva so that the warden at the Domus would believe I was Isaac's granddaughter which, upon my oath, I am. I thought he would not believe me with a different name."

"A clever move, my child. Had I been you, I would have done the same." He laughed.

Burghley's assurance, even more his laughter, accomplished its end. Her body relaxed and she let out a breath of air as though she had been holding it in ever since coming into the room.

"Johane. A rare name, a pretty name," Burghley said. "What does it mean, child?"

"*God is gracious*, my lord. That's what it means, or so I have been told."

"A good name, then, for so He is allowed, by Jew and Gentile. And you are the granddaughter of Isaac Silva, lately dead?"

"I am, my lord."

"Your grandfather was my friend," Burghley said. "I have known him for several years. He was once a guest in this house, staying in the very room you now occupy here. He provided me with valuable information regarding an object that had come into my possession, which I may later show to you, since you too have an interest in it. He helped me ascertain the significance of it, the value of it."

Johane said nothing. Burghley went on. "Tell me, Mistress Sheldon, are you of the Jewish faith and blood?"

She hesitated again, cast a quick look at William, and then said, "I am of the blood of Israel through my father, but not my mother."

"This would be Isaac's son?"

"Yes, my lord."

"Isaac never spoke to me of his family. I never knew whether he had married, had children, family. He never spoke of these matters," Burghley said.

"My grandfather was a very private man, your lordship, as I learned when first I met him. One must needs be so in England if he is a Jew, and then if he converts he must become even more careful in that which he discloses to strangers, who may be Jew-haters or spies, or both. He may be hated by all sides, condemned as a traitor to our ancient faith, or if a convert, then secretly still a Jew."

Burghley nodded. "You speak truly, Mistress Sheldon. I'm afraid it is so. Converts, *conversos*, are rarely congratulated for their change of heart and many of my countrymen believe that it is impossible for a Jew to become a true and devout believer in Christ save his intent is to deceive."

"That was not my grandfather, my lord. He was an honest man, a true Christian. He was nothing but what he professed to be."

"I have no doubt he was honest and think of him daily since he died."

"With all respect, my lord, I believe he was murdered."

When she said this, she turned for the second time to look at William. William said, "And so do I believe, my lord, as I have told you previously."

"All evidence suggests the truth of that," Burghley replied. "But tell me more, mistress, about your father. What was his vocation?"

"Vocation, my lord?"

"His calling, his trade?"

"He was a tailor, my lord. He had a shop in the town where I was born."

"Which was?"

"Neigh unto Halstead, Essex, my lord."

"Has it a name?"

"Plimpton, my lord."

"I do know it, have passed through it many times and have some acquaintances there, and some property as well."

"My father died of a wasting illness when I was eight. My mother struggled as a widow, and when I came of age to work, I went into service, first in the manor house of a rich silk merchant."

"How old would you have been then?"

"Twelve, when I was first employed."

"But you came to London. Why?"

"A guest of my master, a wealthy lady of London, secured me a place. She was pleased by my appearance and service to her while she was a guest. Said that she had delighted her and pleased her more than a dozen such maids. She bought me, in a sense, from my old master, who cared for me but who found he had too many servants in his household and at too great a cost to him. That brought me to London, where Doctor Gilbert found me employed."

"And the doctor here has told you of my wishes. You are to go with him to the isle of Livesey to wait upon the lady of the manor, while he ministers to Sir Arthur Challoner. Is that your understanding, Mistress Sheldon?"

"It is, my lord. Doctor Gilbert has instructed me in my duties."

"And did he say your mission was to discover what is known about the search for a certain hoard of wealth, Jewish wealth, stolen and concealed there many years past."

"That is my understanding, my lord."

"You said you were from Halstead."

"Neigh unto there, my lord."

"There was a burrow found near there, was there not? Where it was said the Saxons buried treasure."

"I heard tell of it, my lord."

"And it is said certain gold was discovered there, and arms and helmets?"

"So it was said, my lord, but whether it was true what was found I do not know. One hears many things. Besides, by then I was in service in Master Alexander Burton's lodge. When in service, we who are maidservants know nothing of what happens outside the house. The affairs without are distractions from our duties. So said Master Burton many times."

Burghley said, "Well, then the truth of it was that nothing was found there—all was a fraud, as is often the case. There are indeed many burrows in England, discovered and undiscovered. Some hill-diggers, as they are called, are nothing more than tricksters, securing funds from the avaricious—more fool they."

Burghley went on about the recovery of treasure, a subject in which he had a great interest, as William had already discovered. As he talked, Johane seemed to listen carefully, her face showed genuine interest, and William confirmed what he had already inferred from her studies with him—that she had a quick, curious mind, not a maidservant's mind surely, not even that of a great lady of the court, most of whom he thought, in his experience were beset with vanity and ambition but no more curiosity than a goose. This cankered view did not apply to the queen, of course. The great Elizabeth was strong-minded and scholarly, and an adept politician—but she was exceptional. So, he believed, in her own way was Johane Sheldon.

Burghley wanted Johane to see his cabinet of curiosities, the one he had shown William earlier. William was not surprised. He could see that Burghley was as taken by Johane's intellect and beauty as he, and Johane's excitement at the prospect of seeing Burghley's collection was readily apparent. Her confidence returned, her dark eyes flashed with pleasure as a servant entered to escort all of them to Burghley's great library and that section of which was given to the cabinets.

The manservant bowed low and withdrew, casting a curious glance at the maiden who was dressed no better than a serving maid but had the attention of his master and the London doctor who came frequently to Theobalds to attend to the young, misshapen son of the master of the house.

Burghley showed first the items he had shown William on his last visit: the Saxon swords, the silver cups, the rings, and Saracen blades, some from Asian lands with unpronounceable names. William could see Johane's interest in these objects. She was fascinated, as he expected her to be. She expressed her delight and marveled, said she had never seen such things, imagined such things, or heard of the places from whence they came. She had served in the houses of wealthy men and seen the jewels of their wives and their bags of silver and sometimes gold, but such a display as this was beyond what she had ever conceived—more wealth, more splendor, a king's treasure, William supposed she thought.

But Burghley reserved for last what was dearest in his collection: Solomon's golden tablet.

"That's what my grandfather described to me," she said, breathlessly.

She asked if she could touch it. She said it would be like touching her grandfather one last time, an experience she was deprived of by his treacherous murderers.

"It is most marvelous, my lord."

"Yes, it is marvelous. Unique, one of a kind. To think Solomon had it made for himself, revered it, gazed upon it nightly."

Burghley told her how he had come by the tablet. It was the same story he had told William about the settled debt, the country lord that did not know what he had, what was written upon the tablet, thought it was but gold.

"It is most sacred, my lord," she said.

"When the Jewish treasure is recovered, the twin tablets will be one, as they were meant to be, for God did not give Moses the Commandments that they should be halved by man's mischief or become the booty of thieves and robbers."

"I am most grateful, my lord, for your having shown me these things."

"I am pleased to do it, Mistress Sheldon. But I must remind you of this: It would not be to your advantage for someone on the island to connect you to your grandfather. You will be there as a stranger. You will tend to the needs of Lady Challoner, and become, if you can, her confidante. She must not know why you are really there, nor whom you really serve."

"I will do as you command, my lord."

"Whatever you learn from your mistress, or from servants you might converse with, touching upon these matters—I mean of Jews, treasure, hidden hoards—you must share with the doctor here."

"Upon my oath, I will, my lord."

She bowed to her noble host and made a curtsy. A very neat curtsy, that William supposed she had learned in the houses where she had served.

Two of Burghley's maidservants entered and led Johane to where she was to sleep. "Treat her as if she were a lady, a guest of Theobalds," Burghley called after them. "That is my wish, and I expect it to be observed."

William watched the three women leave. Both of the maidservants were better dressed than Johane, but he noticed she followed them with a confident stride, as though she knew her own worth, if they did not.

William stayed behind at Burghley's behest, waiting for more about his mission. But for the next hour, as the fire in the hearth slowly died, Burghley went on as he was wont to do in the late evenings. He talked of his life at court, his relations with the queen, his fears for his country, beset by enemies at home and abroad. William marveled that he could so suddenly set aside what had preoccupied him all evening in his conversation with Johane.

But then, just before sending him to bed, Burghley said, as though it were an afterthought: "I am most impressed with Isaac's granddaughter. According to the proverb, the apple does not fall far from the tree. I see the truth of that in this girl's intelligence, her perceptions, her curiosity. What maid of her age takes an interest in metallurgy? Or your magnets, Doctor? I trust you had a difficult enough time getting your colleagues at Cambridge to take your interest as more than a foolish hobbyhorse. But here you have a young woman of, what, twenty or twenty-one? Who can read, write, cipher, and endure an old man's ramblings without falling asleep. She is indeed a wonder."

William agreed. Johane *was* a wonder.

"And quite lovely as well. Her dark looks do not please every taste, besotted as we English are with yellow hair and pink flesh."

"True, my lord. She is an attractive young woman, though she be more brown than fair. It's likely among her ancestors is a Spaniard or perhaps even an Italian."

"Which reminds me again, Doctor, to exhort you to protect her virtue while you are in her company. I would not want to hear reports of your abuse of her."

"Never, my lord. Never would I think of such a thing, much less do it."

"Ah, an oath often made, but commonly violated."

"You have my solemn word, my lord. I will regard her as a sister."

"Sister? Yes, that's good, Doctor," Burghley said, smiling. "A sufficient guarantee, I would hope, for her chastity."

Burghley had other advice to give about their upcoming journey, but William half heard it. He realized to his embarrassment that he was on the verge of sleep. It had been a very long day. His host must have noticed him drifting. Burghley rang a bell by his side and within a minute a servant entered the room.

"Show the good doctor to his room," Burghley said to the servant. "See that he has all that he needs, for he shall not find the manor house on Livesey isle half so accommodating."

Thirteen

They were to travel by coach to the island; a coach provided by Burghley, not the fine one his lordship traveled in with its armorial insignia, footmen, mounted, pennant-bearing guards, and a team of six, but a more modest conveyance without insignia and with four horses and a single driver. He assured them it would take half the usual time to make the fifty-mile journey. "And it will be much easier on the buttocks," Burghley said, laughing genially, he who was accounted a good rider and rode upon a mule each afternoon for exercise.

It was a two-day trip, made worse by constant rain and muddy roads. They spent the first night at an inn, at some town whose name William could not remember later. This was an expense not foreseen by William, although he was gratified to discover Burghley had provided for that, as well. An embarrassing episode occurred when the innkeeper assumed that William and Johane were husband and wife, or at least a couple, and offered them a single room with a "very capacious bed where all four legs can be stretched to their delight."

Before Johane could protest this misunderstanding, William did, explaining that while they traveled together, they both were in the service of Lord Burghley and that was their sole connection. They were traveling companions, not lovers. They would require separate accommodations.

"As it pleases you, sir," the innkeeper remarked, with a look suggesting he didn't believe a word of what William had said. William turned to Johane, expecting her to be blushing, but she was not. She was covering her mouth with her hands to disguise her laughter, William suspected at his own embarrassment. He felt his face burn.

They ate a simple supper provided by the innkeeper's wife, and then went to bed in the separate rooms provided. William read for half an hour, then fell asleep with the book in his hand. When he awoke it was dawn, his book was on the floor and the innkeeper at his door, announcing that his *traveling companion*, a phrase the man was careful to emphasize, was already below, breakfasted, and prepared to continue on their journey.

William hurried to dress himself, but was pleased at Johane's demonstration of enthusiasm for the journey. It was, he thought, a good sign, a portent of success, despite the parade of potential obstacles he had envisioned.

During the journey next day, the girl was strangely silent and sometimes seemed to have fallen asleep, which was easy enough with the rocking of the carriage. The rain had stopped, the sky was clear, and the country that passed through was quite beautiful, William thought. He had not before been in this part of England, the wilds of Kent. He had never had occasion to travel there or ambition to do so. But here he was, sitting opposite a young woman he had not known or heard of but a few weeks before, sworn to protect and bound to her in a common enterprise.

William studied the girl's face as she slept. It was a fine face with smooth, flawless skin and full lips that needed no coloring beyond what God had given her. He wished for a moment he could read her mind. He hoped she was not having second thoughts about their mission. He wondered, had he pressured this innocent girl unfairly into accepting her new role, in dragging her from the city into an obscure corner of Kent and to an island? If he had, he felt shame for it. After all, he might have a duty to Burghley born of gratitude as much as respect for him. But she had no special duty. He was a great lord. Her acquiescence to his plan was appropriate and predictable. She yielded to his power, probably without understanding she might have said no.

Before their arrival at their destination, the girl had revealed her thoughts. They were not of hesitation at going forward, only reflection on her own past.

"You asked me, Doctor, if there was anything the men—I mean the men who visited my grandfather and probably murdered him—wanted of me. I said I could think of nothing. I have so little, and certainly nothing of such great value that they should dog my steps, threaten my peace, much less my life. But now I do think they may want something."

"And what is that?" he asked her, watching from the window of the coach the green Kentish countryside, swollen with spring, verdant to a madness with the recent heavy rains.

He heard her whisper behind him, as though it was a sacred utterance: "My memories, I think. It's all I have, but they want them."

"Your memories…your memories of what?"

"Of my grandfather, I think. Or something I know that I don't know I know. You think I'm silly for putting it like that. You think I'm speaking nonsense." She blushed and looked down to where her hands were folded neatly on her lap.

"No," William said. "Not at all. You may be perfectly right. Everyone's memories are worth something, at least to someone. And now that your grandfather is dead, what can be known of his final days and thoughts depends upon you. It is all in your head now, your grandfather having gone to heaven."

"That makes me fearful."

"That your grandfather has gone to heaven?"

"Because you make me sound like one walking about a city with a purse full of gold, prey of every cutpurse that passes me."

"I do pray you are not so endangered."

"Prayer is good, but will you also protect me, Doctor, from such threats?"

"I will, Johane. I swear on my honor."

"Your honor, Doctor?"

"You have my word."

Fourteen

On the second day, they arrived. It was cold and overcast, and the air smelled of the sea.

Burghley had told him about Livesey, said it was not half as big in ground as Theobalds, its coast gravel and sand, a rampart of rocky cliff, a forlorn, isolated piece of earth. He'd said the Challoners, whose land it was, were an odd couple; reserved, never came to court or seemed to care to. "All this, Doctor, you will discover for yourself in due course," Burghley had said.

The island had but a single village, a "scattering of wretched cottages" as Burghley had described it, pasture and marshland and a hill rising, by William's estimation, two or three hundred feet above the level of the sea. A causeway linked the island to the mainland, except at high tide when even that was covered with water, or so William was told by the driver of their coach, who had been to the island before and knew people in the village. He was a store of information.

"All the island belongs to Sir Arthur Challoner. It's his manor, He governs it after the old ways."

"Old ways?" William asked.

"As a sort of fiefdom. He lives in the big house, you can see it from here, or at least the hill upon which it sits."

William looked to where the coachman pointed. In the distance he could see the hill, but nothing upon it. "I see no manor house," William said.

"You wouldn't, Doctor. It faces the sea to the south and lies a little below the crest of the hill. But you'll see it soon enough. You'll be living among them, and good luck to you."

"Why do you say that?"

"Because they are strange folk, given to strange ways. It comes from living where they do, at the edge of the sea. Livesey is different, Doctor. You shall presently see for yourself."

"You will tell his lordship that we have arrived safely?"

"I will, Doctor, you and the girl."

"You mean Mistress Sheldon."

"Mistress Sheldon—if you say so, Doctor."

The coachman looked at William, apparently expecting a gratuity beyond what Burghley had paid him for getting them there safely. William resolved the man would get nothing: he disliked his rudeness in dismissing Johane as a serving wench quite above herself.

"I say so."

Disappointed, the coachman hurried away to hail a boatman. The tide was at its fullest and Livesey now appeared truly an island. William felt a sudden chill. This was the fateful place—where the Jews were drowned. He felt the heavy weight of the island's history all about him. He wondered if Johane felt it, too. Livesey was, after all, her ancestral place. How could she not feel what he did at the very sight of it?

He helped her into the boat, which she regarded fearfully, saying that she had never been in a boat before and was afraid of the water. It was no more than a shallop. They were rowed by a boy who couldn't have been older than twelve or thirteen.

William reached for her hand and told her not to worry. She smiled a thin smile. "I can't swim," she admitted.

"You won't have to," he said with a confidence he didn't feel. He could swim, but he wondered if he could swim strongly enough to save her if the boat capsized or sank under their weight.

The boy who rowed them said nothing during the journey, which was short, the channel created by the tide not being more than a hundred of so yards by William's estimation. And then they were at the village, a narrow street beginning at the quay, a handful of thatched-roofed cottages and shops, and further inland on a rise a stone church with needle-like steeple. No inn that he could see, a tavern called the Saracen's Blade by its sign, fishing nets outside most of the cottages, the stink of fish and decaying matter on the shore, gulls and other sea birds flying above, their shrill cries like those of souls lost at sea.

"It's as my grandfather described it, the village," Johane said. "How will we get to the manor?"

"Walk, I think."

"Is it far, do you think, Doctor?"

"Not far. I see it ahead of us." In truth, he did not. He saw only the hill where he had been told the manor was, facing the sea to the south, but he trusted in what he had been told. He saw the hill; the seat of the Challoners would soon appear.

He carried her bags, one small, one larger. He had himself but one. She was beneath him in station, but he did not mind being her porter. She was, after all, a woman, thus his gesture was common courtesy, although he knew some of his class would disdain to do it.

The street, first cobbled, then a mix of gravel and earth, extended beyond the church and then began to rise to the hill he had seen from the mainland. They began to walk. Theirs would not be an auspicious arrival. Unmounted, unheralded, unattended, they might as well be wandering pilgrims come a knocking for a night's rest or a free meal.

He carried a letter of introduction from Burghley. William thought that would be more than sufficient to gain them entrance to the manor. Also, Burghley had said he would write a letter to Sir Arthur Challoner, announcing the good news that he had found a London doctor who could work miracles and was sending the same straightway, along with an attendant for his lady wife. Burghley and Challoner had some connection, though Burghley had never made it clear what it was.

The manor house stood at the edge of a cliff and seemed almost to have been built into it to give it a backbone to the weather, which he had been told could be fierce in winter. It was of gray sandstone, two storied, with a wide porch and shuttered windows. It stood a stark edifice, its placement full of authority, looking defiantly across the narrow sea separating his own country from its traditional enemies, France and Spain. It had a small, untended garden, no orchard, with a small copse behind the house and reaching up to the crown of the hill. He could see a stable, horses in a pasture, a flock of grazing sheep. These, he assumed, were all owned by Sir Arthur.

A tall, smooth-faced man with dark, short-cropped hair, square jaw, and air of self-importance admitted them to the house. He was dressed neatly in dark doublet and hose, suggesting he was an upper servant, and perhaps not a servant at all, but some friend or associate of the lord of the manor. He said he had seen them approach from an upstairs window and knew who they were and why they had come. William hadn't needed to show his letter from Burghley.

"I am Doctor Gilbert. This is Johane Sheldon. She is to care for Lady Challoner."

"I am John Broderick, Sir Arthur's personal secretary and steward," the man announced solemnly. "My master lies abed. He will awake soon. I am to show you to your rooms for now."

Broderick looked doubtfully at Johane and asked, "And you, mistress, have you had experience tending to the sick? You seem quite young and frail for such a duty?"

Before Johane could reply, William said, "She's experienced, and trained as well. Your mistress will find no fault in her, nor have I. She has worked with me in my practice for more than a year."

This was a lie, of course. Johane had studied with him less than a month, but William saw no reason to tell the truth about it, not to this uppity servant, whatever he was.

Broderick looked Johane up and down a second time. "Very well," he said.

"We are here at the behest of Lord Burghley, the queen's chief minister," William said.

"I know of Lord Burghley," Broderick said. "And Sir Arthur told me you were coming."

The manor was dark and deary-looking, wearing its age poorly. William could not imagine living there for long before his mission met with either success or failure and he could go home again, either to Burghley's approbation or disappointment.

A narrow vestibule opened into a great hall, darkly paneled and with so few windows it would need to be lamped and candled even at noon. Upon the walls were dark, barely discernible portraits that William assumed were Challoner ancestors, and several coats of arms, all proclaiming lineage, connections, some distant family achievement or trial. A long table, stools—not benches—and at the end a banistered stairway leading into an even more obscure upper floor. William and Johane followed Broderick up, their footsteps echoing on carpetless stairs.

"This is the mistress's chamber," Broderick said, stopping before a door in a long corridor. "And you, girl," Broderick said, looking aside to Johane, "you shall lie within her earshot should you be needed. When your mistress calls, you come straightway. Do you understand, girl?"

Johane said she did. William looked at Johane. She must be terrified, he thought, yet she stood with her chin up and didn't hesitate to answer. "If the mistress calls, I'll come," she said.

Broderick opened a door and motioned for Johane to enter. Johane passed into the room and closed the door behind her, gently, without a sound and without a glance toward William. It was a signal to him that their new relationship had now begun. She was a servant again, he a doctor, a guest in the house. They knew each other from before but now must keep each other at an arm's length.

The two men proceeded down the corridor, Broderick leading the way, holding a single candle above his head as though it were a little torch. They came to the end of the passage to a door.

Broderick seemed to have forgotten William's name.

"Doctor Gilbert."

"Yes, quite so, Doctor Gilbert. Here is your room."

His room, as Broderick had called it, was hardly larger than a closet, with a single window, plastered walls that were spotted and yellow with age, and an unpleasant odor he could not quite place. There was a narrow bed with a stained sheets and rolled up blanket at its foot. He saw a washstand with a cistern without water, and a clay chamber pot sitting beside it, smelling slightly of previous use. There was no pillow or bolster on the bed. He might have found more wholesome lodging in a cheap London inn, or country poor house.

He wondered if Johane had fared better than he, ensconced in her room, waiting, as Broderick had said, for the summons of her new mistress. He wondered if Burghley realized the genteel poverty of this lord of the island. Certainly, if Sir Arthur Challoner had found Jewish treasure he had benefited little from it, or was a miser, content to feast his eyes on his wealth in the privacy of a cellar or some other obscure retreat, the golden hoard for his eyes only.

"I hope, Doctor, these accommodations meet your expectations," Broderick said.

"I had no expectations, Master Broderick," William said, throwing his bag upon the bed, not wishing to give the man the satisfaction of seeing his dismay at the room.

"I will let Sir Arthur know you and the girl have arrived, Doctor," Broderick said.

"Please do, Master Broderick."

Broderick shut the door behind him.

It was a relief to William to see the back of the man, who was impudent and doubtless sycophantic when he saw it to his advantage. William knew his type well enough. They thrived in the households of the gentry, even more so in the palaces of the nobility. A little tyrant over the servants below him, insolent to guests of the master until he discovered what sway they had with the master or what benefit subservience might be to himself. A threat to all below, who were his to bully and demean. Yes, but an hour in Challoner's manor and he already had an enemy, or seemed to.

William walked to the window, opened the shutter, and looked out. Below him stretched the sea. There was land beyond it, but now beyond his view. He saw no ships or boats upon it, just blue-gray water, as smooth and glassy as a lake, and gray sky above, as though this were the edge of the earth even as it was of England. Immediately below him was a narrow stretch of sand. It widened slowly, even as he stood there. He thought at first it was his imagination, but it was not so. The tide was ebbing. He wondered how far, how much of the depths would be revealed. A shipwreck or two perhaps, or the bones of drowned sailors and Jews.

He was sad now that Burghley had told him that story of the treacherous captain, the hapless passengers. It was the stuff of nightmares, provokers of melancholy and despair. He shook himself to rid himself of the thought, but he knew it would return, and soon. He had complied with Burghley's request. With that came the inevitable consequences.

William had been born near the sea. As a man, he had sailed upon it more than once back and forth to Amsterdam where he had friends. It was not a part of the planet he feared or disliked. On the contrary, its hidden depths suggested to him the vast unknown of his universe. Even more than the land, which was a thin crust by comparison. But today, looking out at it, he felt its subtle threat. Why? His mission on the island had just begun, and yet somehow he already felt the specter of defeat. A mission that would come to nothing but wasted time and failure in his great patron's eyes.

He waited nearly an hour, by his reckoning, sitting upon the narrow bed since there was neither chair nor stool in the room. He had not unpacked his bag. There was no chest or cupboard to put anything in. He might have been in a monk's cell, having so little to accommodate him. While he waited, he thought; about his visit with Burghley, about the gold tablet, about the dreary place in which he now found himself, about Johane Sheldon, occupying the room but a dozen or so steps away. What might she be doing right now? Had she already been called to serve her new mistress? Or, like him, was she waiting for a summons, staring from a window at the distant sea, perhaps regretting coming to the island now she saw the forlorn place it was with her own eyes and had experienced the rude treatment of the household's steward?

A soft knocking came at his door. It was not Broderick, but another servant. He said his name was Dawson. Dawson was older than Broderick, graying and stoop-shouldered, his garments shabbier than Broderick's. He said he would show William to the master's bedchamber. The master was ready to see him now, Dawson said with a stiff bow, and moved forward slowly to the other end of the long corridor like a housebreaker fearing detection.

William prepared himself mentally. His mission was about to begin in earnest. He was himself, but not entirely so; not a physician with his cures, but a spy with his own agenda.

Fifteen

John Broderick was with his master, standing by a huge and ornate four-poster bed upon which lay a hairless old man of sixty or more. The lord of Livesey, Sir Arthur Challoner, had a long, narrow face, almost ascetic, as though he were the victim of a prolonged fast. His dark eyes had a hollow look and were accentuated by his pallor, for he looked ready enough to meet his Maker and be gone by nightfall to his heavenly reward. He was, at least, sitting up. A good sign, William thought.

"Doctor Gilbert?"

William made a stiff nod. "I am. Lord Burghley sent me to see to you and to your wife, to provide what medical services you may require."

"Ah," Challoner said in a dry, raspy voice as though even speaking was an intolerable drain on his bodily strength. "Lord Burghley is a friend of long standing. We were at school together. Did he tell you? He sent me a letter about you, said he was sending you to heal me. I knew him when he was but Master William Cecil. Before he was raised to his present honors."

The old man began to ramble on about his earlier association with Burghley. He had once had dealings in London and Burghley had assisted him in some suit at law, in which Burghley also had an interest. The suit was complicated, plagued with legal distinctions. It involved the purchase of some land, a trespass, even an assault by one servant upon another. William could make no sense of it. Perhaps his lawyer father could have.

William half listened, eager to examine the man to find out what was wrong with him besides age, which anyone might see was heavy upon him. Broderick, however, was very attentive, although William was sure the secretary, if that is what he was, had heard these stories before, just as the man would have heard his employer's incessant complaints.

"I am not well, Doctor. I have not been well for some time."

"Can you tell me, sir, your symptoms?"

"Symptoms?"

"Your complaints, Sir Arthur."

"I am always tired, I sweat of nights and sometimes of days. My joints ache constantly. I have no appetite, no desires. You see my pallor. Is it not ghastly? Do I not already appear a dead man?"

William thought it best to evade the question although he had, indeed, seen healthier looking corpses. "With your permission, may I examine you?" he asked.

The invalid was wearing a nightshirt, unbuttoned to his navel. William pulled it aside revealing the old man's hairless, concave chest; bloodless, like his face. William had brought into the room a small bag in which he carried his medical instruments. He opened it and pulled out a conical object. One end was enlarged like an ear trumpet. It was an instrument he had devised himself, to magnify the sound of a heart beat beyond what could normally be detected by pressing an ear to the chest. He placed one end upon Challoner's body, just above his heart, and listened.

The old man's heartbeat was weak. William could hardly hear it, and the beats seemed irregular, an unnatural syncopation. He placed his hand on the man's skin. It was cold and clammy. There seemed no purpose in asking how the man was feeling. It was obvious he was not only unwell, but perhaps more in need of a priest than a physician.

He proceeded to feel the old man's shoulders and arms, reached down beneath the sheet to do likewise his thighs and calves, stopping when his patient's wincing became cries of pain.

"Oh I burn, Doctor! I burn, even as you can see."

"Is it always so?"

"Not always, but enough. At night it is often worse. I cannot sleep, and if I sleep I have terrible dreams. So, Doctor, what do you recommend, what will make me better?"

It was the inevitable question and reasonably so. Who did not want to get better, to rise from his sick bed and walk, or open his eyes and see? These were miracles of biblical proportion. But William with all his learning knew well that sometimes there was no satisfactory answer. A failing heart could not be repaired, much less replaced with a new one. William did not say this to the bed-ridden man. He suggested a palliative.

"There is medicine that will steady your heart, others that will bring you relief from pain in your joints. but I must tell you outright, Sir Arthur, that no medication or nostrum will return you to the vigor of your youth. At your age, one must accept a certain decline in energy and a certain quantum of aches and pains."

William had told the truth as he saw it, but obviously it didn't please his new patient. Challoner scowled. He said, "You were recommended to me by my dear friend. But what you say, Doctor merely echoes what my earlier doctors have said. From you, Doctor Gilbert, I expected more."

"And I promise, sir, that I will try to do more," William said. "I am merely acknowledging the limitations of my profession. Still, we shall see if I can exceed them. Tell me, sir, is there an apothecary in the village?"

Challoner said there was. "His name is Theophilus Baker. You will find him at the bottom of the high street, next to the tavern. He's as old as I am and hard of hearing. You may have to write out what you want. Write clearly, Doctor. His eyesight is poor as well."

"I will visit him in the morning. I pray he has what I need."

"You mean what I need, do you not, Doctor?"

"Quite so, sir."

As he had visited with his patient, he took in the room with a sweeping glance. It was not as commodious as some master bedchambers he had seen, nor was it richly furnished. A large window opposite the bed probably looked out on the sea, but who could tell, funereally draped as it was? Doubtless the man in the bed feared drafts more than the melancholy that often settled on those so enclosed. The bed posts were carved with what he first thought were serpents, but then realized were long entangled vines wrapped about Greek columns. The tapestries on the walls were faded, barely discernible by candlelight, but seemed to depict rural scenes of places William was sure existed only in the weaver's fanciful imagination. There were but two chairs in the room, both of older design with backs so straight it seemed one would be tempted to stand rather than sit. There were several chests and a a tall, imposing wardrobe. If Sir Arthur Challoner had money to spend, he was certainly not spending it here. William saw no crucifixes or religious art that might indicate the devotion of his patient or its depth. No paintings of forebears. No mounted weaponry such as was often found even in the matrimonial bedchamber of a house such as this.

"In London, what other patients have you, Doctor?"

"I regularly attend Lord Burghley and his family," William said.

"But there are others, I assume?"

"There are, Sir Arthur. William dropped names, some of whom had come to him with only minor complaints, some who had only consulted him briefly, and at least two lords who had rejected his ministrations flatly, the first because of his youth, the second because of his perceived religion. The lord was a Papist and preferred one of his own as a physician.

"And the conditions they suffer from?"

"I cannot, sir, say what ailments individual patients complain of, but I will say they range from migraines and ulcers to ague and the French pox."

"French pox? Another benefit from that cursed nation," Challoner grumbled. Challoner went off for several minutes on the ills of the age, condemning immorality, licentiousness, false seeming, and the entire French nation, which he evidently held in great contempt, as though on a clear day he could see it across the narrow sea and observe French vices firsthand. William was amazed at the scope of his condemnation. A ranting Puritan in his pulpit could not have offered a more resounding denunciation.

Finally, Challoner stopped, breathless. William looked at Broderick. Broderick's head was bowed, and William assumed he had heard his master's screed before, doubtless many times.

"I assure you, sir, I am fully experienced in a range of illnesses and complaints. Were I not, Lord Burghley would not have commended me to you."

For the first time since William had entered, Challoner turned to his tall, austere secretary, who had maintained his watchfulness throughout his master's conversation with William without comment.

"What think you, Master Broderick, of this young doctor? Will he serve?"

"I do believe he will, Sir Arthur, if Lord Burghley commends him. I have no doubt his lordship knows what he's doing."

Challoner said to William, "Broderick here, you have already met, Doctor. He is my secretary and steward, my factotum. Though he has been with me but six months, yet I trust him implicitly in all matters. Bed-ridden as I am, I must, must I not, Broderick?"

"My master does me too much honor," Broderick said, giving a brief bow to his employer and then to William.

"Although only a servant, Broderick is endowed with many gifts. He has an excellent hand as a secretary, not merely legible but even—what shall I say—elegant. He is well-spoken. And he has certain other talents which I trust will be of benefit to me in the days to come."

Broderick soaked up the praise, his lips curled in a subtle smile. He bowed again to his master. William regretted that Challoner did not proceed to explain what these talents were, but he thought it impolitic to ask.

"You are to see to Doctor Gilbert's every need while he is here, Broderick. Make sure he is comfortable in his rooms. And this young woman you have brought with you to tend to my wife, what is her name?"

"Johane, Johane Sheldon."

"Is she competent in her duties?"

"She is, Sir Arthur."

"She better be. My wife, Doctor, is most particular in who serves her."

"I promise you, sir, that your lady wife will find no fault in her. She is well-trained, most courteous, a virtuous young woman."

"I would hope so," Challoner said with a snort. "For my wife will abide no sluts or slatterns in this house, nor will I."

William looked at Broderick. He smiled thinly and nodded, as though he were of the same mind.

Challoner said supper would be served at eight. "I won't be joining you. My meals are brought to me here these days. I eat in bed, what little I eat at all. My wife likewise eats in her room, she's finding it difficult to walk down the stairs. I do hope that will not prove an inconvenience to you.'"

"An inconvenience, Sir Arthur?"

"Eating alone. The servants eat earlier. You are the only… gentleman in the house."

"I am accustomed to eating alone, Sir Arthur. I live in a large house in London and have no wife or family."

"And no mistress, I presume?" Sir Arthur gave him a hard stare.

"No mistress, Sir Arthur."

"You are a fit and handsome young man, Doctor. You surprise me by your abstinence. Have you taken a vow of chastity, or perhaps you prefer those of your own sex?"

"Neither vow nor am I inclined to boys or men, sir. My practice absorbs all my time, leaving little for courtship."

The old man muttered something under his breath. He gestured to Broderick. "Show the doctor to my wife's room. I think she's ready for him."

"You have made a good impression on Sir Arthur, Doctor," Broderick said when they were in the corridor and out of the old man's hearing. "But beware, sir. He distrusts doctors in general, and he will look for any occasion to complain of you, to be rid of you, as he has done the others. He has allowed you here only because Lord Burghley recommended you and Sir Arthur would not offend Lord Burghley. I warn you only out of charity, you understand. Should he send you packing within the next few days, don't take it personally. That's his way."

William didn't know whether to thank Broderick for this counsel, or to chide him for criticizing his master. That was what the comment was, was it not? A negative judgment delivered to a guest of the house, or at least to a fellow servant, for that was his status, wasn't it? He decided to set aside his disdain for the man and his comment. He didn't like Broderick, but there was no need to drive the knife in deeper.

"I appreciate your charity, your counsel, Master Broderick. It is always good to know where one stands with a new patient—the sooner, the better."

"You will find the Lady Challoner easier to deal with," Broderick said as they proceeded down the corridor. "She is a most elegant lady, generous to a fault, and much beloved by the entire household."

"Sir Arthur thinks highly of you, Master Broderick."

Broderick smiled. "I have worked hard to win his esteem, through doing what needs to be done on his behalf. But here's the lady's room. Knock and enter when you hear her voice, and with that I bid you goodnight, Doctor Gilbert, and good luck."

It was the second time that day he had been wished good luck. First by Burghley's coachman who had brought them to island, now by the knight's factotum. Why did these seemingly innocuous wishes do nothing to bolster his confidence that he would get from the denizens of Livesey what he came for?

Sixteen

Lady Challoner's bedchamber adjoined her husband's, the door no more than a dozen steps away down the narrow corridor. William knocked, identified himself, and heard a woman's soft voice within inviting him to enter. When he did, he saw Mildred Challoner was sitting up in bed. Beside her stood Johane.

He could see Johane had already assumed her duties. She was outfitted as a maidservant, with a plain dark skirt and white apron and a round white cap that hid her dark, luxuriant hair. She stood where Broderick had stood next to his master, attentive, silent. They were counterparts, it would seem. The room itself was pleasant and clean and while not as grandly furnished as he might have expected for the lady of the manor, more feminine in its décor than her husband's surely. The tapestries were mostly floral, some biblical. Christ and the Samaritan woman at the well. John the Baptist's head upon a platter. It was the most inviting room he had observed since coming to the manor. A window was open, letting in the sea air. Like his own cramped quarters, it afforded a view of the sea and perhaps even the village down the hill. He was tempted to walk toward the window, to look out, but could hardly do so now.

Mildred Challoner looked years younger than her husband. William judged her to be forty, forty-five, certainly not over fifty. She would have been beautiful when young, and the evidence was still there in the handsome eyes and soft chin and high forehead indicating, as it was thought to do, superior intelligence. She had a pleasant smile of one determined to work through her illness bravely, whatever it was, and a pleasing, musical voice. William wondered why she had ever married Challoner; he was much older, a sick man, landed but not so rich that she should be wooed by him and successfully won. But then the logic of coupling was a mystery to him, perhaps a mystery to everyone—unless there was money in it, or ambition to climb higher in the order of things.

William started to introduce himself again, but before he could speak, Mildred Challoner said, "I already know you, Doctor Gilbert. Even before you came knocking at my door. Johane told me all about you."

"Madam?"

She looked at Johane. "This young woman was good enough to describe you to me. I know you are from London, sent by Lord Burghley. I know you are a graduate of Cambridge, an officer of the…what is it, Johane?"

"The College of Physicians," Johane answered, and smiled at him.

"Quite so. My husband probably told you that he has had a succession of doctors, none of whom were able to cure him of his complaints."

"He told me, madam."

"They are all bloodletters and mountebanks, but he insisted on having them."

"And you, madam? How may I serve you? For I am told you likewise are in need."

He was surprised when she laughed. "Oh, that is more my husband's fantasy than not. Because he is unwell and aging, he supposes I am unwell, commands me to lie abed, make myself an invalid to please him, for he would not that his wife should be well if he is sickly."

"And you countenance that, madam?" he asked, thinking the Challoners were an eccentric couple indeed, and yet he had heard of stranger arrangements between husband and wife.

"I do, Doctor," she laughed. "I have learned it is sometimes easier to comply with an unreasonable request than defy it. My husband is made happier, and my life with him more bearable, when he believes I am, like himself, a sufferer of a mysterious malady." She laughed again and exchanged glances with Johane.

"Then you have no need of my service, madam."

"Oh, quite the contrary, Doctor. I very much need it. It's not that you need to do anything for me, only seem to. My husband, however, is ill indeed, as I judge you have already determined."

"Yes, he is," William said. "I have told him that I can prescribe medication that will dull the pain in his bones and joints, but as for his heart…"

The smile left Mildred Challoner's face. "I know, Doctor. Despite what you think from what I've said, that I treat his condition lightly, I do love my husband and already mourn in anticipation of his passing."

"Which may not be for years, dear lady," William said. "Take comfort in that."

"It is the theme of all my prayers, Doctor."

"Then Mistress Johane here has little to do either. Since you have no need of a doctor, why have a nurse to attend you?"

He no sooner said this than he regretted it. He had spoken without thinking. It was solid logic, the question, but should she concur, their mission might be at an end before it started. He was relieved when she responded otherwise.

Mildred Challoner glanced over to Johane and smiled. She extended her hand and clasped Johane's hand warmly, as though the two women had known each other a long time or were related, a mother and daughter perhaps, or two sisters, an older and younger. "Oh, I am much in need of Johane. Call her nurse if you will but I haven't had so good a companion to talk to since I left my father's house to come to the island as a bride. We have been talking for a good two hours here, isn't that so, Johane?"

"I am at your command, lady," Johane said cheerfully, not looking at William.

Two hours conversing, mistress and maid. William would have fain been a fly upon the wall. He looked at Johane. "And may a simple man inquire what you converse of at such length and upon so short acquaintance?"

"You may indeed, Doctor," Mildred Challoner said. "No great mysteries of life, such as its beginning and end. Or matters political or theological. Womanly things, rather. And Johane was telling me about the town in which she was born. She asked about the locket I wear about my neck, telling me it was like unto one she found in a field when she was a child."

"A rare piece," Johane said. "Perhaps lost or deliberately buried there."

"I told her people on the island have often searched for treasures buried by earlier inhabitants. The island has long been settled, you know. Before us, there were Romans here. My husband has a special fascination with such things. But perhaps he's already told you about that."

"No, he mentioned no such interest."

"Well, trust me, Doctor, he shall in time do so. Some gentlemen are obsessed with their horses, or their gardens, or I know not what. For my husband, it's buried treasure."

"Treasure, madam?"

"He thinks we sit upon a mountain of hidden wealth, what the Saxon, the Romans, the Danes, the Normans, and even pirates left behind them."

"And how does he know this, madam? Or is it only wishful thinking on his part?"

"Wishful thinking, I suspect, since none has been discovered of any great value. Oh, from time to time something of value washes ashore and much is made of that in the village, for the villagers are likewise obsessed, thinking they might grow rich because of the discovery. You shall see for yourself, Doctor, when you have occasion to walk abroad on the island. You shall see holes dug in the earth; hillocks made flat, old barns ripped apart. A great deal of wasted effort, if you ask me, for very little reward. Thank God the villagers have left the dead in peace, or every grave in the churchyard would have long ago been desecrated."

Mildred Challoner laughed and grasped Johane's hand again. "Oh, I am so glad you have come, Johane."

William was glad she had come, as well. He regarded Johane admiringly. She had begun well as Burghley's agent, using her admiration for Mildred Challoner's locket as a means of bringing up treasure hunting. Had Johane really discovered a locket as a child like unto one her new mistress wore, or was that merely a fabrication to elicit information? Either way, he had learned something about the island. Treasure hunting was something people on Livesey did, at least some people. Mildred Challoner had described the state of things, at least at present, assuming her account was true.

Seventeen

He returned to his room, having nowhere else to go. He doubted there would be nightly entertainment in this house, no musicians to delight or jester to amuse or pleasant conversation by the fire. Not with the lord and his lady bed-ridden, the lord by need, the lady by edict.

He decided to lie down for a rest before supper, but the bed was so uncomfortable he couldn't fall asleep. He sat up and noticed his bag on the floor. It was not where he had left it when last in the room. He remembered exactly where he had left it, because one of the wooden planks of the floor—there was no carpet—was splintered and he had moved the bag away from it. Now, it covered it again.

He had brought few things with him. The bag, of Italian leather, had been his father's, given to William when he went off to Cambridge and used by him since; a memory of a happy youth and home life in Colchester. When he traveled, he carried it with a sling over his shoulder. He had brought with him a change of shirt, a spare doublet should his become stained, a jerkin, a dressing gown, a few books without which he was unable to travel or rest easy, and a few articles for his toilet.

There was also a notebook, and two quill pens and a bottle of ink. Almost as indispensable to him as his books. He examined the bag's contents. Everything was there that should have been, but he could tell things were disordered. His notebook, which he customarily kept at the top of other contents, was on the bottom. It was as though everything had been removed, examined, and then stuffed back in, without care that the disruption be detected.

He paged through the notebook. Was there anything there that could conceivably be of interest to a searcher? He carried no official commission or letter of instructions from Burghley. The pages of the notebook were full of jottings, ideas for experiments, notes on discourses and treatises he had read—but these were all about medicine. There was nothing there to suggest his purpose on the island was anything other than what he had represented it to be.

A secret pocket within the bag held a handful of silver he carried with him in case of emergencies. The money was still there.

There was an inference that was inescapable. The violation of his privacy was a message to the new doctor. In sum, that he should know his bag had been searched, that the privacy of his room was an illusion, perhaps even that his real purpose at Livesey was known and the searcher was looking to confirm it, find some letter, some warrant, some directive, some token.

He left the bag disordered as he had found it. If his room were entered a second time the intruder would suppose William never noticed the intrusion, the violation. It would serve the violator right.

But serve *whom* right? Broderick, who would be his principal suspect, had been in his sight until he left Arthur Challoner's room. Perhaps after that? He had been in Lady Challoner's chambers less than a few minutes. Would Broderick have dared to enter his room then? Or perhaps Dawson, the older servant who had led him to master's bedside. Dawson would have had time, and doubtless the opportunity. But would he have reason? Unless of course he was directed…

A soft knocking came at the door. Two knocks in rapid succession, a delay, and then a third. It was a signal he and Johane had agreed upon. He opened the door to find her standing there. He beckoned her to come in, but she shook her head. She whispered, "We're being watched."

She nodded toward the far end of the corridor. Broderick was standing there, eyeing them.

Johane said in a louder voice, a voice to be overheard: "My mistress wanted me to ask you something, Doctor. Something she forgot to ask when you visited her. She said she sometimes had a complaint in her side, a sharp pain below her ribs. She wanted to know what it was and what she might do about it, what you might do?"

"How often?" he asked, noticing then that Broderick had moved away, heading back to his master's room.

He told her that someone had entered his room and rummaged through his bag.

"Did they take anything?"

"Not that I can tell. I believe they just wanted me to know they could, if they wished."

"Maybe they were looking to find out why we were really here."

"I thought that. We must be very careful now. Broderick was looking at us suspiciously."

She shrugged and smiled. "Maybe he is of the same suspicious mind as the inn keeper who tried to put us in the same room."

He felt himself blushing again, a tendency he hated in himself. "Perhaps yes. But we must be careful about him."

"I'll be careful," she said.

"Any news?" he asked.

"Only what you heard, that the island's inhabitants are given to treasure hunting."

"That was clever of you, to invent that story about the bracelet you found in a field when a child. It invited her to share with you her own observations about such a pursuit. A fact valuable for us to know."

"Ah, Doctor, I didn't invent it. That was a true story, upon my oath. I had the bracelet for years and wore it for a while before losing it."

"How?"

"I don't know. Perhaps the Roman girl for whom it was made returned as a sprit to snatch it back." She laughed.

"I suspect the spirits of the dead have better things to do than retrieve their worldly goods, even if they are gold."

They stifled their laughter.

"Anything else from the lady?"

She shook her head. "Nothing more. We talk familiarly like two women, like friends. I like Lady Challoner. She's not haughty like most of the women I've worked for. Believe me, Doctor, I think she'll open to me if she knows anything about the Jewish treasure or anything about my grandfather's murder. Give me time. I must get back to her now."

"Oh, about the pains in her side. Find out how often she suffers them. It makes a difference in what may disturb her."

Johane laughed, and whispered: "That I *did* invent, Doctor—to not make Broderick suspicious. If she suffers from anything but good nature and common sense, I am yet to discover it in her."

"Will I see you at supper?" he asked, and then remembered he was to eat alone, not with the household servants. He told her that before she could respond. He was gratified when she looked disappointed.

"We shall have a place to meet in secret—to exchange information," he said. "When I know the manor better, I'll find a place. In the meantime, beware, Johane, of spies. And beware of intruders. They searched my room, they may search yours. If you have aught with you that could hint at our secret purpose, dispose of it."

"I have nothing, Doctor," she said. "I foresaw the risk. From my few years of service in great houses, I know how little that is personal is safe from prying eyes and hands."

"Then, Johane, you were more prescient than I."

"Well, I'm a woman, Doctor. Those of our sex must always be more careful than men, being as we are the weaker in body and mind. Fear makes us prescient."

"I think not the weaker in mind," William said. "Too much humility is unseemly, Johane."

"Then I take back what I have said… as you have instructed me, Doctor Gilbert. Not fearful, only prudent. Will you allow that women are more prudent than men?"

"I will allow it. It has been my experience that it is so."

He had once set out on a journey when a storm was upon him, foolishly went on, had become lost and nearly died of cold. He had, as a younger doctor, agreed to a procedure in which he had no belief, put himself in needless danger in a dozen ways. Prudence would have prevented the consequences of both. Yes, he was prepared to concede that women were more prudent than men, if he himself were typical of his sex.

She smiled radiantly. "You have been my teacher in so many things, Doctor, for which I give you thanks."

"You are more than welcome, Johane. We've been on the island but a day and already we have made progress."

She looked at him doubtfully. "Progress?"

"You shall see," he said.

William waited for the summons to his solitary supper. He was hungry, not having eaten since breakfast, but the thought of eating alone in the dark, cold house didn't appeal to him. It was not merely that he wanted company; he would learn nothing in solitude.

He lit a candle and put it on the little table next to his bed. It was hardly more than a stub. It would not outlast the evening and he made a note to himself to ask for another, for he doubted one would be given him otherwise. This was not Theobalds, where his needs had not only been met, but anticipated.

He walked to the window and looked out at the night. The moon was full, hidden in part by mist that seemed to spread out over the water like a veil. Strangely, he felt closed in, enveloped by something he did not entirely understand. He could hear the murmur of the sea. The tide was coming in. He imagined it rushing over the sand and trying to creep up the rocks where the manor was. He imagined it swelling so high that come morning the front steps of the house would be awash. As for the village below, it would be covered completely, its inhabitants drowned, food for fish.

That had never happened before, such a mighty tide, but who was to say it could not happen now? If there was one thing he had learned in all his science, it was that the world was a strange place, full of inexplicable things, many of which might never be understood until the world's end, when he trusted God would make all things plain, even to the learned such as himself.

Eighteen

Shortly before eight o'clock, he made his way down the stairs to the great hall, where Broderick had told him he would eat alone, there being none other in the house of his rank or station to join him there. He was, after all, a gentleman by birth, thanks to his father's office. When he arrived, he found a place set for him. He sat down, and shortly a servant came to him with food and drink.

It was a modest meal, some sort of fowl—duck he thought, remembering the creatures he had seen in the field upon his arrival—and a soup with some unidentifiable meat floating in it. But he was very hungry. He ate the duck and some of the soup, sipped the wine. The chamber was cavernous and poorly lit, with only a brace of candles, which sat at the table's center while he had been seated at the end. He had said he did not mind eating alone, but now he had second thoughts. He missed Johane. He would have liked to have her at table even if they did not speak to each other, even if they must sit in the dark, wordless.

Shortly, the servant returned. He was a young man, about sixteen, thin and pale, with narrow shoulders. When he brought the food he had said his name was Joseph.

"Joseph," William said. "Where do the others eat?"

"Others, Doctor?"

"The servants, Sir Arthur's household."

"In the kitchen, Doctor. The servants' hall. We have a big table there and keep merry when we can."

"And are you merry in the household?"

"Doctor?"

"Merry. Are all who serve happy, contented with their lot?"

Joseph paused for a moment, then he said, "Some, Doctor, some not so much. We are fed daily, though mutton stew grows wearisome."

"What a shame that not all are happy. I suppose in so large a house the work is hard."

"Oh, it is not just the work indoors, Doctor, but the work outdoors."

"What, herding sheep, gardening, what manner of outdoor work?"

Joseph hesitated. "Whatever Master Broderick directs, sir."

"Master Broderick, is it? Not just Broderick, or John?"

"He is Sir Arthur's steward. He directs us to call him master."

"But this outdoor work, you do, Joseph, I'm one who loves orchards, gardens. What manner of work do you do, outside the house?"

Joseph hesitated, looked about him nervously.

"I have said too much, Doctor. I'm sorry. I must return to the kitchen."

William watched the young man leave, then looked around him, as Joseph had done. The great hall seemed empty, save for himself. But there were dark corners the candlelight did not reach. Corners where an observer, a listener, might stand.

As William had done many times in his life, he imagined a time when a source of light might be found to render dark houses such as this illuminated at any hour. It was a dream of his. No more candles with their timid light, no more oil lamps. Something better, greater, more powerful, rivaling the sun. What might it be? Perhaps, he thought, he himself would discover it before his life ended.

Joseph returned to ask if William wanted aught else. The kitchen was closing soon, he said. He spoke quickly. William knew he would get nothing else about the household from the young man, but he did ask about Lady Challoner's new attendant.

"She's a fair maid," Joseph said. "All say so."

"Does she break bread with the household?"

"She does, Doctor, at least she did tonight."

"Is she still in the servants' hall?"

"She was there when I came up, Doctor, talking and laughing with the others. But I'm sure she'll be gone by now."

"Well tomorrow, I will join you all. I find I like not eating alone as much as I thought."

Joseph looked doubtful, but then he said, "Very well, Doctor. You may do as you please, sir. But it will be strange to have a gentleman, such as yourself, amongst us common folk."

"I have spent much of my time as a doctor among common folk, Joseph. They are as pleasant company as some who live in great houses, often good conversationalists, and very often more intelligent than those whom they are obliged to serve."

Joseph bowed and left. William did as well, and quickly.

On his way back to his room he took the chance of knocking on Johane's door. He gave the signal twice, and when there was no response he started to move away, thinking perhaps she had gone in to meet some need of her new mistress.

Then the door opened slightly and Johane looked out at him. He could see she was prepared for bed. Her sleeping robe was wrapped tightly about her, her dark hair loose about her shoulders. He asked her if she could talk. She shook her head. Of course, she would not invite him to come in. That would raise questions of propriety. But where could they talk and not be seen or suspected of being lovers or, worse, conspirators?

"In the morning I'm going to the village, to the apothecary's. Can you get away?" he whispered.

"I'll try, Doctor, but Lady Challoner keeps me on a leash. I am her pet, she dotes on me so."

Her face, William thought, expressed more pleasure in the compliment than complaint. "Do your best, Johane," he said. "I want to learn all that you have learned about the house."

"Watch for me, Doctor, but I'm afraid I have learned little thus far."

"No matter," William said. "I think she will open up to you more as the days go by."

He told her about his brief exchange with Joseph.

"I know him. A good-looking boy."

"He admitted not every servant in the house was happy. I asked him why. He said something about work out of doors."

"Out of doors?"

"Yes, implying it was an added duty, an onerous duty."

"What manner of duty?"

"Ah, then he fell silent. He would say no more. I think my question invited answer beyond what he was permitted to say."

"Not permitted by whom, Sir Arthur? My lady?"

"Master Broderick. He runs the house, with his master's permission."

"Well, Sir Arthur is an invalid. Someone must command the servants. He's not the first steward who has assumed such power. I could tell you tales, Doctor."

"No need, Johane. I have seen the same. But I don't think Broderick is much liked."

"Few of his rank in a household are. I doubt he expects to be. But It matters not, Doctor, whether he be liked or not, as long as he is obeyed. That is the way of it in great houses, or even such a house as this be."

That night, William slept restlessly. The mattress, such as it was, was lumpy and the blanket he had been given was worn and thin, so that he shivered beneath it. It was midsummer, but cold along the coast, and he could hear the rumble of the sea. And all night he thought he heard strange sounds coming from other rooms in the house. Voices, whispers, then occasional cries, whimpers. He got from his bed and listened against the walls, trying to determine which rooms they came from. He had noticed there were six rooms on the second floor, his was one, Mildred Challoner's another, Johane's a third, the fourth was Sir Arthur's. Which left two unoccupied—or were they?

But when William awoke, the first thing he thought of was Lord Burghley. The impression was so strong, the man might have been sitting at his bedside chiding him for oversleeping when he should properly have been getting on with his work. Work, a strange way to think of, but what else to call it, this scratching for information, listening at keyholes? It all was now his work.

It took him a few moments to clear his head, to distinguish asleep from awake. And then the full burden of his task came back to him, in a flood of second thoughts. It took him even more time to settle his mind. For a moment, he wished he were back in London in his own house with his customary patients and their familiar ailments, not on Livesey, with an eccentric lord and lady, an arrogant and mysterious steward, and a village full of rustics and descendants of criminals.

Nineteen

It was almost light when he fell back asleep; he then awoke abruptly when he heard voices again, this time actual voices, voices of servants, and once Broderick's snarl calling one of the maids to account for some infraction.

William dressed quickly, hurried down to the kitchen and found most of the household staff had already eaten. One of their number was cleaning away the table. She looked up, startled at seeing him, a stranger in the house, in the smoky kitchen, amid the hanging pots and pans and other kitchen paraphernalia. A place in the underbelly of the house where gentry and above rarely went. She was a young girl, hardly more than a child, with long yellow hair and green eyes, and the pretty, innocent face of an angel.

William said, "I'm the doctor, Doctor Gilbert."

He could see by her expression his name meant nothing to her, not even the fact that he was a doctor. But she could tell by his speech and silver-button doublet that he was no fellow servant, no villager, and she regarded him with a mixture of fear and awe.

He tried to put her at ease. "Don't be afraid. I'm come to tend to your master, Sir Arthur."

"He's upstairs, sir," she said, as though she supposed William was lost and needed directions.

"I know where he is."

The girl said her name was Catherine. She said she came up from the village each morning early to help in the kitchen. He was disappointed at not seeing Johane, but supposed she had already been called to attend her charge. He wanted to ask the kitchen maid if there was any food left, but she anticipated his wish and brought him bread and cream before he could ask for it. He sat down at the table and ate quickly. When the kitchen maid returned to see if he wanted anything else, he asked her where he might find the apothecary.

"Why, sir, he lives just beyond the Saracen's Blade."

"The Saracen's Blade?"

"A tavern, sir. It's the only one in the village. If you walk down the high street toward the quay you won't miss it. It's the finest house in the village."

"Have you always lived here?" he asked.

"I was born here, sir, and lived here thirteen years. My whole life. I've never been anywhere else. My family has lived on this island for years and years."

"Since Adam and Eve?" he asked, laughing.

She smiled pleasantly. "Not quite so long, sir."

"You've never left the island?"

She looked as though the idea were so foreign to her that she could hardly conceive of it. "Why should I want to do that, sir?"

"Then you must know everyone in the village," he said.

"I think I know everyone on the island," she said. She had a radiant smile.

He made a note to himself: the girl might prove a useful informant. She was easy, not suspicious like Broderick. But later, not now.

It was a cold, gray morning, the sea flat and featureless. A slight breeze blew in from the mainland. The village of Livesey, unlike on his arrival, now showed some signs of life. On the long street that led from the church to the little harbor, he saw men and some women walking about, some on their way to the quay. The business of a village. Most of the houses were homes of the villagers; humble, weather-beaten structures, some appearing on the verge of collapse. It was evident to him that prosperity was more a stranger here than he was. Most of the inhabitants seemed old, at least older than he. He saw no children, heard no young voices chattering or singing.

When he drew close to the tavern, he saw the sign of the apothecary just beyond but decided to visit the tavern first. He knew that in a village so small, the tavern would be the center of things, more than the church, more than the quay with its half dozen bobbing fishing boats. Even more than the manor house on the top of the hill, overlooking all.

The tavern was a small house of two stories, bricked and timbered, with a faded sign of a curved blade hanging from the door to identify it as a public house. He waited a moment before entering; it was now mid-morning and he wondered if the tavern would even be open this early. But it was. He entered and inside the dark low-ceilinged interior he saw a half dozen tables, a bar, and eight to ten men, some at the tables, some at the bar, all staring at him as he entered as though they had been awaiting him.

At first, he was unnerved at being the object of such scrutiny, then realized any stranger to the island would probably have provoked the same response, a healthy curiosity. A small population starving for novelty, something to relieve the tedium of their ordinary lives, something to talk about over supper or before prayers, something to hate or fear or weave stories about.

He nodded to the stocky, aproned man behind the bar, who he thought was probably the proprietor, walked over to him, ordered an ale, and then sat down at a table in the corner. He took a few sips of the ale and waited. He was still the subject of unnerving stares from the others in the room, most of whom seemed to be laborers or fishermen by their dress, or fishermen who had given up the sea and now spent their days drinking and telling stories—although none was speaking now.

There had been the murmur of talk as he entered, and then all had gone silent as though a religious service were about to begin. He was finishing his drink and thinking about leaving when the tavern keeper came over and took a stool across from him.

Except for an apron greatly in need of washing, the man looked much like the others in the room—a round, guileless face, short but scraggly beard, and a thick chest as if all his work were hard, physical labor, not just serving drinks and chatting with customers. William realized that travel to strange parts would be pleasant if it didn't stir up so much animosity toward strangers, as if the only intent of someone from afar was to poison the water or ravish the women.

"You've never been here at the Blade before, have you, sir?" the tavern keeper said, "If you had, I would know it, but I see by your dress you are a gentleman."

"I'm a physician, a doctor," William said. "I've come to attend to Sir Arthur Challoner and his lady up at the manor house."

"Have you now?" responded the man, whose face seemed to soften at this. William put him at about fifty, perhaps a seaman before he turned tavern keeper, his skin wrinkled with the salt and sun, probably a tippler himself, sober every other day.

"We've had doctors here before for the Challoners," the publican continued. "Still ,they have their complaints, I understand. There's just so much medicine can do, don't you agree, Doctor, when a man is as old and ill as Sir Arthur is?"

William agreed medicine had its limits. He was not in the habit of discussing his patients with strangers, but he felt challenged by the proprietor and said, "Well there is treatment to relieve pain in muscles and joints and encourage the workings of the heart."

The man looked convinced. He said he was the owner of the tavern, and that he had had little experience with doctors, preferring the use of home remedies and the occasional resort to a wise woman. He said he was happy to wait upon so distinguished a gentleman as William was.

"So, where are you from, Doctor?"

"I'm from London, though originally from Colchester, in Essex." William liked to say he was from Colchester. He was not ashamed of the town of his birth, and he believed that identifying himself as a Londoner often put patients off, even patients who were born and reared within the sound of London's bells.

"Well, sir, I've been in Colchester, but not in London, though I have heard of the place. It's where the queen has her court, is it not?"

"That's the place," William said, marveling that any man living now should be so ignorant, but then wondering if the man were just pulling his leg. As an outsider and a city man he would be an easy mark, vulnerable to cleverly-crafted fictions and gossip. He had experienced it before, in other rural places where he'd traveled, been made a fool of, or at least a dupe. He hoped he'd learned the lesson: take nothing at face value. Prove all. It was a principle he tried to practice in his relations with others as well as in his scientific investigations.

William looked beyond the man. He noticed that conversation had resumed in the room and he was no longer the sole object of attention. The tavern keeper sitting down with him had apparently broken the spell.

"Sir Arthur has fetched a doctor from a great distance to come to this place, a village with no more than hundred folk by my count, most of them old and tired, a few more animals, and a sad history to endure."

"What sad history would that be, Master Tavern Keeper?"

"My name is Parker" the man said, "Israel Parker. People in the village call me Parker."

"They don't like your Christian name?"

"Well it's an odd name for a Christian, is it not, being that I am no Jew?"

"I have known Christians of that name," William said. "One a righteous churchman, another a knight of the realm."

"It is the name I choose for myself. Parker."

"Then Parker it shall be." William extended his hand. The gesture apparently surprised Israel Parker. Gentleman in such circumstances usually kept their hands to themselves, but Parker took William's hand, squeezed it hard, and then let it go. He smiled amicably.

"And I am William Gilbert."

"Well, Doctor Gilbert, I suppose every town and village in England has its story, and the story of Livesey is a strange one."

"A strange story, Master Parker," William said. "Pray tell me it. It is my favorite kind of story."

Parker stretched out his legs, relaxed his hands, and stared at a spot on the wall. He let out a breath of air. "Corsairs, raiders from the north, pirates, Dutch, French, Spanish. All would use Livesey as a doorstep to the riches of England. And did, Doctor."

"When was this?"

"It has ever been so, Doctor. I remember such a raid when I was a boy. Africans, armed to the teeth, as black as night. You should have seen them. They came in two ships. Not like English ships, or even Dutch. They landed at dawn, or just before. We had no defenses here, no defenses but raised arms praying for mercy, but they were no Christians, the raiders. They took some of our women, killed most of the men and boys, stole everything of value and burned down half the town. I was spared because I hid in a rain barrel. When I climbed out, the raiders were gone. So were my mother and father. I found my father's body in the street, just outside the door here. I never saw my mother again. That's only part of our history, Doctor, only a part of it."

"More stories of corsairs, pirates?" He was still alert for deception, but somehow he thought the story of the raiding Africans was probably true.

It accorded with stories of pirate raids he had heard himself as a boy in Colchester. But the raiders there had been Danes in their long ships, not black Africans, and hundreds of years earlier.

Israel Parker laughed. "A hundred stories of pirates, Doctor, but I wasn't here to see them. I tell you the truth, sir, when the sea around us dries up, as it will in God's good time, it will not only be sand that's seen but dead men's bones , and if there's a resurrection as our clerics claim, a mighty army of the dead will appear, marching toward land. Ah, Doctor, my flesh crawls at the very thought of it."

"It would be good business for you, Master Parker, should after so long a time the dead have a mighty thirst to quench."

Parker laughed, a dry laugh that ended in a cough. "I never thought of that, Doctor," Parker said when he could speak again. "Maybe you're right, and I should welcome all those dead mariners with open arms, even the pirates."

"I would like to come back soon and hear more of your stories, Master Parker. And I promise you it will be before God's good time."

"And you may, Doctor, if you choose. Welcome to Livesey. We call it that here, just Livesey, since it's an island without saying. I hope you find what you're looking for here."

"Looking for?" William asked, studying the man's face, fearful that somehow his secret purpose had been discovered. Parker's face seemed not as guileless as before. Had William said something to give himself away, and on his very first visit to the village?

"Why, every man is looking for something, is he not?" Parker said, rising from his stool.

William remembered what Mildred Challoner had said about the pervasiveness of treasure hunting on the island.

"I'm told some on the island spend time looking for buried treasure."

Parker laughed. "Oh, they do that when the fishing's poor, but find precious little. Or if they do, they don't spend it here. Where did you hear about treasure hunting, Doctor?"

"I heard it up at the manor."

"Not from Sir Arthur or his lady?"

"From one of the servants."

"Hardly a trustworthy source." Parker laughed.

"He complained about being made to work out of doors. When I asked what manner of work, he wouldn't say. I thought the work might be treasure hunting."

"Well, if so, that would be Master Broderick's doing. Sure, nothing is done at the manor, but he has a hand in it."

"It was he who greeted me at the door and escorted me to his master and mistress. He seems a most able servant, more than what one might expect to find in service."

"Oh, Broderick," Parker said. "He's a sad case, a man that hardly knows how to laugh. He's well suited for the Challoners, for he needs no help in grieving over their ills—he's a natural at it."

"I did find him somewhat saturnine," William observed.

"Found him what, Doctor. Satur…is that where he's from then?" Parker said.

"Saturnine," William said. "Not a place but a temperament, a gloomy disposition."

"Well, that would be him, Doctor. For I have never seen him merry, not even on feast days."

"You said he was not from the island," William said.

Parker shook his head emphatically. "No, Doctor, he's from somewhere on the main. But I know he's not a local. He came here to work for the Challoners but a year ago, maybe less."

"He seems an able man. I wonder that he could not find a place elsewhere, a more, more…"

"Go ahead and say it, Doctor," Parker declared with a grin. "You'll not offend me or any else on this spot of earth. None here think this is the Garden of Eden or any such place. It's mostly a barren rock, what's left over when a more pleasant land was made, such as England is."

"I did not mean he could have found a better location, but a place, a position, with some more prosperous master," William said.

Parker shrugged. "Well, Doctor, Master Broderick is an odd bird. I suppose he may fly where he is able and land and shit where he chooses. You should ask him yourself."

William thought about this. For some reason, he couldn't imagine asking Broderick anything personal. At least not directly, but what he had just learned about Broderick from the proprietor did arouse his suspicion. Why had Broderick come to the island? Was it for the same reason he had, or was that an assumption too far?

Parker said, "I do hope you enjoy your time here, Doctor, and that you receive good payment for your service."

"Should I be worried I will not? William asked.

"Well, to speak the truth there are some who provided services to the manor who have yet to see a penny of what they were promised. None in this village is a tithe as rich as the Challoners, and it is supposed they have more than seems, yet they are not above avoiding their debts. I just thought you should know, Doctor, should your reason for being here was the hope of a fee for your services."

"Thank you for your warning, Master Parker. I will keep it in mind. The truth is I do hope for a fee for service rendered."

"And one thing else, Doctor."

"And that is?"

"Should you walk about the island while you are, pray take care."

"Of what, Master Parker? Raiders, pirates? Please don't tell me Livesey is still vulnerable to attack. Should I go armed to defend myself?"

William asked this in jest, but Parker's expression was serious. The tavern keeper hesitated, on the verge of saying yes.

"Just *thing*s, Doctor."

"What things?"

Another customer came in the door and beckoned to Israel Parker before he could answer. William finished his drink and rose to go. He'd learned some things about the island's history, but the tavern keeper had said nothing about drowned Jews or their treasure. Didn't he know the story, or was he keeping mum for some reason of his own?

William walked into the street thinking that his conversation with the tavern keeper was more unsettling than informative. That Sir Arthur Challoner might not pay him for his services was a standard caution. During his short career as a physician, he had been so abused more than once, often by patients more than able to pay fees they owed but determined to pay as little as they must. Besides, Lord Burghley was his paymaster. He was confident he would lose nothing on Livesey, at least financially speaking.

But the other warning gave him pause. Parker had not expanded on the dangers of walking abroad on the island, even when William had more seriously inquired what there might be to fear. Parker had merely said "things".

Parker could hardly have chosen a vaguer word for what was to be feared, but William could not get him to be more specific. "Things," Parker had repeated, and in its very vagueness the word was even more unnerving to William.

Twenty

The apothecary's shop was hardly more than a shed, leaning against the larger building like a child leaning against a parent. Its tiny door was just wide enough for William to fit through without twisting his body and bending his head at the same time.

The apothecary was in the process of weighing out some powdery substance to an old woman. He gave it to her in a bag; she paid and left. Then, the apothecary looked up at William without any of the curiosity that been displayed by his fellow villagers in the tavern. "Sir, can I serve you?"

William told him he was a doctor, a doctor attending on the Challoners. The name of Challoner was clearly enough for the apothecary, who was a short, squat man of middle years, as bald as Samuel Challoner, but with a reddish beard. William told him what he needed. Of the three items, the man said he had but one. William mentioned some alternatives, and these proved more successful. The shop was cluttered with shelves full of bottles and vials, some labeled, some not, but he thought himself fortunate that the island had an apothecary at all.

Unlike physicians—who were trained, often at universities in England and abroad—apothecaries learned their skill as apprentices to other apothecaries. They were neither licensed nor otherwise approved by authorities, so that although the maxim *caveat emptor* applied to physicians as well, it was even truer of apothecaries. William patronized a half dozen or more in London whose substances and labeling he trusted, but others he did not. And unlike the kitchen maid at the manor and the proprietor of the tavern, the apothecary seemed to take William's presence in the village as a matter of course. He displayed no curiosity, asked no questions, filled the order as if William were a regular customer, took his money, never asked what the substances were for, or whom they benefited. William considered the man might be a half-wit, the village idiot but high functioning. He thought it all very strange, but then the whole village was so.

And then Johane walked in.

She hardly gave him a glance, walked up to the apothecary and bought something William recognized as a woman's cosmetic, then popular among ladies of birth to enhance the eyes, make them more lustrous and enticing. He assumed it was for Mildred Challoner. Johane's eyes were lustrous enough and besides, it would be inappropriate for a maid to use cosmetics to enhance her appearance. It would only get her in trouble, with her employers and doubtless everyone else in the household who would think her a tease or minx, or above herself. But that Mildred Challoner should want such a cosmetic puzzled him. That she might appear more desirable? To whom? He doubted it was her husband she sought to enchant, bed-ridden as he was, impotent as he claimed to be.

They walked out together, neither wishing to converse in front of the apothecary, or even suggest they knew each other. In the street, he whispered to her to follow him, but not closely.

He walked up the hill toward the church. Behind him, he could hear her footsteps on the cobbled street. When he got to the church, he entered a gate and instead of heading for the front door he diverted toward the little churchyard adjacent to it. It was a small plot of earth, with a sprinkling of trees bent over by the wind. It was an old burying ground; most of the monuments and crosses leaned over, the names upon them barely legible.

Except for the two of them, the churchyard was deserted. It was not the best place for a meeting, William thought. They might be seen there by a passerby—who observing them alone might arrive at a plausible but incorrect conclusion that they were a couple, lovers, or would-be lovers—but it would have to do. At least for now. Whatever danger presented itself by their meeting here, it was far less dangerous than meeting in the manor with John Broderick sniffing around.

"If anyone comes, pretend you're mourning a lost loved one," William said. "I will do likewise, but at another grave."

"A good plan," she said.

"How did you get away from your mistress?"

"I suggested something to improve her sleep." She pointed to a little bag she carried.

"You mean her appearance, do you not? I heard what you requested of the apothecary."

Johane blushed. "You caught me in a lie, Doctor," she said. "I was only protecting my lady's vanity from your scrutiny."

William laughed. "A good idea. And I forgive you for the lie. So tell me what you've learned in these long conversations of which your mistress boasts."

"Not enough to satisfy my curiosity about what we seek," she said. "Mistress Challoner is a pleasant woman, good humored, the soul of generosity. By her own account, she is mismatched with her husband, who, as you know, is older by at least twenty years or more. That they sleep in different bedchambers is as satisfactory an arrangement for her as it is for him, for I think the age of happy coupling is ancient history for them both."

"Many married couples do the same, at least among those that can afford to live in houses with many bedchambers, such as the Challoners." William said, although his father and mother had always shared a bed.

"She said she appreciates me being in the house," Johane continued. "She says she doesn't trust most of the servants."

"Not trust most of her servants?"

"Things of hers have disappeared, been taken—stolen, she thinks."

"Perhaps she only misplaced them," William said, although he knew complaints of household larceny were common in great houses, even in not so great houses like the Challoner manor.

"She thinks not. And there's something else," she said.

"What?"

"Broderick. John Broderick."

"She doesn't trust him?"

"She fears him."

"Why?"

"She thinks he's a cold fish, arrogant, imposing. He makes her nervous, his creeping around, giving orders as though he were master of the house. She cannot understand why her husband hired him, and having done so, tolerates him. There were others qualified, or so they claimed. Still, he chose Broderick."

"Has she complained of Broderick to her husband? Surely, he wouldn't keep the man on, if his wife objects? By all signs, Challoner is besotted with her, for all the oddities of their living arrangements. Her wish is his command, he practically said as much, and with Broderick standing there in the master's room."

"She has told him more than once, but her husband laughs, tells her she imagines things. It's because of her illness, he says."

"Why should he laugh it off? Did she tell him why she feared Broderick?"

"That's the difficult part, Doctor, she doesn't know. He watches her, she says. She looks up and he's watching her."

"She's older than he. Broderick couldn't be more than thirty," he said.

"Men have been known to fall in love with women older than they."

"True, but Broderick doesn't seem to be the amorous sort. It's hard for me to imagine him as a jolly wooer."

She rolled her eyes and sniggered.

William told her what he had learned from the tavern keeper about Broderick's having come to the island only months before. How his birthplace was uncertain, how his reasons for coming to the island were unclear. At least to William.

"Broderick doesn't look like either of the men you saw at the Domus?"

"He is nothing like either."

"Then watch Broderick. Your new mistress may misread his attentions. Granted, he is a disagreeable and sour soul, but what of that? There are many more like him. Shall all be hanged because eccentric and disagreeable?"

"Yet I trust Mistress Challoner's instincts," Johane said.

William looked at the girl. Instincts. What were they? Did they have a place in the human anatomy, a seat in the brain, or in the heart, or in the viscera? If one cut open the body as he had done in his anatomy classes at Cambridge, were the instincts there, nestled among some other recognizable organs? Could they be plucked out and displayed to industrious medical students who could then draw them, dissect and discover their parts. Did the word have any meaning at all?

William reminded her of his earlier conversation with Joseph. "He told me he dislikes working out of doors but would not tell me what he did there, what he was made to do. I suspect it's treasure hunting."

"Broderick is a treasure hunter?"

"Perhaps that's why he was hired."

She thought about this. Then she said, "if that's true, then we should observe him even more than his master and mistress."

"Speaking of whom, you had better get back to your mistress," William said. "She'll be suspicious if you delay. She'll think you've found a lover here in the village."

Johane laughed. "In this place? I would be more than desperate, Doctor, were I to find someone here. No man from this place interests me, not in that way at least."

He was tempted to ask her what kind of man *would* interest her, but decided that she would not welcome the question. It seemed presumptuous. Her amorous inclinations were her business, none of his. She had a pretty face; certainly she had had men after her, men other than her employers looking for a quick embrace in the dark, an unchaste kiss, a tumble on the mattress. But she had said nothing about having someone in her life. The more he thought about it, the stranger it seemed. Perhaps she had come to London to get away from some romantic entanglement. To escape some arranged marriage. He knowing her as he did, her intelligence, her curiosity, her studiousness, it was not easy to imagine her finding a suitable husband in the town she was from. No, London was the place for her, just as it was for him.

Her voice brought him back from this reverie.

"I'd best go now. My new mistress will be lost without me, so firm am I in her affections."

"Has she said anything at all about the Jews who were drowned here, anything about Jewish gold, treasure?"

"Nothing," she said. "Nothing about Jews."

"That doesn't mean she knows nothing," he said, and felt at once he had insulted her intelligence. Of course, she would know that. That Mildred Challoner would disclose secrets to a complete stranger upon her first meeting was unthinkable, no matter how cordial that first meeting had apparently been. He was sure Johane would have to pry it from her. There would be no silver plate with the secret sitting thereon.

She said suddenly, as though an afterthought, "Before I go I want to show you something, Doctor."

He followed her over to remote corner of the churchyard where there were even older monuments, slabs and crosses, some sinking into the earth or leaning toward it, some half buried in the weeds. "These are my people," she said solemnly. "Look at the names and dates."

The names inscribed in stone were not easily read. They were markers of the long dead, the barely remembered forebears. The oldest he saw was more than a century old. A man named David Forest."

"Your relations?"

"David Forest was my grandfather's grandfather," she said.

"You have deep roots here, then?" William said.

"You see I do, Doctor. These graves bear witness to it."

They stood quietly for a time, side by side, looking down at the monuments. He wanted to keep their conversation going, but he dared not speak. She seemed lost in thought. He felt at that moment an unusual intimacy with the young woman beside him. As though they were bound, not by any relationship that had a name, but by some deep, spiritual tie. It was not simply that they were engaged in a common effort at a powerful lord's direction. William knew it was more than that, and he wondered if Johane Sheldon felt the same bond and that was also something she thought about in her still meditation, not just her family's dead, sleeping securely in the ground of an obscure island, but the man standing beside her, the young doctor named William Gilbert.

He looked down at the graves again. They weren't Silvas buried there. The name was Forest, a dozen graves bearing that name. But he knew *Silva* meant forest or woods. It was a place name. Sons and daughters of Abraham all, but outwardly Christians for safety's sake, victims of persecution otherwise.

He wondered if they had practiced their faith in secret, observed the holy days, praised Abraham and Moses in their discreet assemblies, quoted the Talmud in reverential whispers. Did they circumcise their sons in secret? Abstain from forbidden meats? Think of themselves as God's peculiar people? Deafen their ears to the sermons of Christian clerics, especially when they heard the Jews denounced and defamed from the pulpit?

He knew this was what some Jews did, that so it was widely believed. It was a race inured to oppression, but one that had learned to survive despite it. As the Silvas had done, as Isaac Silva himself had done before acknowledging his blood and converting to a new faith.

And as Johane Sheldon had done in her own way. Survivors all.

He thought he saw a tear in Johane's eye, but he might have been mistaken.

"Let's go back," he said again, worrying now that they might be discovered.

"Yes. I'm off to a good start with Lady Challoner," she said with a resolute smile. "I don't want to ruin it."

"You won't," he said.

He put his hand on her shoulder, as a gesture of comfort and encouragement. Through the cloak she wore he could feel the delicacy of her small bones, the heat of her blood, and he felt a sudden thrill that surprised him. It was the first time in their association that he had touched her, and he removed his hand at once suddenly fearful he might have offended her in so doing. Touching between man and woman, if not betrothed, could be easily misinterpreted, easily offend. Even if the touching involved no private body part but was simply a hand or an arm that was touched, a cheek that was brushed, or a kiss exchanged in a friendly greeting. He also remembered Lord Burghley's admonition. She was under William's protection, and by extension, his lordship's. Johane might welcome a kiss or embrace, but Burghley would kill him for it.

But she didn't look offended. She had not shrunk from his touch. Her face wore an expression of placid acceptance of their relationship, their shared mission, as though the touch were not only appropriate but expected, perhaps even needed by her, given the circumstances of their isolation. Would she have responded the same way if he had kissed her, here in this private place, amid the graves of her honored dead?

He imagined his lips meeting hers. He saw it in his mind's eye and almost felt the sensation. William let that thought have a place in his head for an instant and then he dismissed it. There was no purpose in encouraging a desire he could not satisfy, would not attempt, should not attempt. It would lead only to frustration, restless days and nights, obsession. And it might bring their mission to naught.

"Good night, Doctor," she said with a sweetness in her voice that stirred his blood. "Sleep well."

"You too, Johane."

He watched her as she walked toward the manor house, watched her until she entered the door and disappeared. He imagined her passing through the great hall of the manor and walking up the stairs to her room. He imagined her alone there, and then being called to the side of Mildred Challoner, the two chatting companionably, more like sisters than mistress and servant. He imagined her discovering more of the island's secrets, finding what was sought, disclosing it to him in furtive whispers, her lips close to his ear so he could sense her warm breath.

He waited among the graves until his heartbeat returned to its normal steady rhythm. He had wondered earlier what he had gotten into, in accepting this strange mission. Now he knew it was more than he had foreseen.

Twenty-One

He gave the medication to Sir Arthur Challoner under Broderick's watchful eye.

"This powder, taken with water or wine, will ease your pain, sir. This other, will steady your heart."

He had had patients who resisted any medication of which they had not heard. Preferred the old treatments of their grandmothers or their neighbors. The education and training of their doctor meant little to them. They distrusted both and even pretended to take medication rather than endanger their lives with something that might poison body and soul. For the two were bound together in the minds of most. The soul and body might be separate entities, yet the soul inhabited the body. How could one not affect the other? The issue was debated by theologians and physicians, and had been for centuries, but it was also a matter of speculation among the poorest and least learned. William knew this from his own observation.

But Sir Arthur, to William's surprise and pleasure, took both medications with neither complaint nor apparent suspicion. He drank each concoction down, with claret, as though there was nothing in the glass at all, and the result of which would be his immediate relief of whatever ailed him. He even looked better after he had taken his medication. He seemed more alert. Had the medication worked so well and so quickly? William doubted it. Both medications were effective, but they took time to do their work, sometimes days, even weeks. Perhaps the ailing knight might have only imagined it so.

It was, rather, Broderick, who seemed more cautious, suspicious, stood aloof, said nothing but expressed in his face a deep-seated suspicion of this London doctor no older than himself and, by extension, whatever he prescribed. Resentment, too. The signs were clear to William, as if the household steward had his designs imprinted on his forehead, like the images he had heard were carved onto the faces of savages in the new world.

It was clear that Broderick saw William as a rival for influence with his master, an interloper in the house. William wondered if the man would have preferred his employer to remain bed-ridden, wondered even that Broderick had designs on the lonely, older widow who might in her need find Broderick a successor to her former husband in her bed. Broderick was tall, manly, and unlike his master, undoubtedly potent. There was precedent for it; women who had married below themselves, driven by love or lust to become bedmates of their servants. William wondered if that was what Broderick was thinking, along with whatever treasure hunting goals he had in mind.

"Take the powders with wine, twice a day. We shall see how you do thereafter," William said.

Sir Arthur smiled broadly. "I'm happy you're here, Doctor," he said, reaching for William's hand. "I truly believe that you will do me good. And I will write to Lord Burghley to tell him so. Broderick here will draft the letter himself. Will you not, Broderick?"

Broderick said he would, but William detected little enthusiasm in his voice.

William went to bed and slept soundly; at least until morning, when he awoke before dawn, and lay awake thinking of his conversation with Johane in the cemetery, then fell asleep again. He dreamed, a vivid dream, but not about Johane. He dreamed about Broderick, dreamed he was in Broderick's place and Broderick in his. They were in a strange room with Sir Arthur lying abed as was his custom. Broderick was on one side of the bed, William on the other. It was not the same room as Sir Arthur's. It was larger, more elegantly furnished with tapestries, more airy. It was a strange and bewildering dream of which, upon awakening, he could make little sense. Broderick had been the doctor, William the steward, worrying that his master in the bed was about to be poisoned, poisoned by Doctor Broderick.

It was very curious and a bit alarming, because in his dream he felt exactly what he supposed Broderick had felt: a simmering resentment at Broderick as the rival, the interloper, the alien from a world off the island. Broderick, of course, was in real life also an alien. He was not from Livesey. He was from the mainland; from Essex, the Lady Challoner had said. And freshly appointed, an outsider therefore like unto himself. Perhaps that was why Broderick felt so insecure about William's presence. But surely he could not suppose William coveted his position. That William was temporary was known to all. It was in the letter of commendation Burghley had sent. Sent by Lord Burghley's commendation, as a favor, not for the long term. Long term was unthinkable. William had a busy and successful practice in London. Who would forsake London for Livesey, an armpit, the end of the world? Lord Burghley had said as much.

But there he was in the dream, very much himself except for the important thing. Broderick was in his place, a detested interloper, and William in Broderick's. The only thing in the dream that was true was the rivalry. In what exact way, he had yet to determine. But then, he thought, perhaps it was Johane. William didn't like the way Broderick looked at her. He didn't like it at all.

Twenty-Two

The next morning, he was out the door by sunrise. Israel Parker had warned him, mysteriously, that walking alone might be dangerous, but had not explained why. William decided to see for himself. Besides, even after a day on the island, he knew he could not stand to be cooped up in the dark manor house, with Johane there and he with little ready access to her. The temptation to see her, to talk to her was too tantalizing, too dangerous.

He had been told by Burghley's coachmen that the island was not more than three miles across and was roughly circular, like a full moon or a woman's breast, except for the hill where the manor had been built. He assumed that if that was true, he would have no trouble walking its shoreline in several hours, assuming that the shore was sand and gravel and not outcroppings of rock. Lean and wiry, William was a good walker. And he was prepared to take in all that he could of Livesey's sights.

He decided to return to the village to begin his journey. He walked back down the single cobbled street, noticing this time not merely the tavern and apothecary, but the few other shops in the town. As he had observed before, most of the houses were simple dwellings of fishermen or laborers, or even farmers whose fields lay beyond the village. At the bottom of the street there was a little harbor, a quay of stone and weathered planks, and beyond a dozen or so small boats anchored, none longer than a dozen feet in length. They rocked gently in what was now a retreating tide, and he imagined that within the hour all would be resting on the sand. A few fishermen were mending nets, chatting among themselves, tending the boats. None paid any attention to him. He wondered if some there had been in the tavern when his strangeness made such an impression, when all eyes were fixed upon him as though he were a freak of Nature.

He continued down the sand, walking along the water's edge. He looked out at the sea. Was it here the Jews had walked, only to find themselves betrayed by one entrusted with their care? The question chilled him, and he wondered at his own reaction. The atrocity had been hundreds of years before, as many perhaps as a dozen lifetimes. If he had never heard of it, he would have looked for no evidence of it now. His mind's eye would have seen only a placid sea, retreating into the distance.

He continued to walk; the air was fresh, and the walk was not otherwise unpleasant to him. On one side, the land rose to a height above his head. Much of it was pasture, green and full. He saw sheep, goats, cattle. Presently he found himself walking beneath white cliffs like those at Dover, although not so high or imposing, perhaps a dozen or more feet above him. The gravel beach below was exposed, the tide out. Suddenly, he heard himself hailed.

"Good day, sir. Are you lost, that you wander aimlessly?"

He turned toward the voice. Ahead of him, an old man sat on a rock, perched like one of the island birds. In the gravel of the shore he had made a fire for himself and was roasting something. Not a chicken or duck, but something smaller, probably a sea bird of which the sky was full. He had long white hair flowing over his shoulders, wore a ragged coat, long pantaloons and no shoes. His bare feet were white, a dead man's feet, bloodless. Around his neck he wore an amulet of a fish, crudely carved from wood.

William said he was just taking a walk.

The old man eyed him curiously, as though the idea of taking a walk without a specific destination or evident reason was unthinkable to him. He removed the bird from the spit, bounced it from hand to hand to let it cool, and then took a bite out of it. He had ripped the neck from the bird, and the feet, but had left the wings and the breast.

He waved the bird before William. "Will you eat, sir? I have more than enough for myself."

William politely declined. He had rarely seen anything so unappetizing. Besides, he considered the old man's conversation an interruption in his way. He wanted to circumnavigate the island but knew if he were gone from the manor too long it would raise suspicions, if not those of Sir Arthur, then at least Broderick's.

"If you will not eat, sir, I suppose you do not mind if I do."

"I am a doctor, come to tend Sir Arthur and his lady," William said.

The old man asked where he was from, mentioning towns on the mainland.

"I'm from London," William told him.

"Then you've come far to tend the sick," the old man said, stretching himself to his full height, which was a good foot shorter than William's. "And I, Doctor, am a hunter of what washes up."

"What washes up?" William asked.

"Well, sir, on a good tide I might find some flotsam from some vessel, a barrel of this, a few pieces of that. Many a dead fish, some edible. Occasionally the body of a hapless mariner, which I let rot upon the beach, since the man's burial is no duty of mine as it once might have been."

"And do you make a living thereby?"

"Well, my food I get from the sea and the air." The old man gestured toward the sky, which at that moment was full of birds and their cries. "I have few needs and hope to have less, with time." He wiped his mouth with the sleeve of his ragged coat. "All of us will have fewer needs in time and then none at all. Will you sit with me, sir? Few come out from the village as you have done. I've spoken to no man for a month or more and would enjoy the pleasure of your company."

The old man pointed to a rock and nodded his head invitingly. William sat down, unsure if the old man's invitation was motivated by a desire for free medical advice or had some darker purpose. Perhaps, he thought, it was no more than the old man's professed loneliness behind the invitation. But something told him his host might be the repository of valuable information.

"And what think you of Livesey so far?"

"I think it's a very small island," William said, laughing.

"Aye, Doctor, it is indeed. Yet in all the world there is none like to it, for its mysteries."

"Mysteries, you say?"

"You heard me right, Doctor. Look about you, sir."

William did. The shore was virtually featureless, widening with the retreating tide. The land itself was green with low-growing plants and occasional outcroppings of rock and then the cliffs. "Tell me, what should I be seeing?"

"Oh, Doctor, more than what seems."

"What do you mean?"

"History, sir."

"The tavern keeper said something similar when I spoke with him earlier today."

"Israel Parker of the tavern is a fool, if I may say so. He thinks he knows all there is to know about the island, but it is but a little of what there is to know. You can trust me on that score, Doctor." The old man looked at William for a moment without speaking, then he said, "You would not by any chance be a son of Abraham?"

"Abraham?"

"I mean a Jew."

The question took William by surprise. What about him might have provoked the old man to ask such a question?

"Do I look like a Jew, talk like a Jew, dress like a Jew—however Jews look, talk, dress?" William asked.

The old man laughed a dry laugh, "I only ask because the last time I conversed upon this shore and spoke about the island's history, it was a Jew I spoke with. He wasn't young as you, Doctor, but of my own years. He said he was new to the island like yourself, but he had roots here, roots meaning forebears."

"When was this?"

"Oh, I know not. This year surely, or perhaps the one before. I am no longer good at keeping track of time."

"Did he say his name?"

The old man thought for a moment. "Isaac, Isaac something, I don't remember."

"Isaac Silva?"

"I do believe it was."

"I think I know the man, or did."

"He's dead?"

"Yes, he was murdered," William said without hesitation.

The old man looked down and leaned forward on his knees. He shook his head and then looked up again. "I'm not surprised, sir, not surprised at all. What with the questions he was asking."

"And what questions were those?" William asked.

"Well, Doctor, he was curious about something that happened a long time ago. Something we who live on the island don't want others to know."

"Something that happened on the island?"

The old man paused, stared out to sea. William knew he was trying to decide whether to tell this stranger from London. William waited. Was he now to learn what he had come to the island to learn? If so, it all seemed too easy. He waited some more. He could not just walk away now.

Finally, the old man spoke. "Some Jews that were drowned, Doctor. Long ago. When there were Jews in England, before they were cast out."

"An accident, this drowning?"

The old man smiled. "Well, you could call it that, Doctor, if you were inclined to paint a good face on an evil deed."

The beachcomber proceeded to relate the same story as Burghley had related, the story Isaac Silva had learned from his family's history.

"And you believe the story true?" William asked.

"More likely than not. I told him that when the news was heard on Livesey, I mean the news of the drowning of all those rich Jews, the priest at that time proclaimed a feast day, the bells of the church here rang out as though a new king or queen had been crowned. That's not in writing, not official history like that studied by scholars such as yourself, Doctor. That's local legend, but true I warrant you, for if there's one article of faith Livesey folk have in common, it's their hatred of Jews. Not that many have ever seen or known one, but it does seem that hatred for some race or creed is required of good Christians, lest they spend too much time inquiring into their own failings."

"And your own feelings about Jews?"

"I have naught against them. Christ was a Jew, was he not?"

"So the scriptures affirm."

"And all are children of God?"

"Also affirmed by Holy Writ. These Jews were possessed of considerable wealth?"

"I suppose they were. They could afford to hire the shipmaster to convey them to a safe haven."

"What happened to their goods?"

"Some of it was sewn into their clothes; small things, jewels, rings, precious stones, that sort of thing. As for the rest, what they had in chests in the ship's hold, I suppose they went down with the ship. The ship was lost in a storm, you know. And not far from here, or so we understand."

"Have you ever found any of it? I mean in your combing of the beach."

"Jewels, rings? I can't say I have. I live in hope, as do we all."

"Isaac was murdered in London. He was living in the Domus, a place set aside for converted Jews."

For a moment, the old man said nothing. He stared out at the sea again, a thoughtful look on his face. "Murdered, you say?"

William decided not to go into details. It would involve explaining how Isaac's apparent suicide could not have been so, reciting again all the evidence to the contrary as he had done for Burghley. But why should this strange man, this beachcomber, be interested? Why should he even believe William's theory?

"Murdered."

"Poor fellow. I tell you, Doctor, I liked him. When we talked, he didn't treat me like an outcast, as my former neighbors on the island do. He was a convert. A Jew by blood, but a Christian by choice. I could hardly fault him for that. I believed him to be sincere."

"He *was* sincere. I knew him well. He was my friend. We talked often."

"What is your name, sir, may I ask?"

"I am William Gilbert, Doctor William Gilbert."

"And I am Tobias Wincott, Doctor."

"It's my pleasure to know you, Master Wincott."

"Call me Tobias. *Master* confers too much dignity on one such as I."

William laughed. "Tobias it shall be, then."

"I see you looking, Doctor, at my pendant." It was the carved fish hanging about Wincott's neck where some other might have worn a crucifix. "I found it, Doctor, one day on the rocks as if Nature had placed it there, especially for me. I wear it as a symbol of my new-found faith. Nature is my God, if I have one at all, if there is a God. I wear it that it might bring me good fortune."

William was about to rise, feeling the need to get on with his tour and worried about the time. But then he recalled that he had spent an hour in the tavern talking to the tavern keeper, and had learned about John Broderick's probable treasure hunting activities. That was a step in the right direction. Now he had the opportunity to learn from this aged beachcomber, as he had called himself. And what had he learned? That Isaac Silva had returned to the place of his birth not a year before his murder, asking questions about the lost Jews and their hidden treasure.

So William forgot about time, about getting back. If his long absence from the mansion aroused Broderick or Challoner's suspicion, then so be it. He would deal with that later, make something up. That was a skill he had not learned at Cambridge, but acquired through recent experiences.

"I would gladly learn of these strange things you spoke of."

Tobias Wincott smiled. William saw he was missing most of his teeth and wondered how he managed to chew on the bird he had roasted. "I would gladly tell you, sir. I rarely meet strangers, and those few who come here have no interest in talking to me. They think me mad, you know. I have that reputation. But I'm not mad, just old and perverse." He laughed dryly. Another toothless grin.

"I can show you some of the antiquities of the island, some our long-time islanders know not of," Wincott said. "I showed them to Isaac Silva."

"How do you know of them, when they do not?"

"I have not always lived here by myself. You have seen the church in the village."

"Yes."

"I was once curate there, many years past."

"You have retired from that post?"

"Well, sir, you could call it a retirement if you will. But the truth is, I was expelled."

"Expelled?"

"Defrocked is the proper word. For certain *doctrinal perversions*, as the bishop chose to call them, and a few indiscretions with my parishioners, to which I will give no name but to say that even men of God are still men, with the flaws of their sex, if you know what I mean. As a priest I was consoler of the wounded and suffering, and many women of the parish needed to be consoled. They have no curate now. A priest comes once a month from the mainland to serve the faithful. I hear he preaches to two or three of a Sunday, offers communion. What good would that serve anyway, since none come? I know it is a dangerous thing to disregard God's word and sacred ordinances, but there's none here eager to cause trouble for anyone else. It's the one thing that can be said for Livesey. People leave each other alone."

The beachcomber got up from his rock, using his arms and a cane for support. William surmised he was afflicted with the same condition as

Challoner. Every joint would protest the movement. "Come, and follow me, Doctor. What was your name again, by the way?"

"William Gilbert."

"And I am Tobias Wincott, as I said. I don't know what I am now."

"A man still. As you were before," William said. "And my guide to the antiquities of the island."

Wincott smiled and shook William's hand. The old man's grip was firm, the hand spotted and veined.

"Come then, Doctor. You're not afraid of an old man, are you?"

"Have I some reason to fear?"

"None, Doctor, that I can think of."

Twenty-Three

William followed Tobias Wincott along the shore that was sometimes sand and sometimes rock. The tide was out now, a good a hundred yards off. During the march, Wincott fell silent, then stopped. They had walked only a short distance, but the old man was already out of breath. Yet he had an excited look in his eyes, as though he were on the verge of revealing something wonderful.

"What do you want to show me?" William asked.

"Part of the island's history, Doctor. You're from London. You've doubtless seen many an ancient monument there. We are not without such things here on Livesey."

William doubted this tiny island could offer the sights of London, or anything near to them, but he decided to indulge the old man. He ahead of them what appeared to be a stone tower, rising over a clump of trees growing near the shore. Only the crenelated crown appeared. He might have missed it, had Wincott not called attention to it. He might have walked right by, his eyes on the rocks, anxious not to stumble and break an ankle and concerned, remembering the drowned Jews, not to be taken by a suddenly turning tide.

"Built by the Normans?" William asked.

"No, while it would appear so," Wincott said. "It was built by one of the Challoner ancestors, or built *for* him by a man named Maxwell, hence its name, Maxwell's Tower. About a hundred years ago, aping the Normans as our nobility often will, because we think them better than us who have come after. The man had delusions of grandeur. Hoped to build an even finer manor house than the one his great grandson lives in today, but ran out of money, and completed only the tower. As it says in the scriptures, a fool builds what he cannot finish. So he built the tower to resemble some Norman castle he had seen elsewhere in England, maybe over in Queenborough, I don't know. He built it upon the foundation of an older structure, a Roman fort, and that was built upon an even older foundation. All to save money, I think, but maybe not. Maybe to show that he was better than those who went before. Challoner pride. Might as well make use of the past to build for times to come. That seems to be the philosophy of those who build for eternity, only to find time takes its toll on buildings as it does on man. People on the island call it Challoner's Folly, but not to Sir Arthur's face. Not that we see his face that often."

For a while, Wincott said nothing. The old man stared at the tower as though it were an object of veneration, not just an abandoned testimony to a single family's ambition. Then he said, "Come, Doctor, you'll want to see what's within."

They climbed up through trees and came quickly to the base of the tower, which William estimated rose at least forty or fifty feet into the sky. The opening at the base had doubtless once held a door, but now stood agape. He followed Wincott inside and stood, looking up a winding staircase tight against the inner walls.

"You may go up, Doctor, if you will," Wincott said with a wave of his hand. "I'm too tired, or too old, or both. The view of the sea is most pleasing. On a clear day you can see all the way to France. Or at least, that's what I remember."

William climbed the stone stairs. They were narrow, hugging the wall, and unevenly spaced, as though he that built it had had no rule to determine the rise of each step but guessed haphazardly, or planned perversely to make the ascent perilous. There was no rail or banister, and he well understood now how Wincott was fearful of the climb. At the top he climbed through an opening, probably once a trap door, also rotted away, and stood upon a platform open to the sky.

Tobias had been right. The view was breathtaking. Far off, he could see a ship under sail.

He turned then toward the north, to see across the tidal creek separating the island from the mainland, the causeway. He could see the village and even the manor, with its chimneys and its mossy leads.

He was struck at how small the island was when viewed from above, yet for all that, its own little world of myths and secrets. For a moment he imagined the peoples that had inhabited it—the Celts, then the Saxon, the Danes, Normans. He imagined the sail-shrouded ships that had sailed or rowed up the Thames. Each had left behind some evidence of themselves, that the layered history of Britain not be entirely forgotten. That the violence perpetrated by each might not be completely absolved by time.

He turned all about him and saw at a distance a small island to the north and east—from what he could see hardly more than jagged rocks, treeless, no habitations that he could see, a desolate piece of earth afloat in a hostile sea. In his imagination, he saw the fated vessel that had taken the Jews on board and then left them to their fate, imagined it dashed upon the shores below him, the crew lost, their dream of recovering the Jewish treasure lost as well. Beneath the water, calm now, lay their bones; Jew and Gentile lost together.

After a few minutes he started down, finding the descent more fearsome than the climbing up, made it to the bottom with a sigh of relief, and looked about for Wincott. For a moment he thought the former curate of Livesey had deserted him, but then saw the old man leaning against a tree, looking out on a clearing where he could view the sea from a much lesser height.

Wincott turned at the sound of William's approach. "Not disappointed, Doctor?"

"It's a wondrous view," William said. "I was born near the sea but am never weary of viewing it in all its moods. I noticed another island, at a distance."

"Little Livesey," Wincott said. "This is Great Livesey, but we don't call it that, not very often at least. Just Livesey. No one lives there on the smaller island, save for gulls and other winged creatures. In times past the two islands were one."

"How do you know that?"

"Island legends, Doctor. Nothing written, just remembered by generations of island folk. I don't know, maybe it isn't true. But it's what's believed here, and what's believed might as well be true, don't you think, Doctor?"

William did not think that. To him, belief and truth were sometimes the same, but as often, not. Often they clashed violently, as in many a scientific theory he had considered. Yet he would not debate the old man. No, there was no point in that.

"I have more to show you, if you can spare another hour," Wincott said.

"I think I can, Tobias, you are an excellent guide."

"Your friend the Jew was not so complimentary."

"Isaac Silva."

"Yes, Isaac. I don't think he trusted me, when I told him I had once been in holy orders. I don't think he trusted the Christian clergy, and no wonder."

"What do you mean?"

"He thought we were all Jew-haters, the priests, fomenters of conspiracy theories involving Jews, the blood libel, Jews castrating Christians, stealing children. Vast plots to take over the world."

They had followed the shore line, making their way around the island, and came now to marshy tract, fenland. He noticed it was full of pools of water—sea water, he imagined.

"You know what those are, Doctor?" the old man asked, pointing to the pools.

"Holes, ponds."

"Dug to find the Jew's treasure, every one of them. The hunters would dig a pit, thinking that's where the ship's crew hid the treasure, then it would fill with water from the sea. Those aren't fresh water pools. Sea water, all of them. If there was ever treasure there, it's far under water now. Except for the mount where the manor's built and the cliffs, much of the island is barely above the level of the sea. You can see that for yourself, walking around the island."

"Who's digging for the treasure?" William asked.

"Ah, that would be Master Broderick from the manor house."

"Broderick?" William found this hard to believe. He couldn't imagine the tall imposing secretary handling a shovel.

"Well, not Broderick himself, he's the treasure-finder general. It's his crew that does the digging. Lower servants of the house. He himself does no more than walk about, waving a large staff, which I've heard he claims can find what's buried. Gold, silver. Sir Arthur's put him up to it, hired him as much for that as whatever secretarial functions Sir Arthur believes he's in need of."

So William had guessed rightly. This was indeed the talent Sir Arthur had alluded to when speaking of his secretary. A gold hunter—and perhaps it also explained Broderick's hostility toward William. Did Broderick suspect that his master's new doctor had a similar interest in treasure hunting? The rivalry among treasure hunters was both well known and predictable.

"Of course, some believe that it's all false, the story, a flight of fancy," Wincott said. "A man could say, your friend Isaac wasn't on the beach when the Jews were drowned. It was a story someone reported to him, and you know, Doctor, how that goes. One man tells another man, the second tells a third. By the time the story has passed to two or three others, things have been added, others subtracted. Who knows the truth of it? Maybe there were never any rich Jews, no brutal shipmaster, no treasure. Perhaps not even a ship, either sailed or sunk. Some might say this, even some on Livesey might say this."

"But you do not say this."

"I do not, because I have proof otherwise. Come, Doctor, I have something more to show you."

Wincott led him back toward the tower to a copse of elms, within which William could discern a hut made of driftwood and stones. Its roof was made of dead branches, braided together artfully and so tightly that William imagined they might indeed keep out the weather.

Wincott invited him in.

There were few accommodations for man within; a filthy pallet of dried seaweed and a piece of sailcloth to cover him, a battered chest without a lid, a vast collection of sea shells, other assorted finds from his combing of the beach. He was a rabid collector, but no organizer.

Wincott knelt down by the chest, dug deep within it, and withdrew a notebook of the sort that William used to record his scientific experiments. "When I was still a cleric, I wrote in this book my sermons, but I've torn all those pages out and used them for kindling. Now, I record my searches."

"Your searches?"

"For treasure, Doctor. Look."

Wincott had opened a page and there William saw what at first seemed an incomprehensible drawing, an uneven circle with intersecting lines at the periphery. There were numbers, too, on each of the intersecting lines."

"What am I looking at, Tobias?"

"The ragged circle is the island, Livesey, and these lines you see here are the sectors of my search."

"And what are you searching *for*?"

"What was stolen, what was lost."

He reached even deeper into the chest and pulled out a metal object. It was a piece of silver, a long spoon, a ladle.

"Look close, Doctor. What do you see?"

William took the ladle. "Where did you find it?"

"On the sand, or in the sand. The tide is like a great rake, Doctor, it buries and unburies, a continuous cycle of concealment and discovery. That's part of why I like where I live now. I spotted the handle, pulled it up, but I pray you look closer at the handle to see what is written there."

William looked. On the handle was an inscription, but not in any European language. It was Hebrew. William couldn't read it, but recognized the script. It was like the script on the golden plate Lord Burghley had shown him.

"I reason, Doctor, that there's but one source of this."

"The Jews' treasure?"

Chuckling, Wincott nodded. "Exactly, Doctor. Since then I've continued to search. I record it in my notebook. It makes more interesting reading than my sermons, in my humble opinion."

He put the notebook and ladle back into the chest.

"When did you find this?"

"But two months past."

"And where, exactly?"

"Ah, Doctor, that's my secret. But be assured I did find it, and I know not to whom it belonged but some well-heeled Jew."

"I wonder that Broderick hasn't found it, given he has a small army to search."

Wincott laughed. "Well, perhaps his magic staff doesn't have the power he claims. But if he found the whole hoard, then why should he still be searching? That's what I think."

He promised Wincott he would visit him again. He told him he hoped to learn more of the island's history, although the truth was that there was only one story among the old man's stories that he was really interested in.

Twenty-Four

Within the hour he was at the door of the manor, and facing Broderick, who demanded to know where he had been. William thought the query insolent, and bristled at it, but tried to keep his composure. He had dealt with uppity servants before. Who had not? It was all a matter of standing one's ground, not letting them see their impudence had rattled you. Casting a cold eye, letting them know their insolence would not go unnoticed or, ultimately, unpunished.

"Sir Arthur has asked for you all morning."

"I have been fetching medication," William said.

"You went to the apothecary's?"

"Of course, but he did not have all I needed."

"Where would you find it if not from him? He is the only apothecary on the island."

"I plucked it from the salt marsh on the other side of the island," William said. "An apothecary isn't the only source of medicinal herbs. Don't you know that, Master Broderick? Some of us have them from where God planted them, not in a glass vial in a shop window."

It was enough to shut Broderick up. He grumbled something about his master expecting him and led the way through the vestibule and up the stairs. William followed. After the stark light of the outdoors, William's eyes struggled to adjust to the darkness of the interior of the house. This was Broderick's natural habitat, it seemed, when he wasn't secretly digging for treasure.

Broderick left him at his master's door. William knocked and entered.

"Ah, Doctor Gilbert, you have returned, finally," Challoner said with a sigh of relief. He was out of bed, sitting in a chair with a book in his lap. He looked to William at the moment almost like a healthy man of his age; not robust, but probably mobile and intellectually alert.

"How do you do, sir?" William asked. The necessary question. What doctor did not ask it a dozen times a day, a hundred times a month?

"Better, I think, Doctor. You see I have risen from my bed of affliction."

"So I see. That's always a good sign," William said.

"I do believe your very presence in this house has improved my condition—in anticipation of proper treatment, I think."

"A happy anticipation often does give one a sense of well-being," William responded. He asked what Challoner was reading.

"Oh, it's a history, Doctor, very dry, very dull reading, and it does put me to sleep from time to time."

"A history of what?" William asked.

"Of our own nation, the wars between the Saxons and the Normans. It's a special interest of mine."

William had not studied English history at Cambridge. It had not been in the curriculum. To his knowledge, it was not taught at any college or university in England, and he had been too preoccupied with his medical studies to divert his attention to his own country's past. In fact, he had heard more historical lore in the past few days than he had in as many years. His busy practice allowed him little leisure to read anything but medical texts, of which there was an increasing number, both translations of the ancients and contemporary works.

So, in response to Challoner's interest, he merely nodded and withdrew the medication he had obtained from the village apothecary from his bag, the story about plucking some natural herb from the island's marshes being a convenient fiction to explain his long absence from the house.

"I think you'll find this, taken with wine or water, will provide ease from your muscular pain, Sir Arthur."

"I will be without pain?" Challoner asked hopefully.

"Well, you will experience less pain, and perhaps *far* less pain. Different people respond differently," William said.

There was a carafe of water sitting on a bedside table, along with a cup. William poured the water, then mixed the powder in the cup. The man hesitated for a moment, looked up at William uncertainly, then took the cup and drank all of its contents. He smiled with satisfaction, as though his taking the medication was a thing for which he should be congratulated.

William stayed almost an hour, while Challoner got back into bed and commenced a long recital of his aches and pains, most—in William's opinion—inevitable, given the man's age and his lack of exercise. *He who lies abed all day, will hardly keep the pains at bay.* It was a silly rhyme he had learned as a child, from a stepmother insistent on exercise as a cure for a great many ills. But he believed it, and had seen its effect in patients given to hypochondria, as he was persuaded Challoner was, in addition to the ills that were in fact his to suffer.

"I think it is time for me to visit your wife, sir, if you will permit me."

"And how is my lady wife?" Challoner asked, looking up from his book, to which he had returned, holding the page close to his eyes and squinting to read the print.

"Why, she seems to improve."

"Improve?"

"So she reported when I spoke to her last," William said. "She is by all signs that I can discern a healthy woman of her age, in good spirits, I would not be surprised were I to find her risen from her bed, even as you, and prepared to enjoy a good supper—in the great hall, perhaps."

"Ah, beware of false impressions, Doctor," Challoner said. "My wife is no more healthy than am I, although her afflictions might be different. She is capable of putting a good face on her distress. If she is in pain, she will deny it. If her mind is confused, she will declare otherwise. Trust not her answers to your probing. She is quite capable of lying to your face."

Challoner chuckled and nodded, inviting William to join in the joke. "I only jest, Doctor," Challoner said when he saw William's expression had not changed. "She's a most honest woman. If any lie ever flew from her lips, I know not of it."

William knocked on Mildred Challoner's door and entered when he heard her pleasant voice. He found the lady, not just risen from her bed, but standing and looking out of the window. She was no longer in her sleeping garb but was fully dressed in an elegant silk gown that she might have worn for some public occasion. Her cheeks were rouged, her eyelids hooded with dark, and her lips were accentuated by some glossy material. She looked to him as though she might be expecting a lover, not her doctor. Her appearance could not, he believed, be for her husband; he was certainly an old man in decline, and by all appearances interested in his wife chiefly as a foil for his own ailments.

He had expected to find Johane with her, and was disappointed. He was eager to share what he had learned from Wincott about Broderick's treasure hunting activities and what he had seen on his island tour, especially Wincott's discovery of the ladle with the Hebrew inscription.

Suddenly, he felt awkward being alone with this woman. Why? It was not that he had treated no girls or women in his practice or been alone with them during examinations and treatments. He could not account for his feeling.

"How do you do, madam?"

She didn't answer the question, as routine as it was. Instead, she said, "I saw you today, Doctor, walking along the shore."

He told her the same lie he had told Broderick, about needing some natural substance found only in a saltmarsh.

"How did you know where to find what you sought, being as you are a stranger to this place?"

"The apothecary told me. When he didn't have what I needed, what your husband needed, he told me where I might find what I sought. He was very helpful that way."

She turned away from him and stared out the window. "Walking alone on the island can be dangerous, Doctor."

"I wouldn't have thought so, madam, the island seems a peaceful place, with its own unique beauty."

She turned to face him again. "It is remote from civilization, Doctor. We are a little island, cut off from the mainland by a tidal river that ebbs and flows as the moon dictates. Every year, more of Livesey washes out to sea. I have come to hate the sound of it, especially in a storm. Were it up to me, we would live elsewhere. But my husband loves this place, and would rather die than live elsewhere, even though he has the wherewithal to do so. This house is falling down around us, not because he lacks money to repair and replace, but because he is indifferent to it. That is my situation, Doctor. You are an outsider, still perhaps you can understand."

William was taken aback by the intimacy of this disclosure. He had not expected it, did not feel comfortable with it. Why was she telling him this, dismissing her ailing husband for his failings? It was not that he disbelieved her description of her life, her marriage, but that it did not seem necessary for him to know, not appropriate for him to know. It was not a medical problem. He felt himself blushing with embarrassment; he couldn't help himself, even though it was a tendency in his fair skin that he disliked. He couldn't conceal it with a decent beard.

"I see I have made you uncomfortable, Doctor," Challoner's lady wife said. "I beg your pardon. I did not mean to do so. I am a lonely woman in this house, Doctor, which is why I have so appreciated the attendance of the young woman who accompanied you here, Johane. She is a jewel. I saw it at once. No typical serving girl."

"I would agree, madam. I've found her a most excellent assistant in my medical practice."

Mildred Challoner went on. "A woman needs someone to listen to her, someone to talk to, a friend, not just an obedient servant. As you've seen, we are the only persons of our station on the island. I have friends elsewhere, even family members. I invite them to come to Livesey, but they decline, make up excuses, some quite fantastical. They are not interested in coming to so remote a place—or perhaps it's me they dislike."

"I think that unlikely, madam," he said.

"Oh, you don't know, Doctor. When I married my husband I cut myself off, and he never encouraged me to resume friendships formed before our marriage. He's a jealous man, Doctor, not that I should take lovers but that I should have *anyone* other than himself. For which reason, I pray you not to tell him how fond I am of Johane. He might even become jealous of *her*."

"Trust me, madam. Your secret is safe with me. That I should say anything that would result in Johane's dismissal is abhorrent to me."

Her eyes began to glisten with tears. William didn't know what to do. Now, more than before, he wished Johane was here. She would know what to do, what to say. He did not.

But then he said, more as a distraction than a response to her need, "You said it was dangerous to walk alone on the island. Have there been incidents? I mean, acts of violence against lone walkers?"

"There was one, several months past. It involved someone in our household."

"A servant, a family member?"

"A servant, he who my husband employed before Broderick came. His name was Peter Audley. He was the steward in my husband's father's time, connected by blood to half the village. He was born here, you see, not like Broderick."

"What happened to him?"

"No one knows for sure. He disappeared one day. A week later, his body was found down by the tower."

William told her he had seen the tower while walking. He did not tell her he had a guide, nor that he had explored the interior, nor that he had spent hours with the disgraced cleric listening to his stories.

"I assume it was not a natural death," William said.

"His head was crushed," she said. "I would not call that natural, would you, Doctor?"

"Perhaps he fell from the tower, climbed to the top and slipped on the stairs?"

"You have seen the inside, been inside, Doctor?"

"I was curious, madam. I could not help but look inside."

"It's a horrid place," she said with a shudder. "My husband took me there to have a look at it when we were first married. He said an earlier owner of the manor had intended it to be a bulwark against invaders, that its foundation had been a Roman fort. I hated it from the very first view of it. I hate the thought of it now. No, Doctor. He didn't fall from a height. It was not that manner of wound. He was bludgeoned. On the left side of his head. I hate to think of it. It was a terrible wound." She shuddered again.

"And robbed?"

"He carried nothing with him typically; certainly no great amount of money. He was a servant, after all. He was a good, honest man, a most faithful servant, devoted to the family. At his funeral, all the island turned out. As I said, almost all were connected to him in some way, cousins of one degree or another. My husband appointed John Broderick in his stead."

"Did your husband not investigate the death? The facts you recount suggest foul play."

"My husband sent Broderick to make inquiries, but nothing came of it. My husband always thought Audley was somewhat of a fool. He only kept him on for his father's sake."

Then William thought to ask, "What was this Audley doing at the tower in the first place?"

"That's the thing," she said. "I cannot conceive. It wasn't his custom to walk out alone. Indeed, he more than once warned me and the maidservants not to do so. He would tell us stories of corsairs, Moroccan pirates who once raided these coasts and stole women to become slaves."

"Pirates, really?"

"Oh yes. I think some of his stories were just to admonish us to be careful. Women alone, you know. Every woman's nightmare."

"Madam, it sounds like good counsel, pirates or no. And it would seem your husband's steward was murdered, if not for his money, but then for some other reason. Do you have any thought as to why?"

"Why he was murdered?"

"Yes. And by whom?"

"None at all, Doctor," she said. "None at all. He was much loved in the village and in this house, honored in his station. A man without enemies."

At that moment, a little rapping came at the door. "Come in," Mildred Challoner said.

It was Johane. She looked in, saw William, then asked, "Am I interrupting, Doctor?"

"I was just about to examine your mistress," William said.

"Please proceed, Doctor," Mildred Challoner said. "I presume I will not need to unclothe?"

"No need, madam, my examination will not require that, and Mistress Sheldon may stay."

He proceeded with the examination. Mildred Challoner's pulse was normal, her heart rhythm likewise. Her eyes, rather fine eyes he thought, were clear and luminous. She had yet to show any untoward symptoms to suggest she was anything other than a healthy female of her age. She had already admitted to him that she feigned disability to please her husband. For one dedicated to healing the sick, he felt repelled by the couple's perverse marital charade. He suddenly found himself blushing again, not because of anything Mildred Challoner did, but at Johane's witnessing his participation in it.

"Have you ever borne children, madam?" William thought to ask.

"No, Doctor, my husband and I were never so blessed."

"Did you desire to have them?"

"It was my wish, my husband's as well. But I was unable to conceive."

William noticed Mildred Challoner's casual acceptance of responsibility. Doubtless, her husband had been quick to assign to her the blame, but he knew it was as often the husband who was unable.

"Will I live, Doctor?" Mildred asked, with a rather charming grin.

"I think it highly likely, madam," William answered. He laughed.

"Johane helps a good deal in that effort," Mildred Challoner said, turning an appreciative glance at her nurse. Johane made a little curtsy in response.

"Lady Challoner is an excellent patient, Doctor Gilbert," Johane said.

"But I do wonder, Doctor, wherever did you find such a jewel as Johane is?"

Johane answered before William could. "I found him, madam. I had some training in nursing from my mother and wished to set out in that vocation, having been a common maidservant before. I had heard of Doctor Gilbert's fame so appealed to him to be his assistant. Knowing that woman assistants are rare these days, I greatly feared he would scorn my offer, but he did not."

"That is my benefit then as well as yours," Mildred Challoner said. She said no more about her appreciation for Johane, at least not in so many words, but it was evident in the talk that followed. The weather on the island had discouraged excursions out of doors, but she said if it improved, she would like to take walks around the grounds of the house, to see the garden, to visit the village where she believed it did the people good to see her up and around, concerned for their well-being. She said Johane should accompany her, and perhaps William as well. She said she believed sea air was healthful and that she had missed it during these long weeks of her confinement.

"But will Sir Arthur approve?" William asked.

"I shall win him over to it, Doctor. Perhaps with your help."

"My help, madam?"

"You may tell him that sea air improves the appetite, invigorates the mind, suppresses contagion," she said.

"I shall, madam, if that's your wish, for what you say is largely true."

"Oh, it is my wish," she declared ecstatically. She reached forward with both hands, grasped William's hand and at the same time did likewise to Johane's so that the hands of each of them were bound together in a confirmatory clasp. "I'm so happy," she said.

William's cheeks burned. He thought Johane's did as well.

Twenty-Five

William ate with the household staff in a low-ceilinged kitchen as dark and gloomy as the rest of the manor. His presence among them created more anxiety than he had intended—in them, not him. As a doctor he was accustomed to mingling with all manner of folk and often broke bread with the poor and the needy, lower servants and upper when he took his fee in a meal. Disease and affliction cared little for the social order, striking down the great as well as the common. But others at the table, the gardener and three downstairs maids, he had not seen before. William counted sixteen in all. They filled a long trestle table and spoke little as they ate, intimidated no doubt by the presence of the London doctor, who was by his dress and manner a gentleman and whose presence among them would surely be inexplicable to them all.

John Broderick presided at the head of table, scowling while he ate and occasionally making sharp comments to the other servants. William ate and exchanged glances with Johane, who was seated at mid-table between two of the maids, who kept talking around her as though she wasn't there. It was clear to William both he and Johane were guilty of the same offense. They were strangers in the house, on the island, and therefore to be kept at arm's length.

After dinner, some of the company lingered. William signaled to Johane with a nod. She followed him up from the kitchen, eager to avoid Broderick who had been the first to leave the table and might, he knew, be lurking anywhere in the house, perhaps even waiting for him, for them, listening to any conversation he and Johane might have, anxious to report it to his master.

Or maybe not, William thought. Perhaps Broderick had his own reasons for disliking the London doctor and suspecting his mistress's nurse, who had arrived at the same time.

"Come into the library," Johane whispered when they were on the main floor. "Lady Challoner told me where it was, had me fetch a book for her. It's nothing compared to Lord Burghley's library at Theobalds."

"Few libraries are," William said.

The library was off the great hall of the house and was notable for how few books it contained and, for that matter, how little furniture. It was a square, cold room, nominally the master's domain but hardly used, if its musty smell and bareness were any indication. There were two chairs facing each other with a modest hearth in the center. A fire had not been laid. The Challoners, William realized, largely lived in their own rooms where they ate, slept, and conversed with visitors, were there any to visit with.

Johane sat down in one of the chairs and leaned forward. She placed the candle on a little desk beside her chair. William knew this was risky business, but he dared not meet in her room or she in his. Were they discovered here, sitting in near darkness in the master's library, he had no idea what plausible excuse might be offered. They would look like lovers, or worse, conspirators—which in truth they were.

"Lady Challoner saw you walking on the shore," Johane said.

"I know. She told me before you joined us."

"She was suspicious?"

"No, concerned, rather—for my safety. She told me the former steward of the house, a man named Audley, had been murdered on the shore at a place where there's a tower. She was worried about me getting murdered, I suppose. But it was interesting to learn of Broderick's predecessor. Try to find out why Sir Arthur chose Broderick. Why not someone else, another islander, as steward? An old man, who I met while walking, told me he thought Broderick was from Halstead, not far from Colchester where I was born and raised."

"Did you know any Brodericks there?" she asked.

"Not that I remember, but my father might know the family. He's a lawyer and a judge there. He knows everyone, or so he claims. I'll write him and put his knowledge to the test."

"This old man you mentioned, Doctor. Was his name Wincott?"

"Yes, Tobias Wincott, a defrocked curate, now living as a hermit, a beachcomber. He gave me a tour of the tower and a stretch of marshland where treasure hunters had dug. He told me something else, something important."

"Which is?"

"He confirmed that Broderick is a treasure hunter, as we supposed. Wincott says that he supervises a crew of servants from the manor, looking for buried treasure. In the marsh. Wincott pointed out the holes. He said Broderick has a long staff he uses to locate the treasure. He waves it about him, and if it trembles in his hand when he points it to the ground, then that's where treasure lies."

Johane laughed. "Seems a silly business, if you ask me, Doctor. I have no faith in such magic, either in its capacity to cure or to find gold or silver. Has he found anything?"

"Not that Wincott reported."

"It's hard for me to imagine Broderick doing that. He seems a man who stands on his dignity, at least when he's not chasing skirts. Are you sure this defrocked curate is not merely telling stories to entertain a fancy gentleman from the city?"

"I think he's telling the truth," William said.

"Lady Challoner says the man is mad. She says he was a horrible person, full of every manner of inequity and heresy and was imprisoned for a season, after which he has never been right in the head. She warned me, as she warned you, of walking alone on the shore."

"I spent an hour with Wincott, more than an hour. He told me about his history on the island. He was quite open about it. I never felt any fear in being with him. And by the way, he met your grandfather."

"My grandfather?"

"He said Isaac Silva came to the island not long before his death, asked questions about the Jews who drowned and the fate of all their goods. Wincott showed him what he had showed me, a ladle inscribed with Hebrew letters. Wincott took it to be proof that the Jewish treasure was buried somewhere on the island."

"My grandfather never told me he had been back to Livesey. Never said anything about meeting one of the locals or talking to him about our family history."

"Maybe he didn't want you to know, or wanted to put all that behind him. He never seemed interested in money. More concerned,

I think, that justice somehow be done for his betrayed ancestors—*your* betrayed ancestors."

"Will you see Wincott again?"

"Tomorrow, if I can get out without being noticed," William said.

"By the way, I told my mistress that you went walking because of your hobby," Johane said.

"What hobby?"

"Your love of birds and sea shells. I told her you had a notebook in which you recorded birds you saw on your walks. I told her it was an experiment you were conducting. Sea birds, gulls, ospreys, and so forth. Observing the pattern of their flight, their migrations, their mating habits."

William couldn't help but laugh. "I admit to having a special interest in chickens, when they are roasted properly, and I like a good, juicy duck on occasion, but as for taking notes on their flight and recording their species, well that would be some other gentlemen of your acquaintance, not I."

She reached toward him and pressed his hands. "Oh, let it be you, Doctor, at least for now. I worry about you walking alone. Besides, if you deny it, you will make a liar out of me. I have given you a plausible reason for your wandering. When I told my mistress of it, she expressed no disbelief. Indeed, she said she once had a cousin given to the same peculiar interest."

"Very well, a student of birds and their habits I will be, at least while on the island. And if it serves to discourage suspicion of my actions, then it will serve us well. But I don't know if our friend Broderick will believe it. Speaking of that worthy, have you had any trouble with him?"

Johane laughed. "Trouble? He has accosted me twice in as many days."

"What do you mean *accosted*?"

"Come up to me, stood next to me close enough so I could smell his fish breath. He fancies himself God's gift to women, I think. He said he was most happy that I had come to serve his mistress, and that should I wish I might become his special friend."

"Special friend? I think I know what that means."

"I suspect he has more than one in the house."

"And your mistress?"

"My lady? She says she loathes him. No, she's an unfulfilled woman indeed, but not *that* desperate for a secret lover, especially her husband's steward."

"There is ample precedent for it," he said.

"I have known this manner of man before," Johane said bitterly. "The great houses of England are full of them; they're common as rats, the serving maids are their prey, that is, what's left after the lord of the manor has picked the bones."

"Stay clear of him, then," William said. "He's dangerous."

"How do you know he's not just an ordinary lecher?"

"Instinct," William said. "But I have another favor to ask of you. I do want you to learn more about this previous steward, this John Audley. His death—murder—is a mystery. Lady Challoner told me her husband had assigned Broderick to investigate and had discovered nothing."

"I am hardly surprised," Johane said. "But your mention of that odious man puts an idea into my head."

"What idea would that be?"

"Broderick. Perhaps I can use his interest in me to discover what he may have found about the last steward."

"But he found nothing."

"So he claimed to his new master, but he may have learned more than he told."

"Or may have good reason for not having told what he knew."

"I'll worm it out of him," she said. "You watch me do it, Doctor."

"I appreciate your confidence, Johane, but you must appreciate the risk. I believe Broderick to be a dangerous man."

"Oh I think, rather, that he is an annoying fool. Believe me, Doctor, I have met his kind before—and have handled them without danger to my life or to my virtue."

"I pray you not be so foolhardy, Johane. Let Broderick be. I will in due course find him out. That he should have so quickly occupied the murdered man's seat of authority in the house is but one mark against him."

"Do you suspect Broderick of killing the man—to make room for himself in the house?"

"I would put nothing past him."

"Then what should I do?"

"Proceed with the greatest caution," William said. "Trust no one. Not even your mistress, gentlewoman though she may be."

"I will in all ways be ruled by your counsel, Doctor. But you said you had still another favor to ask. Tell me, what it is that I may do it."

"You are privy to your mistress's secrets, her rooms. Look out for any jewel, plate, or other item that may be part of the Jews' treasure. Look for marks, Hebrew letters. You have seen what they look like."

"I am already doing the very thing you ask of me, Doctor, but regretfully, I have found nothing yet."

"She may have secreted them away," he said. "In some chest, in some closet."

"I will continue my observations," she said. "But my mistress seems so sweet a lady, of so heavenly a disposition, that I doubt she would secrete anything to deceive. She does not seem to have such motives in her heart."

"Perhaps she does not know the value of what she has, thinks it but a common plate, or some jewel of paste. Some of the latter are so exquisitely crafted that a master jeweler must distinguish the real from the imitation."

"I promise, Doctor, I will keep a watchful eye. You can trust me."

"As I have from the beginning, Johane."

She made a little bow.

"And be circumspect around Broderick," William said. "He suspects me already of some devious purpose in the house. You, you, he's interested in only because you're…"

"Vulnerable flesh," she said.

"I was going to say innocent."

"Yes, that too, Doctor. But I pray you keep in mind, Doctor, that though I am a countrywoman born, I am not a silly maid. I have seen much of men and their wiles. I have no fear of Master Broderick or his devices. You may trust me on that score."

Twenty-Six

Later that very day, Broderick confirmed William's worst fears.

It was shortly before supper and William was in his room looking from his window. Suddenly, his gaze dropped from the sea to the earth below, the miserable excuse for a garden with its tangle of weeds and stumps and weathered trees. He saw two figures going into the copse that formed the border between the garden and the little wood.

One was Johane. He recognized her walk, the slope of her delicate shoulders, the incline of her head. But who might the other be? A man, clearly, by his height, shoulders, confident stride. Broderick. He was sure of it. Where were they going and why? Was she being followed by him?

William bounded down the stairs, not caring who observed him, and rushed from the house, almost colliding with Harris along the way. Harris asked what was wrong, but William didn't answer.

Johane was in danger. It was his instinct again.

It wasn't long before he saw the two persons; they were almost enveloped in the trees, but he had been right. It *was* Johane and Broderick he had seen, and the picture verified every dark fear that possessed him. Broderick had his arms around her, and she was leaning back against the tree, trying to escape him but trapped by his eagerness and his strength. Rushing forward, William called out her name, and then again, crying out the second time. They must have heard him in the manor. He didn't care. He would explain later, if explanation was needed.

Broderick released Johane and turned abruptly. Sir Arthur's steward looked first startled, then furious at the interruption of what William surmised must have been a rape, or a fumbling attempt at one. It was what William had feared, what he had warned Johane of. Now it had happened. He struggled to catch his breath before he spoke again, glaring at Broderick, and then turning to Johane.

Johane, standing now apart from Broderick, smiled thinly, almost embarrassed, as though the fault had been hers. William wondered, did she blame herself for this, for going with him? What pretense had he offered her for this meeting, what threats had he made?

"What's happening here?" William demanded, although it was obvious to him. Did he really need to ask, was it not plain enough?

It took a few moments before William received an answer. Broderick stood there, his legs parted defiantly, searching, William thought, for some plausible defense of himself. Then it came.

"Doctor, I was merely giving Mistress Sheldon some instructions on how she might better please her mistress. Lady Challoner is most particular as to how she is served. The supervision of the servants is part of my duty at the manor."

"Instructions *here*, in these woods? Am I to believe that? You were pressing her, forcing her, I saw it for myself."

"Then, Doctor, you misinterpreted what you saw," Broderick countered calmly. "It is easily done. These woods are dark, you came from the trees. I was in no way forcing Mistress Sheldon, nor would I do so. Upon my honor."

His *honor*? William wondered what honor the Challoner steward had, that he should swear upon it. William would have laughed in the man's face, had the circumstances not been so dire.

He turned to Johane, whose face was flushed, her white cap askew on her head and her hair ruffled. Her breath came rapidly, as though she had been running.

William asked her if she was alright, even though he could see she was not. Johane took a breath and said, "He's telling the truth, Doctor. He was advising me on my duties."

For a moment, William was speechless. It was the last thing he had expected Johane to say, and he could hardly believe he had heard her correctly. He asked her to repeat herself. She did, in the very same words.

"What *duties*? Duties to succumb to his advances?"

"He made no such advances, Doctor," she said.

William turned to Broderick, whose face was calm, if composed, relieved perhaps at Johane's response. He had looked furious when William suddenly appeared. Now, he acted as if the interruption was nothing more than an inconvenience, something to be explained away easily.

"What we have here, Doctor Gilbert, is a misunderstanding," Broderick said. "A natural one, if I may say so. I took Mistress Sheldon here aside, to confer with her privily. So that the other servants wouldn't talk, wouldn't think I was scolding her for some neglect of her duties. You know how servants are. They gossip, and a new servant, as Mistress Sheldon is, is a ready target for malicious tongues. I didn't want to ruin her reputation."

This time, William laughed. It was the poorest excuse for lechery he had ever heard. One that would have provoked laughter from an audience at a comedy, or from a jury in a court of law.

"Master Broderick is right, Doctor Gilbert," Johane said. "He was telling me that Lady Challoner prefers to have those who serve her knock before they enter her bedchamber, not to assume she is alone, or perhaps asleep and would mind being awakened abruptly. She may be in conversation with another. He told me to take care that while she may from time to time speak ill of her husband, she will not abide a servant doing so."

William looked at Broderick. He was grinning an oily grin, as though he had just got away with something. William turned again to Johane.

"He had his body pressed against you, your face in his hands. I do not think that's common in conversations between higher servants and lower, although maybe things are done differently here on Livesey island. He looked as if he were hurting you, he had his hands around your neck."

"Were he doing so, I would show signs upon my neck, would I not?" she said. "And would I not complain thereof?"

"You dropped your cap. Your hair is mussed and tangled."

"An accident while passing through the trees, from the branches. Please, Doctor, do not make of this what it is not. For my sake, I beg you."

She looked at him pleadingly, as though she really meant what she said. William decided she did but could not fathom her justifying Broderick. She had said the man disgusted her, was the worst of lechers. Now she was defending the scoundrel. William would talk to her about it, have her explain. But not now, while Broderick stood there gloating.

Broderick said he had business back at the house, responsibilities. He said he didn't have time to talk more over what was a simple misunderstanding, which he assured the London doctor it was. "I respect womanhood," he said, throwing his head back as though it were a boast. "Besides, I have no *need* to force my attentions on a woman."

William made no reply. Broderick made a bow to him; abrupt, like a sudden jerk, and started back to the house. William turned to Johane.

"Are you really alright?"

"Just shaken," she said, her eyes filling with tears.

"Why didn't you denounce him?"

She took a moment to respond. Then she looked at him squarely, almost fiercely. "Had I done so, the assault must need be reported. He would have countered my charge and I might have been dismissed from my lady's service and our joint effort here frustrated. In supporting his lying account, I have done him a favor, from which we both may benefit."

"Benefit? I see no benefit from tolerating his lechery. He could have…"

"Raped me, stolen my maidenhead? Yes, he might have done so. I do believe that was his intent, to have a taste of the new girl in the house. I am no weakling as a woman, but he's a tall, muscular man. I would have been no match for him. You came just in time, Doctor, for which I thank you, but as you can see, my virtue is still intact, my bodice unripped. I have no bruises about my neck or anywhere else upon my body."

"What if he does it again, this time with more success?"

"I doubt he will dare try it a second time. He's made excuses for what he did, what you saw, and I have confirmed them. The same excuses will hardly work a second time. Trust me, Doctor, I will not follow him into any private place again, where I will be vulnerable to his importunities."

"It wasn't his importunities, it was his violence I observed," William said.

"I carry beneath my skirt a knife," Johane said. "It is a short blade, almost as wide as it is long, but deadly, I think. I found it buried in a field when I was a girl. I think it belonged to some ancient person, maybe a Dane or even Roman who had hid it there or lost it. When I came to London, I brought it with me, thinking I might need it to protect myself. Beginning at this moment, Doctor, I promise you I will carry it always on my person. And if Broderick tries a second time to have me, I will give him something to remember me by. My oath upon it."

William looked at her. Her face was hard, her eyes fixed on his. He imagined the blade she had described. He had seen one like it in Burghley's cabinet. An antique blade, but no less deadly for all that. He imagined Johane thrusting it into Broderick's soft belly. It would make her more than a match for his height and weight. Johane was right. If he accosted her again, Broderick would get something to remember her by.

Back in his room, he wrote two letters. One was to his father in Colchester, inquiring if he knew a family in Halstead named Broderick, or a man named John Broderick. It was not a common name, especially in his part of Essex—he knew that much. He realized that even if his father knew the family or such a person, it might yield no information relevant to his quest, but he had not written to or seen his father in nearly six months. The letter would serve a dual purpose.

The second letter was to Burghley. The queen's principal secretary had asked for reports of his findings, but William had found out little so far. Well, he had found out enough to keep him searching. Enough to make him suspicious—of Broderick, of the defrocked curate that Mildred Challoner thought mad, perhaps even of Mildred Challoner herself as well as her husband. And then there was Isaac Silva's visit to the island. Why would Isaac return to Livesey unless he was convinced that the Jewish gold was no mere story in an old book, but concealed on the island?

And why would Isaac have been murdered, if the Jewish gold was all a fantasy?

The letters took longer to write than he expected. His eyelids were heavy when he finished the one to Burghley. Of the two, it had required the most careful wording. The letter was a progress report, if he could call it that, relating what he'd learned. He hoped that it would assure his lordship that he was on the right track. That Burghley had not put his trust in William and Johane in vain.

Twenty-Seven

The next morning, William forwent breakfast with the household and headed for the village. There he found a grocer on the high street, who sold him a small loaf of black bread and some cheese and an apple to go with it. This would serve both as breakfast and dinner. He put the items in his bag, which he wore slung over his shoulder like a traveler setting out for a long journey. If observed and reported to Lady Challoner, she might suppose the bag was for his various collectibles, such as sea shells and bird eggs.

His intent was to see the former curate a second time, but before that he wanted another opinion on the man's sanity. Mildred Challoner said he was mad. Was that the opinion of all who knew him? If so, then he would need to be guarded in accepting what the man said or did. The proprietor of the tavern had claimed to know everyone and everything on or about the island. Wincott had called him a fool. But William wanted to hear the tavern keeper's view.

It was early morning, so the tavern wasn't open, but looking in the window, William could see Israel Parker sweeping the rushes that covered the floor. William knocked at the window and after a little while, the man looked up with annoyance, then seemed to recognize William and unbolted the door.

"Not open until noon, Doctor. Come back then and quench your thirst."

"I'm not looking for drink," William said, "but for reliable information."

"Information? Now that's also a commodity that can be traded or sold."

"You mean you want me to pay you something," William said, reaching to his waist where he carried his purse.

The tavern keeper laughed and held up a hand. "No, Doctor, I shall take no money from you this day. But since you're a medical man and we have none in the village I wish you would take a quick look at my son. He's eight years, a strapping lad, but with a bad rash on his neck and shoulders. Look at him and you shall have your information, if it is within my power to give it."

Some men, William knew, broke into a rash when they touched certain plants or ate certain fruits. William spent an hour questioning the boy, who at eight, had the height and girth of a much older lad but indeed was afflicted with an itchy rash he claimed was keeping him awake at night.

"What do you eat, that you like the most" William asked.

"The pigeon pie my mother makes," the boy said.

"Anything else?"

He mentioned several varieties of fish, the staple diet of the village.

"Any fruit, berries, nuts?"

"Strawberries. I love strawberries, Doctor."

"Try loving them less," William said. "Stop eating them for a fortnight and see if the rash goes away.

"And the itching?"

"Can you read, Master Parker?" William asked, looking up at the boy's father.

"Not well, Doctor."

"How's your memory?"

"Better, Doctor."

William gave him the name of a tried-and-true concoction he had used since he began his practice. "Go next door to the apothecary. He'll surely have it. Apply the salve twice daily. The rash should go away, as long as he avoids strawberries and you apply the salve as I have directed."

The examination had taken place in the tavern keeper's house, which was behind the tavern itself. Now William walked out into the empty tavern. The keeper pointed to a stool. "Sit, Doctor. You've earned your wages. Ask away, this information you want. What would you like to know about our little island?"

"Not about the island, but one of its denizens."

"Denizens?"

"Inhabitants. Tobias Wincott…he claims he was once curate in this place.

"Wincott, sometime priest before his well-deserved defrocking? He was indeed. How did you come across him? It's been so long since I've seen his scurvy face I thought he might be dead."

"He's very much alive," William said. "I spoke to him just yesterday. I met him while I was walking along the shore. We spoke for some time. He told me about himself. Said he was once curate here."

"He was indeed, and infamous for it."

"How so? I heard he was mad."

"From whom?"

"Lady Challoner, at the manor."

"I don't think she was there on the day he renounced his Christian faith, right there In the church, before half the village. He professed himself an atheist, denied Christ and the sacraments—said all was folly and fiction and he who believed otherwise was a fool."

"That must have caused quite a stir."

Israel Parker laughed. When he recovered himself and wiped his mouth with his sleeve, he said, "*A stir?* Why, Doctor, it caused a *riot*. I mean it. All the congregation rose and rushed toward him. The good people of Livesey were ready to skin him alive."

"He said he had no replacement," William said.

"Well, that's true. We had no more curates or priests either who lived on the island as did he. We have an old vicar come once a month from the mainland. He's a dull fellow whose sermons are as dry as dust. Few attend them, claiming to stay at home sick. You want the truth, Doctor? We have become an island of heathens, forsaken by God and His church."

"But for all that, do you think him sane of mind?"

"Saner than the most of us here," Doctor. "He knows a good deal about the history of this place, its dark secrets, its legends. If you listen to him hard he's quite interesting, though some he speaks of I suspect is made up—to entertain curious visitors. Like yourself."

"You have visitors here?"

"Well, there's you, Doctor."

"And Master Broderick."

"A sort of visitor," Parker said. "One who comes from afar and then stays."

"You don't like the man." William phrased it as a statement, not a question. When the tavern keeper said Broderick's name, he spat it out as if it fouled his mouth.

"I do not like the man," he said. "He thinks too much of himself. He is a servant, for God's sake, yet he comes to the village, struts as though he were master of all he surveys. Who can abide such pride in one so little deserving of it?"

"Why do you say he does not deserve it. Is he dishonest, arrogant, offensive in some particular way?"

Israel Parker thought for a moment. "I cannot say he is any of these things you mention, but still I don't like him."

"Tell me, Master Tavern Keeper. Does Broderick have any friends in the village?"

"None that I know of."

"Do you know how he came to come here, to replace the previous steward?"

"You mean Audley? He was a good man, a decent fellow. But he got himself murdered."

"So I've heard. Do you know who killed him, being he was so good and decent a fellow?"

Parker shrugged. "No one knows."

"It's a small island," William said. "Strangers are rare among you. You said as much."

"You mean, Doctor, it must have been one of us who killed him?"

"That's likely, isn't it?"

"I suppose it is, but the real question, Doctor, is why anyone would. He had no enemies."

"He had one," William said. "And in these matters, one is enough."

Twenty-Eight

William left Israel Parker and headed for the shore, where he walked a good hour or more before he came to the place where he had first met Tobias Wincott. The swelling tide had erased all—the ashes, the spit, the footsteps. Wincott was nowhere to be seen.

He went to Wincott's hut, and then searched the marsh with the same result. He had decided to return to the village when he thought of the tower.

He walked until he could see its top rising from the trees and then approached and entered as he had done the first day. There was no sign of the old man. William knew Wincott wouldn't leave the island. He had no reason to; indeed, he had every reason to stay, if only to torment the villagers with his presence.

But then, William saw something on the tower stairs. It was a piece of wood, carved into the shape of a fish with a string to hang around a neck. He had noticed Tobias wearing it the day before. Why was it there, on the third step up? Had he dropped it while climbing the narrow stairs, which the day before he had confessed himself too feeble to do?

His heart racing, William bounded up the stairs and shortly reached the top. He stood in the open air, breathing heavily. He looked all about. He half expected to find the old man there, crumbled up and quite dead from exhaustion. But there was nothing, just the circular platform of the same stone as the tower itself.

He stood for a few moments surveying the scene; he looked back toward the village and beyond to the manor house. In between was marshland, pastures, fallow fields, and clumps of woods. He imagined he might, from this height, spy Tobias somewhere in all that open space. But although he saw some sheep and a few horses, he saw nothing resembling mankind, much less the tottering form of the former cleric. No such form that moved, at least.

The breeze had picked up, blowing in from the sea. He turned in that direction. The wind blew cold against his face. Then he looked down.

William was not afraid of heights, but neither did he enjoy the bracing experience of staring down at the sea below the tower. The tower had been built on a cliff, so the distance from the tower's top to the cliff at the base of the tower he reckoned must be thirty feet or more and then another twenty or thirty to the water's edge. Small waves licked at the base of the cliff. He looked down and saw what he thought at first was driftwood knocking against some rocks, but then realized it was not wood.

It was a body.

He was sure it was Wincott, even though at that distance he could distinguish no particular feature.

He bounded down the steps and shortly found a way to the base of the cliff, sometimes losing his footing and stumbling, grasping at the branches of bushes until he was there, knee-deep in the water, stumbling toward the floating body. It floated face down, but even before he turned it over, he knew it was Wincott. He recognized the tattered coat, the long stringy white hair fanning out in the water. He had no need to listen for a heartbeat to know that Wincott was dead. His head was crushed, the face only half recognizable.

He pulled the body after him by the old man's arms, as though he were pulling a sled. It was an easier task than he expected; the dead man's lungs still contained air. When the tide went out again, the body would have gone with it. Wincott would have simply disappeared and eventually sunk to the bottom, food for fishes or more malign creatures of the sea.

William dragged the old man to a place where the hungry sea could not reach him and sat down, winded by the climb up and the desperate descent. He averted his eyes from the broken body and stared out to sea. He had to decide what to do, what to say, even what to think. The carved fish he had found on the steps suggested Wincott had climbed the tower stairs. But he had told William he was afraid to do so, told him that he was no longer capable of such effort. He was old and lame, and besides that, *why* would he have done so? To see a prospect he had seen a thousand times when younger and more able? And wouldn't he have retrieved the wood figure he habitually wore about his neck? In place of a crucifix, he said, claiming it represented his new faith, a faith in Nature.

Unless he had been dragged up, with the wooden fish falling off in the act—dragged up, to be thrown off the parapet. Of course, he might have done it himself, in a fit of despair, rejecting Nature as he had earlier rejected the Christian God. But Wincott had not struck him as a despairing man. William had known such, had known men and some women who had ended their own lives and then their family covered up for them, concealed the sin, which suicide was, for Christian and also Jew.

But Wincott had not been like them. As impoverished as he was, as isolated from his fellow man, he seemed content with his simple existence, his role as an annoyer of the community, a rebel against God.

No, William could not accept suicide as an explanation in Wincott's case, any more than in Isaac Silva's.

He was about to leave the scene when he thought of the former curate's hut. He had gone there to find Wincott. Not seeing him, William had left abruptly. Now he had reason to search more thoroughly, perhaps for some clue as to the old man's murder.

He went there and at first nothing seemed amiss. He saw the chest in the corner, went over and knelt down by it, unlatched it. He felt the sting of being an intruder, but it lasted for only a minute. After all, its owner was dead.

He sorted through the contents until he found the notebook. The sermons had been ripped out, Wincott had said. But the map recording his beachcombing was also gone now, and so was the ladle with the Hebrew inscription.

Had robbery been the motive for Wincott's murder? Possibly—yet if so, why rip out the map of the island?

He knew he needed to report the death to someone. He couldn't just leave Wincott's body where it lay. It would be an intolerable indecency. Like Jews, even heretics deserved a decent burial. Like Jews, even heretics deserved justice.

He had no thought there was a constable in the village, or even a magistrate on the island, although he supposed if there were one it would probably be Sir Arthur Challoner. But before he told Challoner of what he had found, he would go to Israel Parker. The Saracen's Blade was the center of life in the village and the tavern keeper the unofficial mayor. He would know, and he had, unlike the Challoners, spoken of Wincott with some respect. He had not dismissed the disgraced cleric as a madman.

As for the missing map and ladle, he resolved to say nothing about them. At least not now, at least not until he knew whom he could trust on the island. It was a diminishing number he reckoned, and perhaps only Johane.

Twenty-Nine

"Back so soon, Doctor?" Israel Parker said, looking up, wiping cups with a damp rag.

"Back with sad news, at least sad to me and perhaps to you." William sat down at the bar. The tavern was half empty, which was good. This was a conversation he wanted to have in private, at least for now.

"What sad news?"

"Tobias Wincott is dead."

Israel Parker made no response, at least not at first; he kept wiping cups, then placing them upside down on a shelf behind him. His back was to William. Then he turned.

"He was an old man, near unto seventy, I think. His time had come."

"He fell from the tower, or was dragged up and pushed over," William said, deciding not to mince words.

"What do you mean, dragged up? Against his will? Are you saying he was murdered?"

Parker looked doubtful and William wondered why he should, given the evident murder of the Challoners' previous steward. He was about to recall that to the tavern keeper, when Parker said, "Well, Doctor, there are numerous disadvantages to living alone, one of which is that you have none to help if you are in danger—say, from those who want what you have enough to cause you hurt. An old man living alone is doubly afflicted—with age and solitude. I understand Tobias had found some things of value in all his beachcombing. Maybe that was the cause of his death, or maybe his heretical views finally were more than some righteous Christian could abide. He had many an enemy on the island,

and many more that will hardly mourn his passing. But you think it murder, do you?"

William told him about finding the carved fish on the stairs, told him about how Tobias had explained he was no longer able to climb them because of his infirmities. "I don't believe he climbed those stairs only to throw himself off from the top of the tower. Had he wanted to throw himself into the sea he might have done it without the effort of a climb. The base of the tower is a good twenty or thirty feet above the beach. That's enough to break a young man's neck, and Tobias Wincott was not young."

"He was an atheist," the tavern keeper said. "He had renounced God. Why would he not do so?"

"I believe he was murdered," William said. "Who represents the law on the island?"

"We have little crime here in the village, Doctor. And when we do, we tend to handle it ourselves."

"You're saying there is no constable, no magistrate?"

"Well, Sir Arthur is the magistrate—officially, that is—but I don't know when he's been called to exercise his office, never in my experience. When his former steward died, he appointed John Broderick to see to it, but Broderick found nothing, not a clue as to who or why."

"I must let Sir Arthur know what has happened and what I suspect."

The tavern keeper leaned forward and whispered, "I wouldn't do that, Doctor. It will only upset a sick man you have come to make well again. Besides, as you told me, Sir Arthur and his lady are both convinced that Tobias was mad. What will he think, but that madness has driven Tobias to take his own life? It stands to reason, don't you think?"

"No I don't think, Master Parker. I think Tobias would not have taken his life. Why should he do so? He's proclaimed his disbelief for years, has he not? Why should he act against himself now, rather than earlier? You talk of reason, Master Parker, but how reasonable is that, that he should suddenly decide to end his life? I talked with him but yesterday. To me, he seemed perfectly sane. That he prefers to live alone and survive by combing the beach proves he's eccentric, not out of his mind."

"If you are right, why would anyone on the island want to kill him?" Parker asked. "He's vexed us all, for years, and suddenly he's a victim, a danger to someone or something?"

"Perhaps the latter. I mean a danger. He had nothing anyone would want. He lived like a monk, taken a vow of poverty."

"A vow of poverty? An atheist?"

"I think you know what I mean," William said.

"Go report the death of Sir Arthur, if you must," Parker said. "And good luck to you."

"What about the body?"

"I'll go fetch it," Parker said. "Where is it, did you say?"

"Near the base of the tower. I pulled it up on the rocks, above the tide, I hope. You'll find it there."

"He'll not be buried in the churchyard," Parker said, shaking his head firmly.

"Yet he will be buried, I trust. It's unchristian to let a body rot in the open."

"The carpenter has a cart. He'll help me with the body," Parker said.

To William it seemed futile, reporting Tobias Wincott's death to Challoner. He had little hope that the magistrate, if indeed that is what he was, would do anything. To Challoner, Tobias had been a madman, a public nuisance. William thought Challoner was more likely to celebrate the former cleric's death than seek justice for him, or even a plausible explanation of his death beyond senility and despair. But he had told Parker he would report the death, and now he must. It was unthinkable that the death should go unreported, ignored as though it never happened.

It was noon before he was back at the manor and climbing the stairs to Challoner's room. He knocked, heard the now familiar voice, and entered, relieved that Challoner was alone. It would be harder to convey his news if Broderick were standing there. He could imagine the man's look of disbelief, even derision, should he hear William's theory that Wincott had been murdered. *Murder?* Broderick might think. *That kind of thing doesn't happen on Livesey*, he might say. And yet it *had* happened, less than a year before, which explained why Broderick was now steward and not the sainted former steward who had no enemies and still ended up dead.

"I was walking along the shore this morning and discovered Tobias Wincott's body floating in the sea," William began, but was prevented from continuing by Challoner saying, "It was bound to happen, Doctor. Don't let it disturb you."

"He fell or was thrown from the tower."

"Maxwell's Tower?"

"I believe that's what it's called."

"Why do you think he was thrown?" Challoner asked. He was as usual propped up in bed and seemed to have been asleep when William knocked. He was wide awake now. "It seems more likely he took his own life. Climbed up and threw himself off, and a good riddance as well, for he was a plague to the faithful and a consistent irritant. Few if any will mourn him."

Again, William recited the reasons he had given Parker. When he concluded, Challoner laughed. "I am magistrate of the village, of the island, as was my father and his father before him, but I will tell you truth, Doctor, it is a title without duty, as my experience has shown."

"You might investigate the death. I believe, sir, that comes within the purview of your lawful authority."

"I, investigate from my sick bed?"

"You might appoint a deputy."

Challoner considered this. Then he said, looking up at William with an expression of satisfaction. "I would choose Broderick, my steward. He's a good man. I trust no one more than he."

"I have learned he investigated the death of your former steward," William said.

"Who told you that?"

"The tavern keeper."

"Israel Parker?"

"The same."

"He speaks too loosely of my business," Sir Arthur said, frowning. "He should learn to hold his tongue, lest he lose it. But yes, Broderick did make inquiries but could not find anything, although he assured me he searched most diligently."

"But you think he will have more success with Wincott's strange death?" William asked.

"Oh, I trust he will, Doctor, and doubtless find the man's death is not strange at all but what naturally befalls an old man in his dotage; a careless slip, or deliberate leap to end it all. It is what I have feared myself in my more desolate moments."

"You feared falling, sir?"

"Feared I would yield to the temptation of taking my own life, that my suffering might end, but was stayed by the divine decree against self-slaughter."

"I am most sorry to hear that," William said. "But you were blessed, sir. Life is God's gift. He who scorns it must needs displease the Great Giver."

"Still, have no fear, Doctor. Broderick will do his duty, as I direct him. I have always found him most faithful in doing his duty."

"I trust he shall be in this case," William said, not meaning a word of it.

Thirty

William went to his room and slumped on the bed, uncertain of his next move. His effort to do the right thing and report the death had accomplished nothing, just as he imagined. Broderick in charge of the investigation? What hope had he now that the mystery of Tobias Wincott's death would be solved? At best, Broderick would do whatever proved advantageous to his master. At worst, he would do whatever proved advantageous to himself. What William was convinced he would *not* do was find out what really happened to the much-despised curate and bring the murderer or murderers to account.

Then a knock came at the door, not demanding but tentative, differential. He suspected a servant, probably not Broderick. He went to the door and opened it. It was one of the manservants he had seen at breakfast the day before.

"A letter came for you this afternoon by special post, Doctor Gilbert."

He thanked the servant and closed the door. The letter was from his father.

It was a response to his own missive inquiring about any family named Broderick in Halstead. He had not expected so quick a reply, but he was glad to have it. The letter was brief; no surprise to William, accustomed as he was to his father's love of brevity, an unusual affection for a lawyer.

Dear Son William,
There was a family of the name Broderick or Barwick in Halstead, since gone. Jacob Broderick was a carpenter. He had eight children by the church records of baptism. Five died in

infancy. The others, two daughters and a son, survived to adulthood. The same neighbor says the daughters have married. The son, named John, was a knave, a deceiver, who claimed to be able to find buried treasure.

I hope, son, that what little I've learned of this family helps you in some fashion.

In all your business, forget not your loving father, your stepmother, your siblings, who pray for you daily.

May God bless you, my son,
Jerome Gilbert, Esq.

William read the letter over a second time and considered the likelihood that the John Broderick in the letter was the Challoners' steward. He was certain it was. The qualities attributed to him in the letter were not inconsistent with the Broderick William had come to know. Indeed, the description seemed to fit Broderick perfectly. A hunter of gold. A deceiver. A smooth talker. And Challoner had taken him on, made him his steward, his instrument. It seemed all clear to William now.

William remained in his room the rest of the day, thinking about Wincott. The old cleric had died a horrible death, possibly having been thrown from the tower while he was still alive. William shuddered when he remembered the rocks at the base of the cliff. Wincott would have landed there—head first, by the appearance of the body. At least his death would have been quick. That is, if he was not dead before his body was dragged up the stairs.

He decided to forego supper. He was in no mood to eat alone and less inclined to eat with the household in the kitchen. About seven o'clock he went to Challoner's room to see his patient. He was surprised when no response came to his knocking. Suddenly, from behind him a manservant appeared, pale-faced, anxious.

"The master has gone downstairs, Doctor, to have supper with my lady."

"He was able to walk?" William exclaimed, surprised but not displeased.

"With his cane and a little help. He said if you were to come to him you are invited to join them in the great hall."

William had been in no mood to eat, but now he changed his mind. He had hoped the medication he provided his patient would prove effective. But that Challoner could get himself to go downstairs, even if attended, seemed miraculous, especially because of his professed determination to remain in bed and keep his wife confined as well.

William went downstairs to find Challoner at table and two other persons he did not recognize.

"Come, Doctor, join us," Challoner said, dressed and in obviously a jovial mood. "And do meet my distinguished guests."

The persons to be introduced were both beefy men of middle age, well-dressed but not so well-dressed as to be supposed persons of rank. They impressed William more as well-heeled-merchants, an impression confirmed when they were introduced as relatives of Challoner, cousins living on the mainland, both merchants as William had surmised.

"This is Master George Challoner and his brother Peter. They are sons of my late uncle."

A place was made for William. The others at table were already half finished. He took a portion of cod, some steamed vegetables, and fruit. The table was abundantly set, with fine silver plates and not the pewter he would have expected. The wine was served in goblets of silver. It was the first sign he had seen of opulence since he had been in the manor. Was all before him part of the Jewish hoard, or was it simply some other treasure, perhaps honestly obtained?

Then he became aware he was being commended.

"Doctor Gilbert gave me medication just yesterday. I took it, and now as you can see I am a new man. I feel ten, nay twenty, years younger."

Mildred Challoner, sitting opposite her husband, beamed and added to the praise. "The doctor is a most excellent physician. He has done wonders for us both."

William flushed with these compliments, none of which he felt he deserved, still not believing what he was seeing in Challoner—unless his malaise had been a fraud. William knew that his heart rate could not have been. It was a weak and damaged organ. He had made no mistake there.

Perhaps Challoner was putting on a show now, for these cousins, or for his lady wife. Probably for the former.

He had nearly finished his meal, when another person entered the room. It was Broderick. He had been out in the weather and his face glistened with rainwater, his great coat, which he still wore, was dripping. William had noticed the rain had begun just before he left his room. Broderick apologized for interrupting, looking first at the cousins and then sternly at William.

Challoner asked, "What is it, Broderick?"

"I investigated the death Doctor Gilbert reported, just as you requested I do."

"And with what results?" Challoner asked.

The conversation at the table had stopped. Talk of a death had commanded everyone's attention.

Broderick glanced at William. His lips curled into a smirk. "No body was found, sir. At least not where the doctor said he left it."

"What do you mean, no body was found?" Challoner asked.

"Just that, sir. I and Master Parker and another men searched the entire area and we found no trace of the old man. We looked beyond where the doctor said the body was, and even then we found nothing at all. Perhaps the good doctor only *imagined* finding a body."

Broderick cast a glance at William when he said this, his lips turned up in a derisive sneer.

"Whose body was it?" Mildred Challoner asked, visibly upset by talk of dead bodies.

"Wincott's, Tobias Wincott's."

"The demented old man?" Mildred Challoner asked.

"Yes, but now it would seem he may not be dead at all. Doctor, could you have supposed Wincott was dead but he was not, revived say after you had left him for dead?"

William said, "I could have made no mistake, Sir Arthur. His wound was too severe. He had landed on the rocks, gone over the tower head first. No one could have survived such a fall, such injury as he had."

William looked up at Broderick. "Are you sure you looked in the right place?"

Broderick addressed his employer, not William. "We looked exactly where the doctor said Wincott was and beyond. There was no body, sir, no body of Wincott or any other person."

"Well, Doctor," Challoner said, turning to William. "I trust Broderick's search has been thorough. I don't know what else can be done."

To this point, William had enjoyed his meal. Now it seemed tasteless. He looked up at Broderick, who was staring down at him, his lips curled in a supercilious smile. William felt a surge of anger he knew he must control.

He turned to look across the table at his host.

"I would like to search myself, Sir Arthur. I could not have been mistaken as to the condition or location of the body. It is just as I reported. At first to Israel Parker, then to you, Sir Arthur. My eyes did not deceive me, nor did I lie in my report. Tobias Wincott is dead. I found his body. If it is not where I left it, then it has been removed."

"But who would remove it?" Mildred Challoner asked. "And why?"

"I can answer neither question for the moment, madam, but I am confident the man is dead, and if his body was not found where I drew it up on the beach beyond the tide, then it has been either washed away or removed by persons unknown with motives equally obscure—at least to me, at least for now."

"You can't go out now, not in this weather, and at night," Mildred Challoner exclaimed.

William excused himself, hurried up the stairs to his room, got his great coat and cap then left the house as soon as he could. It was now nine o'clock, but he knew the tavern would be open and on such a night doing a good business. He walked through the cold rain toward the village until he came to the lights of the tavern and, looking in the one window, saw Israel Parker standing behind the bar talking to a single customer. Other tables were occupied by some of the men William had seen on his first day on the island. He recognized their faces.

He walked in and waved to Parker, who looked up at him quickly and then went back talking to the customer at the bar. William took a table by himself and waited. He waited a while, no one paying attention to him now as they had done the day before. The novelty of his strangeness having apparently worn off. Finally, the customer left. Parker walked over to William, his head down.

"Broderick says you couldn't find Wincott's body."

Parker sat down opposite William. He sighed heavily and wiped his brow.

"Couldn't find it, Doctor. Not where you said it was."

"That's impossible, Master Parker. The man was dead. He didn't get up and walk away."

"Maybe you thought he was dead."

"He was dead, Master Parker. You don't get more dead than he was, trust me. I've tended a great many persons as they passed to the next life. I know a corpse when I see one, especially one with injuries such as he suffered. No man could have survived such injuries. Tell me what you saw at the foot of the tower."

Parker looked down. He didn't respond, and William had to ask again.

"I didn't go," Parker admitted.

"What do you mean you didn't go? You said you would go and bring Wincott's body into the village, to the church for a proper burial. You agreed to do that."

"I know I agreed," Parker said. "But Master Broderick said I didn't need to go."

"Master Broderick said that?"

"His very words, Doctor."

"Did you ask him why?"

"Why?"

"Why you didn't need to go with him to bring back the body," William said, not bothering to disguise his impatience. William asked the question and wanted an answer, but he thought he knew the answer already.

"Broderick said he didn't believe you saw what you did, that you had reported falsely, and that there was no point in my going down to the tower when nothing would be there. He said I would probably meet old Wincott on the way, stumbling around on the shore, very much alive for all his infirmities and scoffing at us for supposing him otherwise."

"So, you didn't go?"

"Who was I to defy the magistrate's deputy? I keep a tavern, Doctor. I comply with the law and those appointed to enforce it, else I don't stay in business, especially on this island. I hate Broderick. Most on the island do. But he's Sir Arthur's man for all that, and this is Sir Arthur's island, and he rules it as he wills."

William walked out into the dark street, out into the rain. He was soaked and chilled, his great coat not providing the protection he hoped. The servant who had bid him come to supper admitted him, not Broderick, for which he was thankful. The last thing he needed was another confrontation with Challoner's steward, now elevated to deputy magistrate. He would not be able to hold his anger and frustration. It was not merely the implication that he had falsely reported Wincott's death, but that he had made himself an obstacle to confirming it. Had Broderick gone himself to where William had said the body lay and found nothing, or had he gone there, found the body and hidden it somewhere? He would not put it past the man to do that, would not put it past Broderick to do anything.

In his room, he removed his sodden clothing, wiped his body dry with a blanket and crawled into his bed. The manor house was quiet now, but outside the rain still fell. He could hear it against the window, could hear the wind penetrate and shake the old house. He hoped it would all stop before morning, because his intent was to return to the tower to see for himself and he would rather do that if it was dry, if there was no wind, if the tide was out exposing the stretch of sand.

He fell asleep thinking of Johane. He had not seen her all the day and he wanted to tell her about Tobias Wincott, what had happened to him and why he was certain that what he saw was real, not fabrication or false imagining. He also wanted to tell her what a devil Broderick was, not that she did not already know that since she had bitterly complained of him, been assaulted by him. But this was a new offense.

If Broderick had *not* found the body and then concealed it, buried it, or weighted it down and cast it into the sea, then it might still be where William laid it and in that case he would bring the body back to the manor if he had to drag it behind him and say to Challoner and his deputy, "See, sirs, is this not Tobias Wincott, and is he not dead, dead as a stone, even as I said?"

He would share all this with Johane. But then he fell asleep. The rain and cold and his anger had undone him for day.

At breakfast, he joined the household again in the kitchen where he would be able to see Johane and give her a sign that they should speak. But when he came down, Johane was getting up to leave and talking to one of the maidservants. He wasn't sure she even noticed him.

He was tempted to follow her back upstairs, but decided that wouldn't be wise. He was more than ever conscious of the need for discretion. His accusation against Broderick for his assault on Johane and the man's resolute denial there was a body to be found meant Challoner's steward would do everything in his power to undermine William's efforts. Who could trust a doctor who imagined dead bodies, who lied about finding them, whose resolute insistence on their existence disturbed the peace of the island, displeased its lord and master, Sir Arthur?

He ate a little, then set out for the tower.

The rain had stopped and the morning was clear and bright. He walked briskly and confidently. The tide was out, leaving the exposed sand littered with seaweed and debris, some wooden planks, bottles, rotting fish, things he could not identify and might, on a less pressing business, have stopped to examine, to collect. It wasn't long before he saw the tower rise before him. He climbed up to the rise to the base of it, pushing his way through the underbrush so thick it almost hid the door. Then he made his way to where he had left the body. Where he was *sure* he had left the body.

He remembered there had been a slight depression in the ground. He remembered when he had pulled the body over to it and pushed it in, like a grave half dug, that the corpse had been left half buried, open to the sky. He remembered when he had pulled the body up, dead weight out of the grasp of the tide, and laid it down in the depression in the earth, reverentially even, remembering that for all his eccentricities Tobias Wincott was another soul. Irreverent perhaps, not even likable, but still a human soul.

But the body was not there now. There was nothing. Not even footprints around the half-grave to hint that someone had come before him, found the body, moved it away, hidden it.

He considered that if the body were hidden, or even buried elsewhere, it would be close at hand. He began to search the foliage. The branches grew thick as though it was all part of the tower's defense. For an hour he searched, until his clothes were covered with dust and leaves and dirt, insisting in his mind that his discovery of Wincott had *not* been a dream or a hallucination. There was nothing.

For a while he sat on the stone step into the tower, his head in his hands. He thought about Challoner and Broderick back at the manor. If they could see him now in so dejected a state, what pleasure and satisfaction might it give both of them. Especially Broderick. He envisioned the man's face the night before, preening before his employer and looking down at William condescendingly, and wished he could smash it. It was an un-doctorly thought, and he was ashamed of it even as he nurtured it in his imagination.

He shook off the image. He felt he should continue his search; he felt he *must* continue it. He knew what he had seen and what he had done. Wincott was dead, as dead as any corpse he had ever seen or examined.

After a while he got up and decided to return to the manor the way he had done the day he met Tobias Wincott. He walked on rather than back and soon came to the marshland where Wincott had shown him the pits where treasure hunters had dug. There were three of them, all visible from the path he and the former cleric had followed that morning. All filled with water—sea water, Tobias Wincott had said. Had Wincott not told him how they had come to be, he would have supposed them to be natural features of the marshland.

He made his way through the uneven ground to where the first pit was. The level of the water was deep into the pit, maybe ten or twelve feet. He stood at the edge and looked down. He was surprised to see the water was clear. He could see at least another ten feet down into it. He reached down, found a pebble near his feet, and as he would have done as a boy out of mere boyish curiosity, let it drop.

He heard the splash, saw the concentric circles, like one of his diagrams, and then something more when the water was still again, clear, translucent. There was *something* in the water, something moving. Could it be a fish or some other water creature? He started to turn away, but some impulse made him stay to take a second look. He had imagined that whoever took the body—Broderick, he expected—had dragged it to be carried out by the tide. But maybe what he saw below the surface floating was the old man himself.

Another question came into his head. Why should Broderick conceal the body? Was it just to make William seem a liar? It seemed to him a petty motive, not even worthy of Broderick, such as he was. More likely it was to conceal his own hand in the death. He imagined Broderick or one of his henchmen attacking Wincott, dragging him up to the top of the tower and throwing him down onto the rocks below. Why? To rob him of his few treasures? To extract information from him?

He stared down into the pool a third time. The water was still. Full of shadows. He saw nothing now, nothing floating below the surface. Had he imagined it?

He went back to the manor. Broderick opened the door to him.

"Did you find what you were looking for, Doctor?" Broderick asked, smiling, but falsely.

"I found enough," William said.

Broderick looked at him uncertainly. His smile suddenly vanished. "What do you mean, Doctor?"

William pushed past him, went through the great hall and up the stairs. He could hear Broderick's footsteps behind him. He made it to the door of his room when he felt Broderick's hand on his shoulder.

"Doctor, tell me what you mean."

William turned to him. "You shall learn…in due course, Master Broderick."

William shut the door in Broderick's face. He experienced then a sense of satisfaction that surprised him. His own mission that day had proved a failure. Somehow, in these last moments he had found a reserve of determination. Broderick had looked mystified and unnerved by what William had said to him. William wasn't sure himself what he had meant by finding enough. He would have to find out.

Thirty-One

The next morning, he pulled Johane aside just as she was leaving the breakfast table. He told her they needed to talk. She had learned of Broderick's role as deputy magistrate from Mildred Challoner, who in turn had learned it from her husband. Johane knew about William's finding the body of the former cleric, Broderick's claim that he couldn't find it himself, and even William's failure to find the body again. Challoner had put it all down to the young doctor's feverish imagination. His wife agreed.

"But what do you believe?" he asked her.

Johane smiled. "You don't seem to me a man who needs to imagine dead bodies, having seen so many real ones."

She reached out and touched his hand reassuringly.

Later, a man came to the manor from the village. He said he was a friend of Israel Parker. He was a tall, lanky man of about thirty dressed in fisherman's garb. He said his name was Jeremy Locke.

"Would you be the London doctor, sir?"

"I am." William said.

"Master Parker begs you to come to the tavern."

"For what purpose? I spoke to him only last night."

Locke seemed surprised at the question. "Why, he said it was important, sir. He said that was how you would see it, sir, Doctor. Important, I mean."

"When?"

"As soon as possible, sir."

"I'll come now, then," William said.

Within minutes they had arrived at the Saracen's Blade. Israel Parker was behind the bar. He looked up, saw William, and left his station to come where William had taken a seat. Locke had gone off somewhere.

"I'm come at your behest, Master Parker. What news?"

"News to gladden your heart, or at least relieve your worries," Israel Parker said, all smiles.

"My worries? Worries about what?"

"Why, Doctor, the belief about the village and at the manor that you're mad."

William knew what Parker was speaking of. But he waited. He wanted to hear Parker say it. It did not please him to learn that his claim to have found the dead body of Tobias Wincott had created such an impression of him on the island.

"That you've been seeing dead bodies that aren't," Israel Parker continued.

"And now I will be believed?"

"Proof, Doctor. Honest to God proof."

"What proof?" William asked.

"Two fishermen have seen the body for themselves. It floated up on yonder island."

"What island?"

"That would be Little Livesey."

He had seen Little Livesey from the tower. A pile of rocks rising from the sea. Wincott had told him about it, how it used to be part of Great Livesey, several hundred years earlier.

"They found his body floating in the shallows just off the island. They pulled it ashore and left it there."

"Did they know who it was, the body?"

"Everyone on the island knows Tobias Wincott, Doctor."

"Why didn't they bring him back to the village? That would have been the decent thing to do. Why leave it on the island where it might never be found again or washed away?"

"Ah, that's a good question, Doctor, but easily answered. They were afraid. Afraid they would be thought to have murdered the man had they brought the body back."

"I would think they should still be suspected in reporting their discovery," William said.

Parker shrugged. "You will want to go to the island and see with your own eyes, Doctor."

* * *

Jeremy Locke was one of the two fishermen who had found the body. The other was a shorter man, somewhat older and stockier with a ruddy, windburned face partially concealed by a red beard. William didn't catch his name. They led him down to the quay to a small boat, hardly big enough to hold the three of them. William sat in the bow, Locke sat midships and rowed with strong powerful arms. The other man, Locke's companion, sat in the stern, looking uneasily at the water.

It was mid-day and the water was calm, the skies clouded over, as though a gauzy veil had been placed just above the island. It was cold and William wished he had worn his winter coat, not the thinner jerkin he had chosen which was good enough to withstand the chill of the manor but not adequate for the open sea.

Wincott had told him Little Livesey was hardly more than a mile off Greater Livesey. Locke said, "It'll only take a bit, Doctor, and you'll stand upon the island and see for yourself. I know, or knew, Tobias Wincott. It was he who baptized me, but I can't say it ever made that good a Christian out of me for all that." He laughed hoarsely, as though there were something caught in his throat.

It hadn't occurred to William to ask before setting out whether with the three of them in the boat there would be room for a fourth. He asked now. The man whose name William hadn't caught assured him there would be room aplenty, even if they had to tow the dead man behind them. "The man's dead. We can curl him up as we please without fear of him complaining or offending his dignity." He laughed.

William supposed they might be halfway to the island when a dreadful thought came into his head. He looked at the two men. Something was familiar about them—not individually, but as a pair. He looked at their faces and realized that they might have been the very embodiment of the two men Johane had described as having visited the Domus, the two men William suspected of hanging Isaac Silva. It was cold in the open sea, but the chill he felt then far surpassed anything caused by the weather.

He considered that his fear was imagined. These were two men, two fishermen as Israel Parker had described them. Islanders. Neither had probably ever been in London, may never have heard of the city. There was that much ignorance in the far-flung counties of England. Why should he suppose these were the same men? Neither of whom had features of face or body that one might call unusual. Johane's description might not even have been accurate. He breathed easier. Reason had rescued him from panic, and he was grateful for it. The last thing he needed now was panic, the urge to run, or in this case to cast himself into the sea and swim desperately for land.

"Almost there, Doctor," the man without a name said. William turned to look. The features of Little Livesey that he had observed from the tower now stood out in sharper outline. It seemed at this distance nothing more than a cluster of sharply pointed rocks. He saw no sand, no graveled shingle, and certainly no trees, although there did seem to be low-growing shrubs, not green and verdant like those on Great Livesey, but a stark, a desolate, God-forsaken remnant of the larger island that once was.

"The body's on the other side, but we'll land here and tie up," Locke said. "It's just a bit of a stroll from there. You'll see it for yourself, Doctor. Then we'll carry the good reverend back to the boat and be enjoying an ale in the Blade before supper."

Jeremy Locke shipped the oars, leaped out and pulled the boat up onto a gravel beach, his long, muscular arms exerting all of his strength. William started to get out, but before he could Locke's companion grabbed his elbow and helped him out as though he were an invalid. William resented it a little. He was strong and sinewy himself, and clearly younger than the unnamed man. He needed no aid in getting out of the boat.

Locke led the way, maneuvering around rocks and tide pools as though he knew the island well, not as an object in the sea, but as dweller in the place. William followed. The other man brought up the rear. They came to a rise and at once William saw ahead of them the open sea and more immediate to him a gradual slope to the island's other side. Like the rest of the island, it was a field or rocks of various shapes and sizes and no vegetation that he could see. He had observed no animal life amid the rocks, but the air above was filled with clouds of birds and their shrill cries as they circled overhead and then, suddenly, dived into the sea.

Then he saw the body on the rocky shore, sprawled out as William remembered putting it. It was Tobias Wincott without a doubt. Israel Parker had been right.

"There's your man, Doctor," Locke said, as they drew near to where Wincott lay. "Doesn't he look right dead to you?"

"He does," William said, "And has looked dead ever since I found him so two days ago."

The bigger man laughed. His companion remained silent.

William waited for the next thing to happen. It wasn't what he had imagined, but was what he should have foreseen.

Before he felt the blinding pain, there was a flash of light. He didn't feel himself fall to the sand, face down.

Thirty-Two

They must have supposed him dead, the two men who'd brought him to this desolate island. With all that blood, how could they think otherwise? So they left him where he had fallen, stripped of his fine jerkin, his purse cut, even his shoes taken. They had spared him his shirt and his hose. Otherwise he would have been quite naked.

He lay next to the dead curate, whose body was already rotting and attracting a variety of loathsome creatures to the feast. Some of these were already advancing toward him. Then he fainted away again.

It was dark when he came to again, his head afire, his face caked with dried blood. He lay motionless, unable to do much more than groan in agony. He couldn't remember where he was or what had happened to him. Despite the pain, he felt himself succumbing to sleep, but somehow he understood sleep might prove fatal. He had treated patients with injuries similar to his. He remembered one in particular, a young laborer who had fallen from a roof to the cobbles. His head streaming with blood, passersby standing about unsure what to do to help, a woman weeping her eyes out, his wife perhaps, or mistress. He remembered the man had recovered. But then William lost consciousness again.

When he awoke yet again it was morning, and for the first time since the attack he could remember clearly what had happened. And he knew where he was and why, for the stink of the dead man lying next to him was almost unbearable.

He had been struck from behind. A rock, he supposed, since neither of the two men had cudgel or staff with them. The pain in his head was unbearable. He tried to stand but staggered like a drunken man and fell forward on his hands and knees. Half blinded by pain he saw a few feet from him the edge of the water. He crawled toward it and buried his face in the sea. The water was frigid, but he didn't care. The sensation was good, and it would wash off the sand on his face, the dried blood, perhaps even the pain. He knew his head would ache for a while. He also knew the pain would end.

By the time the sun was high in the sky, he was able to stand, not walk but move from rock to rock, up the way they had come in crossing the island. Had Locke and the unnamed man left him here, or were they waiting by the boat with some utterly unconvincing explanation as to what had happened to him? Why they had abandoned him. Why they had robbed him.

The journey took him most of the day, or so it seemed. He crawled on his hands and knees over the rough rock, stopping from time to time exhausted, face down—for he had no idea what wound existed in the back of his head, and applying pressure on it would be unbearable. He had touched it once and experienced a flame of fire so intense that he had retched uncontrollably until his stomach was empty, until there was nothing but bile. Then he had crumpled on the ground.

He had reached the highest point on the island, a rocky mound like a cap. Old rock, he estimated, rock of the sort the manor house was built of. He looked all around him as he had done when standing on the tower. That had been two, three days earlier, before Wincott's murder. It seemed ages ago now. He fixed his eye on the island from whence he had been brought the day before. It was little more than a mile away, but in his present state it might have been a thousand.

He had seen what he came to know was Little Livesey from the tower. But he could not see the tower from Little Livesey, or the the manor house, or the village. gratified that evidence had been found of Wincott's murder, but also, he now remembered, fear of his companions, which he then dismissed as a foolish fear. He had had reason to be fearful. Maybe the two were not the same men Johane had seen in London, the men William believed had murdered his friend Isaac. But they *were* responsible for the condition in which he now found himself. Badly injured, alone and, he feared, stranded. He thought it unlikely the men would return for him, and even if they did, surely they would try to kill him again.

Back at the manor house, they would have missed him returning for the day. Sir Arthur would have asked Broderick to look for him. Broderick would fail to find him. William was certain of that. He imagined Broderick inventing some story about how the London doctor, unwisely walking along the shore, had met with some misadventure. Or humiliated by the discovery of his lies about the dead cleric, the doctor had fled. Although it had been Israel Parker who had arranged for his voyage to Little Livesey, William had no doubt Broderick was author of the conspiracy against him.

And what would Johane think—that he was dead, drowned, murdered like Isaac? Would she report it all to Lord Burghley? Given their short acquaintance, would she grieve for him, or think the worst—that he was a coward for deserting her?

He knew he had to get back to the manor house. But he wasn't sure how, or even if, he would survive in so desolate a place in the meantime.

He had no shelter, no food, not even water. He could swim but not well enough to make it to the bigger island, not in his present state. He might build a raft, but that would require wood, nails or binding, and he had seen none. He set out to survey the island, deciding that if he were to survive and escape, he must know more clearly what resources were available to him.

He remembered reading, while he was at Cambridge, a book presenting travelers' tales. One, he remembered vividly. It was an account of a mariner marooned on a desert island, very much like Little Livesey. His comrades, corsairs all, had left him there to punish him for some treason against them, thinking that he would either die quickly or even take his own life in despair. But the hapless mariner had survived, survived long enough to be rescued at last. He had learned in the meantime what sea creatures he could eat, what puny grass or plants could sustain him. He had discovered a spring of fresh water. He had dressed himself in garments made from twigs and dried seaweed, and sheltered himself in an island cave. And he had found a wreck not far from shore from which he salvaged what else he needed to provide for himself.

William had loved the story, had imagined himself as the solitary mariner. Had imagined himself marooned on a desert island. And now here he was. His fantasy come true. But he was resolved not to be a victim of Broderick's machinations. He would survive. He would use his skills, not as a resourceful mariner, which he was not, but as a doctor of physic, a man of science. And in so doing, he would live to accomplish the mission Lord Burghley had assigned him.

Thirty-Three

That afternoon, it rained again; at first a drizzle, then a downpour, soaking him completely since he had yet to find a shelter. William remembered Wincott's notebook, the diagram of the island by which he had methodically surveyed the shoreline in sections, numbering each to mark which he had searched. By his own admission Wincott had found nothing, except for the ladle with the Hebrew inscription, which was no small thing. William resolved to do likewise. He had no notebook, nothing to write with, but he had a good memory. He would create a diagram in his head, he would imagine it as the numbers on a clock. He would begin at the place where they had beached the boat and move from there until he had surveyed the whole island.

His first impression of the island was that there was nothing. It was a barren outcropping of rock, a remnant of the larger island that once was, ages before. But his next impression would be formed from a careful search for resources. His approach would be as exacting as his experiments with magnets, carefully testing the properties of magnets and their power over various elements and substances. It was science again, a methodology with which he was familiar. And thinking all this, he was suddenly full of hope, a hope that transcended the pain in his skull and his fear of dying, for the worst for him was to have nothing to do, to surrender to despair, to find a rock to sit on and wait for a rescue that would not come. Or to do the unthinkable, which was to drown himself in the sea and end all. Both his faith and his natural instincts rebelled against the thought.

And so he began his work, as he might have undertaken new experiments, with the same dedication, the same single mindedness.

*   *   *

He did not remember when he had last eaten, perhaps breakfast of the day before, yet he wasn't hungry although he knew he would be soon. The pain in his head would end, and his belly and its needs would reassert themselves. His first aim was to find food and water. The island's stark barrenness gave little promise of either, but when he had crossed it, following Locke, he had been paying little attention to his surroundings or the shore of the island, except where they had landed and where they had found Wincott's body. He decided the water's edge gave the best hope. He set out, walking upright now, his head still pounding but the rest of him sound.

He realized at once that there was no sandy strand to walk on. The margin of the island seemed to be rocks, some quite large, some seemingly impossible to climb over. To avoid them, he had to step into the water, sometimes up to his thighs. The rocks were bare and slippery. As he moved, he would see from time to time things floating, things the tide had brought in, occasionally what looked like dead fish which rapacious gulls and other sea birds quickly snatched up before he could do so himself. Indeed, the sky was full of the cries of birds. Their droppings were everywhere above the waterline.

He had struggled about what he estimated as half the way before he made his first find. It was a cask, wedged between rocks. It filled him with excitement. Even before he recovered it from where it had become lodged, he imagined its contents; wine perhaps, ale, something drinkable. Suddenly a powerful thirst seized him. But when he lifted it out of the water, he could see the top was cracked, the cask nearly empty except for some sand and seawater at the bottom. Whatever the original contents had been were long gone and there were no marks on the outside of the cask. The cask would have settled on the bottom, not floated, the wonder was it had made it to the island, pushed along by the incoming tide, rolling and rattling along the sea bottom until pushed up into the crevice.

William took the cask and climbed higher onto the mound and set it upright, using smaller rocks to keep it firmly planted, its opening to the sky. If it rained, the cask would collect water. The rain had stopped, but it would rain again and it never hurt to think ahead.

He made his way back to the water's edge and moved on. The island's southern coast was irregular. There were inlets, some going deep into the island like probing fingers. Each of these he explored, thinking they might be good places to find driftwood. He was surprised at how he found none of any use. He knew he could build a fire by friction, by rubbing stones together, but he needed fuel to keep it going, even to get it started. He thought dried seaweed might work, and he had noticed scanty grass on the upper level of the island. Fuel to make a fire, to cook if he found anything to cook, to signal if there was anyone to see.

In time, he came to where Wincott's body sprawled. The two men had not moved it, nor had the tide—retreating now—carried it off, as he imagined the men might have intended. It had been two or three days since William had found Wincott dead, and his body, exposed as it was, was horrible to look upon, although as a doctor, William had seen far worse. Tiny creatures had continued their feast, finding joy in this windfall of decaying human flesh.

William turned away in disgust, prepared to move on, but then stopped and turned again. The corpse stank. But he had no time to think of that. He knelt by Wincott's body and began to remove the dead man's clothes. They were worn and fetid and clung to him. He removed the man's ragged coat, his pantaloons and shirt, a short length of rope Wincott had used as a belt, and continued until he lay naked; his sunken, hairless breast and scrawny arms were white as his face, as though blood never ran through his body. William felt uncomfortable despoiling the dead, but he had no idea what he might need during what he hoped was a sojourn on the island, rather than it being a final resting place.

He disliked leaving Wincott's remains so exposed. But a burial was impossible, given the lack of soil. He thought he might drag the body into the sea, but there was always a chance he might be rescued, and Wincott's body remained the best evidence of the truthfulness of his report.

He took the bundle of ragged garments over to the water's edge and washed them of sand and dried blood. He eyed the rope. It was short of a yard in length, but it might serve to bind together planks to make a raft. The marooned mariner in the account he had read had done that. William might do the same.

Now he continued on. He knew he would return later.

It took him what he thought might be an hour to complete his survey of the beach. On the northern side he found a stretch of gray sand. In the sunlight it sparkled. He sat down and crossed his legs. His headache was subsiding.

For the first time since regaining consciousness, he had enough of himself to review what had happened. He remembered his conversation with Israel Parker, the man's feigned excitement at the fishermen's report of finding the body. He knew it was feigned because it was completely at odds with his earlier satisfaction that William was thought mad, a victim of delusions.

And the two men, Locke and the unnamed one, the ones he imagined might be the murderers Johane had described…he remembered every lying move, every deception practiced upon him, everything until the moment of the blow. If he was conscious of any of that, it was gone completely from his memory. He knew only that one of them, probably Locke, had tried to crack his skull and was satisfied he had done, or they would never have left him behind.

Everything now was falling into a pattern. First, the former steward meets a mysterious end, murdered by persons unknown. Broderick takes his place, a man with a mysterious history, an outsider like himself, but as Challoner probably knew, an experienced treasure hunter. And then the devious tavern keeper and his friends…

He was thinking this, when he heard a sudden swish over his head and ducked. He looked up. A bird with the largest wing-span he had ever seen circled above him and then made another dive, apparently thinking William was prey, fresh meat.

He scrambled for cover. He felt the bird's wings a second time, brushing by his head. He knew there would be a third attack, this time probably successful. He fell forward onto his stomach now, covering his bare neck with his hands, bracing himself for the bird's attack. Then he looked ahead of him, not an arm's length away. He saw a flat rock beneath which there was a crevice, a shallow cave, but it would suit to protect his vulnerable head. He turned to look above him.

Now there were two birds of the same kind, white-tailed eagles he thought, by their enormous wing-span of six or seven feet. Raptors, birds of prey. He had seen them hunt many times along his own coast, circling around; their victims were usually small creatures, but they were known to attack larger. He remembered a story about one snatching up a child from his mother's arms, the child never seen again.

Terrified, he scrambled forward and wedged himself into the crevice. Not a moment too soon. He heard the swish of air, shrill cries like needles.

Somehow, he knew more of the birds were coming after him. Then he was in darkness.

Breathless, he tried to see where he was wedged between one rock and another. Slowly his eyes adjusted to the darkness. He was in a shallow cavity, too small to be called a cavern. He could hardly move his arms or legs, he could not raise his head, the smell within was stale air, and it was cold. For a moment, he imagined himself dead and buried, but it was only a brief sensation. He knew he was alive—and for the moment, safe, from the birds. He was thankful for that. He would not complain about his present circumstances. The cavity had saved him from this most recent threat to his life.

He lay there for a long while, even fell asleep. He forgot about the lingering pain in his head, his thirst, his hunger, which had grown as he circled the island. His experience had been a nightmare. Sleep could present no more threatening scenario than this.

When he awoke it was dark and his throat was dry as dust, his belly like the empty cask he had found the day before. Slowly, he backed his way out into night, thinking no birds would attack him then. Above him the skies were clear, the stars brilliant. He rolled over on his back and lay staring up at them. What hour could it be? He thought he saw a suggestion of light in the east. Early morning, then, with the day ahead, a day in which he must find water, must find food. The cavity in the rock had proved to be a kind of shelter. That was the beginning.

He soon discovered that the crown of the island, or what he called the crown, since it was the highest point, was a field of rocks, all jagged and standing or leaning at odd angles. So the cavity in which he had taken refuge was but one of such features, many larger than his first place of refuge. One he found was a real cavern with a gaping mouth, and a descent like a stairway. Sunlight illuminated the first ten or twelve feet, beyond which all was dark. He entered and, using the side of the cave for support, descended the stones that formed natural stairs. The interior was dry, but somewhere he thought he heard water dripping. He wondered if what he heard was only what he wanted to hear; an imagined sound, a dream of water, percolating through the rock.

He walked beyond the sunlight, feeling his way against the rock, tentatively like a blind man, and stepping carefully, until shortly he felt drops of water fall on his head, run down his face, and moisten his parched lips.

The water was cold and sweet. He took another two steps and stepped into water up to his calves. Fresh water, a pool. He got down on his knees into the water and drank as an animal would, thrusting his face into the water, slacking his thirst that had left him weak. He had known he could go for a week or more without food, but without water he would be dead in three or four days. Now he had water. Was it good water, or contaminated with dead things? He imagined it seeping down from above, perhaps a shallowness in the rock where rain water collected. He didn't know. For now, he didn't care. He didn't have the luxury of caution, or even of reflection. He drank until he could drink no more.

Later he crept out of his cave, feeling now not like a distinguished member of his profession but as a primitive creature, his learning and academic distinctions irrelevant. His fine clothing distinguishing him as gentry had gone, his blood-stained shirt was clinging to his body like a second skin and mocking the miserable creature his dire circumstances had made of him. His aim now was mere survival. He had taken the first few steps. The next was to find food.

All along the shore he had observed seaweed, long strands of it drying in the sun. He knew from his reading that it was eaten by his own kind, in far Cathay and other remote lands. Marco Polo had written of it. He was fond of travelers' tales, that strange mixture of fact and fiction, leaving the reader never sure which was which. But William thought it probably true. When a boy, he and some of his friends had sampled various plants as a lark, challenging each other to eat what other children dared not. He had eaten the leaves of trees, sampled grass growing in the pasture, thinking if the cattle ate it and received nourishment, why shouldn't he?

His experiments and bravado had usually produced nothing more than a bitter taste in his mouth, once a violent retching, but he had survived. He had not heard that seaweed caused any such reactions. He had not read of anything in the medical literature, had heard nothing from his colleagues, no anecdotes of dead or dying patients their mouths still crammed with the seaweed that killed them.

He thought the chance was worth taking. He collected an armful of seaweed and climbed up again to the crown of the island, where the cave was, and laid it out on a flat rock to dry. Then he looked around for a way to make a fire. For this he drew not on his reading but on his observation of the smiths of his native town, the ironmongers, the metallurgists, who created fire by friction, creating sparks that when properly fueled burst into flame. He lacked their iron tools, even their skill, but he understood friction, and he knew rubbing two stones together would produce the same effect, at least theoretically.

He looked around for fuel, and found an armful of driftwood from some wreck that had accumulated on the beach. Ordinarily, he would use dry sticks for kindling, but sticks were the product of trees and there were none on the island. Something else combustible, then, perhaps the stumpy grass, whatever it was. He came upon a patch of it, pulled it out by the roots and made a pile of it. He knew the pile would generate heat in and of itself, making combustion all the easier. He found a stone, carried it to the pile and began to rub it against the rock.

It seemed to him forever before the rocks sent a spark flying, the kindling ignited, and he threw the driftwood atop it.

It wasn't until the smoke rose above him that he realized the riskiness, even foolishness, of his success. Were the smoke seen from a passing boat or on Great Livesey, he might put his life at risk a second time. His two assailants might see the smoke and realize he remained alive. He stomped out the fire. He had found two dead herring on the beach and had brought them up along with the seaweed. These he put in the ashes. Within the hour he would eat, though the fish be half raw and he gagged at eating it. Though the seaweed taste like bile, he would suffer it.

The seaweed was bitter and salty but edible, and the mostly raw herring had a not unpleasant taste. He ate part of the seaweed, and all of the herring, and thanked heaven for his good fortune. He would not feast like a king on Little Livesey, but neither would he starve nor die of thirst.

His next step was to find a way to escape the wretched place.

Thirty-Four

The next day he continued to forage, until he believed he knew every inch of the island. But then, on the fourth day, he discovered he was wrong. He had missed something. On the same flat area in which he found shelter, he came upon the remnant of a fire, evidence of some earlier visitor. It was just outside a mound of rocks like unto the one he now thought of as his own, and as he examined it more closely he found the mouth of yet another cave under an overhang of rock.

That it was larger, more spacious than his, and the floor was more even—as even and smooth as pavement, he saw at once. He resolved even before going beyond the opening that it should be his new abode. Had he a light, a candle or torch, he would have explored further. As of now, he was content to possess what few yards of cave the afternoon sun penetrated.

For the next hour he moved what things he had accumulated in his searches of the island to the new cave, including the bed of dried seaweed he had made for himself to sleep on. He laid it just within the cave where the dark shadows of the interior began, lay down upon it to test its softness, and was satisfied. He lay there for a while, thinking what his next step should be. As he did, he fell into a state in which he half-dreamed, half imagined himself back on the larger island, Great Livesey, at the manor conversing with its lord and master.

In his imagination, Arthur Challoner stands upright, no complaining invalid, but clothed fully, even elegantly. He listens without response as William denounces Broderick. Provides to Broderick's master the strong proofs of his perfidy. Recounts what he had learned from his father's letter, that Broderick before his current appointment had been a hill-searcher, a treasure hunter, a perpetrator of frauds and deceptions to gull foolish investors in his dubious enterprises. In William's half dream he tells Challoner how Broderick has used the tavern keeper as his tool, how he secured ruffians disguised as fishermen to take him to the desert island and knock his brains out and, failing that, maroon him instead.

In his imagination he recites these facts like a lawyer reading out an indictment, then he waits for Challoner's response. But in his dream, he waits in vain. Challoner says nothing. It is as though he does not comprehend what William has said, or does not hear him, or understand his language. Or hears and understands but rejects all.

And in the dream, William starts over, with the same frustrating result.

So real was this scene, so obsessive was he in reliving it, that when he came to himself again, he wondered if he was going mad. He had heard of such things. Men isolated, marooned, left to the devices of their imagination, a cruel taskmaster to make a healthy mind a pitiful mess of confusion and delusion.

He turned on his side and toward the interior and yet undiscovered part of the cave and then sat up of a sudden, as though he had been bitten by a serpent. The afternoon sun had penetrated deeper into the cave and he now saw what darkness had prevented him from seeing before. It was a primitive encampment of the previous occupant like unto his own: a seaweed mat, several canvas bags against the cave wall. A battered chest, and a store of driftwood, random objects retrieved from the gravel and sand of the shore, and unlit torches, three of them. He leaped up, knowing the light was precious to him now. He seized upon the torches first, and threw them outside the cave. Then dragged everything after into the open, including the chest. As he did so, he saw the cave went deeper into the island's heart, down to where the sunlight would never reach.

He took one of the torches. It was wrapped in oil cloth—he could smell it. Any flame there would not last long, but perhaps it would last long enough. He made a fire, lit the torch. Within minutes of its discovery, he was beginning the descent into the dark.

The cave widened as he went deeper, although the ceiling was lower and he had to bend over as he moved, bend over like an aged man, his back beginning to ache. Soon, the cave walls pressed inward, and he started to be afraid. He was about to give it over and inch himself back up, when the torch illuminated a kind of shelf in the wall, not made by human hands, but part of the cave's natural contours, made by water or the shifting of the rock or whatever hand of God shapes the nether regions of the earth.

And on that shelf sat a second chest, smaller than the first and more curiously crafted, more like a coffer in which jewels and coins might be stored.

The sulfur and lime that fueled the torch were almost expired. He seized the chest, thrust it under his arm and escaped. As he moved, he thought for a moment he heard footfalls behind him. He went faster, once almost dropping the torch which was giving off less and less light. By the time he reached the opening of his new dwelling he was breathless, his heart racing. It took him time to recover. For a moment he had indeed felt pursued. Was it his imagination, made more distorted by his isolation, or some spirit of the deep, or perhaps even the old, disgraced cleric enraged by an interloper in his cave?

He didn't know which it was, but he had felt its effect and it had been a powerful one. He was a man of science, of learning, a scorner of superstition; yet he was a man, and he could not ignore the cold hand of fear gripping his heart.

When he opened the first chest he had found it confirmed what he had originally imagined, that he had come upon another Wincott redoubt. The old man had said he came to the island from time to time, William supposed to search the beach, even as William had done. Before him on the rocks lay the fruit of Wincott's efforts.

The first chest contained rags, shreds of clothing, doubtless once worn by drowned mariners and salvaged by Wincott—for what? William thought it unlikely he would ever wear them, stitching the fragments together for other use; as a blanket, say. There was also a book there, a slender volume. A well-worn prayer book. Wincott was a self-described atheist, a scorner of religion and its ordinances. Yet he kept a testament to his former faith. Did he read it in the silent watches of the night on the island? Was there a true believer skulking beneath the blasphemer all the time?

William remembered his talks with Wincott. It seemed unthinkable. Wincott had seemed sincere in his rejection of all that was holy, sacred, venerated. He seemed an honest atheist.

Then he turned to the other chest. It was smaller and more ornate in its design. No common carpenter had crafted it, and no ordinary man had owned it. It was a casque fit for a nobleman, or a prince. Yet Wincott had found it, washed up on the shore or buried in the sand, a relic of some storm-stricken vessel.

William noticed there was a lock affixed to it. He looked about him, found a stone to use as a hammer and smashed the lock in the first determined blow.

Now he looked within and found no rags there, no mere detritus of storm or shipwreck.

He found, rather, leathern bags, two of them, that when untied revealed coins: some Spanish pieces of eight, a scattering of less valuable coins, and one silver piece. Hardly more than a diligent pick purse could have earned in a day of filching. But where had Wincott found them? Probably, William supposed, in the exposed sand; mementos of human disaster. Doubtless, the Jewish outrage was only one of many wrecks, all littering the seabed with coins and other objects.

While daylight remained William examined every coin, turning each over in his hands and estimating its worth. He was a physician, no jeweler, no courtier for whom these things were the be all and end all of mortal success. This was indeed a treasure. Perhaps even the treasure of the drowned Jews long sought for. How had the old man come upon it? Had he found it in this very chest, washed up on the beach after the murderous captain's ship ran aground upon the shore? Or had he found the chest empty and used it to hold things he had recovered from the sand when the tide was out?

Lord Burghley must know of this. That was William's thought. All that was left now was to offer proof of those who had stood obstacle to that aim—Broderick, Israel Parker, the whole murderous pack of them. He knew he must get off the island, get himself somehow to London. There was no going back to Livesey, the manor house, the village. He would never survive a second attempt on his life, which would be forthcoming as soon as he showed his face at the manor's door. He could not go back there. And he couldn't stay marooned as he was.

He also thought of Johane. His heart sank. She was vulnerable to Broderick's lust before; she would be more so now, without him to protect her. For all William knew, Broderick had somehow become aware of his secret purpose at Livesey. And would he not suspect that Johane, having arrived with him, shared that purpose?

His worst fears suddenly gripped him. Perhaps Broderick had already acted. Perhaps he had arranged an accident for her. Perhaps she was already dead, or at least expelled from the house, alone somewhere on the island or on the road back to London where she would be vulnerable to God knew what.

Thirty-Five

In the afternoon of the next day, black skies appeared over the Channel and advanced quickly toward the island. He watched the weather with a close eye, wondering how he would fare if the storm came upon him, unprovided as he was. Within an hour by his reckoning there was a roaring wind accompanied by a torrent of rain that drove him into his first redoubt and kept him there until nightfall. The concave rock above him, that had retained rainwater and saved him from thirst, overfilled, and the water that had been a mere drip became a steady stream that filled the pool at his feet and drove him to find refuge on a higher level in the cave.

By the time the rain had stopped it was nearly dawn, and he was thoroughly soaked.

He might as well have stayed in the open, for all the protection his cave supplied him. He was wet, cold, and began to despair of ever escaping. He cursed his fate. He owed too much to Lord Burghley to include him in his cursing, but he recognized that had he never agreed to come to Livesey as his lordship's agent, he would be enjoying the comfort of his London house and the approbation of his well-heeled patients and not shuddering in the cold on a desolate island.

The new day brought some relief. The storm had passed on to ravage the mainland. He lay upon a rock in the sun to dry himself, spread out his arms, shut his eyes and slept. Since he had had no sleep the night before, it was well after noon when he awoke and looked up to see a clear, blue sky above him and a host of circling birds; thankfully, no ravenous eagles or he would have awoken to his eyes being plucked from their sockets.

As it was, despite his suffering, he had had a dream in which he was indeed back in his London house enjoying a bounteous supper. Isaac Silva was alive, sitting across from him at table, hale and hearty, as he had never been when William knew him, and Johane was dressed not as a serving maid but elegantly in silks and jewels, with her dark hair in curls and her cheeks rouged like a lady of the court. In the dream he was telling them a story, he could not remember what, although he did remember that he was struggling to tell it. He could not remember the details of the experience and kept confusing time and place. And he kept his eyes fixed on Johane. In the dream he felt drawn to her, but she looked at him mockingly, which made it all the more difficult to tell his story.

Now, awake, he could not remember what the story was about. All he could remember was his helpless confusion, his embarrassment at being so poor a raconteur. In the dream he very much wanted her attention, her approval. He remembered now, awake, that the table was abundantly set, but neither he nor Johane nor her grandfather were eating.

It took time to shake it off, the dream, and by that time he was dry again.

Had it been an ordinary piece of God's Earth, given the strength of the tempest, he would have seen around him a ravaged landscape, fallen trees, uprooted bushes and plants. Dead beasts of the woods and fields. Drowned men afloat in lingering pools. But in so rocky a terrain, so barren from the beginning, there was hardly a thing that suggested the storm had ever happened. It might have been a part of his dream, for all the tempest had left its mark.

He walked over to where he could see the beach below. The little fringe of sand was strewn with seaweed and what appeared at a distance to be the wreck of a vessel. No great ship, only a small boat. It lay on the beach, garlanded with seaweed.

William made his way down the rocks to where the wreck lay, wedged between two rocks. He turned it over and saw at once that the boat's hull was breached. No great hole, only a sliver-shaped crack, but fatal to its seaworthiness. He pulled the wreck up onto the sand, out of the reach of the tide, and examined it more carefully. It would have been too much to hope that it could have survived the tempest without damage. Given the violence of the storm, that would have been more than a miracle. The question now was whether it was beyond repair.

He remembered that he had saved Wincott's clothes; his hat, shirt, and pantaloons. At the time, he wasn't sure what use they might do him. Now he realized when Fortune deals the hand he had been dealt, nothing is useless.

His plan was to stuff the breach with the rags and then somehow caulk it. He doubted it would prevent a leak, but if he could slow it he might have time to make the distance between Little Livesey and Great Livesey, at least at low tide when the distance between the island might be no more than a mile of open water. And if not, if the boat sank before he made dry land, he might swim the rest of the way, as Isaac's ancestor had in escaping the tidal flood. Unlike most of his countrymen, he could swim. He had learned as a child, when he and his boyish companions would swim out into the sea almost beyond sight of land and then swim back. He was often the winner and once helped another boy whose strength had failed make it safe to shore.

But that was when he was a boy. He had not been in the water for years. Did he still have the skill? And given his head injury, did he have the strength?

He searched the beach for an oar, or something that could be used as one. It took him most of the rest of the day and it was near dark before he found what he wanted: two short planks from a wrecked vessel, perhaps the one the small boat had belonged to. He gathered these up and took them back to his cave with him. At first light, he would shape them into oars. He had no saw or blade, so he would give the planks shape on the rocks, creating grooves for the oarlocks. As for caulking, tar would have been ideal, but where would he find it?

Then he thought of excrement. How could he not? It was all over the island, especially on rocks nearest the beach. He knew the dung of birds was rich in chemicals, and that it hardened into a crusty substance if not washed away. He had a friend in Colchester, an apothecary, who collected it and used it in his garden. The apothecary was ridiculed for it by almost everyone who knew him, yet his garden flourished. The apothecary said the excrement was rich in potassium, that the seabirds' diet of fish supplied what nourishment plants needed.

William thought it was worth a try. The ancients—Aristotle, Galen, Pliny—had nothing to say about this, but what of that? Their silence meant nothing. It was William's instinct and practice to experiment.

Given his dire circumstances, what had he to lose?

That night, he lay awake planning his escape. He was already beyond weary of his diet of raw herring, seaweed, and, more rarely, birds' eggs, although he was aware that it had strengthened him, being rich in nutrients. He caulked the boat, stuffing the breach with the dead beachcomber's shirt, folding the garment several times over until it had the thickness of canvas, and then covering it with excrement, to which he had added sand, like a thick, gummy paste. Now he would wait for the caulking to harden and the tide to work in his favor.

He kept count of his days on Little Livesey—the number of them, not the names. Why, he wasn't sure. Perhaps so if he survived to return to the mainland he might tell the story of his ordeal, the loneliness of it, the terrible fear. A chapter for each wretched day. It would make a good story if he lived to tell it, or be the stuff of his nightmares, probably both.

On the sixth day of his sojourn on the island the tide retreated farther than he had ever seen, leaving an expanse of water between the two Liveseys no wider than a half mile by his reckoning. It was late afternoon. He had resolved to take nothing with him but the coins he had found in Wincott's chest. Its value would serve his needs to make the journey back to London and make up for the purse Jeremy Locke and his friend had stolen from him.

He waited until the last rays of light, then he pulled the boat after him across the exposed sands. It was heavier than he thought it would be, and the distance to the retreating tide was farther than he expected. By the time he reached the water's edge he was breathless. He waited a few moments to regain his strength. He looked out over the dark water. Then he pushed the boat into the water and climbed in, noticing that, already, the patch he had made leaked. There was a half inch of water in the bottom of the boat. He put the oars he had fashioned into the oarlocks, and he began to row, keeping a wary eye on the patched breach in the boat's bottom. He did not fool himself into believing the leak would somehow seal itself. He knew it would grow greater. Now, he was racing against time.

He was an inexperienced oarsman, and it took him a while to establish a rhythm that moved the boat in the direction he intended at the speed he wanted. From time to time he looked behind him to measure his progress. The sea was calm. He thanked God for that. His boat he knew would not survive a rough sea, nor would he, even if the patch had held.

But then he felt his shoes were wet. The boat was slowly filling with water. It was a slow leak, but fatal for all that. He had originally hoped to row around Great Livesey, to make it to the mainland, perhaps to Queenborough, but now he had no choice. Great Livesey was the nearest land.

He rowed faster, breathing hard, keeping an eye on the rising water. Beyond him he could see lights—the lights of the village he thought, what other lights could they be? He imagined the tavern, its host, full-bellied and roaring, with his devious friends, the ones who had left him for dead. Still enjoying their triumph over the London doctor with his airs, his big-city arrogance and pride. Would they feel guilt or shame for what they had done to him? He doubted it.

He rowed faster, his muscles protesting, and then it was useless, the boat was settling beneath the water. For this eventuality he was not entirely unprepared. But he quickly realized that there was no ground beneath him. The water was cold, just as he expected. He had grabbed the oars to keep his head above water but they provided only a slight advantage over swimming freely. He clasped the two planks together and kicked his feet. It was not much to enhance his own body's buoyancy, but it was something, and he made use of it. He was moving now only a little slower than he had when he had the boat beneath him.

He knew that if he maintained his course he would end up at the village quay. Virtually in the hands of his enemies. The cold of the water was beginning to make his legs more difficult to kick. He felt he wasn't going to make the sand. He stopped and maintained his grasp on the planks, but felt himself slip under the water.

And then his feet touched sand, or he thought they did. He walked forward, bouncing on the bottom so his head came up to give him air, and as he walked the water became shallower and he realized he was within a dozen paces of the exposed sand.

Within moments, the water came no more than to his waist. Now he moved not toward the shore, a good quarter mile beyond he reckoned but parallel to it, away from the village, around the island toward the tower from which he had first viewed that barren rock on which he subsisted for nearly a week.

This took more time than he expected, as he trudged on the wet sand until he could climb up onto the path to the tower. It was full dark now, but the moon was round and shiny as a newly minted coin. He was shivering with cold, yet he felt exhilarated. He had, within the week, been bludgeoned, marooned, faced with starvation and the good possibility of drowning in the sea, and had survived it all. Surely all of this meant something, some beneficent deity blessing his efforts, saving him for some redeeming work ahead.

He could not see Maxwell's Tower rising above the trees. It had been difficult to see even in daylight, but he knew where it ought to be when he made his way up the rocks upon which Wincott fell, and came to the tangle of trees and bushes that concealed it. He stood on the threshold and listened. No sound came from within, although he had not expected one. Still, if he had learned anything while on the island it was to take nothing for granted, to act out of abundance of caution.

He entered the tower, trusting that no ghost of the old cleric would bother him, despite his having despoiled his corpse of ragged clothes no longer of use to him and taken for himself his hoard of coins.

He would not go up to the top. He was too weak and unsteady to climb the narrow stairs. He had no reason to look back at the island from which he'd fled, even if it could be seen in the dark. Besides, it would be too cold on the roof, when he was already cold enough. And trusting that exhaustion would ensure his sleep and oblivion would make him forget his shivering body, he laid himself down on a pile of leaves and thanked God for his deliverance.

His gratitude was only half uttered before sleep overtook him.

Thirty-Six

When he awoke, it was already light and his body was sorely racked. He touched his face. It was hot. It was a fever—he prayed not unto death, but rather a transient reaction to the cold water and the hard physical exertion of rowing and trudging across wet sand and gravel. His goal now was to escape this new and even more dangerous island where friends were far outnumbered by his enemies and where he could do nothing of himself to right the wrongs done to him or to Isaac Silva, Tobias Wincott, or the earlier steward whose murder William was sure was part of the same deadly thread.

He knew the path that led to the causeway joining Great Livesey with the mainland. He had traveled it with Wincott and remembered every detail of the journey. His immediate purpose was to make it there without being seen, or at least remarked upon or reported. The chances of being seen by anyone from the manor house were remote indeed. They would have supposed him gone back to London abruptly, or dead, whichever story Broderick had told to explain William's disappearance. But there were people from the village who had taken note of him on his arrival who might bring word of his presence on the island to Israel Parker. That would put him in considerable danger. His assailants would not fail a second time.

He had seen an old hat in the cleric's hut; he went there, found it, and planted it on his head. He found a moth-eaten coat, a wretched garment, but serviceable for disguise and warmth. He had no mirror about him to see what others might see. So he imagined himself now fully transformed. No longer the London doctor, but a simple rustic, a husbandman or low fellow on his way to his labors. Nearly invisible, although not quite enough to make him feel completely safe.

During his journey he saw no one, at least no human sort. He saw sheep, cattle, soaring birds, and once a deer.

He was almost to the causeway. He was grateful to see that, while overnight the tide had come again, the causeway remained above water. He looked across to the mainland. Once there he would find a way to London. With his store of coins he would secure a horse, better clothes, and a decent meal.

He was still standing looking across the water when he was startled by a voice behind him.

"Good morning to you, my good fellow."

He turned around abruptly to see a frail, elderly man, dressed in a simple smock and shepherd's cap. The man supported himself with a staff and stood in such a way as to indicate he was lame. The left leg, William surmised. No, a bad hip. He knew the signs.

"Good morning to you, sir," he replied, trying to seem as though this unforeseen meeting with another traveler caused him no disturbance.

"You are on your way to the mainland, I see," the older man said.

"I am," William answered.

"Would you be pleased then, for company? I am heading in the same direction, to visit my daughter and her family, and you can see the way is hard for me."

"Is it your hip that pains you?" William said, noticing the man wince as he stumbled forward.

"You have a good eye, my friend," the old man said. "Most would have supposed me lame of limb."

"I noticed how you stand," William answered and immediately regretted it. He had never seen this man before, did not remember him among the crowd at the tavern when he first became a recognizable figure in the village. He added, "My father suffers from the same complaint. He stands and walks as do you. And so I recognized your affliction."

This was not true, and suddenly William felt a tinge of guilt at having used an imagined illness of his father as an excuse. Jerome Gilbert was a good twenty years younger than the man before him and as hardy and straight of limb as a man half that age. But as for now, he wanted to give this stranger no clue as to his identity.

"It has been my affliction for many year," the old man said. "I am accustomed to it, since there's no help. I would I had a new one, and suppose in some time to come creatures such as I can have some estimable surgeon provide me with a replacement."

"I should not think that would be any time soon," William answered, laughing. "Were they to do so, they must surely make it out of iron or brass. And it would be a miracle indeed."

The old man laughed and raised his staff to suggest they set out across the causeway.

As he walked with his new companion, it passed through his mind that this was a happy meeting. Anyone observing the two might well think them father and son, traveling together. William took the old man's arm, and they set out.

"And what is your name, may I ask?"

"You may well ask, my name is William…Coggeshall." William used his birth mother's maiden name.

"Coggeshall, is it?" the old man asked. "I don't think I know the family. You are not from the island then. I know every family that has ever lived on Livesey."

"No, I'm not from hereabouts."

His new companion seemed to wait for William's explanation of just why he was on Livesey, but William was not prepared to say.

"My name is Joseph, Joseph Martin," the old man said, breaking the silence.

"I am pleased to know you, Joseph," William said. "And where does your daughter live?"

"Beyond Queenborough. Do you know it, Master…Coggeshall?"

"Not well. My journey will take me through it."

"Then we may be companions, then," the old man said.

"So shall we be, Master Martin."

"Call me Joseph, for I care little for titles I have neither earned nor deserved by birth."

Now they were near the middle of the narrow, road-like causeway that linked Great Livesey with the even larger Isle of Sheppey, with water licking on both sides of them and a stiff breeze blowing over the water. William knew the rising tide would overcome them soon, but he was confident they would make the other side before it did. His companion did not seem worried at the least, and William supposed the old man had made the crossing many a time in all manner of weather and was as tuned to the tidal rhythm as a German clock.

"May I ask you, William, what you do to live?" Joseph asked as they walked.

William thought quickly. He had offered the old man a false name, he might as well offer a false vocation. "I am a trader, I trade goods from abroad, Holland, France, Italy."

"Ah, William, have you been to all those lands, then?"

"I have been in Holland, several times," he said, which was true. He had been in Amsterdam and had friends there, one very precious friend, yet no longer among the living.

"Tell me of it, William. It gives me pleasure to know of distant places that I will not see in my lifetime."

William told the old man about the port, the great houses of the rich burghers, the manners of the Dutch, the learning of the doctors and the scholars. The devices of the Dutch to pump the water out and increase the land of the country. Joseph said the last was of greatest interest to him.

"The scholars, you mean?"

"Yes, sir, the mechanics who build machines, who drain the lowlands there and make them fruitful. How they build the devices to pump the water out."

William was about to explain what he had seen, and the devices used, when suddenly he became aware of a cart and driver approaching from the opposite shore.

He pulled his hat down over his eyes and drew closer to his companion as though steadying him in his walk. Then he heard someone, the driver of the cart, shout out a greeting to the old man.

"Good day to you, Joseph. Make haste, you old fool, or the water will catch you and make you food for fishes."

His companion muttered something in response. The pair took up most of the causeway. Both stood by to let the horse and cart pass. William could smell the sweat of the horse and the content of the cart, a load of grain, and caught a quick look at the driver. It was Jeremy Locke, the man William suspected of trying to brain him. His heart leaped into his throat. He pulled down his hat even farther over his face and stooped a little, trying to conceal his height, mimicking the limp of the old man he accompanied.

He breathed a sigh of relief when Locke passed on without apparent notice of Joseph Martin's companion. "Do you know that man well?" William asked.

"Jeremy Locke? Too well to think well of him," Joseph said. "If you ask me, he's little more than a thief and brigand, but in a place as small as Livesey is, it pays to be on reasonably good terms even with the devil."

"He spoke most disrespectfully to you."

Martin laughed. "He treats all about him the same, except for those who pay him for his services."

"What services might those be?" William asked.

"It would take too long to relate those, Master Coggeshall...William. Just say that if you have an unsavory task to perform, a sly move under the table to undo an enemy, why Locke's your man. He has not an iota of virtue. Pay his fee, and no worries thereafter—unless, of course, it's you he's been paid to undo."

"Has he done murders, this Locke?"

"I shouldn't put it past him, Master Coggeshall. No, sir, I wouldn't put it past him for a moment."

"And does he work alone, this Locke fellow? I mean, has he a companion in his mischief?"

The old man thought for a moment, then said, "He does, a long-time friend of his, another scoundrel as quick as he to do the devil's work. His name is Browne."

"I think I've seen him. A thick-chested fellow isn't he, red beard?"

"That would be he, without a doubt," Joseph Martin said.

Within a few more minutes they had reached the shore, having met no other persons on the way. William turned to look behind him. Livesey now lay at a distance. He remembered when he had first seen it and thought it seemed a pretty piece of earth afloat in a gray-blue sea. He thought differently of it now; as a dismal place of ignorance, deception, and violence.

But he knew he would return—accompanied, he hoped, by a troop of Burghley's private army. Let them sweep the island, arrest the Challoners, show no mercy to Broderick and his tools, and rescue Johane.

Thirty-Seven

William supported his enfeebled companion the last mile or two of their journey, along the road through the town of Queenborough with its oddly concentric castle where, as far as William could observe, they drew little attention. Why should they? An old man and a younger, probably father and son, neither encumbered with baggage of interest, so no passing travelers to be questioned or stayed on their way. In a busy market town, they were lost in a crowd, perfectly anonymous.

As they left, Josiah complained that his hip was to be the death of him and that he doubted he could go much farther. He said, "Should I die, my friend, pray convey the news to my son-in-law. He's a good man. We are within a mile or two of where their farmstead lies."

"I will do as you wish, Joseph, but think it unlikely that you'll pass on before seeing your son-in-law again. Rest will do you good, at least for now."

They sat down by the side of the road where there were trees and a pleasant meadow. It was now past noon. It was a fair day, now with marshland to the south of them and only a few—carters and some horsemen—along the road. While they waited, they talked. Joseph about his daughter, who was his only living child, and her husband, a long-limbed handsome youth who had already fathered two sons. Joseph said he had lived on Great Livesey all his life, and his parents and grandparents before him. He said he was a blacksmith, but had little work, there being so few horses on the island or other work pertaining to his trade. Age had also crippled him, he said.

"How do you live, then?" William asked.

"Ah, poorly, William. My wife is dead. The son we had together likewise, lost at sea. I eat but little, enough to live, and Sir Arthur Challoner has mercy upon me and charges no rent for my house, which I confess is little more than a hovel, yet it is enough."

"This Sir Arthur is most generous. Is he so generous with other of his tenants?"

"Oh I don't know. Some he charges overmuch. If you listen to the complaints of his neighbors. To tell truth, William, I did him a piece of work once he wanted very much, and so he favors me now."

William wondered what this piece of work was, but was hesitant to ask outright. To ask seemed nosey and boorish, and while he felt no need to impress his elderly companion with his good manners, he still thought of himself as a gentleman, despite his own bedraggled appearance.

He suspected Joseph would divulge what he called "the favor" in good time. And if he did not, William would find a way to pry it out of him. The more he knew about the doings of the Challoners, the better.

It was a handsome farmstead with a prosperous look, well cared for, with a freshly-thatched roof and an orchard heavy with fruit. In the pasture beyond, William could see cattle grazing. They had not gotten within a dozen feet of the door when a young woman emerged from the cottage, ruddy faced and dressed in a clean apron. When she saw William's burden, she cried out in alarm. "Oh Father," she cried. "What's happened?"

She looked imploringly at her father, then suspiciously at William as though she imagined he had caused her father's distress.

"Have no worry, daughter, I am well enough off, thanks to my friend here." He nodded toward William. "He has borne me most of the way from the island out of the goodness of his heart."

The girl, slender with a mass of red hair beneath her cap, beckoned William to bring Joseph into the house. They were met by the young man Joseph had described as her husband. He said his name was Robert, his wife Elizabeth. Robert took Joseph from William and went into an adjoining room. William followed.

The arrangement within was typical of the farmhouses William had often seen in his country. A low-ceilinged parlor with a hearth, thus also serving as a crude but ample kitchen. A trestle table with stools, all rough-hewn, doubtless by the householder himself. Two rooms and a simple stair or ladder leading to what he presumed was a single large room under the eaves. The other rooms below, were there any, would be bedchambers; one for the farmer and his wife, the other for the children and the nurse, the space above for servants, were there any. A single cottage could hold a dozen or more persons of the same blood, or not. The hearth would provide heat for the whole of it.

The son laid his father-in-law on a large stuffed bed and covered him with a blanket that had lain folded at its foot. The young husbandman obviously had genuine affection for his wife's father, and treated him with great tenderness. Joseph's eyes were closed, as though he were asleep, or even dead, but William knew what his companion suffered from most was the sheer exhaustion of the journey. The young couple asked him his name, and where he had found their father.

"My name is William, William Coggeshall," he said, giving them the same false name he had given Joseph. "We met along the causeway from Livesey. We became companions on the road. My own journey takes me west, as far as London. I said I would accompany him. His hip is arthritic, it grew worse along the way. So I carried him when he could no longer walk by himself."

"And so doing you performed a Christian act," Elizabeth said. "I thank you, sir. Whoever you may be."

"Your father is not sick, only exhausted from the way, made worse by his hip's agony."

"You called it something," the young husband said.

"Arthritis. The hip joint is inflamed. It is not an uncommon condition, made worse by our English climate, and age as well. How old is your father?"

"Seventy, seventy-two or three. He was never sure," Elizabeth said. "He doesn't even know whether he was christened."

"Right now, he needs rest," William said. "If you heat water and apply it to his hip in a towel or rag, that may bring him relief—that and knowing his journey is ended."

William wished the family well and made a move to go.

"Please, sir. You must be hungry from the way. Please stay and eat with us," she said.

"And stay the night," her husband said. "It's the least we can offer you for your service to our father."

William's instincts were to press on, but the truth was that he was weak from hunger and footsore as well. Joseph was a frail old man, but carrying him the last quarter mile had not been easy, and the prospect of food and shelter before he continued on his way was hard to resist. Besides, he could see in the earnest expressions of the young couple a sincerity that would be rude for him to refuse. As a young doctor beginning his practice, he had often accepted such hospitality from the poor in lieu of his fee. This young family could not be regarded as poor. Still, he could hardly expect a fee for doing no more than making a casual observation about a condition obvious to him. Aching joints were almost inevitable in one Joseph's age, like graying hair and failing eyesight and lost teeth and a host of other afflictions incident to age for which his science had no cure.

"Thank you. I would be happy to accept."

The young farmer showed him out through the door to the well, where he could wash the dust from his journey. A little later, after being treated to a tour of the farm by its proud owner, the three of them and a little boy of six or seven sat down at the trestle table to a supper that, if not remarkable for its variety, was more than adequate in its quantity. Joseph's daughter had killed and cooked a plump chicken, garnished it with vegetables and cheese sauce, and served a beer of her own brewing. It was all a delightsome change from the raw fish, seaweed, and bird eggs that had sustained him while marooned on the island.

Joseph's daughter asked him again how he knew her father, and William told her the same story as before: that they had met on the causeway, two travelers heading for the mainland who decided to keep company along the way. He was still concerned that his identity not be known, for he realized now that it would be to his advantage to be thought dead still and no threat to the conspiracies and plots of Broderick and his fellows, the full nature of which remained unclear to him except for the threat it presented to his life and limb.

"Then you were well met. For years I've begged my father to leave the island and come live with us here, and worried about him making the journey alone, although it is only a day's journey by foot."

"But you are not from the island?" her husband asked.

"No, only a visitor. On some business matter."

"I hope then," the husband said, "you were not cheated. It's a dangerous thing to do business with them on the island. I grew up there, and I know how those people are."

He was tempted to tell them that his business had been with the lord and lady of the manor, but that would have revealed too much.

"I believe I was treated honestly enough," William said, although the opposite was true. He was not prepared to share with them the story of his ordeal, or talk about island murders he had come to know of, and almost experience for himself.

They had nearly finished their meal and were enjoying the plum pudding, when Joseph appeared. He still walked with a cane, but said the warm water on his hip had given him some relief, that and knowing his journey was at an end. He did not seem surprised to see William at the table but pleased, rather. "Oh, William, I see my children have prevailed on you to stay. It is the least that can be done to thank you."

The old man looked around approvingly.

"I do hope you are the better for your daughter's ministrations," William said.

"Oh, I am. I truly am."

Joseph sat down at the table and his daughter spooned some of the pudding into a bowl.

There was more casual talk at the table about the farm. William barely listened, having nothing to contribute himself. But later, the old man drew him aside and the two went out of doors into the pleasant night air. There was a bench near the well and Joseph invited William to sit with him.

What William expected was more expressions of gratitude, not that he felt more were needed, for he had done no more than any decent man might have done to aid another in distress, but he was surprised when Joseph said. "You know, Master Coggeshall, I didn't recognize you at first."

"Recognize me? How do you mean?"

"I knew your face was familiar, but not the way you were dressed. Then when I heard your voice…it wasn't an island voice, not island speech. I knew you were from somewhere else, and then finally I remembered."

"Remembered?"

"Seeing you at the Saracen's Blade, talking to Israel Parker. You're the doctor who was up at the manor."

William could hardly deny it, but Joseph continued before William could speak.

"The one they said had left to go back to London, or had drowned and his body lost at sea."

"Who said that?" William asked carefully.

"Israel Parker said that, and his cronies, the two men I told you of, Browne and Locke, them that will do anything for money and the devil take the hindmost. I heard them talking about it, how you had gone, but they said it so that it seemed you hadn't just left of your own will, but had some encouragement, if you know what I mean. The three are villains through and through."

William thought for a minute and then said, "You would do me a great favor, Joseph, by not telling anyone that you met me on the road. I would be just as happy for them to think I was dead and gone, if you know what I mean."

"Rest assured, Doctor, though I be lame and old, I know how to hold my tongue. Surely, I would do nothing to advance the fortunes of those men, who have ever treated me but as scum to wipe from their feet."

William thought to ask, "Did you know this curate who of late... disappeared?"

"Dead, I think," the old man said.

"You sound sure of that."

"The curate, if I may still call him that for all his sins and heresies, has not been seen for a fortnight, him who one might see almost daily walking the shore line for what the tide brought in. Certain it is that he didn't just get up and walk away. Or swim. So I think for these and other good reasons that he is dead."

"Any idea by whose hand?"

"No idea at all, Doctor, but the island lacks not those malicious enough to do it, and to be truthful, the good man was an annoyance to many, not only because of his damnable opinions but because of persistent treasure hunting."

"Why should that have bothered anyone but himself?"

"Competition, Doctor, I know no better motive for murder."

"Competition of what sort?"

"Treasure hunting, Doctor, if you knew the curate you knew it wasn't just driftwood and odd cast offs he sought. And he wasn't the only one."

"Who else?"

"Why every fisherman and husbandman on the island dreams of finding silver or gold in his garden or in a fish's mouth. Their wives, as well. If it's not buried gold by the Romans, it's some Viking plunder. What else is there to dream of on Livesey?"

"And you, Joseph?"

"I give no heed to rumors about treasure, Doctor. I once had a friend in my youth who found a Roman chamber pot in his cellar, or at least so he claimed. He said if you sniffed hard and long you could still sniff some legionary's piss."

Both men laughed. Joseph went on, drawing his head closer to William and lowering his voice to a conspiratorial whisper.

"I said I had my house on Livesey by grant of a leasehold from Sir Arthur, because of some favor I did for him."

"So you said."

"But you did not ask what favor might have invited such beneficence from a man not noted for it otherwise."

"I did not."

"Well, I'll tell you since we are speaking of treasure, or the discovery of it. Earlier in his life Sir Arthur was as besotted with desire for island treasure as anyone else on the island. He had heard tell that there was gold buried over where the old tower is and had men digging ever so many pits to find it. Somewhere he'd gotten a map. But when the pits were dug they no sooner went down a dozen or so feet, but began filling with water. He needed a way to pump it out. His steward then knew me well, knew I was clever with making… devices."

"Devices?"

"You know, Doctor, machines. He said his master needed one to draw up the seawater, since he believed the gold was buried in the marsh and that it was under water, which if removed would allow it to be discovered. You'd think the Challoners, owning as they did the island, would have had enough money to forego such foolishness, but no, it was otherwise."

"Did you invent such a device?" William asked.

"Oh, I did, Doctor, and I must confess I had pleasure in so doing. I have always been a tinker."

"Tinker?"

"You know, one who loves inventing things, devices, contraptions."

William nodded with approval. He knew the type. While not one himself, he admired the ingenuity that went into the making of new devices which he and others in his profession used themselves. "What was this device of yours exactly?"

The old man went on to describe what he had fashioned out of the iron at his forge; a long cylindrical form to which scoop-like blades were attached, that would capture water and draw it upward when turned manually from above. All was encased in a sheath of iron."

"An Archimedes Screw," William said.

"What did you say, Doctor?"

"Archimedes. An old Greek. I don't know if he invented it or if the device is simply named after him. Some say the Egyptians used such a tool to dig their canals."

"I learned it from no man, Doctor, Greek or Egyptian either," his companion said, bristling a little.

"I'm sure you did not," William said. "History teaches us that men in various times and places can come upon similar ideas, independent of each other. Was your invention successful?"

"In removing the water? Yes, but no gold was found, no treasure of any kind. All that was accomplished was a series of holes, now looking like ponds. You may have seen them yourself, Doctor, while you were there. But for all the failure, Sir Arthur was as good as his word. The house was mine, and my pump was his for all the good it did. You can see it over near the tower, if you ever go back to Livesey. It's all rusty now, being exposed to the weather, but I had pleasure in conceiving of it, making it, and seeing that it worked as I intended."

William remembered having seen the tangle of rusting iron when Wincott gave him his tour of the island. He had thought it some manner of pipe, or old canon. Wincott had said nothing of it on his tour. Perhaps he hadn't known its purpose.

"Where did Sir Arthur get this map you speak of?"

"He said he had it from a gentleman friend of his."

"I trust he didn't pay a goodly sum for this fraud."

"I have no idea about that. I do know that his lady wife railed at him for the expense of time and labor. I heard her at it. Believe me, she's a quiet soul on the outside, but she's a right termagant when she's crossed. I think he gave up treasure hunting after that."

"Tell me, whose gold was this supposed to be?"

"Who buried the treasure? Oh, I don't know. I asked him once, but he wouldn't say."

They talked some more but William, still cautious, withheld more than he gave. He said nothing about Lord Burghley, or his secret assignment on the island, or his earlier conversations with the disgraced cleric. And he was most careful not to say anything about Jews, their treasure, or what he had found while on Little Livesey.

"I pray you, Joseph, don't tell your children who I am. Right now, the fewer that know me and my business on Livesey the better."

"I said I would keep mum, and so I shall. Who you are and what you are, will be known only by me. It's the least I can do for your charity. But tell me, Doctor, how did you escape death by these villains?"

William could think of no reason not to tell him.

"Browne and Locke lured me to the island, Little Livesey, saying Wincott's body was there. I wanted it to prove that he was dead, that I had found him so, and was not a liar or a madman in reporting it. The body was there indeed, but one of them, Locke I think, struck me from behind and left me on Little Livesey for dead."

"Little Livesey. Why, Doctor, there's nothing there but rocks and bird shit."

William laughed. He could laugh about it now, even though he knew in time to come he would dream of it and wake shuddering with relief that it was in his past. Joseph seemed an honest soul, but William wasn't prepared to tell him just how more there was on the island than that.

"Will you return to the island, to Livesey?" William asked.

"My daughter and her husband have prevailed upon me to stay with them. My son-in-law will go to Great Livesey in the morning and bring all worth bringing back here. No, Doctor, I will probably end my days here. There's nothing left for me there, nothing worth saving or weeping over. My wife's body is buried in the churchyard, but that's but dust. I know her soul's in heaven, where I myself will presently go."

"I wonder if your daughter's husband will be so kind as to convey a message to a friend there…a servant at the manor house."

"Not Master Broderick, I trust. He's a devil."

"So I believe," William said. "But the message is for a young woman of the household. Her name is Johane Sheldon. She assists Mistress Challoner."

"I don't know her, and it's unlikely my son-in-law does, but if she's one of the household he can get your message to her. You say she's a young woman? Fair to look upon, I suspect?"

"We have no relationship such as you assume, Joseph. It is not a love letter I will send to her. She came to the island with me to provide service to Lady Challoner. Since her arrival she has done that, and admirably.

I'm afraid she thinks I'm dead, or fled to London out of fear. I would not have her think either of me."

"Will my son carry your words or some writing?"

"Writing would be best. She knows my hand and will have no doubt it comes from me. I will need paper and pen."

"I'll see if my son-in-law has such. Neither he nor my daughter can read or write, nor can I if truth be told, so it is unlikely paper and pen can be found here, but perhaps something else will serve. Come, let us go back in and see what my son-in-law can provide. He's a quick lad, clever and resourceful. My daughter is likewise blessed. Don't worry. Your message will be delivered as you direct. My oath upon it."

Before all went to bed in the farmhouse, Joseph's son-in-law had secured a fragment of cloth, and his wife Elizabeth some pig's blood she had intended to use as a dye. A goose's feather completed what William needed. By candlelight he wrote to Johane.

> *Dear Mistress Sheldon, or Johane, for you have bid me call you such,*
>
> *By this you will know that I am neither dead nor have fled in fear of being so. Who tells you otherwise lies and is not to be trusted. I go to Lord Burghley to tell him my progress in finding what we sought, which is far more than I can convey to you in these few words. Believe that I will return to Livesey—for you and for justice for those murdered by conspirators, most especially your grandfather of blessed memory. In the meantime, be safe.*
>
> *You know my name and my faithfulness, and so farewell for now.*

That night he slept in the loft, on a straw mat covered with a wool blanket he suspected was that of his hosts. He slept like the dead: dreamless, fearless. In the morning they fed him again, and he ate as the night before, ravenously as though making up for what he had lost on the island. Afterwards, the pig blood having dried on the cloth, he rolled it up, tied it with a string and handed it to Joseph's son-in law.

"Give it only to Johane Sheldon, she who is the personal attendant of Lady Challoner, not to the steward, or anyone else at the manor. That is most important. The message is for her eyes only, none other's."

"I will, sir,"

William watched the young husbandman drive off in a cart toward Queenborough, with no misgivings. He had liked the lad's honest face, his obvious devotion to Joseph's daughter, his generosity as a host. No, he believed he had done the right thing in trusting this little family.

Then he said goodbye and set out in the opposite direction. He reckoned it was nearly fifty miles to London. That would be three days on foot, two on horse or wagon. He was not without resources. He had Tobias Wincott's money, the stash from the island cave. At the next town of any size he would secure a horse and decent clothes, and proceed with his plan. Within the week he would report to Burghley, relate what he had discovered, whom he suspected, and with God's help see Burghley had what he wanted of him.

Thirty-Eight

In London, William found his father at his house. That was no surprise; Jerome Gilbert now made regular trips to the city, where he had much business with lawyers and property owners, minor court gentlemen and petitioners.

By the firelight, his face looked heavy and lined. Jerome took one glance at his son and said: "Look at you William, you look terrible, haggard. What in heaven happened to you?"

It was too long a story for William to relate in detail, and he was more than weary from his journey. "Tomorrow, Father. Now, I'm for bed."

"Well, you can at least tell me about this girl who I hear tags along after you as your... I know not what to call her."

"Where did you hear of her?"

"From one of your physician friends, who upon seeing me in London took care that I should know my son was keeping company with a young woman. He thinks she is your mistress."

"Idle gossip," William said.

"But is it true, son?"

His father was obsessed with William's relationships with women, hoping to see William married before long so that he could see grandchildren before he passed—a fate he talked about frequently in his more melancholy moods.

"She is only my assistant. Her name is Johane Sheldon."

"Is she of good family?"

"I know little of her family, father, only that she is an honest girl, intelligent, interested in medicine. She is not what you might call a love interest, if that's what you're assuming with these questions."

"My friend says she's striking, no common drab."

"So she may be considered, but our relationship, such as it is, is purely professional. I am her mentor, she my pupil, nothing more."

His father smiled mischievously. "Well, William, we shall see. You know my fondest hope is that you will marry, now that you are so well established in the city."

"I know, father, you have expressed such a desire many times. And I shall marry at some future time, God willing, but for now I have my work."

"Which brings me back to your appearance. You're disheveled, dusty from the road. Were you assaulted, robbed by the way?"

"Tomorrow, father, I pray you. Then I will tell you how I came here so disheveled. For now, to bed, the both of us. Sleep is the great healer of a weary heart. You always told me so."

Later, just before falling asleep, he regretted not having asked after his stepmother or his brothers and sisters. He prayed, thanking God for his safe return, although he knew the danger was not past. He had made enemies in Livesey, some to whom he could give a name—Broderick, the two villains who had tried to kill him and leave him dead on the little island, the traitorous tavern keeper, and who else? Was the roster complete? Did it include the lord and lady of the island? Sir Arthur Challoner was himself a treasure hunter, and as he had hired Broderick, not just as a steward but as a treasure hunter in chief, as a man reputed to wave a magic staff to detect treasure. Challoner, William decided, was at least complicit in the plotting, if not its principal architect.

At breakfast he was obliged to fulfill his promise to his father, to tell where had been, why, and why he had returned looking more like a vagrant that a prosperous gentleman and physician. But his story needed to be simplified, and Burghley's secret purposes had to be concealed.

"I went to Livesey to secure the health of its lord and lady, Sir Arthur and Mildred Challoner."

"I know him, or of him, a poor knight. The island, his manor, is not much, I've heard. And did you, my son, cure the man and his lady?"

"The knight is beyond cure. He's dying of a bad heart. As for his lady, she is as healthy as a horse. That she is sickly is her husband's delusion, forced upon her that they may be equals in their affliction, or at least that she not be superior to him in her good health."

His father laughed. "An unusual relationship."

"Indeed," William said.

"You wrote to me asking about a family named Broderick."

"I did, and you responded, for which I thank you."

"Who is this Broderick you inquired of?"

"Sir Arthur's steward. I learned he was from Halstead. I wanted to know more about him."

"After your letter and my response, I learned more, from another lawyer who had heard I asked after him."

William leaned toward his father.

"He was reputed to be a treasure hunter, a searcher of mounds and burrows. He was in Halstead, where he dug a deep tunnel to find what he believed was a hoard of gold and silver, deposited by the Danes when they ruled the land. He is said to have possessed a device for the discovery of such."

"What manner of device?"

"Something like unto a compass."

"Compass?"

"Not to find directions out, north, south, and such. And not resembling a compass, something like unto an usher's rod."

"An ornate stick or cane?"

"Something like unto it. His practice was to walk about in fields and pastures, holding the rod before him. It was supposed to quiver in his hand when there was anything metal beneath, and more so if the metal was precious metal, gold or silver. He called it Merlin's Rod."

"A fraud, no doubt." William scoffed. "Merlin's Rod indeed. The tool of one who though famous throughout the land most likely never lived. This all sounds like the vilest sort of trumpery."

"I was told he did find gold, some at least, gold coins," his father said. "More than a handful, but less than a chest. Some swords too, shields, bucklers, cups, the usual."

"And he claimed thereby this device of his worked?"

"He did; the find proved it, so he claimed. He made a reputation in the area, but was not so successful in other enterprises. It is said, he dug enough holes in Halstead to build a fortress and achieved nothing but ruined fields and pastures."

"His device, this Merlin's Rod, notwithstanding."

"Oh, he had an explanation for its failure."

"Did he convince?"

"Some, yet not enough for him to escape the wrath of the farmers whose land he ruined with his holes and tunnels. They ran him out of town and would have hoisted him on Merlin's Rod had they caught him. My friend has no idea where he went from there."

William told his father about John Broderick. "I think it likely this is the same man."

"Has he been treasure hunting on Livesey?"

"By report, yes. Treasure hunting is a popular pastime on the isle. Sir Arthur was, during his youth, similarly minded, or so I've been told."

"And with what success?" his father asked.

"Little, I think, from the condition of the manor house. It's a dreary place and looks as if no improvement has been made since it was first erected."

William decided not to tell his father about his experience on Little Livesey, of how close to death he came. The story would have horrified his father, who detested violence and most particularly violence exerted against his own flesh and blood. Jerome Gilbert would have done everything he could, short of having William imprisoned as a mad man, to stop him from pursuing his goal any farther.

His father sighed and gave him a searching look. "So, what do you do now?"

"I must see Lord Burghley, go to him. I have a message for him he will want to hear."

"You travel in exalted company, my son, but seeing his lordship will not be easy."

"Why not?"

"Lord Burghley is in France, on a mission for the queen. It is said he will not return until month's end, if then. Perhaps your message can be delivered to one of his staff. It is said he has a vast company of them to do the common tasks of his work."

"His lordship has an army of servants but, no, my message must be for his ears only."

"Then your news must be no trivial matter," his father said.

"I assure you it is not," William said.

"I pray not some threat to the state, or to her majesty?"

"Not so grave a business, but important, nonetheless. I'm sorry, Father. I can say no more."

Thirty-Nine

There was nothing to be done but return to his patients and their needs and demands and await Burghley's return, a prospect that offered him little peace of mind. Always before him, he saw the faces of those he had left behind on the island, both his enemies and, most especially, Johane. He realized that in some sense he had not left Livesey at all. It was still with him, its mysteries only partially solved, the guilty yet to be proven so by stronger evidence, and most important, its treasure yet to be discovered—or at least fully so.

Then, but a few days after his return, he received a letter. It was from Johane. A response to his own.

His heart was full of an intense relief, akin to joy. For weeks he had feared the worst, that she was dead. That like him, she had fallen victim to Broderick's machinations. But here was sure evidence of otherwise, evidence that she was both alive and also well, at least well enough to write.

She wrote with a delicate hand, with letters idiosyncratically shaped, a self-conscious artifice nonetheless readable to him. It expressed her joy in learning he was alive, said she was doing well in keeping Broderick at bay, and had discovered new things from her lady she was eager to disclose, but could not do so in the letter. She urged him to return. She said she thought of him always and prayed daily for his safety. His face, she wrote, was always before her.

The last of her sentences he read and reread. What did it mean, his face always before her? Did she return his affection? Or was she saying less than that, a mere expression of regard and respect of one who had been her teacher, her fellow spy? How could he know? He wasn't even sure what he felt for her but regard and respect, despite the assurance he had given to his father that there were no thoughts of love between them, no pledge-making, no compromising intimacy.

The more immediate question was her plea that he return. He had planned to do so, but not alone. He envisioned making his report to Burghley, returning with a troop of Burghley's guards to accompany him. Broderick would be arrested, the tavern keeper and his murderous fellows taken and judged, and even Sir Arthur if it were proved he was complicit as William suspected. The gold tablet would be recovered and delivered to Burghley. But all that must wait. Only Burghley could authorize such an expedition, only Burghley would understand why it must be done. Livesey was not only a treasure island. It was an island of deception, treachery, and violence.

He sat down to write to her.

Dear Johane,

I have received your letter and appeal for my return, and I promise so to do. Not only for this news you have, but to see you safely home again. But I must wait upon Lord Burghley's return from France where he does the queen's business. By the new month, he is to return. I will report all we have learned until now and bring help, a troop. In the meanwhile, I pray you stay safe, both from the vile Broderick and any others that might threaten you.

Your faithful friend,
William Gilbert

Half of the time he spent on the brief letter he spent deciding how he should salute her, and more particularly how he should style himself in closing. He decided to be faithful friend, since it committed him to little and made no reckless assumption as to how she might regard him. He could not use the regular post. He secured the aid of a messenger at considerable cost, to ride the distance to Livesey and present the letter to her personally, as he had done his first missive. She had received his first without interception. He trusted the second would also be read by her eyes and hers alone.

He waited a response, with more anticipation than he waited the end of the month when Burghley should return to England.

He did not need to wait long. Within the week, another letter came. In this, Johane's tone was more urgent and the letter's content more mysterious.

Dear William,
   I write in great haste that you may know our purpose has been fulfilled. My lady has revealed all and the treasure has been found. Yet it may be hard to reach seeing that it is buried deep and beneath water, which I do believe we could recover with your magnets. You may remember we talked of this while I was in your house, and you told me of how powerful magnets were in lifting metals from the depths.
   Do not fear returning. Broderick's treachery has been discovered and he has been dismissed by Sir Arthur. I have it on good authority he has left Livesey. Another, more honest, man stands in his place, a good Christian. No one in England knows more of the lodestone's power than do you, and we will use it to our advantage to recover what Lord Burghley desires above all.
   I wait your return,
   Your friend, and she who would be more,
   Johane

And she who would be more. The phrase stuck in his head, lodged there, and would not leave him. Even while he considered her principal proposal about his magnets. Did she love him, then? Was her plea that he return to the island motivated by love as much as desire to find Jewish treasure.

He believed it was. Her face and form appeared in his mind's eye. Did he love her, or was he simply moved by her apparent attraction to him? It was a question he could not resolve, at least for now. The magnets were another matter.

Assuming that the Jewish gold and silver were not purely so, but alloyed with iron or copper or other metal, then the lodestone, were it of sufficient power, and the objects to be recovered not too heavy, might lift them up from any depth, given they were secured by a long enough rope or cable.

He spent the rest of the day preparing. He would leave tomorrow. If the prospect was as bright as Johane claimed, the treasure would be recovered and justice done before Lord Burghley returned, a much to be preferred outcome since it would surely overshadow any slips of judgment he might otherwise admit in his report.

Forty

His preparation for the return to the island was done in great haste: his own horse to carry himself and his bag, and another, secured expressly as a pack animal, to carry the lodestones. Of these there were seven in the shape of bars of roughly equal dimensions and derived from the same place, a certain iron mine in Bavaria. He knew of their strength from his experiments, knew they could lift when combined a metal object of considerable heft—a sword, a helmet, valuable plate and jewels, bags of coins, certainly a gold plate inscribed with Hebrew lettering that—if like its companion piece—could have weighed less than a half a pound.

With the lodestones, he packed a hoist of his own design with a spool of cedar and steel cable to secure the lodestones. All to lift an object from a depth of thirty feet or more.

His companions on the journey were his household servant, Thomas Denham, and Thomas' cousin Geoffrey Stillman. Thomas was sturdily built, fancied himself as a wrestler, and had begged William to take him along on the journey as soon as he learned the doctor was to return to the island. Geoffrey Stillman had been a soldier in some European war or another, William could not remember which, and could wield a sword deftly and fire a pistol—at least so he claimed.

William did not tell them about the treasure, only that their muscular arms might be needed for a project that required heavy lifting. They were used to helping William with his experiments. They did not question his description of their duties, but probably supposed this was merely another scientific inquiry. Another reason for their presence was obvious. What gentleman was safe riding the roads of England alone, and with a pack animal with him to suggest he carried something of value that might tempt thieves or brigands, either at an isolated inn or on the road?

William's plan was to reach the island as soon as possible, but it was a two-day journey in the best of weather, and he thought it likely rain would muddy the roads before reaching his destination. Still, he could not wait. He was mindful of the urgency in Johane's letter, as if a possibility of recovery presented itself but would not last. But most of all, he wanted to see her, to determine her feelings for him, if they were indeed what the phrasing of her letter suggested, that she loved him, that she wanted him.

William and his companions set out before dawn, leaving London behind them just as the sun rose. Clouds blew in from the east within an hour, and not a mile thereafter rain began. By noon, the road was a quagmire. William reckoned they had only made ten miles from the city walls, if that.

"Will we stop soon, Doctor?" Thomas called out from behind him. William looked back. Both his companions were pitiful sights, their riding cloaks hanging on them like shrouds, their faces half buried in their hats. William imagined he looked no better. No weave could resist such a downpour. Only the horses seemed indifferent to it.

William looked ahead again. Beyond, through the rain, he could see a church spire like a great finger pointing upward. It was a town or perhaps only a village; he did not know which, nor did it make a difference. It might prove a place of refuge against the weather and the advancing night.

"A village is coming up. If there's an inn, we'll stop," he called over his shoulder.

He did not want to stop, but the road, such as it was, was now nothing but mud. Going farther was useless. His two companions would do what he required of them, he was their master, but why strain the relationship that had to now been a happy one, for both master and servants, he believed? He faced the reality. They could go no further until the rain stopped, until the roads dried.

The church came into sight, and not long after an inn—not an imposing place, but one he trusted would provide shelter and hopefully clean beds. But it was the only inn, as it happened, and full. The inn keeper, a cheerful man who seemed more delighted to have his rooms occupied than sad that he could not accommodate these London wayfarers, said beds for them might be found farther down the road, at a farmstead named Blackhart Farm, whose owner sometimes took in travelers.

"But it will cost you, sir, more than me," the inn keeper said.

"More than you?" William answered.

"I charge for my chambers but tuppence a night, sir. The farmer, Abraham Houston is his name, charges six and sometimes seven. He says he's more put out than I, whose business is putting up travelers, whereas he is chiefly a farmer."

The inn keeper gave William the directions, with such exactness of detail that he suspected the inn keeper and the farmer had some mutually profitable relationship. They remounted and pressed on, the storm having become even worse in the meantime.

The farmer, Abraham Houston, was a heavy, dour man with hairy cheeks and flyaway hair as though it had never seen a comb or brush. William put him at about his own father's age—early fifties or a bit older. He spoke with a gravelly voice. At table with him was his wife, a sullen, plain-faced woman, younger than her husband. She had large, pendulous breasts, wide hips, and said nothing throughout the meal. Also present was the farmer's son, a broad-shouldered young man in his early twenties with a cup-bowl haircut, narrow eyes, and large, calloused hands. The farmer also had daughters, three of them, homely girls much younger than their brother, but of marriageable years if husbands could be found for them. In disposition as well as looks, they seemed to take after their mother.

Throughout the meal, a simple one, the girls kept mum, their eyes focused on their plates, never looking at the three strangers their father had taken in for more money than the inn keeper had said—but then the rain had made the roads impassable. William and his companions were at the farmer's mercy.

"Master, where do you travel in such weather, you and your servants?" Abraham Houston asked.

William thought there was no reason to lie. He would not see the farmer or his farmstead again. The question was merely a polite inquiry. At least, that's how he understood it.

"We're going to Kent. To the isle of Livesey."

"Never heard of it, sir, Kent, yes. This isle of...."

"Livesey."

"Livesey, then."

"It's a small island," William said. "Hardly a dot on a map."

"Then why would you go there, sir?"

"I'm a doctor. I have patients there."

Abraham nodded. "A doctor, are you?"

"Yes, in London."

"Are you a good doctor, sir?"

"I believe so, Master Houston."

"Then perhaps you'll have a look at my father."

"Your father?"

Abraham Houston was old. William thought the man's father, if alive, must be truly ancient.

"He's in the next room. He's ninety years old, come Michaelmas. He's blind, sir, has what they call cataracts in his eyes. He can't see."

"I'll take a look at him," William said. Cataracts were not uncommon in the aged. Removing them was surgeon's work, not a physician's. But it was an expensive procedure, and difficult. William knew two members of the barber-surgeon guild in London who specialized in diseases of the eye, especially cataracts, but even they had not always met with success. Some of their patients, desiring to see again, had awakened in the life to come, where—William was assured—they would need no surgeon to open their eyes.

After supper, William was shown into the room. Abraham's father, whom he learned was named Samuel, lay on a bed, covered with a ragged blanket. He too was fully bearded, making both men, although father and son, seem almost the same age. The difference was in Samuel's eyes. Even by candlelight, William could see a gauzy film covering the pupils. The old man stared into the distance and then, seeming to detect William's breathing, fixed his sightless eyes on the doctor.

"Father, our guest is a doctor, from London, would you believe? And he knows someone who can make you see again."

"I did not say so much," William said, turning to his host. He walked over and sat down on the bed. He could see that beneath the blanket the older man's body was shrunken. Nothing in Samuel Houston's expression registered William's protest. He smiled thinly in his beard, as though all the news was good. "Thank you, Doctor. I am very grateful. You're an answer to my prayers."

William took the candle that sat by the bed, and held it close to the old man's clouded eyes. The man responded to the light, not as a fully sighted person would, but enough for William to know the lens still allowed some vision, although not enough for the man to make his way about the house or farm without missing a step or falling into a ditch.

"The cataracts can be removed. I know surgeons in London that could help you."

"None closer?" Abraham Houston said. "My father doesn't travel well."

William shrugged. "I know none in this region of the country," he said.

"And London surgeons would not want to come here, or if they did they must demand a great sum."

"I don't know what they would ask, but it true that everything is more expensive in London."

Abraham shook his head, his thinking plain. His father was a very old man. How many years could he have ahead of him to enjoy the delight of his eyes, even if his vision were restored? If William had pulled from his bag an elixir, an herbal remedy, a concoction of some sort costing but a few pennies, it would have been different.

There seemed nothing more for him to say. William stood, prepared to leave the room, prepared to thank the farmer again for his hospitality and wish all goodnight. The fire in the kitchen had done little to dry his wet clothing. His servants looked equally bedraggled. He was tired and ready for whatever bed was offered him.

"Wait, Doctor."

It was the old man who spoke. His son left, beckoned by his wife from the kitchen. It was the first time William had heard her voice. It was the shrill command of a nagging wife, *come help with something*, or some complaint about the girls shirking their chores. William wondered that she could have kept silent for so long.

"Where are you bound, Doctor?" the old man asked.

William told him what he had told his son at supper. The isle of Livesey. Samuel Houston had heard of it. He said he had never been there, and William was unsure the old man wasn't confusing Livesey with some other island or even village. England had hundreds of them along its coasts. One very much like another, he imagined the old man thought.

"That's a good distance, Doctor. I hope you do not travel alone."

"I have two servants with me, young sturdy men," William said. *Neither of whom are armed*, he might have added, but did not. In his eagerness to get on the road, he had not thought of the need for weapons, only his magnets. He suddenly realized he should have. Both carried knives—what young man did not? But swords or pistols, no.

"Are you carrying aught of value with you? I mean other than your horses and clothing?"

William thought of the lodestones. He had obtained them at some cost, but they were hardly what a normal person would consider of value. They would look like simple pieces of iron. An ironmonger might value them, think of what useful tool or weapon to make of them. They might make useful doorstops, or paperweights in a scholar's library. But to the eyes of a thief, a disappointing haul, hardly worth the effort, not worth getting hanged for.

"No, sir, only our personal possessions, coats, boots, I travel with little money myself, my servants with less. We are no merchants conveying goods to market."

"Ah," Samuel said. "That's enough for thieves hereabouts. The roads are dangerous, thieves and robbers are bold. Did not my son warn you?"

"He did not."

"He wouldn't." Samuel Houston shook his head, look down at his hands, which were large and calloused like his son's. "He says my fears are groundless. He thinks me addled as well as blind. Do you think me addled, Doctor? Do you think me mad?"

"You have given me no reason to think so."

Samuel Houston smiled agreeably. He sat up in bed and looked at William out of his sightless eyes. "Though my vision has failed, still I see."

William waited to hear the old man's explanation of this curious statement.

"I have heard that when sight is diminished, other senses become more...powerful."

"So it is believed, by some, not all," William said. He thought it was not an unreasonable assumption but he had not studied it, created experiments, which he would do before asserting that it was true.

The old man leaned forward, moving his body in William's direction. His voice fell to a whisper. "Sometimes, I see what the future holds."

William didn't know how to respond to this curious statement. Was the old man a witch, then, a teller of fortunes, some other creature with connections to the supernatural, or merely a very old, bed-ridden man losing his mind as well as his sight?

"I see things about people."

"What people? Neighbors, friends, people of name and renown?"

The old man laughed. "Hardly people of renown, Doctor. I know none such, being as I am, or at least was, a humble tiller of the soil."

"Friends then, people you know?"

"Or have merely met, whom I have sounded out."

"Sounded out?"

"Known quickly, come to understand them, and in so doing, come to know what might befall them."

A fortune-teller's trick. William thought not to find it here in a Surrey farmstead, and not from an old, bed-ridden blind man. What did he want from his curious knowledge? Was his motive money? That was what moved most of the tricksters. In London they were everywhere—sorcerers, prophets, soothsayers with their spells and enchantments. Even the nobility of England consulted them. Even the queen. Superstition didn't just exist in dark corners of the commonwealth, but even at the center of things; the universities, the Inns of Court, the throne of England itself.

"You have been kind to me, Doctor, even though you are not the one to help me. My son's concern for my blindness has its limits, as you have seen. The expense of curing me is too great for him, although the farm is prosperous, as you have also seen. It is a burden to have a son moved more by greed than charity for his old father, Doctor, but the burden has been long borne and I am thereby used to its weight upon my heart. But you have been honest with me, and as I say, kind. I would not have expected it, not from one from the great city. When you walked in the door of this room, I suddenly saw something, something dark. It was in my mind's eye, not the eyes in my face, you understand."

"What dark thing did you see?" William asked, not thinking for a moment that he had anything to fear from the old man's ramblings.

"You travel with two servants, you said."

"I do."

"I pray you keep them close at hand, Doctor. They may be of use to you. As I have said, the roads are dangerous. Robbers, thieves, dishonest men. They are everywhere. God help us, they are greater in number than honest men. Take it from one who knows, one who has lived among them."

William thanked the old man for his advice. It was, after all, advice that might be given any wayfarer. The roads were dangerous. Robbers and thieves were not uncommon. He himself had at one time been assaulted on a road, struck down, robbed, and had his face smashed into the cobbles until it had run with blood. It had happened in Chelmsford, not a quarter mile from the town market. It was an unpleasant memory, as was the larger circumstances of the robbery, a witch trial in which he had served as witness for the defense, been defamed, and nearly had his own life taken.

Being marooned on Little Livesey was, of course, worse. Every day he thought of it and willed himself to forget his terror and suffering. When he was at Cambridge studying to become a doctor, he had never thought his life would entail such misadventures, such risks to life and limb. But it had.

And where might it all end?

Forty-One

He was a doctor, a gentleman by his clothing, his speech, and his carriage. And so William was given a room in the farmer's house, upstairs, next to the room where the nubile daughters of the family slept, for he had no sooner entered and shut the door but he could hear the twitter of their voices through a wall he imagined no thicker than his thumb As silent as fence posts during the supper—overawed, he suspected, by their father's distinguished London guest—they now chattered in voices loud enough for him to hear through the common wall—an occasional word, tittering, an oath or two, then all quiet. They had been talking about him, he was sure of it, probably ridiculing him for his weather-beaten dishevelment or East Anglian accent, or his long thin legs like sticks.

It was spartan accommodation, much as he had expected, with hardly more than a bedstead and a candle to see his way, but he was grateful for it. Thomas and Geoffrey, mere servants, were to bed down in the barn with the horses. They were given a candle between them and told to mind they did not set the barn afire. William had paid eight pence for each of them. Equal pay for unequal accommodations, but that was the way of it. It was useless to object. William was glad they were out of the rain, in a dry and safe place, and the greedy farmer had not charged more.

He snuffed out the candle and stretched out in the darkness.

Exhausted, and cold despite the blanket he had been given, he was adrift in that mysterious space between sleep and awake, when he heard—or thought he heard—the door of his room open and then shut again. Then, the almost inaudible tread of bare feet and someone climbing into his bed beside him; the mattress he lay on yielding to the additional weight.

He dreamed it was Johane and became aroused by the image of her face, her body, her touch. He turned toward her and moved to embrace her but he was immediately aware that whoever his bedmate was, it was not Johane.

This body, naked as he could tell with every touch of the warm, smooth flesh, was indeed female, but plumper, bounteously so, slippery with sweat and bent on immediate gratification. He felt a bare leg thrown over his hip, and a mouth pressed upon him in a kiss that sucked breath out of him and was sour. He had never been intimate with Johane, but he knew this was not she. One of the farmer's daughters, he thought, the silent, nubile girls at the table. Quiet and demure maidens, but aggressive now, hungry for a husband, or just experience with a stranger.

He pushed away the face pressing against his own, and struck wildly with his fist, not with the intent to injure but to fend off the assault. He hit her face, or where he thought in the darkness her face was. He felt the impact of the blow, heard a sharp cry of pain, and then fleeing footsteps of the intruder and his door opened and slammed shut.

He was breathless, amazed, confused by what had just happened, unsure if he had dreamed it or really experienced it. His heart raced. He was thoroughly awake now. He would have lit the candle if he believed there was anything to see, but there would be nothing to see. His mysterious visitor was gone and would not return. He knew that. Aroused moments before by the thought of Johane, he was now almost breathless because of the encounter with a strange female. He struggled to catch his breath. Sitting up in bed and staring into the darkness, he thought of the three girls in the next room. Sleeping or awake now, his nocturnal visitor recounting perhaps to her sisters what had just happened and doubtless laughing about it. In his memory, they dissolved into a single person, a trinity of succubae.

He had read stories like this. A traveler asleep in a strange house or inn is visited by a woman, unknown to him or known but unrecognizable. She makes no secret of her amorous intent. She is bent on seduction, an adulterous coupling. In some stories the traveler responds as his unknown visitor desires, excited both by the physical charms of the visitor or the mere novelty of love with a stranger. In others, he resists, fearful perhaps that his visitor is a demon, a succubus, hungry not merely for his body but his very soul.

He knew he would not have disappointed Johane had it been she, not refused the offering, would have responded in kind.

He lay there thinking about her for some time, happy to have the alternative to the more recent memory of seduction. The thought of embracing one of the girls at table was repugnant to him. Doubtless they would find husbands in time, but he would not be among them, not seduced by their nakedness, their wantonness. Was every visitor to the farm offered such a dubious gift, or had he been chosen because he was a gentleman doctor, undoubtedly well-off, a good catch, and vulnerable in a strange house on a stormy night?.

He reminded himself that nothing had happened. There had been no coition, no fornication in the dark, only a clumsy one-sided attempt. The event had not been a dream, but a failed effort, not initiated by him. He turned his thoughts again to Johane. He felt a powerful desire for her, not only for her company which was ever a delight to him but also for her body, the pleasures of which he had yet to experience.

He fell asleep at last, not thinking of the unknown intruder but of the girl who had accompanied him to the island, his confederate in espionage, a girl who in the most recent of her letters had virtually declared her love for him. He carried the letter with him, next to his heart.

He woke at dawn, heard the voices of the sisters in the next room getting themselves up and dressed. Heard their mother's shrill voice calling them down. There was work to do in the kitchen, chores in the yard. *Lazy sluts*, the mother called them. The London doctor and his servants would want breakfast before they continued on their way.

William wasn't hungry. His night's adventure had cut his sleep short. He dressed himself, thinking he did not want breakfast, did not want to see the faces of the farmer's daughters and sit at table speculating as to which had been his seductress. In truth, he didn't care. He wasn't even curious. He yearned to be on his way, to see the farm retreating behind him. To get on to the island and see Johane.

He was coming down the stairs when the farmer appeared and grasped his arm, asked how he slept in a loud, obstreperous voice and bid him come eat before William could say a word. William let himself be led into the kitchen as the night before. The farmer sat at the head, two of the three daughters were present but they looked so alike to him that he could not tell whether they were sitting in the same order as the night before or not. Bowls and cups had been set at each place. Hot pottage and milk, William supposed. That would fill their bellies well enough until nightfall. The mother was bent over the fire stirring something, one of the girls was by her side. William could not see the face of either. Then the hulking son with the calloused hands came stomping into the room with Thomas and Geoffrey in tow.

"I had to wake these two up," he snorted contemptuously.

His two servants looked at William and grinned sheepishly. Thomas still had straw on his coat and looked half asleep. Geoffrey had washed his face in cold water from the well; William could tell by the color of his cheeks.

The third daughter came to the table. None of the three looked at William, but kept their heads down. No grace was said. Everyone began to eat, except for the farmer's wife, who still stirred a pot. The farmer had been voluble the night before but said little now except to make occasional snorting noses of approval or disapproval. Then suddenly he said, "I thank you, Doctor, for examining my father's eyes. You do agree, do you not, that his condition is beyond help and he will go to his grave as sightless as he now is?"

"That is likely," William said. "Save a surgeon removes the cataracts. Even then, the operation is risky. Some patients see afterwards, others do not, and some die of it."

"Some die of it," the farmer repeated.

"I have known some to do. It is not an operation I perform myself, as I said last night." William thought the grandfather was possibly still asleep. Blind as he was, there would have been no pressing reason for him to rise this early in the morning.

"Well," said the farmer, "All's God's will, is it not? My father is blind, then God has made him so, and I would not want my good wishes for the recovery of his sight to run counter to what the Almighty has ordained in His wisdom."

"And the procedure is expensive," William commented drily, but without effect on the farmer's pious expressiveness.

The farmer summoned his wife. "Wife, come eat with us. Breakfast is getting cold, what's left of it." He scowled at his daughters, who had fed ravenously as they had done likewise the night before.

William could now see the round fleshy faces of the girls. All plain and plump and unbruised as before. He was sure he had heard his fist hit home, encounter solid bone, and he had heard a sharp cry of pain, not just surprise. Had his midnight visitor been a dream after all?

The mother did not respond. Her daughters and son got up and left the table, the son grumbling about something William could not hear. The father got up and walked to his wife where she stood, threw an arm around her and led her back to the table. She kept her face down, resisting her husband but without success. She was a domineering wife and a scold, but her husband was physically stronger. He whipped her around and dragging her over to the table where William sat, forced her to look at William.

Her swollen left eye was black and blue.

"My wife's hurt herself, Doctor, as you can see. She says she got up in the middle of the night to answer a call of nature and bumped into the wall." He laughed.

"I'm sorry to hear that," William said, avoiding the woman's gaze.

"Well, it happens from time to time, does it not, Doctor?" The farmer said.

"I believe it does."

The farmer snorted contemptuously and pulled his wife away. He lifted her chin up to his and held it in a tight grip. William could see the woman wince with pain. He spoke to William, but kept his eyes fixed on hers. "At least, that's the story she told me, but to be honest, Doctor, I don't know if it be true or no. I mean, how she came by this bruise." This time he did not laugh. The farmer turned suddenly to William with cold eyes.

William didn't know what to say, so he said nothing. The farmer pushed his wife back toward the stove, and then went out into the yard after his son and daughters.

William stared at his plate. He had eaten but half of what was there, and he was left with a bitter taste in his mouth. For a moment, he couldn't speak. He could hardly apologize to the woman for striking her, or upbraid her for her licentiousness. He could only pretend what had happened during the night had not.

It was the option he chose, for want of a better one.

"Thank your husband for his courtesy," William said to the woman.

She said nothing in response, stared at him blankly, wearing her bruised eye as a kind of badge, defying him to explain himself or the cause of her injury, at least in her husband's presence. William motioned to Thomas and Geoffrey that they should go.

"What was that all about, Doctor?" Thomas asked as they crossed the muddy yard to where the horses were.

"Nothing you need to know about, Thomas. The poor woman is unhappily yoked. Her husband's a brute. We're well gone from this place and will endure any weather before we'll stop here again."

But William wondered if the farmer knew more what had happened in the night than he let on, and he wondered if it had happened before to lodgers at the house, but with different results.

Forty-Two

The three of them hadn't traveled more than a mile or two before he heard the riders coming up behind them. He sensed trouble even before he turned to look. Even his horse sensed it. He could see the riders approaching at a gallop, and then he recognized them, at least two of them. It was the farmer and his son and two other men he didn't recognize. Their faces were hard and threatening. He didn't know whether to rein in and wait or run for it. But then it was too late. They were surrounded.

The farmer hailed William, his voice raw with anger. It went through William's mind: had the farmer's wife admitted what had happened, told a different story? His question was immediately answered.

The farmer said, "You violated my wife, Doctor. Abused my hospitality. And for that you must pay."

The son echoed his father's threat in viler phrases, calling William a *ravisher*, a *lecher*, a *fiend*.

"I did no such thing, Master Houston. If she says I did, your wife lies."

"Then how did she get that black eye? She says you gave it to her."

William hesitated before answering. The farmer's son and the other men looked at him angrily and he saw now that they were armed. Each wore a knife at his belt, and the son's weapon was the longest and most threatening.

"She came to my room while I was asleep. She woke me when she climbed in bed with me. Maybe she was confused about which room it was, which bed, took me for you, Master Houston."

William didn't believe that for a moment, but he thought it might give him, the wife and the husband a way out.

"So why did you strike her?"

"I was taken by surprise, awakened from sleep. I didn't know who it was, who'd come into the bed."

The farmer looked at him skeptically. "You knew it was a woman, didn't you?"

"Yes, I could tell that." William recalled vividly the touch of the woman's body, moist, fleshy. Yes, there had been no doubt about the sex of his visitor.

"Not very convincing, Doctor," the son snarled. "You tried to rape my mother. That's what she's told us. When she had entered where you were by mistake."

William glanced at the servants accompanying him. They were looking at him with confusion in their faces, and some fear as well. Did they believe these false charges against their master? The farmer was the very image of the outraged husband, the cuckold, the wronged party. Their master was a respectable gentleman, but perhaps beneath, a common lecher, a ravisher of other men's wives.

"My wife is a good woman, Doctor," the farmer cried. "She would not bear a false witness were she to die for it. You took advantage of her, ripped off her gown."

"She came naked to where I lay. I did not disrobe her," William said.

Suddenly, Thomas spoke. "I've been Doctor Gilbert's servant for almost three years. I know him well. He would never do such a thing as your wife accuses him of."

"You would say that," the son spat out angrily, glaring first at Thomas, then back at William. "It's the doctor that pays your wage. He might as well have had his mother here to proclaim his innocence." The son moved in closer to William until the noses of their horses touched and William could smell the sour breath of the son, the bad teeth, the swollen gums.

The conflict was interrupted for a few moments as another group of riders passed, laughing and swearing, They glanced at William and the farmers, but showed only minor curiosity about what was keeping such a group in the middle of a narrow muddy road. The farmer and his company said nothing until the other men passed. Then the attack began again. William was breathing heavily, the son was pushing his face forward, his hand on the hilt of the knife.

"The question, Doctor—if you are really one—is what are you going to do about it?"

"What do you mean, *do about it?*" William shot back. "I did nothing wrong. You gave me a bed, for which I thank you. I gave you money in exchange, for my lodging and for my men. Your mother came into my room, either by accident or design."

"By design?" the father exclaimed. "Are you calling my wife a whore?"

"I call your wife nothing more than your wife, sir. I am only saying that I did nothing to invite or provoke her. She was naked when she entered my room, naked when she slipped into my bed, and no less virtuous when she left than when she entered."

"I am tired of his damnable lies," the son shouted at his father. He pointed an accusing finger at William. "He violated my mother and your wife and must pay for it."

There was a moment of silence. On one side of the road was a spacious field—barley, he thought—on the other side woods; thick, perhaps even impenetrable. They were far, he knew, from the next village. Certainly far from any help.

William steeled himself against the attack he knew was coming. He could see it in the son's eyes, full of hatred and desire for revenge. If he managed to avoid the son's thrust, he would ride hard, but he knew escape would be nearly impossible. His two servants were not armed, his antagonists fully so. For a moment he thought about Johane. He would never arrive at Livesey. What she had called her worst fears would be realized at last. He would be dead and buried, probably secretly, in the woods or the desolate field. His two servants would meet the same fate. The farmer and his son would feel justified, the adulterous wife vindicated. Until the next guest at the house, who might not take a swing at her but enjoy what pleasures her body afforded.

All of this passed through his mind in a second.

"You must pay for what you've done, Doctor," the husband said, more calmly. "It comes to that. If you do, we might let you pass on your way."

So this is what it is, William thought, watching the eyes of the son. Not a killer's eyes now, sweeping to his revenge, but a dealer—father and son, and whoever the two scoundrels were who accompanied them and looked on at the exchange of accusations and denials with mild amusement. They'd seen this all before, he suddenly realized. A no doubt frequent performance. Blackhart Farm was not much more than a bawdy house with extortion as its purpose. He wondered if the daughters too were put to work.

He began to breathe easier. He glanced at Thomas and his cousin. They still looked frightened, sat on their horses uneasily, Thomas gripping the packhorse with its cargo of magnets and equipment.

"You want money…as compensation for your loss, the violation of your wife's chastity?"

He put it the way his lawyer father would, coldly, as a simple transaction, something for something, the law mediating between the bargainers. The alleged assault would be treated not as a crime to be punished but a bargain to be struck, a wrong to be absolved in coin of the realm.

"We can start with that," the son said, now obviously in charge of the matter. The father sat watching it all, his face blank as if the transaction now had nothing to do with him, was fully and properly in his son's hands.

The son looked at the packhorse. "What's in the bags you carry, Doctor?"

"Nothing of value, nothing that would interest you," William answered. "You can have what's in my purse and whatever my servants have with them. You can take it and go. I admit to nothing you've charged me with, but understand we are outnumbered and are not armed."

"More fool you," the son said, suddenly bursting into cruel laughter. He swiveled around and looked at the two men who had come with him, men who were also armed with knives and were smiling now with the same cruel faces as the son as though they were taking their cues from him. These was merriment in their eyes, delight in intimidating the travelers, the London doctor. Now the dispute was all about compensation. No one was to die that morning in the road. William saw it all. They would be allowed to go on, without their money, without the precious lodestones in the pack. And if that were the outcome, they might as well return to London.

William's relief was replaced with a seething anger. He saw all this moral outrage now for what it surely was, a show in which farmer and wife were surely involved. It was a like a play, more comic than tragic, for although it was William who was the victim, not the perpetrator of any crime or wrong, the heroes were the extorters, the fabricators of the trick. It was they who would receive the acclaim of the audience for their cleverness, deception, a nice trick on the London gentleman with his gentlemanly airs.

"Let us see what's in the packs," the son said. He motioned to one of his friends to go forward to see. William nodded to Thomas, who surrendered the packhorse. William watched as the pack was removed. Then suddenly, Thomas broke from the circle and bolted off. In a second his cousin followed at a mad gallop. William was alone.

"Let the vermin go," the son cried to his fellows who looked ready to pursue the fleeing men. "They'll have little more than the shirts upon them. Cowards all. We have here what we want with the good doctor."

Thomas and his cousin soon disappeared over the rise.

At this, William felt not so much abandoned and betrayed by his companions as relieved. While he worried about his own safety, he worried as well about that of his servants. They had come with him at his behest, on a mission they had no understanding of, and had they been killed by the men, their deaths would have been on his head. It would have been a fate they didn't deserve.

He looked down. One of the farmer's son's confederates had the pack off the horse and on the ground and was opening it, pulling from it the spool and bracket, throwing them aside into the mud. He pulled out the lodestones and unwrapped them, throwing them aside as well. "It's all metal bars and wood, worthless stuff," he proclaimed, turning his head up to the son.

"Cut his purse," the father said. It had been a while since the father had said anything. William had almost forgotten about him, the brooding cuckold, now turned robber.

William handed over the purse. It was fine-tooled Spanish leather and he had paid a goodly sum for it. It was worth more than the money it held. He did not remember how much money he was carrying, but he always had money hidden in the lining of his traveling cloak, or in a secret compartment of his satchel. He had made it a practice to do so ever since he was robbed in Chelmsford a few years earlier. At least this time he might escape a beating, or worse, if he was lucky.

"The iron and the wood may be worth something," the father said.

His son scoffed and cursed and said it might be useful to weigh the London doctor down until he drowned. The younger Houston's face was full of malice. William wondered if the son really believed his mother was an innocent victim of William's lust, or knew quite well she was a fraud—she and her husband, the whole family. The younger Houston picked up one of the bars and held it tightly in his fist.

"I would beware of doing that, sir," William said.

"Why, Doctor, are you going to try to take it away from me?"

He held the bar with one hand and pulled his knife from its sheath. He pointed it at William. William imagined a quick thrust, one he could not defend against and would end him here in this Surrey wilderness. He thought quickly.

"Those aren't mere iron bars," he said.

"Not iron? I know iron when I see it," the younger Houston scoffed.

"They are lodestones, magnets."

The father said, looking at his son, "May they not then be of greater value?"

"They are of greater value indeed, especially to them who are sick," William said.

"Sick of what?" the son asked.

"Sick of the plague," William said.

For a few moments William's assailants stood silent. Then the father spoke.

"How valuable? What does it do?"

William said, "Magnets can draw that which causes one to suffer from the plague out of the body."

It was the rumor his father had once asked about and William had cast aside as a false belief, but he could read the fear in the faces of his assailants and knew that false though it be, it might prove his salvation—and the salvation of his magnets.

"I've never heard that," the father said, his face white, his hands trembling. He told his son to drop the magnet he was holding. He told him a second time. The son obeyed the father, letting the bar drop in the mud.

"It is a new discovery of their use, the magnets I mean. The magnets are fixed to the sufferer's body. The poison of the plague is drawn out of the body and then absorbed into the magnet itself. But after, it is important that the magnets be covered, infused as they are with the plague."

Hearing this, two men stepped back. The father whispered something

William couldn't hear, a prayer perhaps, or a curse. The son returned his knife to the sheath.

"I've touched the bar." The son cried. "I've touched the damnable bar." He turned to his father, his face a mask of terror and desperation. His lips moved but nothing came out.

"Yes, you have," William said. "You've touched it. Which means the plague…"

"What can I do?" the son cried, his terrified eyes fixed on William.

"Lie down, rest, sleep," William said. "It may help. It has helped some. Wine helps, claret is the best."

"I think, Doctor, you are making all this up, this story of the plague," the father said, glaring at William.

"The use of magnets to extract poisonous substances from the body is attested to by many an ancient authority," William said, in his lecturer's voice. "I might mention Galen, the Roman doctor, and… Meretricious, he who was accounted like unto him. You've heard of those persons and places, have you not, Master Houston?"

Houston said he had, although it was clear to William the man had not. Galen had said nothing of the kind, and as for Meretricious, William had made up the name and therefore Meretricious had no opinion at all in the matter.

"Still, I don't believe it."

William detected the uncertainty in the farmer's voice. "Well, then you risk a great deal, don't you, in touching these magnets? Look, Master Houston, you and your fellows have my purse. Consider that as sufficient compensation for any indignity your wife may have suffered by mistakenly stumbling into my bed, and then let me pass, for God's sake and the queen's."

For a moment, father and son and their two fellows said nothing. They seemed dumbfounded and too terrified to speak. Finally, the son said, in a much less assertive voice than before, "But I've already touched the… magnets. What will happen now, Doctor? I beg you to tell me, for I've seen what befalls those with the plague and would not die before my time."

"Undoubtedly, the pestilence has passed from the magnets to you," William said, giving the youth a false look of sympathy. "I'm sorry, I can do nothing for you. I suggest you go home and pray. You are in heaven's hands, not mine. But for your father and mother's sake, do not touch them or they will share the same fate."

His assailants rode off as hurriedly as they had come. He watched them grow smaller and smaller until they topped a hill and disappeared on the other side. They had taken his purse but left the magnets, the bracket and the hoist, the steel cable. He had his horse, his satchel with the hidden money, and the pack horse.

He spent the next little while repacking the magnets and worrying that the Houstons, father and son, and their friends would realize they had been deceived and come back, angrier than before, more dangerous than before. Knives would be out again, and this time they would be used.

As a doctor, it was his duty to heal and console. Here, he had done the opposite. He had instilled terror with a falsehood, undone his enemies, and sent them flying. He had violated his oath. It did not set well with him on reflection, but then the device had saved his magnets, maybe even his life. Maybe that evened the score, made what he had done allowable in the scheme of things.

But then he was on his way again, the packhorse with its precious cargo behind him. He traveled most of the day, and slowly his fears of pursuit vanished. He imagined his servant and his cousin back in London, explaining to whomever what had happened to the young master at a farmhouse in Surrey. He didn't blame them for running. He would blame them however if they revealed the thing he was accused of, violating the farmer's wife. Had they believed it, despite witnessing the doctor's resolute denial? They had seen the farmer's wife—no great beauty there to inspire lustful thoughts, much less acts, and yet, one never knew. There was no logic in what drew a man to a woman or woman to man. Attraction was unfathomable, more a mystery than the design of the heavens or the depths of the sea. Still, If his servant gossiped, or his cousin, and it spread around the city, it would not serve him well. What would his colleagues think? What would his father think? And, even more important to him now, what would Johane think, should she hear of it? Would she think of him as a common lecher, another Broderick, an assaulter of women, a liar and betrayer?

William rode on, the packhorse behind him. He would not stop now.

He would ride through the night if needed. When he stopped again, he would be on Livesey. Johane had said Broderick was gone. He assumed Broderick's flunkies, Browne and Locke, had gone with him.

A safe harbor now, God willing.

Forty-Three

By the time he crossed the causeway to the island he was half asleep in the saddle, swaying like a drunken man, gripping the reins of his horse with all his might and occasionally drifting off, images of the duplicitous farmer and his son in his head, along with occasional appearances of Johane. More of the latter, thankfully, as he drew closer.

Before dawn he passed through the village, and by the first rays of light he stood at the door of the manor house and knocked, having put his horses in the stable and concealed his precious cargo beneath a stack of hay, since he was not prepared to explain what this cargo was or its purpose. At least, not yet. Not until he had confirmed all that Johane had said in her letter.

It was a while before there was an answer. Harris opened the door to him, dressed not in livery as before but in a suit of good clean clothes in somber colors. William surmised that Harris had succeeded Broderick as steward to his master. Harris had impressed him as a decent sort, probably a good choice for Broderick's replacement, but then who could have been worse?

Harris looked at William without surprise, his lips parted in a kind of smile. "Good morning, Doctor Gilbert. Her ladyship said you would be arriving today, or at least in the next few days. We are most happy to see you again, to see that you are well, and not dead or vanished into thin air as reported."

"I was reported dead?"

"Yes, Doctor. Broderick said as much. Sir Arthur and his lady believed it."

"And did Master Broderick say how I died?" William had to ask.

"Drowning, if I remember, Doctor. He said you were walking along the beach and fell into the water, or were caught up in the tide and carried out to sea. It has happened before."

"Well, as you can see, Harris, I am very much alive. Master Broderick was mistaken, or he underestimated my ability to swim. I'm told he's left the island."

"He has, Doctor. He was dismissed by my master at Lady Challoner's behest. I saw him leave the island with my own eyes."

"He left in good humor, I suppose?"

"Hardly, sir. No dismissed servant leaves his lord's house in good humor. He cursed us all, Sir Arthur and his lady, indeed, the whole household. In truth, Doctor, none has missed him. He rode roughshod over us all, curried favor where it was to his advantage, and would not leave the girls alone, especially Lady Challoner's nurse."

"You mean Mistress Sheldon."

"The same. I saw him at her many a time before he left, and it was such attentions that made Lady Challoner urge Sir Arthur to let him go."

"I hope all you are well in the house," William said.

"Oh, Doctor, we are a sad house, at this hour."

"Wherefore?"

"Lady Challoner must tell you, sir."

"Tell me what?"

Harris didn't answer.

William followed the new steward up the stairs, expecting at any moment to see John Broderick again, stepping out of the shadows to declare he had never left, or was back to plague William the more.

He was surprised to find the lady of the manor out of bed and fully dressed, but dressed in mourning clothes. Mildred Challoner wore black well. It made her pale face luminous in the dim light. He saw too that the heavy drapes that had covered the window of the room were pulled back, showing an exhilarating view of the sea below.

"My lady." William bowed and followed her direction to a chair.

Before he could ask what the occasion of her mourning was, she told him outright. "I am sorry to say, Doctor, that my husband suffered a reversal in his health, not long after you disappeared. He has died but a few days ago. His funeral was yesterday. He now lies buried in the family crypt with other lords of this island."

"I am most sorry to hear it, my lady."

"Had you been here, Doctor, perhaps he could have been saved—or at least his life extended a few days, or even months."

William listened for the tone of reproach in her voice but detected none. She did not blame him then.

Her eyes filled with tears. William leaned toward her and took her hands in his. Her hands were like ice. He could see that her grief was real, not feigned.

"It was indeed only a matter of time, my lady. I could relieve his pain, but not rebuild a weakened heart."

She said she understood. She said her husband had died in his sleep.

"He could not have asked for a more peaceful death, then, to stand before the Maker even before one is aware."

She continued to talk about her husband—not his passing now, but his merits as a husband. It was a different account that she had given before, when she spoke of Sir Arthur as a domineering person, causing her to play the invalid that she not seem healthier, more vital, than he; a silliness she tolerated while he lived. All that seemed forgotten now in her sorrow at his passing.

"And you, Doctor? While I am most happy to see you again, you see now that I am hale and strong... I have no need of a physician."

"I can see that, lady. You do look well, but then you always were. May I ask about Johane, Mistress Sheldon?"

"Oh, she's here. Or will be here soon. I sent her into the village on an errand. You will see her soon. I know she is most anxious to see you, to confirm with her own eyes that you are alive and well. She told me so. By the way, Doctor, perhaps you have already noticed. There have been changes at the manor since you left us."

"Changes, lady?"

"For one, John Broderick is gone and gone for good," she said. "It was the last act of my husband before his death, to send that vile man packing. I think I told you once how much I detested and feared him. I finally persuaded my husband to do the right thing, for my sake as well as the sake of the women of the household, upon whom he was constantly pressing himself. I think he also stole from the accounts. There was a good deal of money missing, unaccounted for. I think that was what impressed my husband the most. He could have abided

Broderick's lechery, but not his larceny. Anyway, Broderick is now history."

William admitted that he had found the former secretary unpleasant and suspicious. "I found him once pressing his attentions on Mistress Johane, but prevented it."

"And you were right to do so, Doctor. Johane was not the only one. I had complaints from one of the kitchen help as well, a young girl no more than twelve or thirteen years."

He thought of the girl in the kitchen he had talked to. A lovely child, innocent. Easy prey for one of Broderick's proclivities.

"You met her?"

"Once. But you said *changes*, madam, I'm presuming it is not only Broderick who has been replaced."

"Ah, yes, well, in addition to my now being no longer bed-ridden and confined, I have decided to fulfill an old dream of my husband's, which is to rebuild the tower his grandfather first began, Maxwell's Tower. It will be a monument to him. And a new chapel as well. It was, indeed, his final wish that he be buried there. I have told Harris to hire stonemasons to assure the foundation is secure. Let me show you my drawing. It expresses my plan."

She moved away from chair to a wardrobe, and opened it to reveal within a chest of drawers. From the top of this she took a rolled parchment, unfolded it, and laid it out before him.

It was a crude drawing, lines vertical and horizontal, done by one with little architectural talent, presumably Mildred Challoner herself. He recognized Maxwell's Tower, at least in its present form, but there was another structure next to it, an extension. William asked about it.

"That will be the chapel," the lady said. "It will be where my husband's body will eventually lie. Beneath the floor. When I pass, I will join him there." She said this happily, as if the reunion would be joyous. The two of them, side by side, beneath the floor, stepped on by casual visitors. Perhaps it *would* be joyous, although William's impression of her affection for her husband had been otherwise—a stoic tolerance of his curious demands—all now apparently forgotten in his passing.

She folded the parchment and walked to the window. She stood there, staring out like a pilot estimating the distance to land.

"When will the construction begin?" William asked, if only to break what had become an awkward silence.

"It has already begun," she said, her back still to him. "I ordered the work to begin the day my husband died. The stonemasons have come from the mainland, which is not cheap by any means. He who is head mason told me it will take a month or more to lay the foundation of the chapel. As you can see from my drawing, the chapel entrance will be from the base of the tower. When finished, it will be a single structure, and will look as if it had always been thus."

"Will it be a private chapel?"

She turned at this and looked at him directly, as if the answer to his question was obvious to any rational being.

"Of course. What interest would the people in the village have in it? They have the church, St. Andrews, if they must needs worship God or hear the gospel preached. The chapel will be for me, for the household, for my family that may now come to visit me here."

William imagined the chapel that Mildred Challoner conceived. If he read her plan aright, it would cover the ground where Tobias Wincott's hut had been, where he had hidden—not successfully—the more valuable of his discoveries. William's memories of that place were not pleasant. It was where the earlier secretary, the one before Broderick, was murdered. It held the tower from which Tobias Wincott's body had been hurled. The tower in which he had taken refuge on the night he escaped from Little Livesey, his body shaking with cold, and he wondering if, having survived the swim from the island, he would also survive the night. Mildred Challoner might think of it as a fitting memorial to her husband. For William it had all the appeal of a mausoleum.

"I think your husband will be pleased that you carried out his wishes," William said, if only to say something. Mildred Challoner seemed to have fallen into a trance, staring wordlessly at the sea before her. Was she thinking of her late husband, or something else?

A soft tapping came at the door. Without turning from the window, Mildred Challoner said, "Enter".

It was Johane.

Forty-Four

Like Harris, whose elevation in the house was signaled first by a new, or at least better, suit of clothing, Johane appeared not as maidservant with black skirt and white cap, but as an upper servant in pearl-buttoned bodice and worsted skirt in sad colors, her dark hair flowing below her shoulders. She wore a necklace, silver, with a pendant that was circular, with a stone in the middle. In the half-light he could not tell what gem it was. She was radiant. Somehow, he knew these were gifts from her new mistress; her own clothes, her own jewels, bestowed upon Johane. Seeing him, she smiled, and William felt his desire for her run through him like a hot flood.

"Doctor Gilbert," Mildred Challoner said. "May I introduce to you my new companion—nurse no more, since I was never sick to begin with. But Johane has consented to serve me as my personal companion, my secretary."

"Is that true, Johane?" William asked.

"It is, Doctor. Lady Challoner has been most gracious to me, in advancing me to a higher state, where I pray I may serve ably and fulfill all expectations."

William looked at Johan, uncomprehendingly. She smiled thinly and then, when her mistress turned away, she raised a hand to William, bidding him be patient.

A secret signal, he was sure of it. He breathed a sigh of relief. She was still with him, still involved in the search. In an instant, he saw her strategy. With Sir Arthur dead and his widow without complaint, Johane would have been sent away. Like William, she would have been redundant. Her new appointment gave her reason to stay, long enough to recover what they both still sought.

"Doctor Gilbert," Mildred Challoner said. "You've traveled all the way from London and for no reason, it would seem, since I have no need of a physician or a nurse. But please be a guest here, stay the week if you will, to rest before returning. Johane, of course, will not return with you."

She advanced toward Johane and put her arm around her lovingly, as though the two were mother and daughter, and they did seem to resemble each other, if not in coloring, Lady Challoner being the lighter of skin, but in expression.

"You are most gracious, lady. My journey here was somewhat of an ordeal."

It was an understatement. He knew it when he said it. With the memory returning of the farmer and his son, the dangerous encounter on the road, he was exhausted. He had ridden almost all of the day before and through the night. His weariness must have been obvious; on his face, in his dusty, sweat-stained clothes. He realized he was hungry, starving. He suddenly felt physically weak, as though his legs wouldn't hold him up.

"And we will provide you with a better room than before. Not that terrible closet Broderick stuck you in," Lady Challoner said.

"I think the doctor needs to eat," Johane said, taking him by the arm. "When did you eat last, Doctor?"

"Yesterday, at breakfast."

"Then you are past due for meat and drink. I'll show you to your new room later. For now, the kitchen."

He followed her down the stairs. They did not speak; they would not speak of what was important, not yet.

It was too late for breakfast, and hours before a mid-day meal would be ready, but the cooks found something for him to eat among the breakfast leavings and it was enough. Johane sat with him, but still there was no talk of their secret purpose, nor did she confirm his interpretation of her signals to him that all was as before, despite what Lady Challoner had called the "changes in the house."

William enjoyed Johane's company even more than the food. It was, after all, what he had dreamed about. But he was eager to tell her all that had happened, his island misadventure, his journey to London and back. He wasn't sure he would tell her about the Surrey farmer, his lascivious wife, and the attempted robbery. The false accusations against him still stung. It was enough that he had brought the magnets Johane had requested and that they were safely concealed in the stable.

"Come, Doctor, walk with me," she said, when he had devoured what was put before him and felt himself a whole man again.

She led him into the ragged garden and into the little copse of trees. It was where he had, weeks earlier, interrupted Broderick's attempt to assail her—a most unpleasant memory, he was sure, for them both—but it had at least the virtue of being as private a place as was in the house. He looked to her to see if the memory of that event lingered enough for her to choose another place for their conversation, but it had not. There was a stone seat there, overgrown with weeds, but enough surface to sit on.

"I accepted my mistress's position so I could stay. I tell you, William, we are on the verge of a great discovery, which I spoke of in my letter. And when I have accomplished that, I assure you I will return to London... with you."

"Your mistress believes you will stay."

"She shall be disappointed, then, I promise you. I want nothing more than to fulfill my obligation to his lordship—and my promise to you, of course."

He told her he wanted to know everything, everything that she had discovered and everything that had happened to her in his absence. He had been hungry for food before. He was even more hungry for information now.

"We have found the Jews' treasure, Solomon's gold," she said triumphantly, her eyes alight. "Or at least, I believe so."

"Where?"

"The stonemasons who are building the new chapel discovered it, but did not know what they discovered. It's a hole in the earth, a hole beneath the foundation of the chapel Lady Challoner's having built. It's a miracle, William! Had Sir Arthur not died, Lady Challoner would not have commissioned the new structure. It's a hole, a hole in the earth. A hole too narrow for a man to descend into, but when the sun is right, or a lamp is lowered, you can see from above the glittering."

"The glittering?"

"Gold, or the appearance thereof. Cups, plates, swords, chains, I know not what. I'm sure we've found what we and Lord Burghley are looking for. It's where Tobias Wincott had his hut. The hut was built atop it, right over it, ruins that were there before the tower was built."

"Ruins that were there before the shipwreck?" William said, finding it hard to contain his excitement. "And after all the years of searching, he never knew how close he was to what he sought. Does Lady Challoner know of it?"

"Yes and no," Johane said. "She knows the ruins of the old Roman fort are being uncovered, what was there when Maxwell built his tower. She knows there are passages going down to a sea cave, the stonemasons told her that. What she *doesn't* know is about the treasure, for which I suspect she cares little. She's obsessed with building a chapel in memory of her husband. She said she wanted the holes filled."

"Are you sure it's there?"

"Look at this. You tell me, if aught is there to bring up."

She reached into the folds of her skirt and pulled out a bracelet. It had been designed for a woman with a very small wrist and it had the appearance of gold. It was inscribed with a Latin phrase from a Roman poet, if his memory served.

"This was found on the first day of the excavation."

"By whom?"

"By me. I walked among the workmen, some of whom had been recruited from the manor's household. They were dredging up earth and I saw it glitter, picked it up when no one noticed, concealed it well."

"Do you remember where you found it, the exact hole?"

"Your magnets will tell us. Several of the passages, they look like chimneys, vertical and narrow, too narrow for a man to squirm into, but wide enough to admit a load of magnets, which I trust you brought with you."

"I did." He told her where he had hidden them.

"Then tomorrow we will go fishing for whatever's down there, let the magnets do their work. We can let the magnets down into the chimneys."

He could see in her face that she was as excited about the prospect as he. Her finding the bracelet gave promise that more could be discovered in the same ground, but as yet nothing was certain. His instincts told him the effort was well worth it. Besides, it gave him chance to see Johane again, to work by her side, to conspire together.

"It must be at night," she said, "our work. After the stonemasons and the diggers have done for the day."

"Of course," he said. "At night it shall be."

Forty-Five

His new accommodations in the manor, as promised, were better. He now occupied a larger, more spacious room next to that of the late Sir Arthur. The room connected to it, he was sure. There was a real bed, solid, canopied, with a mattress of goose feathers. A serving man, whom William didn't remember from his last visit, was there to make sure there was fire, oil lamps—not just candle stubs—blankets. He slept that night like a dead man himself and didn't wake until nearly eight o'clock, later than he had ever slept before.

He joined Lady Challoner for breakfast in the great hall. Now in full control of her schedule, she needed no more to eat in her room like a convalescent. He was pleased to see the lady of the manor had invited Johane, as well. While servants saw to their needs, Lady Challoner spent most of time talking to Johane about her plans for the manor house. It appeared her late husband had a good deal more money than she had thought. Inheriting it all, she was now determined to make repairs in the house. To "brighten things up," she said. The house, she felt, was much too dark and gloomy, a house of shadows and painful memories. Johane gave her ideas, Mildred Challoner said. Johane had served in great houses in London, she had an eye for design, for what was in fashion. "She's been at Theobalds, Lord Burghley's house, isn't that true, Johane?"

Johane nodded.

He would have liked to talk to Johane alone, but he knew it would be impossible now, with Mildred Challoner sitting there. Later they would talk, perhaps in the copse again. Certainly, toward evening when the laborers and stonemasons were done for the day and the recovery of the treasure was to begin.

In his room later in the morning, he thought about Johane's words. Chimneys, she had called them, vertical shafts reaching down into a subterranean chamber, carved out by the sea, filled with water. A sea cave, the entrance to which had been sealed by rubble when Maxwell's Tower was built, built upon the foundation of the old Roman fort. He imagined a sequence of events that made sense to him. Jewish treasure concealed in the sea cave, accessed by the cave's opening. Then, two centuries later, blocked when the earlier lord of Livesey built a tower upon the ruins above. Now to be accessed through the narrow shafts, if to be accessed at all.

His magnets, bound together to increase their power, would be put to a test. He knew magnetic power was not unlimited. There might be more below than his magnets could lift. But wasn't the experiment worth the effort?

It crossed his mind that since the tower and the chapel to be were on Challoner land, Lady Mildred might have some claim to treasure buried beneath, or at least some right. But then he remembered Lord Burghley had told him that since the treasure was stolen property, the current lord or lady of the island must surrender it to its rightful owners, and since the original owners were long dead and their posterity impossible to track, it would naturally come to the crown.

These thoughts put to rest any reservation he might have had about depriving Mildred Challoner of what she might claim as her own. Burghley knew about these matters, probably William's own father did as well. These were all matters of law, not moral right or wrong. He would abide by their judgment.

They made their way by lantern light, like the conspirators they were, not along the beach, the way he had first come there, but over land and through the marsh, a way Johane had discovered. William led the pack horse with its burden of equipment. When they arrived it was fully dark.

"How did you get out from under Lady Challoner's thumb?" William asked her as they walked.

"I told her I had a terrible headache. She insisted I take to my bed."

"She's a kind mistress," William said.

"Too kind, perhaps."

He asked her what she meant.

"I do think she loves me."

"I'm sure she does," he said.

She stopped and turned toward him. Because she led the way it was she who bore the lantern. Her face took on a serious look, which was difficult for him to read.

"She loves me in a way I would not wish to be loved—at least by another woman," she said. "Let's hurry, William. Time is precious to us. The water in the chimneys rises and falls with the tide. The rubble from the Roman fort prevents a man from coming in, but not the water."

Suddenly they were there, at the base of the tower, and an acre or more cleared of marsh grass and what remained of Tobias Wincott's wretched hut. It resembled in the darkness an unfurrowed field, leveled for the construction to come. William imagined the foundation of the projected chapel, the stone walls rising, redeeming the emptiness, then the beams, and at some future time a slab upon which doubtless the effigy of the late lord of the island would rest, face upward toward the rafters.

He imagined Mildred Challoner and the household worshipping there. He remembered that Livesey had no priest. One would have to be brought in, perhaps the same cleric who occasionally served in the village church.

Johane showed him where the shafts were, what she had called the chimneys. There were four of them. She had covered the openings with rushes but marked their place with sticks, inconspicuous sprigs, cuttings, the significance of which only she could identify. While she held the lantern above him, he knelt down in the soft soil and brushed away the covering, revealing a roundish shaft, no wider in its circumference than two or three feet. Below, all was darkness, although he thought he could hear water like a whisper coming up from the shaft. He thought he could even smell it, but perhaps that was only his imagination.

He unleashed the equipment from the pack horse, then set up the hoist. The cable was, he reckoned, about thirty feet in length, maybe a bit longer. The magnets were in a separate bag, like a large leather purse. These he removed. There were six bars; these he bound in two straps with buckles, making of them one magnet, which he attached to the cable, using sailor's knots to secure them. "I think we're ready," he said.

The pack of magnets disappeared into the darkness of the shaft. He let out the reel slowly, worrying that it would catch on a rough edge of the shaft or encounter a turn that would make any further descent impossible. The cable on the reel slowly diminished. He thought it was probably thirty or forty feet out now. At last, he felt the cable grow slack. The magnets had touched bottom, whatever bottom was.

"That's all," he said, looking up at Johane whose gaze was fixed on the shaft's opening.

He wound up the cable, moved its position slightly and then dropped the magnets again. He did it a third and fourth time.

"Nothing?" Johane asked, behind him.

"Not here," he said.

They tried the second hole, like the first a column of darkness descending into the earth. The results were the same. He wound up the cable, and found the magnets had attached themselves to nothing.

"Let's try the third hole. If there's nothing, we'll go back to the manor."

She held the lantern above the third hole while he moved the winch and then dropped the magnets into the ground. They touched bottom earlier than in the others. William estimated he had reeled out no more than a dozen feet, if that. He thought he could hear water lapping from the hole, an expulsion of sea air. "The tide's coming in," he said. In the near distance he could hear the waves come rushing toward the island.

He raised the magnets. Johane's lantern illuminated the object it had attracted. It was a flat object. Of metal, clearly, at least part iron. In the candlelight of the lantern it had the appearance of gold. It was a seven branched candelabra, he recognized it. A menorah, a Jewish ceremonial candle. Its base was missing, broken off, but the significance of the object was unmistakable. Johane recognized it, too. She gasped behind him, and held the lantern directly over it. It was covered in part with sand. William wiped it away.

"Gold," William said. His excitement that his magnets had achieved their purpose was even greater than his pleasure in having recovered not only something of monetary value but an object that tied itself to the Jewish hoard. Was there more treasure below? He could not know for sure, but certainly this single discovery was promising—more than promising. He would be a fool to suppose this was all there was to be discovered, and his magnets had made it possible.

He was preparing to send the magnets down a second time, but Johane reminded him about the hour.

"Very well," William said. "That is enough for tonight. More than enough."

"Is this not the proof we have sought, William?" Johane asked, almost breathless with excitement.

"Well, it is a treasure, this menorah, it is Hebrew without a doubt, and ample warrant for us to continue searching."

He began to gather up his equipment. They were now very close to the base of the tower. Surrounded by rushes before, the foundation of the tower was now exposed in the soft light of the lantern, a stone platform. He stepped backward and suddenly his left foot sank into the freshly turned soil. He let out a little gasp. Johane rushed forward to support him, grabbing him beneath his arms and letting out a little cry of alarm.

Johane helped him up, and he realized he had stepped into an as-yet-undiscovered shaft. This one was larger. When he had recovered his footing, he told Johane to bring the light closer. He dug around the new opening and saw as he looked down that this was a hole like the others, a passage to the sea cave beneath. He could hear water swirling, water penetrating the old opening now covered with debris from the old Roman fort.

But this passage did not drop straight into the earth. He could see it worked its way down at an angle, like the slope of a roof, and even more importantly, it was a large enough passage for a man to descend into it if he were not a hefty man, if he were thin as a reed as William was, and not afraid of the dark and whatever else lay below.

"If I descend, we will not be exploring. We will not need the magnets." In a way, he was sad at that. He was proud of what his magnets had accomplished. That they might no longer be needed in the next step of their search caused him to pause, but only for a moment. The important thing was not the means but the end, and the end was about recovery of what had been lost, stolen.

He turned to look up at her and saw at once her own recognition of what he had said. No, the magnets might not be needed if there was more below, more of what they sought. He might bring it up in his arms, like a lost child, or a bundle of laundry.

Johane helped him to conceal the newly-discovered chimney. Its existence would be their secret, and tomorrow, at low tide, he would descend.

They would need more light, a lantern not merely a candle. And he would have to muster more courage.

He remembered his earlier experience on the island, Little Livesey. Exploring Wincott's cave. A nightmarish experience. But it had to be done. It wasn't just to please Burghley, nor even Johane who expected him, he was sure, to be brave. He felt he must do it for himself. He had invested too much in this search to give up now.

The oil in the lantern was spent when they reached the manor. They passed through the copse by moonlight; Johane led the way. Then they separated, William to return the packhorse to the stable, Johane to find her way up to her room. They had agreed to slip out in the morning, when the tide was low.

"Are you hopeful, William?" she asked.

"Very," he said.

"You're quite wonderful, you know. You and your magnets."

Suddenly, she embraced him and pressed her lips to his. It was brief, the kiss, but full of promise. He could see her eyes shining in the dark. Then, in a movement as sudden as the embrace and kiss, she turned away, deciding to enter through the kitchen, a door that was rarely bolted.

He re-entered the house, and was half way up the stairs when a figure appeared at the top of the landing.

"Doctor Gilbert?" It was Harris, the steward.

"Harris? You're up late."

"I am, Doctor, but so are you—and so was Mistress Sheldon."

William said nothing.

Harris continued: "I saw you both coming out of the copse together, Doctor."

William saw no way to deny it and could think of no explanation he was prepared to give.

"I do think Lady Challoner would be displeased to know you and her most beloved Johane were in the woods together, doubtless doing that which cannot be done in the light. At least, not decently."

"We were doing nothing there."

"Nothing, Doctor? That speaks little for Mistress Sheldon."

"I mean her no disrespect, Master Harris, She is a most admirable woman."

Harris chuckled, then became serious again.

"Lady Challoner is of the same mind. It's late now, but I will inform her tomorrow of what I have seen and let her draw her own conclusions, which I believe will agree with my own."

Harris started to turn away. William reached out to him, grabbing his shoulder.

"Wait, Harris."

"Doctor?"

"It would be…I would not want Lady Challoner upset by the thought that anything transpired in the woods contrary to her own wishes. It would disturb her at this delicate time…this time of her mourning Sir Arthur."

Now it was Harris's turn to wait. He stood erect. He was not as tall as William, but broader in shoulder and girth. William imagined him holding out his hand.

"I have my purse in my room, Master Harris. Perhaps we can work something out, something between us that will not require disturbing Lady Challoner at her time of grief."

"That might be a good plan, Doctor."

"Could I trust your discretion, Master Harris?"

"Oh, Doctor, I am nothing if not discreet."

In his room, William handed Harris what he thought it would take to keep his mouth shut. Harris looked at the coins and nodded.

"And this for your discretion on any other occasion while I or Mistress Sheldon are here."

William doubled the amount. He thought it was an unsavory transaction and was ashamed of himself for playing into it, but it was a concession to the way the world worked.

He went to sleep not thinking of the marvelous find his magnets had secured, but of Johane's mouth, her lips, the sweetness of her breath, like the purest honey.

Forty-Six

Before dawn they were back at the site of yesterday's discovery. Johane brought the lantern. Everything depended on whether the opening on the surface was wide enough to admit him and continued to be so.

Johane uncovered the passage she had carefully concealed the night before, and within moments William was wedging himself into the opening, his hips fitting comfortably and then his shoulders. He reached up to her. Johane handed him the lantern and wished him good fortune. Her face reflected the same look of excited anticipation as it had the night before. Had their kiss been real, or part of a dream? For a moment, he wasn't sure. But then she was out of sight and he was in the dark, or would have been but for the lantern, whose light showed no more than a foot or so around him.

As he descended, the passage widened. He inched himself down, extending his feet into the darkness below, looking for something solid, but there was nothing. The angle of his descent stayed the same, a gentle slope without serious impediments, a few sharp rocks and round stones, nothing to injure him. He thought, *I am a London physician, a graduate of Cambridge, but have become as a worm, a snake, other things that burrow in the earth, yet in a good cause.*

Then his feet touched something: not dirt but hard like brick or stone, and flat. He stretched beyond it and found another of the same feel and shape. A third effort convinced him. It was a stair, stairs, descending. No banister or handholds, just steps equally spaced, or relatively so. He twisted his body so he was facing the roof of the passage, for he thought of what he was crawling through now as a passage, no more a mere hole in the earth. He leaned against the rough wall, realizing it was masonry. He held the lantern up to it. Not just masonry, he thought, but a faded mural, ships at sea, ancient vessels with single square sails moving with oars across a still sea.

He thought then it must be Roman, and this passage the nether regions of the old Roman fort. The stairs ended. He held the lantern aloft and revealed a large chamber with brick ceiling and at his feet a kind of porch, which upon closer examination was a dock of sorts. Then he understood this had been a port to receive boats when the space was open to the sea, before the building of Maxwell's impudent tower had sent a mountain of building rubble down to close the cave mouth and seal it off from the invading waves, except for what water seeped in. Yet the tower had been built but a hundred years before. Before that, the cave would have been an accessible hiding place, accessible to the shipmaster and his crew who had robbed the Jews. How else could the menorah have gotten there, but by being deliberately concealed? The question in his mind now was whether it was a lone deposit or one among many, and this the site of a treasure trove.

He was now able to stand upright. He moved to the rear of the cave and looked up at the roof. He could see where the holes were, into which he had dropped the magnets. He looked around him. The pavement of the dock was covered with a film of sand and gravel, having worked its way through the wall of debris. When the tide returned, the cave would slowly fill again. Probably not to its roof, but above William's head. He needed to be quick.

He went to the far end of the cave and begin to explore the cracks and corners, the uneven spaces in the pavement of the dock. He knew that coming across the menorah had been a kind of miracle, but he hoped it might be repeated.

Then he saw something shining over to the right of him. It lay on the floor, half buried in the sand. He knelt down and examined it. It was cup, a silver cup, with jewels inlaid in its rim. William had brought a canvas bag with him. He placed the cup in the bag and continued his search. He would have called up to Johane to let her know what he had found, but he doubted she would be able to hear him.

Then he found what he had hoped to find, not an isolated object, valuable though it might be, but in one recess of the cave a battered chest.

It lay on its side. Its lid was gone, and one side was bashed in as though a vengeful sea had thrown it against the cave's wall. All around it were strewn what must previously have been its contents: coins, rings, arm bands, plates. All lay upon the sand, some half buried. He began picking the objects up, not taking the time to examine any in detail, knowing their value and convinced he had found the lost hoard.

And then he saw it, or a mere corner of it. He might have missed it entirely, but God be thanked he had not. He drew it up from its resting place in the sand and held the lantern over it.

At last: a thin, rectangular plate upon which Hebrew letters were inscribed.

It was so much what he had hoped for, it took a moment for him to realize that it was all real and not merely a figment of his imagination, stimulated by the dark and solitude of the cave, created by his desire, his wish to find it.

For a few moments, he disregarded everything else and held the gold plate in his hand. Like the one in Burghley's cabinet, this was rectangular, and had a hole drilled in its upper corner. He could not read the script, but it was clearly the companion piece that Burghley had coveted and would now possess.

Solomon's gold.

He gathered as much of the treasure as he could collect in his bag and carry, moved back to the stairs, and began to climb. The climb was more difficult than the descent had been and when he reached the top, Johane, who had a concerned look on her face, had to help him out of the hole. He had thrown the bag and its treasure out before him, but she paid no attention to that.

"God be thanked, William. I thought I'd lost you." Her face reflected the anxiety in her words.

"Then I am found again," he said. He struggled to stand.

He motioned toward the bag and told her to look inside.

She undid the tie that bound it, opened the mouth, and gasped. She turned to him. "I can't believe it," she said.

He reached deep into the bag, pushing aside the plate and goblets, the cups, the silver knives. He pulled out the gold plate. "God's Commandments to Moses. I believe, the last five."

"It is like the one Lord Burghley showed us," she exclaimed.

"It is its twin. See where the two were coupled." He pointed to the holes.

"And the rest?" she said.

"Not a king's ransom, but a goodly hoard."

She did not hide her delight; she giggled like a child.

"And there's more, more below. The bag would not hold it. I have to go back."

"Back down?" Her face fell.

He explained about the battered chest, its spilled contents, swept about in the thin sand of the cave floor at every rise and fall of the tide. He told her about the muraled walls he'd seen below, the paved floor, the dock where Roman boats tied up when the cave mouth was open to the sea. Ancient times, before the building of the tower and the destruction of the Roman fort.

But she only half listened to him. He could tell her mind was elsewhere. "But I am worried about the danger below. Is this not enough?" she asked, pointing to the bag, the contents of which were now strewn upon the short grass.

"Not enough if there is more to find. And I know there is."

He wondered, having said that, whether he was driven by greed, or just the desire to be thorough. He imagined reporting his find to Burghley. Burghley would surely ask if what he had brought back was the whole of it. Even if Burghley might forgive him for having left much behind, he would be disappointed. The lord treasurer was thorough. He would expect William to be likewise.

"We must have something to put this all in," he said. "Some chest, some crate or box."

"If all this is so contained, it will have the look of something worth stealing."

He admitted this was true. He said, "Then let us find something that will arouse no suspicion, that will suggest nothing of worth is within. A suitable hiding place until we can get all we've discovered off the island and back to his lordship."

"I think I know what will serve," she said brightly.

"And what might that be?"

"Tell me, Doctor Gilbert if you know, what thing is it that no one wants to be, nor to be near, or to find buried in his garden, much less hidden in his bed?"

"A riddle?" he asked.

She smiled mischievously. "Think hard, William. You're a doctor. Not all your ministrations are successful. And when they are not, you have…?" She paused, looking at him with a droll expression.

"A corpse."

She laughed. "Exactly."

"You are proposing we stuff all in a dead body?"

"No, good goose," she laughed. "But in a coffin, where such a body is placed. A box large enough, I think, For what it will hold."

She was a clever girl. It was an excellent idea. A coffin would excite no one's curiosity. Death, after all, was as common as birth, and in some seasons more so. He could imagine himself and Johane traveling back to London, riding a cart, the coffin in full display. Husband and a wife, burying his or her old father, perhaps. A victim of some terrible, disfiguring illness. Even the plague, which was better, since no affliction was more terrifying. Who would want to look inside to inspect its contents, who would dare to do so? He thought of the strategy he had used with the outraged farmer and his brutish son. Was it not the same: instill fear to drive the threat away, disarm the enemy?

"We'll need a coffin," he said.

"One of the grooms has carpenter's skills. He's been following me around like a puppy dog since I arrived on the island. He's in love with me, or thinks he is, but have no fear, William. He's a mere boy with a scrawny chest and a pimply face. I think I can persuade him to make a coffin that will serve our purposes."

"And what will you tell him as to the reason? We have no corpse to occupy it."

"Trust me. I'll think of something."

They restowed the canvas bag, William threw it over his shoulder, and they headed back to the house.

"Sea shells, for my collection. That's what we will say if we're seen, and someone asks what I carry."

"That's a great many shells," she said, nodding toward the bag he carried.

"I'm an obsessive collector," he said. "Isn't that how you described me to Lady Challoner?"

She laughed. "I've described you in a number of ways to my lady.

You'd be surprised, Doctor. By the way, Harris saw us last night, together, coming from the copse. He accosted me this morning after breakfast. He thinks we're lovers and threatened to tell my mistress. I realized quickly that he would not be persuaded otherwise. I paid him in exchange for his discretion."

"How much?"

She told him.

He did not tell her that he had made the same bargain, and for quite a bit more.

Forty-Seven

For the next two nights William continued to explore the sea cave, bringing up a dozen gold chains of various sizes, more cups and plates of silver, another candlestick, and various knives and spoons. All were good silver or gold and in remarkable condition, given the buffering they had taken beneath the water.

During this time, except when he and Johane assisted him at the tower's base, they saw little of each other, which was according to their plan. Neither trusted Harris to keep his word, despite the bribes he had been paid. And even if he did, others of the household might be observing them, ready to report their secret meetings to the mistress or try to secure more money from them for their silence.

William made a final descent into the cave, found nothing though he spent longer there than ever he had done until the tide was rising to his ankles, and he decided he had done all he could. There was no manifest listing the goods the betrayed Jews had lost, so he would never know whether he had found all there was to find. But he was eager now to leave Livesey and return to London. He had written to Burghley the day after their first positive discovery, describing the menorah as evidence that the Jewish treasure had indeed been found. He wrote a second letter the next day, when the precious gold plate inscribed with the last five of the Commandments was discovered. But he had received no response.

The question in William's mind now was how they should take leave of the island. Johane had agreed to stay as Mildred Challoner's secretary, but William understood that was a pretense. They could, of course, merely vanish, both of them. Could not leave without explanation, as Johane had done from her employer's house in London. They could say Lord Burghley had summoned them home. The problem was not William's leaving—that had already been decided by Mildred Challoner herself. He no longer had a purpose there, to her way of thinking. Then he thought of the coffin.

"When will it be ready?" he whispered to Johane on the evening of his last expedition into the cave.

"He said tomorrow, at end of day."

"Whom did you tell him it was for?"

"I said I had a relative in the village, a distant cousin. The coffin was for him."

"Did he believe you?"

"I made him believe," she said, smiling. "As I said, he's a foolish boy, enamored with me. He would believe anything I told him."

"Perhaps we can make use of the same dead cousin," William said.

"What do you mean?"

"Tell your mistress about the cousin. Tell her that he has died and his last wish was to be buried on the mainland, in some town, give her the name of it. Move her to tears in your telling of it. Say to her that I have agreed to accompany you on your way, since my plan was to return to London anyway, at her behest if you remember. Swear to her you will return afterwards."

"I doubt she will let me go," Johane said.

"Trust me, Johane. She shall. You are like a magnet. All who know you adhere to you," William said, smiling.

"Do you adhere to me, Doctor?"

"I do." He moved toward her, embraced her, lifted her chin and kissed her.

He felt her response as she dissolved into him, pressing her body against his. They had been talking in the old garden, in full view of the windows. It was a reckless move. William realized that even as he was making it. He didn't care; she didn't seem to, either. Her warm response more than compensated for the danger to his way of thinking, of feeling.

"I will find a way to convince her, to put out of her mind any thought that I am abandoning her," she said.

"I know you will," he answered.

The house was quiet. He might have had it to himself. He went back to his room, seeing no one on the way and hoping that no one observed him. He had never been so happy. His mission was accomplished, and now he had every reason to believe that his affection for Johane was returned. Had she not said it in so many words, manifest it in the kiss, no mere token but full of passion?

He went to bed thinking not of the treasure they had recovered, or the dangers he had escaped, but of her. He imagined her at his house in London, not now as a servant or even a pupil or assistant, but as his wife, the mistress of the house. His painful memories of the Dutch girl he had loved were now receding into the shadowy past. Her image was replaced by Johane's As for their marriage, the difference in degree, an objection almost surely to be raised by his father, was a difficulty he could deal with later. He would point out to Jerome Gilbert that times were changing. That rank and lineage were beginning to yield to a new social order in which the quality of mind and heart were rapidly becoming the standards by which marital fitness was judged, and that the new freedom would infuse in the tired blood of aristocracy a quality and vigor that would strengthen the race, and certainly enhance England's place among the nations.

Sleep came in the midst of these lofty thoughts, along with Johane's smiling face and her pert query, "And do I adhere to you, Doctor?"

He hoped she knew she did.

The next day, she came to his room before breakfast and before he was fully dressed. She waited while he buttoned his jerkin and put on his shoes, like a patient wife, watching him as though the simple act of his dressing was a thing of great interest to her and not a routine of his day. It filled him with a strange excitement, her watching him that way. That she should allow herself to be alone with him was bold enough, as though she didn't care anymore what Harris thought or her mistress thought. She wanted to be with him. At any price, it seemed. She spoke.

"My mistress says I must go. She says the final wishes of the dead must be observed. It is for that reason, she says, she is having the chapel built and the tower refurbished. Although she wondered that I had a cousin in the village."

"How did you explain never having mentioned him?"

"Easy, a relative recently discovered."

"A name you've invented, I assume?"

"In part. Roger Skelton bullied me regularly when I was a child. For which he deserves to die and serve as our corpse." She laughed. "As to never mentioning my dear cousin, I said I had only recently discovered the relationship. I am his only living relative. What could I do but honor his last request?" She laughed again.

"If the coffin is ready by end of day, then we'll leave in the morning, before breakfast. The sooner we're back in London the better."

Before noon, William was at Mildred Challoner's door, feeling excitement of another kind.

"I am most sorry to see you go, Doctor. I hope your stay here this week has given you the rest you need for your return journey."

"It has, madam. I am very rested and thank you again for your hospitality."

"And I thank you, for agreeing to accompany Johane along her way. To Queenborough, I think."

Yes, Queenborough. Which I believe is the place where her cousin should be laid to rest."

"The roads are dangerous," Mildred Challoner said, her face heavy with concern. "I would be devastated if anything happened to that dear girl on the way."

"Trust me, good lady, I will guard her with my life."

He made a low bow and thanked her again for the week of rest she had offered, although in truth it had been one of the hardest of his life. He had slept little, his recent nights having been spent in cave exploring, in lugging the trove up from the depths, in fearing the tide would overtake him, that the cave would collapse, or they would be found out. It had been almost as bad as his sojourn on the little island, when he feared at each moment his presence there would be discovered by those who had marooned him. He had not become inured to fear. It was always fresh to him, as though no peril he had survived before had prepared him for what faced him next.

Forty-Eight

Harris had secured a cart for them, by order of Lady Challoner and with an additional sum from William to make sure all was done properly. William would ride his horse, Johane one of Lady Challoner's from the stable fitted out with a fine Spanish saddle. The groom's boy, a more comely lad than Johane had described and certainly neither scrawny nor pimply, would drive the cart.

The more challenging part was filling the coffin with its intended contents, without the boy seeing it. But Johane had foreseen this difficulty and provided for it. She and William had placed the Jews' hoard in three different bags before anyone else was up and about and these in a shroud she had prepared earlier from one of her bedsheets. Johane told the boy that the body of her cousin had been brought up earlier from the village by his friends. William was relieved to see the boy accept this account. The boy even helped William lift the supposed body into the coffin.

"How did your cousin die, Mistress Sheldon?"

Johane looked at William. "Of the plague, I think."

"So were his symptoms," William said.

The boy's face, before ruddy with good health, went white.

"I fear to go near it," he said, terrified. "I have touched the shroud. Will I die then?"

"We shall all die, Arthur, sooner or later," William pronounced solemnly.

"I much prefer it be later, Doctor."

"Don't we all?" William said, now employing his best bedside manner. "Don't worry, Arthur, I'll drive the cart myself. You go about your duties here. Mistress Sheldon will return within a few days."

He had wished to ride his horse, not drive the cart, but the boy's reaction had proved the unlikelihood that anyone would want to look within the coffin. Human curiosity rarely extended so far, and a well-seasoned corpse was often enough to give the casual viewer nightmares forever.

By eight of the morning, William, Johane, and the cart supposedly bearing the body of Roger Skelton were crossing the causeway. William turned to smile at Johane, who was following on her horse and at the same time took a last look at the island. It was a cold, gray day. But it was dry, and he reckoned it would be no time at all before they passed through Queenborough and were well on their way to their real destination.

About the effect of the coffin on passersby, William had been right. Johane drew attention first, an attractive young woman well mounted, then William driving the cart, then the cart's contents, a long box—obviously a coffin—and then observers with Papist instincts crossing themselves, heads turned away or eyes averted, not the dramatic response of the stable boy whose infatuation with Johane did not overcome his terror of the plague. But then the passersby, a mix of farmer's carts and wagons, an occasional coach, and many a poor person on foot, did not approach to ask what he within the coffin died of, or where the coffin was being taken. A troop of Burghley's guard would not have provided them with greater security.

By evening they had arrived at a small village with three inns. It was not as before, when William was driven to find lodging in some nearby farmer's house. He was glad not to risk that danger and indignity again. And the first inn they came to was not full, but there was only a single room available. William had asked for two.

"Will we share a room, then, Doctor Gilbert?" Johane asked when William returned from seeing to the horses and cart. The stable boy at the inn had not asked about the coffin. The innkeeper had not asked about the couple who applied for lodging, not caring whether they were married or no. His blank expression assured him that monitoring the chastity of his guests was no business of his.

She asked him again about the room, the sharing of it. She did not blush at the question.

"If you wish," William said.

"I wish," she said, not smiling now—serious, rather.

"I would not dishonor you, Johane, or have any misunderstanding between us."

"There is no misunderstanding, William. We have kissed and embraced, a thing neither of us found repellent, I believe, nor would we have joined so were there not love between us."

"I believe the same," he said.

"I wish to share the room with you," she repeated. She laughed. "But first, let's eat. I will not be bedded on an empty stomach."

The inn had a kitchen from which they were served a middling meal—fruit, fowl, a kind of pudding. Later, he would not remember. There was much for them to talk about, much that pushed nearly everything else from William's mind.

When they had nearly finished their meal, Johane said, "So, Doctor, I have been your pupil and your confederate, do you now desire me for your mistress?"

Her candor took him aback. What she'd said was farthest from his mind. He quickly recovered.

"No, Johane, I desire you for my wife. It's marriage I'm proposing, nothing less."

She smiled, and looked pensive as though he had presented her with a problem. "I see." She looked down at her half-empty plate.

Her hesitancy to respond suddenly filled him with fear. He wondered if he had assumed too much, taken her tokens of affection, even her remark about mutual love, for more than it was. Had he misread her so badly?

Johane seemed to perceive his dismay. She leaned toward him and put her hand upon his, as though to comfort him. "Doctor, William, you are a gentleman, a noted physician in London, a friend of Lord Burghley and other persons of name. You have a brilliant future ahead of you. I, on the other hand, am a servant and have been so since I was a young girl. My parents are dead. I have no living siblings. All of which means I have no dowry to bring to such a marriage. Nothing to give you but my poor self."

"You have what you are, Johane. Your intelligence, your sensitivity, your virtue. All these are of great value. I care nothing for a dowry. I don't need money. I have sufficient."

She thought about this, looking away from him for a moment and then back again. She seemed worried.

"Would your father agree, William? You have told me of him many times. A man ambitious for his son. What would he think? You are his eldest son. Would he cut you off, were you to marry contrary to his wishes? Would I be welcome in his house, by him and your stepmother, your brothers and sisters? Think about it, William. I would not wish to be the source of family conflict, would not wish to be an outcast or make you one."

She had gone to the root of the problem with unerring and painful precision. William thought of his father, a man who had pressed him to marry ever since his leaving Cambridge. But to marry up, not across, and certainly not down. His father would hardly approve of this serving girl, of no family of name or rank, of no distinction beyond her beauty, her intelligence, her wit. To Jerome Gilbert, it would not be enough. He could hear his father now: "William, you've always had a weakness for a pretty face. Remember the Dutch girl. What was her name?"

"Katrina, Father. Katrina Weinmere."

"Yes, you gave your heart to her, only to have it broken."

"True, but…"

He put the imagined conversation aside. Johane sat before him, studying his face, waiting for a response.

"Johane, I can't see myself happy in this life without you."

"Not your work, your science?"

"They fill my head, provide my living. They do not fill my soul. I think I can win my father over. We have butted heads many a time. I usually prevail."

"But would you prevail this time?"

"I will prevail," he said.

"There is something else," she said.

He waited.

"You mentioned my virtue."

He nodded. "Along with your intelligence, your sensitivity."

She sighed heavily. "The night on the island when you found me with Broderick, when he was accosting me."

"I remember it well," William said. The memory was still bitter to him.

"You thought he threatened my maidenhead."

"I thought he did."

"William, you must know that I would not come to your bed as a virgin bride."

She paused to see his reaction, but went on before he could speak, speaking tearfully in a way he had never heard her speak before. "The houses where I served in the town where I was born, and later in London, in both places I was accosted, violated; in the first instance by my master's son, who seeing me, wanted me, and insisted on having me. I was fourteen. In the second instance it was my master himself who preyed upon me, night and day, that I should give in to him. He threatened me with arrest for theft should I not let him have his way, which he claimed was his right as lord of the manor. I was terrified of going to prison, perhaps even being hanged. They do that, you know, for the smallest of thefts. I gave him what he wanted and having satisfied his lust, he let me go."

She stopped, dissolved in tears. He reached across the table and took both her hands in his. He said, "All this doesn't matter to me."

"My past lies heavy upon me," she said. "Like a huge weight."

The inn keeper approached and addressed William. "Sir, we had no second room before, but do so now. If you wish, you may have it."

"That would be fine, Master Inn Keeper," Johane said before William responded.

The inn keeper said what room it was, said it would be suitable for the lady. William looked questioningly at Johane.

"I need some time to myself to think of what you have proposed, William," she whispered when the inn keeper had gone. "My heart is not settled. Not because I do not love you, but because I fear what burden to you I should be, were we to marry. I pray you be patient with me. At least for tonight. Tomorrow, I promise, you shall have my answer."

"I will be patient," William said. Although his patience was in short supply, still she commanded his heart. What else could he be, but patient?

He couldn't sleep. Johane's stricken face, her tearful voice, was ever before him. He longed to comfort her, to hold her and let her bury her head in his chest. Her past did not diminish his love for her or his respect. Hers was a common story of abuse and betrayal. He relived their conversation at supper dozens of times, until sleep overcame him. Even then, he dreamed of her in his arms, sharing his bed, bearing his children. Then his father would appear, his stern countenance judging, advising, predicting the worst.

Johane had been right about that, without even knowing his father, only knowing *of* him, the Colchester lawyer and judge. To his father, Johane Sheldon would simply not do.

A deeper sleep finally came, the cure for nothing.

Forty-Nine

Awakening, he thought at once of her, in the room next to him. Sleeping still, perhaps, or awake an hour or more. She had said once she was an early riser. What serving maid was not? In his England, even the rich and titled rose before dawn.

He doused his face with the cold water in the pitcher by his bed, dressed quickly, and went into the corridor. He approached Johane's room and knocked. Knocked again. There was no response.

He ran down the stairs. Where the inn keeper had done business the night before, a heavy-set woman perched on a stool. He asked her if she had seen the woman he had come with the night before.

"What woman, sir? We have by my book at least five here at the moment. Which is yours, sir?"

William described Johane. The woman on the stool shifted her weight and looked up at him. "You speak well of her, sir, in your description. By which I suppose she is a special friend, for no man speaks with such grand words of his wife. But to be brief, I have not seen such a woman, neither this morning nor before, and I have been on this stool since cockcrow."

"Is there another way down from the rooms above?"

"No, sir, there is but one stair. If a body wishes to leave otherwise, they take the window, which one of our guests once did, to his great hurt when he landed." She laughed. Her whole body shook.

William went back upstairs, thinking he might have knocked at the wrong door. But no, it was not the wrong door. He pounded, called out her name, and went in. The room was identical to the one he had occupied, but it was empty not only of Johane, but also of her bag.

Except for the unmade bed, there was no sign that she had ever been there at all.

He was overcome now with a nameless dread. Had his proposal of marriage so alarmed her that he had driven her off? Or had he imagined her as his companion for the journey back to London because he wanted it more than he wanted the treasure he had recovered from the island cave? One of his London colleagues had once such a patient. A man who imagined what he wanted, who hallucinated daily. Bleeding him had done no good. He remained quite mad.

He thought, then, that she might have slipped past the woman on the stool and into the street. He went down again and in a moment was walking the high street of the town looking for her. He spent an hour or more so occupied and then decided to return to the inn and the stable. If she had indeed left, she would hardly have done so on foot.

In the stable, he looked about for the cart.

It was gone, and the coffin with it. The horse Johane had been provided by her mistress was also not in its stall where the stable boy had put it. His own horse, the big gelding, was there, staring at him with soulful equine eyes.

For a moment he was overcome with confusion. He could not imagine her driving the cart off on her own, leaving him without a word, without an explanation for her disappearance—no, more than that, her treason. For wouldn't that be what it was, to leave him so? To steal the treasure while he slept dreaming of her in his arms, listening for her breathing on the other side of the wall?

He felt at the thought an almost physical pain, a seizing of his heart in a vice.

"Good morning, sir."

The stable boy had come up behind him while he was in his stupor of thought.

"Good day, sir. Would you be wanting your horse?"

"Where's the cart, the other horse my companion rode in on?"

"They were gone when I came here this morning, sir. I thought you and your lady had gotten them and been on your way."

"So you did not see woman I was with?"

"Nay, sir, I never did, save when you two arrived yesternight. Your horse is here, sir, right where I stalled him."

"I can see that," William said, more sharply than he intended.

"Oh, but I almost forgot myself, sir. Are you a doctor, by any chance?"

"I am."

"Then I have this for you, for I found it pinned to the stall where the lady's horse was."

The boy drew a piece of paper from his pocket. He handed it to William, regarding him expectantly as though he hoped for some reward for his poor memory.

William read it. At once he recognized the hand that had written it. It was Johane's.

Dear William,

This will find me in great distress. I am abducted by our common enemy. I will not offend heaven by writing his name for you know him as well as I. We thought he had gone away. He had not. I am now his prisoner.

He says if you follow you will not see me again, not in this life. I love you but would not have you grieve for me or think yourself responsible for my untimely death.

Adieu. Johane.

William's confusion was now replaced with rage, but also relief. That Johane should have betrayed him was the worst of his fears. She had not done so. Her sudden disappearance was, by her own word in the letter, John Broderick's doing. *Our common enemy.* Who else but John Broderick?

William saw now what had happened. They had been followed from the island by Broderick and probably at least one other of his companions, Browne or Locke. Probably both. He imagined Johane abducted during the night, easy enough to do in the ramshackle inn with rooms no more secure from intruders than a chicken coop. They would have stolen upon her while she slept, muffled her cries of alarm, and driven away with horse, cart, and coffin—and Johane as well, for William had no doubt he would use her for his hostage.

The thought of Broderick hurting her almost drove him mad. It was not in William's nature to hate so, but he acknowledged now that he hated no living creature as much as he hated John Broderick, thief and abductor.

The letter warned against following them. But what else could he do? He could hardly think of riding back to London, not more than a day away now, as if nothing had happened on the island, nothing found and nothing lost. Anger raged within him, it warred with any sense of caution. Despite the letter's warning, he would arm himself and pursue them.

He read the letter again. He looked for any clue she might have provided as to where she had been taken or in what condition. The horse Lady Challoner had given Johane to ride was gone. Presumably, she would be mounted, not merely tossed into the cart to ride along with the coffin. But how did Broderick know of its precious contents? Had he been spying on them even while William explored the sea cave, brought up the treasure—or was this information had by some other means? Or perhaps only discovered by chance. Broderick's only goal may have been the abduction of Johane, with possession of the treasure an unexpected windfall when the contents of the coffin were examined or disclosed by Johane herself, tortured until she revealed all.

"Make my horse ready," William said to the stable boy. "I'll leave within the hour. And tell me where I might acquire a pistol."

"A pistol, sir?"

"You heard me, boy. You know what a pistol is, do you not?"

"I do, sir, but know not where one can be found."

"There is no armorer in this place? No gunsmith?"

"I think not, sir, perhaps in Queenborough. At the castle."

William would not retrace his steps. He would kill Broderick with his bare hands, without benefit of a pistol.

Fifty

It was less than an hour before William returned to the stable yard to find the boy standing by William's horse with his hand out. William did what was expected of him, giving him a coin and then climbing up into the saddle. He tried to think of Johane as he remembered her, her face calm, her face filled with love for him, but all he could imagine now was Johane threatened, abused, even murdered.

Would he find her dead body along the road, should Broderick become aware that William was in pursuit? He was in an impossible position. He could not let her go, could not simply ride away, but he could hardly think of pursuing because of Broderick's threats. There seemed no middle ground to his dilemma. It was not a problem he could reason through. He decided to follow his instincts. God help him, God help her.

He rode through the town slowly, surveying each house and cottage. He reckoned Broderick had been on the road for hours, but what if that was only what Broderick wanted him to think? What if he were concealing himself in some nearby householder's garden plot or farmer's field, beneath a bridge or behind a hedgerow, laughing as the love-sick London doctor galloped past in hot pursuit?

He knew he could take nothing for granted. So he kept a watchful eye even until he came to the town's end and fields and hills lay before him, and always the road, wretched though it was from recent rains and neglect. He rode on, realizing there was one assumption that he needed to make, and that was Broderick's ultimate destination. William reasoned that must be London.

London was where the goldsmiths were, both the honest who would be guarded in accepting gold and silver from a stranger and those indifferent, those who made a regular practice of dealing in stolen goods. London was also where those with money felt no compunction to inquire where something they wanted came from. Stolen or honestly obtained, it made no difference. God judged all, but that was in the life to come. In this life, all was vile practice.

There was a hint of this in Johane's letter. The warning against any attempt to rescue her. Why bother, if Broderick's intention was to flee to some remote corner of England, say Yorkshire or Cornwall, where William would be unlikely to pursue him anyway? No, William's instincts told him London would be Broderick's goal, at least until he had liquidated the Jewish hoard and what was for William and Burghley its greatest treasure, Solomon's gold.

For the next hour or two he rode at a brisk pace, making by his reckoning nearly twenty miles before he was forced to stop to give his mount a rest. On horseback, he had the advantage of speed over the cart, but Broderick had the advantage of a head start. William stopped at a town, went from tavern to tavern, asking anyone who would talk to a stranger with a desperate look on his face whether they had seen a mule cart accompanied by horsemen, one among them a woman, the cart conveying a coffin.

His question drew more than one strange look, given that business of a coffin. It was an unusual question, a sinister question, their expressions told him. Then he realized that if Broderick was smart, he would have covered the coffin with a tarpaulin, more concerned to disguise his burden from William than from the possibility of drawing the interest of robbers.

Finally, he found one man, a middle-aged bricklayer, who said he had seen such a cart, but that it contained no coffin he could see.

"I've seen many a coffin in my life, sir. I can tell you that. But there were two, nay three men ahorseback, and a woman too, a young woman. She rode between two of the men. They talked over her as they rode. I do remember that, sir."

"But no coffin. What did the cart bear?" William asked.

"I couldn't tell. Something oblong in shape, I think. Like a trunk or a large chest. It was covered with a canvas and bound to hold it from moving about."

William hadn't considered this, but wasn't it an obvious device? What easier than to remove the coffin's contents, discard the coffin, and repack all in an ordinary chest? Broderick would undoubtedly be armed and his fellows likewise, so more confident in handling himself and keeping the hoard to himself against robbers.

"Can you describe the men, or the woman?"

The bricklayer looked thoughtful, put a finger to his forehead as though the gesture would quicken his memory. "The woman was young, as I have said, and as much as I could see of her face she seemed a fair piece of female flesh. Dark-haired, I think, her complexion more brown than fair, a nose of no particular quality that I could tell, neither hooked nor pointed. She wore a cap pulled down around her ears. As for the men, they are much of a blur in my memory, which is not what it once was. Ah, yes, I think the man who seemed to lead them was tall, taller than the average man."

"Tall? How could tell if he was astride his horse."

"Why, by the length of his legs, sir. They were quite long, and he had a stern look, although that may have only been because I stopped along the way, I being on foot, to watch them pass. I did not know their rank or condition, so I held cap in my hand out of respect. Better safe than sorry in such matters. That's my view."

"When did you see this company?"

"Why just after dawn, sir. I was on my way to my work. I lay brick. For a gentleman's house, here in the town."

"And they were on their way to London?"

"Well, in that general direction. Where a man may go I have no idea once he is over the hill, and there are many hills about here."

William thanked him for his help, fairly certain the company of riders the bricklayer had seen was Broderick's. Broderick was long-legged, stern in countenance, and the woman with them sounded like Johane, although it may have been some other woman. Johane wasn't the only dark-haired young woman in England and while the cart may have been carrying a chest, the chest might have contained clothing or some other personal item, or perhaps even grain.

He *wanted* it to be Broderick, and the woman, Johane. It was the only lead he had, the only support for his instinct that those he pursued were heading for London, a sprawling city of contiguous neighborhoods numbering, what? Several hundred thousand souls, according to those who kept count of such things.

The terror of this impressed itself on him when he entered the city in the late afternoon. The narrow streets were alive with wagons, carts, horsemen, and even more on foot, making their way from this point to that, coming in and out of shops, courtyards, taverns, public buildings. Gentlemen and women, secretaries, clerks, servants, soldiers, tradesmen, apprentices, unemployed youth, fallen women, and not a few foreigners, by their dress. How was he to find Broderick now in this multitude?

More important, how was he to find Johane? Perhaps, he reflected darkly, she was already dead, her purpose in Broderick's plan fulfilled. Broderick was a devil. He would show her no mercy. His only concession to mercy was that he might not ravish her before he left her for dead.

He knew there was no point in searching farther, at least for now. His horse was tired, he more so, his mind blasted with worry and frustration and anger. It took him the better part of an hour to ride through the streets until he came to his own house, where he hardly said a word to the servants who welcomed him home, and went to his room and his bed too exhausted to dream.

Fifty-One

William had told Burghley in his letters that he would report his discoveries upon returning to the city. He dared not delay. Despite his fears for Johane's safety, he had a duty that if breached would not sit well with his great patron or with himself. Besides, he felt it not unlikely that Burghley could be of help in recovering the treasure and Johane, and in bringing justice for the dead, Isaac Silva and Tobias Wincott.

The servants who had deserted him in Surrey—Thomas and his cousin—looked at him sheepishly, hats in hand, preparing for an onslaught of recrimination and probably dismissal from service, but William waved it off. He assured them no harm had been done to him, told them how he had terrified his attackers by claiming his magnets had cured the plague but now they were contaminated thereby. By all appearances, the two enjoyed the story. They laughed, but William could see in their eyes how relieved, and perhaps surprised, they were to find their master so forgiving.

Burghley had a fine and imposing London house. It was not Theobalds, but then, what house was? In his London residence Burghley did his business of state, conferred with his fellows in the government, heard a host of petitioners for this privilege or office or honor, occasionally entertained the queen. William arrived there at nine o'clock by the tolling bell and went at once to a side door where, as on other occasions, he was met by one of Burghley's personal aides, a man named Samuel Harper. William knew Harper well. Harper had been his patient on two occasions and on the last William had treated him gratis, for friendship's sake. He knew the man's family, from Gosford in Essex, not far from his own birthplace. They were good, honest people, the Harpers.

"Doctor Gilbert? Abroad early? Here to see his lordship?"

"Is Lord Burghley in residence?" William asked calmly, without explanation of his purpose. Still, Harper seemed to sense the urgency of William's request. Maybe he had it written on his face. How could it not be written there, like a disfiguring scar? A man does not go through what he had and remain unscathed.

"He'll be here presently, Doctor. He had an appointment with some of the lords of the Privy Council. You can wait in the antechamber."

He went upstairs to the imposing room, not one wall of which did not proclaim the wealth and culture of its owner with tapestries, armorial bearings, or silken drapes. He found a chair, not comfortable, but straight-backed to discourage lingering or even coming at all. He wasn't alone in the room. Burghley had others, petitioners, wanting to see him, to see the great man. The room buzzed. Faces were serious, some anxious. He wondered if he looked like them, men hungry for what Burghley could provide, angry because of some offense done them, real or imagined, fearful of some impending fine or other punishment.

He sat for an hour and then another. Burghley didn't return. William had planned to spend the time thinking how he should explain the theft of the Jewish hoard, justify his actions on the island, but all he could think of was Johane. Where was she now? Did she still live? And had she not been taken, what answer would she have given to his proposal of marriage? Would love dictate an answer, or fear of his father's disapproval, her unworthiness, her lacking a dowry, her having nothing to bring to the marriage except her "tainted" self? She had been eloquent as to her own disqualifications. He had been inept in refuting them, or why would she have needed to sleep on his proposal? If there was love between them, why could she not have simply said yes?

It was past noon when Burghley appeared, surrounded by a flock of assistants and clerks so that the antechamber, crowded before, was packed with bobbing heads and voices raised to get his lordship's attention. Burghley spied William, smiled and nodded to him but waved another person—who was elegantly dressed and obviously someone of note in court—into his office first. William had to wait another hour before he was summoned, during which time he squirmed with nervousness.

At one time he had anticipated this meeting as a demonstration of his faithfulness in following Burghley's instructions. Now he had to tell his great patron that he had both succeeded and failed. The treasure found had been lost, and through his own carelessness. Had he been vigilant—not stopped for the night, not left the cart with its precious cargo unattended, insisted that Johane remain with him—Broderick would have failed. Over-confidence and distraction had undone William at every turn.

Burghley greeted him warmly and pointed to a chair opposite his own, not in front of the desk but beside him, a conversational position that William knew Burghley favored. Two men talking without a large piece of furniture between them is more likely to foster honesty and candor than not, he had once told William.

"You have news for me then, Doctor. Pray give it, I am all ears."

William hesitated for a moment, not sure where to begin. He walked on thin ice now, and he knew it. Then he said, "In my letters to your lordship, I spoke of our findings on the island, proof of a connection with the Jews who were murdered and robbed of their goods, their silver and gold , and then the discovery of the hoard itself."

William took a breath, prepared to give the bad news, but he saw that already Burghley was regarding him strangely. Was it disbelief, curiosity, or confusion William saw in Burghley's face? It quickly became apparent that it was the latter.

"Doctor Gilbert, I received no letters regarding these matters. The last letter of yours I have is the one informing me of Isaac Silva's murder."

"You never received letters more recently, within the last two weeks, my lord? I sent them by special post."

Burghley shook his head. "None," he said.

William remembered the dates of the letters and told Burghley. "Perhaps it arrived here but was not called to your attention."

"I gave Master Thomison, my personal secretary, explicit instructions that any missive from you—or from Livesey island—was to be brought to me at once. Thomison is nothing if not scrupulous in such matters. You know him, as he knows you. Besides, that one letter should be mislaid is one thing, that two miss my attention defies belief."

William squirmed in his chair, his collar felt tight on him, as though he were choking. "Upon my oath, my lord, I did write and send them, informing you of what was discovered and how."

Burghley shook his head, stroked his long white beard with his fingers.

It was a gesture William had seen Burghley make in many a conversation, a gesture not of doubt but of uncertainty, and those two were different. He was thinking deeply, but of what? William wondered. That William was lying about the letters, writing them or sending them? Had he lost Burghley's trust so quickly in the conversation?

William felt his head swim. He felt he was awash in a nightmare of his own making. He had written the letters, given them to the new steward, Harris, for posting. Harris said he would put them with letters his mistress was sending to family members, notifying them of her husband's death. But then he thought of Harris, who had demanded bribes from him and from Johane. Why should he have been trusted with such a duty, he who had proved himself since as corrupt as his predecessor, Broderick? He might have broken the seal of both, discovered the contents, and somehow reported the same to Broderick, who had gone from the isle but probably not gone far. He may have merely cast them away out of sheer malice. He realized now that with Harris, anything was possible.

"Well, we have a mystery then, Doctor, but let that rest for now. Tell me what news these letters contained, what I would have read had I received them."

And so William began—not at the beginning, which was hardly more than paddling his feet, but with his return to the island, armed with his magnets, and faith in Johane's promise that she had found something where the magnets could be of use. "I found first a seven-pointed candle stick, a menorah, brought up from the depths by my magnets, whereby Mistress Sheldon and I were persuaded that there was likely more beneath, the Jewish hoard. Then we found a way down."

William explained about the sea cave, the shafts or chimneys as Johane had called them, the tower constructed over the Roman ruin, and his nightmarish descent to the dock the Romans had built. He described the interior of the cave, the patterned walls, the mosaic, all illuminated by his lantern.

"A Roman ruin!" Burghley said excitedly, interrupting William's narrative. "Marvelous, Doctor. It wasn't enough that the Romans occupied our land for four hundred years but they must leave behind them such mementos of their presence. Were that the totality of your discovery it would be worth celebrating. And those mosaics, tell me what they depicted, for I have seen some in Italy where I have traveled, and much admire them."

"A scene of ships with oars and sails, if I remember, my lord, but I must tell you what else I found there, that which I do swear will delight you even more."

"Tell me, Doctor. My ears are ever open to good news."

"It is good news, my lord, although I regret to say bad news will follow."

William paused to see how Burghley would receive this. Burghley showed no reaction; not the frown that William had anticipated but an almost philosophical calm. Perhaps he was used to news that partook of both bad and good. Perhaps that was the way it was at court, nothing ever purely one or the other.

"As it often does," Burghley said, "but pray let's have what's good first, else we cannot judge how bad the bad news be."

William then recited what he had found in the cave. He surprised himself with the extent and accuracy of his memory, as though the inventory, recorded by a zealous clerk, were before his very eyes. Had he left anything out? Cups, plates, candlesticks, coins, chains, wealth that could be embodied in silver and gold. Portable wealth, not the houses and the land and the shops that were abandoned by order of the crown, but what could be transported, entrusted to a wicked shipmaster, a Jew-hater, a thief, a monster.

"And something more, as well."

Burleigh waited, his old eyes alight with anticipation.

"The other tablet, my lord, the companion of the one you have in your cabinet at Theobalds. The final five Commandments. What Solomon called his gold."

"You found it in the cave?"

"Upon my oath, I did—or we did, for Mistress Sheldon aided me at every step."

Burleigh could hardly contain himself. William had never seen the great man so excited. "Show it to me, I care more for it than all the rest discovered. It is only metal, valuable though it may be, but to have now the complete tablet, the Holy Commandments, the law given to Moses, the tablet Solomon called his gold, not because of its precious metal but because of what was written thereon—that is the chief prize which makes all your effort worth the while."

William could hardly bring himself to say the words. "I would, my lord, did I have it."

Burghley looked stunned. For a moment he was speechless or seemed so. Then he said,

"What, do you mean you don't have it with you, Doctor?"

"I am afraid I don't have it at all, which brings me, my lord, to the bad news I spoke of."

He could have related the abduction and theft with more clarity, had he fully understood what had happened. As it was, he stumbled through the story, avoiding telling Burghley how much of his attention on the night of the terrible event was devoted to paying court to Johane, how little to making sure that the treasure in the coffin was properly secured. Even as he spoke, he felt shame. Burghley deserved more candor from him, William was simply not up to it.

"And so when you awoke and found Mistress Sheldon gone, you looked for her, found no trace of her and then proceeded to the inn's stable where the cart and coffin and her horse were also gone."

He sighed heavily despite himself. "That's the sum of it, my lord, save for a letter, more a note, I received warning me not to follow or harm would come to Johane, I mean Mistress Sheldon."

"And the author of this?"

"Mistress Sheldon wrote it, but I trust with John Broderick looking over her shoulder and dictating her words."

"And who is this John Broderick?"

"Sir Arthur's former steward. A scoundrel who contrived, I believe, to have me killed and was almost surely responsible for the deaths of two other men of the island in furthering his aim. I suspect him also to be the murderer of our friend Isaac Silva."

"His aim?"

"To find the treasure himself."

"Do you still have the note, the note written by Mistress Sheldon?"

"I do, my lord." William took it from his pocket and handed it to Burghley, who read it through, sighed heavily, and then handed it back.

"It's to the point, I'll tell you that," Burghley said. "I have read many such notes over my years, threatening letters, poisoned pens, hateful words. it all is the burden of a public life. One makes more enemies than friends, for all that he can do. Do you think this man means what he says, I mean the threats?"

"I'm afraid he does mean it, my lord, every word. He tried to kill me while I was on the island and nearly did so."

It was not an episode he included in his letters, not an event in his life he cared to recall, but he realized he had said more than he intended and having done so, he could not withhold the rest.

He told Burghley about the death of the defrocked cleric, the disappearance of his body, the two men who had rowed him to the little island, assaulted and robbed him, and left him for dead. He told him how he survived.

"A remarkable tale indeed, and an experience worthy of acclaim should you think to publish it. And you think Broderick was behind this?"

"I'm sure of it, my lord. Browne and Locke were his men. I have that on good authority from several sources."

"It is like a story from a traveler's tale," Burghley said, looking at William as though for the first time. "A marooned sailor on a desert isle. Doctor, you have misadventures beyond imagining. Did you ever think at Cambridge you would endure such experiences?"

"I thought I would die on the island, my lord, but thank God I did not. I returned to tell the tale. To you, my lord, and to you alone."

"You were dealing with some dangerous people here, Doctor. Had I known, I would not have sent you to Livesey, nor Mistress Sheldon, at least not without a troop to protect you. But do tell what happened after your discovery that the cart and Mistress Sheldon were gone."

"I did not heed the warning. I could not come back to London as though nothing had happened. I rode after them, or at least, rode in the direction I reasoned they must have gone. Toward London, toward London goldsmiths and those eager to buy stolen goods. I rode most of the day, until late in the evening I met a man who had seen them, or thought he had."

When he told Burghley about the bricklayer he realized that the man might have been wrong in his identification of the men and woman he had seen, might have been wrong in his description of the load their cart carried. Might have been making everything up, as countryfolk sometimes do, to tease city folk, or get money out of them.

"This bricklayer may have seen correctly and reported correctly, or perhaps not. Yet I do agree that London is likely where they came. Where else? To some country retreat where they could sit by the fire and eye their stolen goods?"

"I fear for Mistress Sheldon, that they will harm her."

"You called her Johane earlier. By that informality do I infer that you and she developed feelings for each other?"

William hesitated, unsure what Burghley would make of the truth. It was the thing Burghley had warned against. He decided to be honest. What had he to lose, beyond what he was sure he had already lost in his patron's estimation?

"We did, to tell truth, my lord."

"Well, she's a beautiful young woman. I would think less of you, Doctor, were you to say you were unmoved by her charms. And did she return your love?"

"We were most chaste in our relations, my lord, but yes, within those bounds set by yourself she did express feeling for me. I did ask her to be my wife."

"And she said?"

"She said she would give me an answer on the morning we were to leave the inn. That was when she was taken by Broderick."

"Why not when you asked her?"

"She expressed concern, my lord, that she was of low birth, that she would bring nothing to the marriage, that such a marriage would work to my disadvantage, personally and with regard to my work. She feared my father's disapproval."

"Your father's disapproval!" Burghley laughed. "I can well imagine your father—a lawyer in Colchester, is he not?—having climbed to become himself a gentleman, treated to the spectacle of a daughter-in-law who is naught but a servant."

"With all due respect, my lord, you have seen that Johane is much more than that."

"With equal respect to you, Doctor, I would agree with your estimation. She is a remarkable girl, but what abilities she has do not make her more than what she is. It's a sad truth. We value blood, not ability. Family ties, not intelligence. I tell you there are lords temporal and spiritual in England who now receive all honors who have half her wit and less than half her worth. Yet I share your father's concern, if she indeed reads him aright, marriage to her would hardly advance your position, either in the public or at court. Indeed, it might be somewhat of a scandal, as if there were not enough of those about as is."

"I do love her, my lord, and would gladly take her as she is, low birth and all."

"No dowry?"

"But herself, It's what I told her when I did propose we marry."

"Then you spoke well and honorably, Doctor. What more should a woman want than to be wanted for herself alone? So our poets of love have said from time out of mind. But as you yourself may have observed, marriage is often—is usually—not about love but about advantage, about land, about money, about power, about everything else *but* love. If love comes, it comes often by accident, an unintended consequence of a family alliance, or plain, unmitigated ambition or greed."

"I must find her," William said.

"And this Broderick as well," Burghley said. "And the treasure, and more particularly the plate of the Commandments, which I must have."

"I don't know where to look, my lord."

William heard himself say this and felt shame. He sounded like a whining child, even to himself. He looked at Burghley for signs of disapproval and found it in his patron's stern countenance.

"You are a scientist, Doctor Gilbert, or so you have called yourself to me many times in our acquaintance. Who better than you to discover what's hidden from common eyes? You know what Broderick looks like, you certainly know Mistress Sheldon by sight, for if you love her as you say you do, her very face is imprinted on your heart. You have inventory of what was lost. No one is in a position such as you to recover it. If you need help in that endeavor you shall have it, I promise you. If you need a company of troops you shall have it. But first you must find out where these miscreants have gone. That's not the work of a troop, but of a single diligent searcher."

"I shall attempt to be so, my lord."

"Don't talk of *attempting* something, Doctor. Attempt is merely an honest effort, an effort that may fail. An effort is not enough. I want this Broderick creature brought before the bar, I want to see him hanged, as he deserves, and his two accomplices as well. I want Mistress Sheldon found and freed, that you may decide if your love for her is greater than your ambition as a doctor. And I want the Jewish hoard. It belongs to the crown now, impossible as it would be to restore it to its rightful owners. And I want personally, for myself, the Commandments, the whole ten of them, as God in heaven intended. Go now, Doctor, you have your work ahead of you. God give you success in it."

Burghley had not questioned his story of discovering the treasure; he had not railed at him for losing it. But he had now given him what was an even greater charge. To find a single man in a great city, a man who would have every reason to remain hidden from him. As well, to find Johane. Burghley did not need to give him that directive. But where was all this to begin? And how would it end? He was already grieving the death of Johane, even before he knew for sure Broderick had killed her.

He went home, canceled his appointments for the afternoon, and went to work.

Fifty-Two

William made his way to Fleet Street, where the goldsmiths of London had their shops and where the Worshipful Society of Goldsmiths, one of the wealthiest guilds in the city, had its headquarters. A benefit of being a medical practitioner in London was that one came to know a great many people of importance, and one of these was Alexander Deane, the warden of the guild.

"Doctor Gilbert, my young friend, how do you do in these days of shame?"

Deane's greeting to William was always the same. As was William's answer: "As well as can be expected, given conditions as they are."

They would always laugh after this gloomy exchange, for the truth was the Deane was a jovial man, who by all accounts enjoyed the full benefits of his place in society. He was happily married with six children, each of whom had attainments for him to boast of, and he was well respected by others of his trade in the city, so much so that it was thought his position as head of the guild was his for as long as he should want it.

Deane motioned for William to enter his study, for Deane was not only an excellent worker of gold but also a man learned in all matters of metallurgy. William had first become associated with Deane in that connection; later, Deane had been his patient, William curing him of a half dozen minor ailments and then quartan fever that had him bed-ridden for a week.

A servant brought in two glasses and a wine William recognized by its color.

"So, what brings you out in such weather? Is your own robust health such that you envy those of us more vulnerable?"

William laughed. "Information, if you can help me."

"Information is cheaper than most things I'm asked for. What would you know?" Deane asked.

"How many goldsmiths are there in London?"

"Easy to answer, there are fifty-six who are members of the guild."

"And of these—and I grant you this is a more awkward question—how many of these are disposed to buy gold from dubious sources?"

Deane frowned and looked at William suspiciously. "Why would you know that?"

"I mean, Master Deane, no disrespect for your guild. I am on the trail of stolen goods, a hoard recently discovered and then stolen."

Deane frowned. "You mean goldsmiths not too careful to ask where a seller got what he offers to sell. A silver spoon from a larcenous serving wench, hopeful that she is not caught pilfering."

"Yes, that sort of thing."

Deane thought for a minute. "I can give you no number. I suppose even the most honest of us may from time to time succumb to a larcenous impulse. But there are a few whom I would not trust within a mile of my family's silver, much less items of gold worth much more."

"Could you give me their names?"

Deane thought about this.

"For what purpose, Doctor? To report to the authorities?"

"For purpose of my own. I was responsible for what was stolen and am under heavy obligation to have it back again. Upon my oath, none shall know you named names."

"It would put me in a difficult position, were it known that I was the source of your information."

"As I've said, sir, none shall know."

Deane opened a drawer in his desk and withdrew a piece of paper. For the next few minutes he wrote down names along with some direction as to where these persons might be found. When he finished he handed the paper to William. "You shall see, Doctor, I have made a mark, a cross, by those most likely to be indifferent to the source of anything offered to them."

William looked over the list. Almost all of these had shops on the same street. Surveying them would be easy, he thought, assuming that trying to sell the stolen goods was the first thing Broderick thought of when he arrived in London.

That inference gave him pause. Could William really know the mind of someone as devious and unscrupulous as Broderick? Nonetheless, it was a place to begin.

He had planned his strategy before meeting Deane. Obtain the list, visit each suspected goldsmith, inquire as to their recent purchase of any gold from a man answering Broderick's description, tell them to give him notice should anyone come to sell it. William set out at once.

There were eight goldsmiths on Deane's list. By the end of the day he had visited three. Some of them, he thought, had the devious look of a thief or brigand, a goldsmith by trade but in fact a buyer of stolen goods, paying far less that what the item was worth but confident the seller would realize the risk the buyer was taking. From each of these he received no response. None admitted to having bought anything from such a person William had described, none confessed to having purchased anything of gold, not for the past month.

William trusted none of these responses. Why should these men tell the truth? What had they to gain? They had more to gain by being silent.

For the next day, he decided he would take a different tack. He would seek to purchase what was stolen. No talk of Broderick or of stolen goods. Just a direct honest inquiry about some items from the hoard. Come across as an avid customer. Say he was looking for Judaica—an unusual obsession for a communicant of the queen's church, but what of that? London was full of persons with exotic tastes. Satisfying those was the very hallmark of the city. Maybe a gold tablet with Hebrew writing, a candlestick with seven prongs. A gold chain or bracelet. Something inscribed, in Hebrew, of course. "This is my name and where I can be found. Let me know if anything comes your way. I'll pay well."

The effect of this in the faces of those with whom he spoke was dramatically different from the day before. No suspicious glances under dark brows. No hesitant responses for fear a positive response would reveal some complicity in theft. Just a customer with money to spend. Who cared if he wanted Jewish gold, as long as the young gentleman had the wherewithal to pay for it?

But none said he had what William sought.

Fifty-Three

Two weeks had passed since his return to London. He had resumed his practice but thought hourly of Johane. During the day, her face was ever before him. At night, he dreamed of her. He rehearsed in his head their parting conversation, their last embrace. He walked the streets to catch a glimpse of her, or Broderick, but it all seemed futile.

Then, on an afternoon of the third week when he was about to write to Burghley and tell him he had failed, a visitor came to his door. It was man with whom he had done some business in the past, a man whose profession hardly had name. He was a procurer of goods who, knowing William sought magnets from remote lands, had promised earlier to keep an eye out for any that should come his way.

William asked him in. The merchant, Simon Willoughby, was a stout little man his father's age, with tired eyes and hair that flew every which way when he removed his cap. He carried with him a handsome leather bag, slung over his shoulder.

William bade him enter. The two sat down and William waited to hear what Willoughby wanted. He knew Willoughby was a man careful of his time, and that he should pay a visit to William's house suggested the bag Willoughby carried contained something to arouse William's interest. Whatever it was, it was a heavy, like a brick.

"I have bought this very day a lodestone, Doctor, a very fine piece, in my humble opinion. I wonder if you should want it for your experiments?"

William had bought magnets from Willoughby before. He had treated the merchant with ever so many lectures on its properties, powers, and importance, both in navigation and even in healing. William had gotten the impression that the lectures may have bored the merchant, but they had at least firmly convinced him that the young doctor, half-mad though he might be from excess learning, was a very good customer, one that Willoughby should cultivate.

Willoughby opened the bag and pulled out a rectangular bar the size of a brick and handed it to William. William took one look at it, and then looked again. He noticed the almost indiscernible mark scratched in the metal: an initial and a number. The magnet was his, one of the bars he had taken to the island. There was no doubt about it.

But he did not tell Willoughby that. He would keep that fact to himself for the time being at least and buy it back if he needed to. He did not want to offend this man by suggesting he had bought stolen goods and lost money thereby.

William reached across his desk, where he had a piece of iron he used as a paperweight. He tested the magnet. The attraction was instant. Magnet and iron stuck fast. It was an effort to separate them. "Excellent," he said. "If you are offering it to me for sale, I am your man. How much?"

Willoughby named a price. William hesitated for a moment, but only for show. Then he said, "Agreed."

His visitor smiled and leaned back in the chair, doubtless glad for the sale but probably also that he did not have to lug it home again.

"Do you have other of these, these magnets?"

"I have, Doctor, or will have," Willoughby said.

"You say *will have*. What do you mean?"

"When he that brought it to me saw I was willing to pay for the one, he asked if I wanted more. He said he had others, and that he would return and sell them to me as well, for the same price. I came to you, Doctor, because I thought you'd want them."

"And he who sold it to you?"

"He was tall, lanky, dark hair, very blue eyes. an imperious air, as though he were a gentleman, though I knew he was not."

"How could you tell?"

"A man knows," Willoughby said, nodding wisely. "Besides, he didn't talk like a gentleman, if you know what I mean."

"Smooth-faced."

"Nay, Doctor, the beginnings of a beard."

"I don't suppose he told you how he came to have the magnets, what use he put them to?"

"No. He didn't say. I didn't ask. It was no business of mine, Doctor."

"I'll buy this magnet from you—and the others as well, although I'd like to talk to the man who sold them to you."

The merchant looked worried. William knew why. Willoughby was afraid William would buy them directly from the seller and he'd miss out on his profit.

"Don't worry," William said. "I only want to know what country they're from. It's important in assessing a magnet's strength. He'll sell to you. I'll buy from you. You will lose nothing in the transaction, I swear it."

Willoughby seemed relieved.

"What time does this person come to your shop?"

"In the afternoon, he said, weather permitting."

"I'll be there, whether the weather permits or not."

When Willoughby left, William sat for a long time marveling at his good fortune and the irony of it. He had yet to find the gold, but he had found the magnets. They had been in the coffin along with the treasure, which was proof positive that this imposing fellow Willoughby described was none other than John Broderick, thief, murderer, and abductor of innocent women. William was glad now that he had not written to Burghley confessing failure. He was the recipient of good fortune. He had not found the magnets, the magnets had found him.

Still, it was a personal victory, which Burghley would acknowledge when he learned of it. A step, a large step, in the right direction.

A Cambridge colleague had once advised him, when benefited by Fortune, claim it as the fruit of your own genius. A fortunate man invites envy and doubt as to his worthiness to receive what he has not earned, the same colleague had said. But a man who finds within himself the seed of accomplishment inspires, gives others hope, defeats the twin evils of melancholy and despair.

That night he could hardly sleep. He kept going over in his mind what he should do when he encountered Broderick, or whether he should confront him at all. Burghley had promised muscle—armed men if needed. But William knew it was too early for that. He was sure Broderick had sold the magnet to Willoughby, but he wanted to see the man for himself.

While he wanted his magnets back, the gold was the ultimate prize, that and discovering Johane's whereabouts. He trusted that if Johane was alive, she would be with Broderick, a hostage perhaps, but alive.

He would station himself all afternoon outside Willoughby's shop and wait until Broderick appeared with the other magnets. When Broderick had finished his business, William would follow him, follow him to where the gold was, to where Johane was.

Fifty-Four

Next day the weather cleared, the smoke returned to its wonted place in the London air, and William made his way to Willoughby's shop, a hole in the wall on the eastern side of the city. Willoughby, after all, was no ordinary tradesman. While honest, William believed, Willoughby procured goods of special interest to his customers, importing most from elsewhere in the world. His business was essentially simple: His customers told him what they needed and Willoughby found it for them, sometimes at the end of the earth, often at an exorbitant price. William had come on him by accident, shortly after moving to London.

There was a tavern on the opposite side of the street, and William found a table there near a window and waited and watched. He waited and watched all morning and then into the afternoon, and Broderick did not come. Indeed, no one seemed to come and enter the little shop as far as William could tell. When dark fell, he left the table he had occupied, paid the tavern keeper a good sum for allowing him to sit there all day and order very little, and approached the shop.

"He never came," Willoughby said, opening his hands in a gesture of helplessness.

"He said he would."

"People say all manner of things, Doctor. I could tell you stories about that. Maybe tomorrow. He was excited when I said I would buy the other magnets."

"Did you tell him you had a customer for them?"

Willoughby shook his head. "He'd ask who it was, find you, and sell them to you directly."

William was relieved. The last thing he would have wanted was for Broderick to hear his name.

"Maybe tomorrow he will come," Willoughby said again, his face hopeful.

"God willing," William murmured, disheartened.

The tavern keeper was surprised when William returned the next morning and gave him money for his chair by the window with a full view of the shop's door. He gave William a queer look, wondering doubtless whether the young, well-dressed gentleman was not mad, or perhaps up to something sinister or illegal. William ordered something that passed for breakfast, and waited.

Just before noon a man appeared, paused before the shop, and then entered, but he looked nothing like Broderick. He was stouter, older, bearded. He carried a bag, a large one. There was something about him that was familiar to William but he couldn't place it. His profession brought him into contact with a great many people. But after the man disappeared inside, William remembered. It was Browne, one of the two men who had marooned him on Little Livesey island. He was wearing a different cap than he had worn on the island, a city tradesman's cap. His beard was longer and shaggier. But it was Browne, without a doubt.

At once he stood, knocking back the stool upon which he had been sitting and startling other customers who wondered if the young man who had been staring so intently out the window had had some sort of fit, for which a physician should be called. It was all William could do to wait. Evidently, the transaction was quickly done. Browne emerged, still holding the bag, slack now, empty.

Browne entered the street and moved quickly to the east, as though he were hurrying for an appointment. William followed at what he thought was a safe distance, finding some comfort in that it was a busy street, full of shop patrons, apprentice boys on errands, clerks and secretaries, a multitude of housewives with children in tow. Browne walked fast, and never looked behind him—to William's relief.

Not long after, they came to the outskirts of the city, where the houses gave way to houses of a different character, farmhouses surrounded by fields. All this time Browne kept the same pace and never looked behind him, never suspecting William thought that he was being followed. William imagined Broderick, being clever, would have been more circumspect. Thinking about that, William was happy that Broderick had not brought the magnets to Willoughby.

And then, suddenly, the street rose to an incline and Browne disappeared. William picked up his pace, almost ran, and when he came to the height of the road he spotted Browne again, this time standing before the door of a two-story house at what was clearly the ending of the street and the fringe of an apple orchard.

William drew back, hid himself behind a tree. After a few minutes, the door opened—William could see that clearly—and then Browne entered. William caught a glimpse of someone admitting him. It looked like a man, but at the distance William was, he couldn't be sure. Was it Broderick who let him in? Browne's accomplice, what was his name, Locke? Or some other person, a servant perhaps? It was that kind of house, old style and dignified, chimneyed, certainly manned by servants, perhaps several of them.

William waited and watched. It was now mid-afternoon. There was no more sign of life within. William didn't know what to do next. Was it now time to see Burghley, to have his men besiege the house? William imagined this and gloried in the very thought of it. In his mind he saw the troop advance, armored and weaponed, the house surrounded, Broderick dragged forth, forced to reveal where he had hidden the hoard, where he had imprisoned Johane. William imagined the glorious reunion, Johane in his arms, grateful for her rescue, grateful to him.

Then he decided it was still too soon for that. On the other side of the road another house stood, and near to that yet another; both more modest houses, the sort owned by prosperous farmers, surrounded by gardens and orchards and pastures. They had barns and the pastures were filled with sheep or goats or cattle. It was the more distant house he intended to visit.

A woman answered the door—the housewife, not a servant. She looked William over, saw that he was a gentleman by his dress, and her initial expression changed from disapproval at being interrupted in her work to guarded respect. William apologized for interrupting her. She did not ask him to come in. He knew she was afraid of him, this stranger at her door. William spoke quickly to explain himself.

"I am trying to find an old friend who has moved into the neighborhood.

It would have been recent," William said. "His name is John Broderick. He has a friend, or servant, named Browne, a big hulking fellow with a beard, who might live with him."

The woman seemed relieved that William's business had nothing to do with her, no threat to her own house or family. She was a plump woman of about forty with graying hair beneath a simple cap.

"I know no one by that name, sir," the woman said. "Nor by the name of the other person you mentioned, Master Benson, was it?"

"Browne," William said.

"As far as moving into our neighborhood, there has been but one in recent time, and that would be in the house near the woods."

"What about the house?"

"He who owned it and his father before him have died, sir. The house is now owned by his sister, and she has leased it out, or so I understand."

"And he who has leased it, his name isn't Broderick, John Broderick?"

"Oh I don't know what the gentleman's name might be. It could be Broderick or some other name. I saw him only once since he moved in."

"Can you tell me what he looked like? Can you describe him? Perhaps he's my friend but I wouldn't want to knock on his door and find a stranger answer."

The woman paused, looked thoughtful. "Well, I didn't see him clearly. My eyes aren't what they used to be. I think he was a tall man because he with him was shorter."

"There were two men you saw then?"

"More, sir, There were four persons. One a woman, I think, or so she seemed, though it might have been a boy. It was the first day they were here."

"And when was that?"

"I think no more than a fortnight past, sir."

"But you've seen no one enter or leave the house since?"

"Nary a person."

"And you have no idea what he who resides there does to earn his living?" She shook her head. "Well, sir, he's no farmer."

"Maybe a gentleman of independent means," William said.

The woman looked at him quizzically. He could see she hadn't understood the concept. *Does not everyone do something to earn his bread?* her expression seemed to say. The concept of permanent idleness was foreign to her experience.

William thanked the woman and started to leave, then hesitated. "I wonder if you would do me a favor," William asked.

"If I can, sir."

"The person you describe, the tall man, is not the friend I sought," William said. "I pray you, should you see your neighbor, don't tell him about my visit to you, or that I asked about him or his friends. Sometimes people are undone when a stranger inquires of them, and I wouldn't want to cause the gentleman distress. God's truth, I mean him no harm at all."

The woman looked fretful. "That's true, sir. Were some stranger come asking about me or my husband, I would be fearful too, that some constable or sheriff's man had come to take me off to prison or give me a fine."

William laughed. "Thank you, mistress, you've been very helpful."

"Oh, sir, I don't see how I was since your friend doesn't live there."

He turned to go, then said. "You said the house was inherited by the previous owner's niece?"

"So it was," the woman said.

"Does she by any chance live around here?"

"She does indeed, sir. She lives in the farmhouse just beyond the woods, the one with the newly thatched roof. Only a blind man can miss it."

The house of the niece was another prosperous timbered farmhouse very much like the one Broderick and his companions now occupied. When he came up to it he saw at once that he would have no need to knock on the door. A man and a woman stood on the front steps berating a third person who seemed, by his dress, to be a servant. The man stood abjectly with a cap in his hand submitting humbly to his chastisement. William was but a few feet away when the couple became aware of his approach and stopped their diatribe, which seemed to have something to do with missing spoons the servant was alleged to have taken.

Seeing William, the man—obviously the master of the house—scowled, and said: "And what would you have, sir, that you come so boldly upon us?"

William was not accustomed to such rudeness, but he let it pass.

"A question about the house down the road, the one your wife inherited, or so I have been led to believe."

"What about it?" the woman said, matching her husband's sharpness. "The property is now mine and I can lease it to whom I will."

William was about to explain when suddenly, the husband looked at the servant and said, "You, get you gone, or I'll put the constable on you."

The servant scuttled off, making a rude gesture over his shoulder as he reached the road.

"So the house is already leased, is it? I was interested in the property."

"Well, as I said, sir, it is leased. To a gentleman and his family."

The couple turned to go back into the house. They shut the door with a slam.

William would like to have asked more about the tenant, this so-called gentleman from the city and the other people in the house. Yet clearly the woman and her husband didn't seem inclined to reveal any more than they had.

But William felt now he had all the information he needed. He was confident he had found Broderick's hiding place. He started walking back to the city and was passing through the woods when he heard a voice coming from the trees. It was the dismissed servant. He was a young man in his twenties, William reckoned, with strong facial features and a cap pulled down to his eyebrows. Before William could speak, the man immediately began to curse his former employers, calling them names, and warning William from having anything to do with them.

"I curse the day I came to serve there, sir. That the house she inherited is already leased to another is a blessing to you, for no one deals with my former master or mistress and escapes their wrath or savagery. It's not that I didn't like being ordered about. That's the life you live as a serving man. But it was worse with her. She's a devil, or his very wife, my oath upon it."

"Do you know the new occupants of the house, the gentleman who leased your mistress's house?"

"I never saw him, or them. They came by one night, said they wanted a house to live in for the year. My mistress had just come into possession and was eager to find someone. She and her husband needed the money and they got it from this London person. All this I know from what other servants in the house told me. And they told me something else. The London gentleman gave my mistress gold."

"Gold?"

"Gold coins. For the lease. Who pays in gold to lease a house, save he's some lord or prince? And this man was neither."

"But how do you know, if you never saw him yourself?"

"Well, you tell me, sir, would a great lord lease a farmhouse to dwell in? Look, sir, my mistress accused me of stealing a silver spoon, and the truth is, I did. No, sir, whatever the man was he was no gentleman, nor his companions, and for all I know he got his gold coins the same way I got my silver spoon, by filching it from him to whom it rightly belonged."

By evening William was back in the city where he found Willoughby waiting for him, grinning from ear to ear. He had brought with him the remaining magnets.

"It was a different man this time, Doctor, him who brought them."

"I know. That's of no importance now."

"He asked me for more for them when he found I had found a buyer so soon."

"Greed will do that," William said. "No matter, I'll pay for them."

Each of the magnets bore his mark. Now the set was safely home again. He thanked Willoughby and saw him to the door.

Now he was ready to approach Burghley with what he had learned.

There was no doubt in his mind that he had found Broderick and probably the stolen hoard as well. The question was whether Johane was the woman the neighbor had seen entering the house. Was she still Broderick's prisoner, or was she dead?

William was shown right in when he arrived at Burghley's house, bypassing guards and the remnant of the day's petitioners.

Burghley sat him down. William reported what he had found. Burghley smiled and summoned his clerk, William's friend.

"Where do you say this house is?"

William told him again.

Burghley said he knew the neighborhood. "Go with my guard. Show them the right house. We wouldn't want to assault the wrong house and terrify some innocent householder."

"My pleasure, your lordship. I wouldn't have it any other way. But my lord..." William paused.

"Say it."

"He may have Mistress Sheldon there as prisoner."

"Don't worry, Doctor. I'm old but not so aged to forget what you told me of your feelings for this woman. I will inform the captain of the guard that there may be an innocent hostage in the house. He is used to such cases, believe me. He has fought Scots many a time, and they do take hostages as a matter of course."

"I would not that he set fire to the house or open up with cannon, my lord."

"The captain shall not, Doctor. Upon my oath. And if your beloved is there, he shall treat her as though she were his own daughter, nay, the queen herself."

"With your permission, my lord, I would like to be with the company."

Burghley laughed. "By God, Doctor, you shall be—and whether I permit it or no. For love makes fools of even good and wise men.

William wondered if Burghley was speaking from experience. It was not a question he dared to ask.

Fifty-Five

Before dawn, William set out with the captain and his men, all in good humor despite the possibility that some of them would not return at day's end or, if so, would be bloody and broken. Burghley had minced no words in his instructions. The men they sought to arrest were hard men, dangerous felons, inured to violence, and unlikely to surrender without a fight. He told them the men would almost certainly be armed.

William counted at least twenty men, fully dressed for war. The troop was commanded by a man William knew, a doughty veteran of campaigns in France and Holland. Rough speaking, but trustworthy. A man who knew how to wield a sword, fire a pistol, storm a castle, or storm a farmhouse in Middlesex if he was bidden.

William wasn't even sure Burghley had told the captain what the miscreants indoors had done to deserve this, but he did trust the captain had been told to take care in case there was a hostage. The captain was a man who knew how to take orders, no philosopher concerned as to why. The question was whether he would restrain himself or his troop when the firing started. William doubted Broderick would give up easily, even if armed only with pitchforks and kitchen ladles.

It was getting light when they came to Broderick's retreat. The house was shrouded in early morning stillness. If there were servants within, they were not to be seen or heard, and it occurred to William that the assault on the house had somehow been foreseen and all within fled. He had discovered Broderick's hideout; but had he also betrayed his purpose in speaking to the neighbors? Had a word of warning got to Broderick, or perhaps even an inkling within himself that his pursuers were near? If heaven could warn of dangers, could not the devil as well, looking out for his children in their time of need?

The column of men formed a line. The captain motioned to them to be silent, to keep the horses still if possible. The element of surprise was essential, he had explained earlier. He would fall upon the enemy and take the house before those within were aware.

The captain motioned his men to advance, then divided his force, sending half around to the back where there was a barn and an orchard, concealing himself and the remainder behind a hedge. William stayed with the captain, hoping for the best, a quick surrender of the house's occupants, the rescue of Johane, and the manacling of Broderick and his companions. The front door of the house lay about a stone's throw away. If it was like other houses of its kind, there would be a postern door as well, ground floor windows wide enough to crawl from, and concealed spaces like priest's holes that might provide refuge from the assault.

"This worked well in France," the captain said, turning to William who had ridden beside him. William supposed he was referring to the strategy he was about to employ. Surround the house, assault the front, prevent anyone from escaping. Just seeing their predicament would cause most men to surrender without a fight. That was the captain's view. He said he didn't expect bloodshed. There was nothing like helmets, halberds, swords, and bucklers to cow the most heinous scoundrels—which he assumed these men were, not trained soldiers, and poorly armed if armed at all.

"How will you proceed?" William asked.

"As I have said, surround the house. Scare the hell out of them inside. If luck holds, we'll not fire or shot or draw a sword. They'll be sensible and come out. You shall see, Doctor."

"And if luck doesn't hold?"

"We'll smoke them out," the captain said matter-of-factly.

William looked toward the house. He imagined it consumed in flames, no great feat since it was all timber, no stone or brick. There was no sign of life within. All windows were shuttered. But he knew that Johane might be there inside, too.

"Let me go in," William said. "Let me go in first."

The captain turned to William and gave him an incredulous stare. "What did you say, Doctor?"

"I want to go in before you."

The captain looked startled, his jaw dropped. "You're mad if you think that will do any good. You're not armed, you've no experience that I know of in these dealings. You'll only get in the way, or get yourself killed. And then his lordship will kill me."

"I can talk to Broderick. He's a vicious knave but not stupid."

"They're more likely to do that if we send a volley of shot at the windows and doors. Besides, Doctor, I tell you again, if you get but a scratch in all this, I'll have to answer to his lordship, who has taken a liking to you. You will not move from this place, Doctor. That's an order."

Ignoring the command, William leaped from his horse and ran toward the door of the house, the captain's curses ringing out behind him. He had seen a shutter open slightly on the ground floor. Someone within would see what they were facing.

William pounded on the door. Almost at once, it opened a crack. Enough for him to catch the quick glimpse of a bearded face.

He thought it was Browne at first, then when the person spoke he saw it was Broderick. He had let his beard grow, but the cruel mouth and lifeless eyes were the same, forming the same supercilious sneer William had learned to hate on the island.

"Doctor Gilbert, I warned you what would happen if you followed me."

"Do you have Johane?"

"I do, and I'll keep her if you please. She'll pay the price of your not minding your own business."

"The house is surrounded," William said. "You've no possibility of escape. Let her go."

Then, Broderick looked up to see the captain and his men advancing. He cursed and slammed the door shut. William could hear it being bolted from within.

William heard a noise behind him. It was the captain and two of his men riding up at a gallop.

"Get back and away, Doctor," the captain cried. "You've had your chance. Speaking them fair's a fool's game. Were they honest men such appeals might work, but for miscreants as these be…"

The captain didn't finish. He barked an order to two or three of the men, who quickly dismounted, advanced upon the house and lay their shoulders to the door, but it was thick oak and would not budge, despite a good deal of effort and cursing. This failed, the captain and the men drew back, dragging William with them.

The captain conferred briefly with his second in command then ordered an attack on the house, first with pistols fired at the window shutters. For the next few minutes William was nearly deafened by the explosions of gunfire, but it was clear lead balls would do little to penetrate the walls of the house and there was no response from within, no returning fire and certainly no signal of surrender or parley.

The captain cursed with frustration. "Burn them out," he cried. "Like rats."

William watched, horrified, as two of the men came forward with bows and arrowheads covered with oil cloth set alight, and sent their missiles toward the roof. It was the very thing he had feared: the captain frustrated by the resistance, Burghley's orders ignored.

The archers' aim was true. The thatch of the roof was old and exploded into flame. Within the next minute, the fire had spread to the upper floor of the house and was quickly consuming everything the flames licked. The smoke poured from every opening, obscuring the scene. William heard the captain say that those within had set a fire themselves to hasten their own destruction and avoid the punishment of the law. William doubted this was true, but then thought maybe it was. It would not be unlike Broderick or his two fellows. Anything to avoid capture, even if it meant death for themselves. Better that than the rope or a dismal existence in one of her majesty's prisons, subject to torture and starvation.

But then he had another thought, one he suddenly felt more convincing. Their motive may not be suicide, but a need to cover their escape. Why else?

He left his appointed station and rode around to the back of the house, where there was a stand of trees, an old orchard, and smoke so intense that he was nearly blinded by it.

Meanwhile, the noise of pistol shots and the conflagration had alerted the neighborhood, and a crowd of men and woman were now assembled in front of the burning house and behind. William had seen fire work this furiously before in his life, but never with such speed. Well had the prophets of Israel viewed hell as a place of eternal fire, for what else conveyed such an image of absolute destruction? Within minutes, the entire house had been consumed and was hardly recognizable as a human dwelling.

He had not let himself think that Johane might be within. It was too painful, and he had been momentarily distracted by the fury of the blaze. He thought about it now with a sinking heart. Broderick had not claimed she was within the house, only implied that he still had control of her. Perhaps she was somewhere else, hidden away and bound, but safe from the destruction visited on the house and its occupants. Was there not a small chance at least of this being so?

It was a hope he held on to, despite its unlikelihood.

It was William who found the first body, which was hardly recognizable as such, but a body nonetheless. A man, he thought, but not Broderick. This was a shorter, more slightly-built corpse. William thought it was probably Jeremy Locke, the other man that conveyed him to the island and left him for dead.

The captain came up behind him and stood staring at the charred remains. Hardened in battle, the captain seemed unmoved by the devastation before him. He had seen it all before on one battlefield or another—the mutilated dead, the near complete erasure of human identity. When he spoke to William, his words seemed almost idle curiosity.

"Man or maid, Doctor, can you tell?"

William looked closer. The body had been almost entirely incinerated; the face and hair were gone, as was the clothing. The body parts that might have permitted a determination of gender were burned away as if some accelerant had intensified the carnage.

Was it Johane? He dreaded to think so. Then he noticed a piece of blackened metal protruding from what had been the chest of the diseased. "He was killed before the fire," William said, as much to himself as to any of the captain's men who had been assigned to search the rubble. "Stabbed in the heart." The captain's men had not done this, that was clear. It would have been Broderick, turning on his own.

He knew the body could be Johane's. He imagined Broderick killing her for revenge, either before William came to the door or immediately after. It was no more than he had threatened from the first. He would have had time, and a mind for murder. But then a worse thought came to him. If it was Johane he looked upon, William was almost as responsible for her death as Broderick. He had after all defied the warning not to follow, had insisted on doing so, even knowing that his pursuit would put Johane in great danger.

His only hope left was that the next body discovered would be clearly Broderick's. But he knew even now that Broderick's death, as much deserved as it was, would not assuage his grief or his guilt.

Behind him, the captain mumbled something under his breath. William didn't hear, didn't want to hear. He turned away, and started back to where his horse was tethered. He tried to shut out the scene by closing his eyes. The stench of burned flesh was awful, but hardly worse than the sight of the dead, hardly worse than his grief.

Fifty-Six

The search continued until noon, by which time the smoke had cleared and the extent of the devastation could be seen. There was nothing left but ashes and a confusion of charred timbers where the house had stood. Neighbors, drawn to the scene by the noise of angry voices and gunfire, had since returned to their homes, except for the owner of the house, Mistress Cable, who loudly complained to the captain that their fiery darts had caused her house to burn.

The captain told her that those within had set the fire themselves. She said she didn't believe it and continued to complain. She only ceased when the captain threatened to place her under arrest and drag her before the magistrate for obstructing the queen's business.

"I knew not it was her majesty's business," she said, her outrage suddenly tempered by a healthy terror of royal authority and the punishment it could impose.

"Well now, mistress, you know," the captain said and sent her off, along with her husband who had also come to the scene, grieving that his house had been destroyed.

William looked out over the ruin. It had scared even the earth around it, the air still smelled of smoke, he could smell burned flesh too, a sweet stench of the battlefield the house had become. Then he had a thought. The house had burned to the ground, but what of beneath?

"Was there a cellar?" William asked the woman who owned the house, and who had yet to comply with the captain's orders that she and her husband go home.

"Yes, sir, and a fine cellar it was," the woman replied, tearfully. "High enough for a tall man to stand without bending over, and dry in the worst weather."

"And a way in and out from the outside?"

"Yes," she said, looking at William curiously.

"A cellar to the house?" The captain called to one of his men to repeat William's question.

"The house fell in upon it," the man replied. He was in fact no more than a boy, the youngest of the troop and, William had noticed, much bullied by the others.

"We must dig it out," William said.

"That would be a good deal of work to do," the captain replied, obviously eager to be on his way. William realized that for him the day had been a victory. The castle had been taken, its recalcitrant occupiers incinerated. Burghley had given the captain a job to do and he had done it to his own satisfaction. That it might have also killed Broderick's hostage did not seem to bother him.

"Our work here is not done until all the house is searched," William said. "The cellar is part of the house. Lord Burghley will not abide a job half done."

The captain considered this, then nodded. His men had been standing by their horses engaged in casual talk, obviously eager to mount and get themselves home, or to a nearby tavern or bawdy house. Now the captain called them to attention. "Dig out the cellar," he shouted, although not with the same vigor that he had earlier shown in commanding the attack. The men grumbled. They were tired. Digging holes wasn't what they had signed up for. But they obeyed the order, none wanting to get on the wrong side of the captain, or worse, his lordship.

The soldiers assigned to the task, reluctantly removed their breastplates and helmets and turned to the task, though none seemed happy to do it, or think it was so important. They had not brought shovels, no one thinking that would be part of their duty, but these were quickly secured from the neighboring farms and within an hour the digging had begun.

By early evening, the task was done, charred beams and planks that had held the house upright in all weathers were now dragged away and stacked to reveal the cavity beneath the house. It had, as the woman had said, been a deep cellar, with walls and floor of stone, a commodious place for storage, and what must have been a doorway to the yard—for the steps going up and out had not burned.

And here was discovered another body as unrecognizable as the first two, although more clearly a man's, despite the crushed skull that had probably killed him before the fire could. Again, not Broderick. Too short and narrow in the shoulders. The man's shoes had somehow escaped consumption. They dangled at the end of charred ankle bones.

Here too was found a chest, saved from the inferno by some miracle, placed neatly in a niche in the cellar wall, to be retrieved easily by any survivor of the conflagration.

William reached the prize before the captain's men could. It had a heavy padlock, which one of the soldiers shattered with two swift blows of the shovel. William opened it, saw a canvas cover, and pulled it back slowly. Within he saw gold and silver plates, cups, candlesticks. All precious things he and Johane had placed in the coffin. He had memorized the contents. He could identify each item. He had carried them up from the sea cave in his arms.

It was the Jewish hoard, or what remained of it, what Broderick and his confederates had not already sold off.

Near the bottom of the chest, amidst the plates and chains and bracelets, was the gold tablet Burghley had coveted above all other items in the inventory. The missing Commandments: Solomon's gold.

The captain looked down on the find and asked what the thing was William held. He said it looked like a serving plate.

"A good deal more than that, captain."

"What then?"

"Have you heard of Moses?"

The captain shrugged. He said he knew no one of that name. "Is he some great lord that I should know him?"

"Or the Ten Commandments?"

"What the priests used to speak of, when they stooped to speak the King's English and not Latin."

"These are the Commandments, or at least five of them."

"I cannot read them," the captain said.

"They are written in Hebrew."

"His lordship will be pleased with that, I do think. He's a great collector, you know."

"I do know that," William said, thinking of his lordship's cabinet of curiosities, where he imagined in the near future the plate would rest along with its companion piece.

"It's a good thing I ordered my men to search the cellar, or we would have missed this," the captain said.

"A good thing indeed, Captain," William said, content to let the captain revise the history of the day as he saw fit.

"We've got the chest up on one of the horses. Two of my men will ride double."

"What of the dead, the bodies?" William asked, thinking of the one he feared might be Johane's.

"Why, Doctor, we'll do what's done in war, we'll leave them where they lie. When they stink enough, the locals will see they're buried. Never doubt it."

Fifty-Seven

For the captain, the return to Burghley's London house was a triumph, worthy of a fanfare of trumpets and beating of drums. The farmhouse had been taken, its occupants killed, a treasure discovered. And the captain had not lost a single man in the effort. All the way back to the city he declared this, repeating the thought like a rote prayer. Not a single man lost. Not a single wound.

William had less to celebrate. The treasure was restored, but he suspected somehow Broderick had escaped to the nearby woods, possibly from the cellar door, hidden from view by the smoke and confusion, which as the captain had surmised might well have been Broderick's work as much as the captain's flaming arrows.

And what of Johane? Had it been her body into which a knife had been plunged? Had Broderick carried out his terrible threat at the last minute, surrounded by Burghley's troop but defiant at last, killing his prisoner to avenge himself on William? Had he escaped, William imagined Broderick stuffing his pockets with as much of the treasure as he could carry, skulking off into the woods, exultant at having escaped. As for Johane, perhaps the body wasn't hers after all. Perhaps Broderick had dragged her with him. She might have been a prisoner elsewhere. He imagined Broderick had found more than one hiding place in London—some cellar, attic, or priest's hole—to place prisoners like Johane, keeping them alive for some monstrous purpose known only to him.

In the library of his London house, Lord Burghley and his secretary, Hastings, had spread the treasure out upon a long table, and Burghley had set Hastings to work cataloging the items, the contents of the hoard to be reported to the queen, to whom they by right belonged. By candlelight, the relics shone as brightly as they might have done when they were first concealed in the sea cave. And chief of these was the golden tablet with the last five of the Commandments.

Burghley had brought from his cabinet the first of the tablets and placed it with the second. The great man could not take his eyes off the pair, joined at last as originally intended, as King Solomon himself had looked upon them and called them his gold because the words of God were of greater value than the gold they were inscribed on. That was mere metal, the work of the forge, a metalsmith's hands and art. But the words, they were God's words, God's thoughts. Eternal truths and mandates for all believers.

Finally, he turned to William. "Doctor, you have succeeded beyond my wildest imagination, both in recovering these relics from the sea cave where the thieves had hidden them and in this recent effort to recover them from John Broderick, who you think may have escaped the fire?"

"I think it likely, my lord, for none of the bodies we recovered could have been his. He is a tall man, easily above six feet. No body found in the debris was of that stature."

"And you are sure he was in the house when the fire started?"

"I saw him with my own eyes, my lord. We spoke. I recognized him at once, though he had grown a beard since last we met."

"Well, justice will come for him by and by, as it does for us all," Burghley said. "A man so hardened in criminality does not discard the mantle easily. He will commit more crimes I have no doubt, and in God's good time, he will face the rope. But what of Mistress Sheldon?"

"I am grieved to say one of the bodies may have been hers, my lord. It was burned beyond recognition of sex. The person slain had died by knife, not fire."

"Killed by Broderick, you think?"

"I think so, and since Broderick had threatened to do her harm if I pursued him, the body might have been hers."

Burghley sighed heavily. "I am sorry, William," Burghley said, reaching across the table and placing his hand on William's. "I rejoice in finding a treasure, but you have lost one. Johane Sheldon was an exceptional young woman, her low birth notwithstanding. May God give her rest if she has indeed passed to the life to come, and may he who killed her burn in hell."

"Thank you, my lord. I share your prayer."

"I have something for you, William. It will not console you in your loss, but it may compensate you for the tribulations you have suffered in being my agent these past weeks."

Burghley nodded to Hastings, who went to a cupboard and brought back a silk purse. "This is for you, Doctor, with my gratitude. When I contemplate the tablet, I shall think of your service."

Burghley nodded to William to untie the bag. Inside William saw dozens of coins, some gold, some silver. Not a king's ransom or even a modest fortune, but sufficient to compensate for his tribulations and his losses, except of course for one. For that loss, there could be no recompense.

"You do me too much honor, my lord."

"Honor you deserve. A lesser man would have kept part, or even all, for himself. You might have returned from Livesey empty handed. Said your search had come to naught. I would have believed you. The treasure was lost for nearly three hundred years. The sea might well have swallowed all of it up, to be revealed only in the last day when the sea gives up her dead. I would have believed you and would have rested content with the tablet I have, as must we all rest content when hope is lost."

"It never crossed my mind, my lord, to take what was not mine."

"I'm sure it did not. I employ you as a doctor because you know medicine, but also because you are honest. A dishonest doctor cannot be trusted to cure an ailing cat."

William laughed.

"Discovered treasure rightfully belongs to its original owner," Burghley continued. "These poor Jews so betrayed are long gone and it were impossible to find their descendants. The treasure belongs therefore to the crown and he who finds it deserves a portion thereof, which I confer on you."

William made another low bow.

"What will you do now?"

"Go home, my lord. See to my patients, if I have any left. Experiment with my magnets, that human knowledge may advance. And have hope."

"Hope?"

"That Johane still lives, somewhere, somehow."

"God be with you, then. Spend that money wisely, Doctor, neither extravagantly nor on loose women and bad practices—as my father used to say. As for Johane, I share your hope that she lives. You deserve to be happy, my friend. After all, in life love is the great thing, is it not?"

"Yes, my lord, I do believe it is."

Fifty-Eight

His grief was a strange thing, a heart-wrenching misery he had not experienced before. He had lost others close to him in death. His beloved mother, and the Dutch girl he had loved and lost, but his grief for Johane was more complex. It was mixed with a disquieting uncertainty as to whether she was really dead, and that added a peculiar pain to his emotions and filled his soul with melancholy, even on days in the few weeks after when he had good reason to feel cheerful and hopeful.

With the money given him by Burghley he had secured a lease on a second house, north of the city, a property with a cottage, a garden, an orchard, and fields of grain worked by tenants. He would stay there when life in London became oppressive, or if the plague drove everyone far afield; or he would take refuge there in times of civil unrest, a condition often threatened by the machinations of ambitious courtiers. His plans for the future were clouded with uncertainties.

He was in that state of disquiet when he received the letter. It had come by special messenger, from someone who had appeared at his door, thrust it into his servant Thomas's hand, and then ran off without the usual expectation that the service provided might earn him some modest gratuity. Thomas described the deliverer as a scurvy fellow of indeterminate age, but definitely of low degree by his ragged coat and rudeness.

"The fellow said nothing?"

"Nothing save whom it was for, Doctor. He looked down all the while so I could not get any decent look at his face."

His heart leaped even upon seeing his name written on the outside of it. It was Johane's writing. Unmistakably. He thought quickly. Either she lives, or she wrote it before death to be delivered after. Praying in his heart that it was the first of these, he broke the seal and unfolded the letter, holding it carefully as though it were a sacred text.

Its first words sent his head reeling.

Dearest William,
  By this you will know I live.
  A great lump came to his throat. For moment he felt breathless and could hardly read beyond that first short utterance. He read it twice over, if only to make sure that he had interpreted it aright, but of course he had. She had spoken plainly. She was alive. Then he read more.
  I am in the city as I write this and eager to see your face, hear your voice. I pray you come to me where I am in hiding, for I still fear our common enemy who has sworn my death. Shortly, someone will come to tell you where I am. Watch for him. You can trust his word, for he has sworn before God and all angels to keep me safe from harm.
  Yours most faithfully,
  Johane

She was alive, in London, awaiting him. Her letter expressed as he understood it the most profound affection, what he had dreamed her feeling for him. Someone would come to tell him where she was. Soon, the letter said. He was to watch for this messenger. Very well, he would watch all hours if needed.

He hardly slept that night. He tossed and turned and when he slept he dreamed of Johane, dressed elegantly in a fine lady's gown, her face bright with joy and expectation and beckoning him to follow her, which in his dream he did, only to become lost in a kind of maze, hearing her voice but losing sight of her, somewhere ahead of him.

The messenger came the next day, about noon, between two patients with the same complaint. A little man dressed as a common laborer, he had dirt beneath his fingernails, a filthy shirt with holes in it, and a cap too big for his head so that it settled down over his brow.

"Doctor Gilbert, is it?"

Thomas had answered the door and was about to turn the man away before he remembered William's instruction that anyone coming to the door should be admitted, or at least acknowledged by the doctor, no matter his apparent station in life or condition.

"I am Doctor Gilbert."

The unlikely messenger made a stiff, unpracticed bow, obviously unused to such civilities, and said, "then I have been bid to tell you where a certain patient resides, that you may come to minister to her."

"A patient?"

For a moment William wondered if this summons were from Johane, representing herself as a patient, or some other woman, who had happened to hear William's reputation and sought him out.

"Does your patient have a name?"

"She does, Doctor, but I am sworn not to tell it."

Ordinarily, William would have found such coyness annoying in the extreme and sent the man packing, but now he was encouraged. An ordinary patient would have no reason to conceal her identity, would indeed have made sure he knew it, especially if it were a person of standing, a rich merchant's wife, a knight's lady, a woman of the court. In hiding, Johane would have reason to be cautious. Yes, he felt it in his bones, this was the message he had been waiting for.

"Pray tell me where this patient might be found."

"I am asked to have you follow me, sir. It isn't far from here. No more than a half hour's walk through the city."

Thomas had been standing behind him during this exchange, doubtless concerned that so unkempt a personage might prove a danger to his master. William instructed him to fetch his cloak. Dark clouds hovered over the city. Rain was in the offing and had been forecast by learned astrologers as well as others wise to the signs of impending storm.

"Shall I accompany you, Doctor?" Thomas said, eyeing the messenger suspiciously and perhaps eager to redeem himself after his flight from the Surrey farmer and his son, when he and his cousin disgraced themselves by their cowardice.

"No, I shall be well in the company of this man," William answered with firm conviction.

"And will we expect you for supper, Doctor?"

"Probably not. I don't know when I shall return."

He could not imagine finding Johane again and then returning abruptly to his house. Why should he do so? She who was lost had been found. He could hardly contain his excitement.

Fifty-Nine

William followed the little man through the streets until he came to the great bridge that crossed from the city to Southwark, a neighborhood that made him uneasy, since he had once been confined there in one of her majesty's prisons, falsely accused of medical malpractice. A disreputable neighborhood of taverns, bearpits, brothels, and poor houses, Southwark was a slum. William became uneasy, his delight at the prospect of seeing Johane again clouded over with concern for his personal safety. Would he again experience an assault, the theft of his purse, or perhaps even be murdered? Such experiences were not uncommon in Southwark. One heard of them every day. A doctor of his acquaintance had been lured to a house there to see a patient, only to find himself beaten, stripped half-naked, his purse and medical bag stolen from him. He still bore the scars upon his head and face. He said he would not go south of the river again, not even if the queen herself commanded it.

His guide showed no fear. This was obviously a familiar terrain for him, for he walked forward confidently through the narrow streets, looking neither to the right nor to the left, a few steps ahead of William, as though working to make the doctor's passage easier. At last, the man stopped, turned to look at William, and pointed to a small cottage at the end of an uncobbled street.

The filthy weather had begun; first as a gentle sprinkle, now as a steady, cold, rain. The street, such as it was, would soon turn to mud. The cottage had but a single window, no chimney. And no light in the window, although it was surely dark enough for one, it being now nearly six o'clock by William's reckoning.

The guide approached the door and suddenly turned to William.

"She whom you seek, Doctor, is within," the little man said, doffed his cap despite the rain, and hurried back from whence they had come.

William knocked at the door.

A voice, a woman's voice—Johane's voice—asked him to enter.

A single candle showed a small, bare room without hearth or furniture. It was Johane, but not the woman he'd known and loved. He had expected, foolishly perhaps, for her to appear as he had last seen her in his dreams: respectably garbed, as perhaps a merchant's wife, not richly, but with modest collar, a skirt of wool. Now she seemed bedraggled, a woman of the streets, her face colorless, her eyes glazed over, her only adornment a pendant hanging about her neck.

It was a pendant he recognized, a silver dolphin with a boy riding atop it. He could not remember where he had seen it before. Not on her, not around her neck. Suddenly, even before he addressed her, he was filled with loathing for John Broderick, her abuser and abductor. He had done this to her, wrought this terrible transformation. He had not stabbed her to death, the body in the fire was not hers, but he had reduced her to this. A miserable parody of her former self.

He started to approach her, thinking to embrace her and kiss the face he had dreamed of. He wanted next to fall at her feet. Never had he felt so overwhelmed with emotion. He felt tears running down his face. But she held her hand up. She raised a finger to her lips and whispered.

"Stay, Doctor, we are not alone here."

It was then, out of a second room, a human form appeared in a doorway. It was a man, and as he approached the light of the candle, William saw that he was tall man with a badly disfigured face. The scars William recognized as burn scars. The man's hands were also burned. One eye, covered with a patch, had been lost in the fire from which John Broderick had escaped. William could see now that Broderick was not so disabled that could not hold a pistol. The man's hand trembled, but it would not prevent his firing. The weapon was aimed at William's chest. The man's single eye with its unremitting glare showed Broderick's intent to use it.

William had not thought of Broderick while he followed his guide through the city. He had assumed that if Johane were free to write him, to summon him, she was free from Broderick himself. It went through his mind now that she had been forced to summon him, to trap him. All he could see before him suggested that. What a fool he had been, he saw that now, now that it was too late. He had been thinking about his colleague who had been lured to a trap. And it had befallen him as well.

"I have lost much because of you, Doctor. The treasure that you found which should have been mine, my face that now causes children to run in horror from me. I should have killed you on the island when I had a chance."

"You did endeavor so to do, at least your fellows, did," William said. "Leaving me as dead on Little Livesey."

"I will not make that mistake another time. Nothing will I gain from killing you, Doctor, save a deep-seated satisfaction."

William looked at Johane. She was motionless, her face terror-stricken as though she herself was the target of Broderick's pistol.

"Shoot if you will, Master Broderick. Shoot and be done," William said, with more bravado than he felt. "But shoot truly. If you miss me, I will be on you before you have time to reload. I see the scars upon your face, beyond remedy as I'm sure you know. I see the tremor in your hand, a failing of muscle. You didn't leave that burning house unscathed. You can hardly hold the pistol."

"I did not," Broderick said. "Thanks to you."

"Whose body was that we found in the ashes? The one who had died by knife."

"That was a fool, a boy we hired while we were there to look after us. To see to our needs. He was an impudent lad and stole a ring of mine. I killed him the day before you found us. I had not time or mind to dispose of his body. I suppose you found the treasure in the cellar."

"I did find it. Lord Burghley has it now."

"Well, damn his lordship and every other lord in England," Broderick cried, spitting out the words. "May they all rot in hell."

His curse ended with a violent cough. His whole body shook. William could see he had not only been terribly wounded in the fire, but was a sick man. What was it? Some fever?

William looked at Johane. He could see now that her colorlessness was also a symptom. She was sick, too, perhaps from the same affliction that had gripped her captor. Some fever, bred from the foul vapors of the river or spread by rats or the fleas that infected them.

"Before you do what you must do," William said. "May I ask a question?"

William could see that his question took Broderick by surprise. Perhaps he expected that William's next words would be a plea for mercy, a futile appeal surely given the malice in Broderick's single eye, the harshness of his voice, the depth of his hatred and thirst for revenge.

But for a moment Broderick hesitated, his curiosity piqued.

"One question, Doctor, one alone?"

"Why Isaac Silva, that good old man?"

Broderick paused for a moment, then said, "Because he wouldn't tell us what we wanted to know, where the Jews' treasure lay. We knew it was somewhere on the island. His family history told us that."

"Did you consider that he might not know himself?"

"I considered that, but then I feared he would talk, about how we forced him, what we wanted of him. He knew too little to satisfy me, and then too much for his own good."

"He was an innocent man," William said. "A good man."

"He was an old man, Doctor, ready to die by your own admission, I think. Besides, no one mourns a dead Jew."

His comment ended in a fit of coughing. He struggled for breath, the pistol shaking but still lethal. He turned to Johane.

"Tie him up," he managed to say.

Johane looked at Broderick, she hesitated.

"I said, tie him up, woman. Do it, do it now."

Another fit of coughing.

She pulled from her sleeve a piece of rope and approached William.

"Sit on the floor, Doctor," Broderick said. "I'm sorry, but your meddling has left me without means to buy furniture."

William did what he was told. He sat down, held his hands out so that she could bind them. For the first time since seeing her last she touched him, and despite the dire circumstances of this meeting her touch filled him with an irrational hope. Would she really take part in his death? If not for love, would she at least show him mercy?

She tied the length of rope to his feet. Now he was completely bound, helpless to defend himself. Struggle would do no good. Broderick had pointed the pistol at his head, not a foot away. There would be no chance of him missing his target. The ball would enter William's brain, the light would go out, and he would pass into the world to come before he knew it.

"Aim at his heart, Johane." Broderick handed the weapon to Johane. She took the pistol, her face blank of expression as though it were not a deadly weapon but some harmless thing.

Broderick went to the dark corner of the room and picked up something from the floor. It was a container of some sort, a pot. He came over and poured the contents on William's head, his whole body. It was whale oil. William could tell from the smell of it and the feel of it, and then he saw Broderick pick up the single candle in the room and hold it over him, taunting him like a schoolyard bully, although William knew Broderick was far worse than that.

The burn scars had altered his countenance. He could have sat for a portrait of Satan, for so he looked at that moment, a ferocious embodiment of evil. William imagined him as a figure in a tapestry, surrounded by a dozen damned spirits. Sitting in the middle of it all, amid flames, his ghastly visage grinning with triumph and delight at the human suffering to come.

"Fire burned my face, it shall burn yours, Doctor. It shall burn your whole body and that will be the end of you. You will die by fire, a very painful death, or so I have observed and been informed by those knowledgeable in such matters."

William focused his attention on Broderick's face. The fire had made him a monster, or at least revealed, at last, his true nature.

But then, suddenly, there was an explosion. Broderick's hideous countenance changed. He dropped the candle so that it fell away from the oil, and turned to Johane in amazement.

She had fired the pistol. Not at William, but at her abductor.

Broderick lay in a pool of blood, motionless. William had no need to examine him to see that he was dead. He had evaded human justice. He would not evade God's.

William looked up at Johane. She was shaking uncontrollably, but then seemed to come to herself. She dropped the pistol to the floor and then, without a word, knelt down by him and untied him. He could see that she was weak, fading away. Even without touching her, he could feel the heat of fever exuded from her flesh.

When he was free, he took her into his arms and held her, but she had fainted away, her breath labored, her face bathed in sweat. He knew what ailed her, what had ailed Broderick as well. The sweating sickness, *sudo*r *anglicus*. Did he not know the signs? Chills, labored breathing, delusions, death within hours of the onset. The horror of the disease was not merely its consequence, but its inexplicable suddenness, before a priest could be summoned to administer last rites, before its victims knew fully they were ill.

She did not have all the symptoms, but she had enough.

He went over to Broderick, placed the pistol in the dead man's hand. If anyone came, they would think Broderick had killed himself. Before his death, he had been a dying man. Afflicted with the same disease as his prisoner. Had William come later to the house, he would have found Broderick dead. And perhaps Johane, as well.

Sixty

He carried her from the house, the scene of death and sickness, and found an obliging carter who delivered them shortly at his front door. He carried her upstairs and put her in his own bed, where he once dreamed of having her alive and healthy and wanting him. Throughout the longest and darkest night of his life, he attended her, applying cold compresses to her head and her body, to bring down the fever.

Much of the time she was delirious, sometimes calling out Broderick's name, sometimes calling out his own. It was nearly dawn when she fell into a deep sleep, breathing hoarsely as though her lungs were afire.

Then, exhausted, he fell asleep in the chair he had drawn up beside the bed.

When he awoke, he saw by the still-burning candle that she was motionless. Her face glistened with sweat. He listened for a heartbeat. None. She was dead, her body already stiffening, her eyes stark, her mouth agape. He sat down beside her and wept, loud enough that his manservant Thomas, alarmed, came to see what the matter was.

Thomas came in, looked at William, and then saw the body on the bed. He recognized it, remembering the pretty girl his master had treated as a pupil, the girl the household had thought was the doctor's mistress, the girl that accompanied his master to the island of Livesey.

"Mistress Sheldon?"

"It is she, Thomas."

"Is she... ?"

"She's gone, Thomas." William wiped the tears from his face.

"The plague, Doctor?" His servant looked frightened.

"Not the plague, the sweating sickness. No, not just that, John Broderick as well."

"John Broderick, Doctor?"

"Another name for the devil, Thomas." William nodded.

"Is there anything you want, Doctor?"

He told Thomas he wanted nothing. Nothing except to have Johane alive again. Nothing but to have his misery staunched. Nothing but to die with her.

Thomas looked over at the body on the bed and looked questioningly at his master. William drew the sheet over Johane's face. He was surprised that Thomas had recognized her. Disease and death had changed her, as it does all mortals. The sheet covering her afforded a modicum of privacy, but did nothing to calm his rage. Broderick had done this, made her vulnerable to disease, stripped her of her beauty and her dignity, robbed William of his fondest hopes.

Thomas moved back and edged toward the door. Given the danger of contagion it was a prudent move, but William was beyond prudence. If he contracted the disease himself, so be it.

"I'll see to her," he told Thomas. "Don't tell the other servants. No need to frighten them. Send for the undertaker, will you?"

"And a priest?"

"No, she wasn't' a believer. She'll need no rites of any church. God will see to her directly."

He had grieved for her so long, fearing she was dead, now that it had happened, now that the truth was known, he almost felt relief. It was an emotion that shamed him, for it seemed to belittle all the feelings he had for her. He asked himself, *have I loved her?* He answered *yes*. Not since the Dutch girl had he been so enamored, so caught up in pleasant fantasies, not only of love but of posterity—what his strait-laced, dignified father wanted; grandchildren, the perpetuation of the family name. William admitted it. Yes, he had loved her, poor as she was, bringing nothing but herself to the marriage bed.

For him it had been enough, more than enough.

She had called out Broderick's name while dying, but she had called out his as well. And she had killed her abductor with the last of her strength, saving William's life in so doing.

She had spoken more than once of the town where she came from, where her people were buried. He would have her buried there. She had no one, her parents and siblings all dead. The decision, he decided, was his by default.

Her people lived north of London she had once said, in an obscure village of which William had never heard. William secured a carter for the conveyance, a means that brought back memories of his last time in her company, riding together from the island, happy in the thought that Solomon's gold had been recovered and danger was behind them, when it was in truth just before them, standing in their way like an invisible sentinel. Now he rode with Thomas, the carter driving his cart with Johane's coffin covered under canvas.

When they arrived, two days later, William went at once to the town's only church, a modest edifice with a stunted bell tower and named after an obscure saint William had not heard of. The churchyard next to it was deserted, except for a lone man standing at the entrance as though he were waiting for someone. He wore no clerical garb and William guessed he was the sexton. It turned out William was right: so the man identified himself.

The sexton was an old man, nearly seventy by William's estimation, who announced, even before William told him what family he inquired of, that he had been sexton at the church for fifty years and knew every grave within and every family that had buried their dead there.

"What did you say the name was, sir?"

"Sheldon."

"There are Sheldons buried here," the sexton said. "A dozen or more, by my reckoning. I knew the family when they were alive."

"All of them?"

"Yes, sir, all of them, every one."

William told him he had brought Johane Sheldon home, to be buried with her kin. He told him he was a doctor in London. Johane had been his patient. She had died but a few days earlier. Sweating sickness, William said.

"That was Christian of you, Doctor, to make such a journey for a dead patient. Most doctors wouldn't have done it, not unless the patient was a family member, and maybe not then."

"She was a dear friend, not just a patient," William said. "Her name is Johane Sheldon."

"I remember Johane," the sexton said, adjusting his cap and looking into the sky as though he were studying her face in the clouds above him. "I remember when she was a child. A pretty girl, Johane. And clever as a whip. Her family still lives here and will be most saddened to hear she's dead. But then the sweats take the best of us, so we are standing at heaven's gate before we know it."

"Her parents are dead," William said.

"Dead, you say? Since when, sir?"

The sexton turned and looked at William. He seemed bewildered, as if William had suddenly spoken in a foreign language. "Oh no, sir, they still live in the town. Her father is a tailor here, and a good one. His name is Simon Sheldon, her mother is Elizabeth, or Bess as we call her. I've known them for years."

"There must be some mistake," William said. "Johane Sheldon told me her parents were dead. Could this Simon Sheldon be some other relative, say an uncle or a cousin?"

The old sexton laughed. "I assure you, sir—Doctor, is it?—that there's but one family by the name of Sheldon in the town and so it has been for near on twenty years. No, I said, Doctor, that I remembered the girl, Johane, a pretty wench but wild, yes, wild, Doctor. And her father is very much alive, at least he was so when I passed him on the street this very morning and wished him well and he did likewise to me."

"Where can this tailor be found?" William asked.

"Why in town, Doctor, on the high street."

"Where on the high street?"

"Come, Doctor, the way is easy," the sexton said. "I'll show you. Leave the cart and coffin and your manservant where they are and come with me. Johane won't climb out and run off, I warrant you. Don't worry, it's an honest town, no thieves or robbers here. And who would want to steal a coffin, anyway?"

William told Thomas to stay with the cart, despite the sexton's assurances. He followed the sexton down the street of small shops and houses. It was late in the day. Already many of the shopkeepers had shuttered their windows and doors. Presently they came to the shop, where the tailor's sign, newly painted by all appearances, which suggested the sexton had been right. It was a prosperous looking shop in a respectable stretch of the high street, wedged between a greengrocer and a lace maker. The tailor himself, Simon Sheldon, could be seen through the window of the shop, sewing in his chair, surrounded by such a store of clothing, male and female, that it looked like a closet in a rich man's house.

William no sooner saw the man but he wondered, if this was indeed Johane's father, why had she said he was dead? From the sexton's account the mother also lived and now, William suspected, perhaps siblings as well. A whole tribe of Sheldons, whose existence Johane had denied. Why?

"Master Sheldon, this is a doctor from London. He says Johane was his patient and his friend. He's brought Johane's body home. She's dead."

The tailor looked up from his work, glanced first at the sexton, then at William. The man's face showed more resignation than surprise or grief.

William said, "You have my deepest condolences, sir."

For a moment, the man's eyes glazed over. It was clear he was affected by the news of his daughter's death, but he made no comment. He only nodded his head.

"There's a place in the churchyard for her, next to her brother," the sexton said to the tailor.

"Yes, bury her there," the tailor said. "They could not abide each other in life, fought like cat and dog. Maybe they'll do better in death."

William gave the sexton a coin and said he would return to the churchyard toward evening.

"We don't bury at night, Doctor."

"That's alright."

William turned to the tailor. The man had an open, guileless expression. "Master Sheldon, may I speak to you about your daughter, Johane?"

Simon Sheldon paused before answering as though the question presented a difficulty for him. Finally, when the sexton had left, the tailor said he would speak of her, though he admitted that she and the family had not spoken or even seen each other for more than five years.

"That long. May I ask why?" William said.

Sheldon groaned. "You have heard, Doctor, of children disowned by their parents, cut from wills, blotted from memory or mention for some transgression?"

"I have heard of it, and known some sons cast out for reasons compelling, some frivolous. It is not a practice I approve of. Blood should be thicker."

"We did not cast Johane out by any means, upon my oath we did not. She was a willful, high-spirited girl, who resisted mightily her obligations to parent and to the religion in which she was reared. But we did not cast her out. The truth, Doctor, was that she disowned us."

"May I ask for what cause?"

"You may ask and I will say. If you don't hear it from me, you will surely hear it from others in this town, where gossip is rife and secrets, even family secrets, are few."

A woman drifted in from the back of the shop. William knew that was the tailor's wife, Johane's mother, Elizabeth or Bess. She had her daughter's same dark hair, dark eyes, full lips. Add twenty years to Johane's face and there she stood, a quiet loveliness marred only by concern about the well-dressed stranger in the room, the atmosphere of silence and grief, the heavy hand of a momentous event yet to be explained. She looked at her husband, read the bleakness in his countenance the way a good wife can. "What is it, Simon?"

"Bad news."

"Is it Johane?"

"This is a doctor...Doctor?"

"Doctor Gilbert."

"Doctor Gilbert says Johane has died. The sweating sickness. He's brought her body home to us."

The mother's eyes filled with tears but she said nothing, holding her hands over her mouth.

"I am grieved to be the bearer of such bad tidings," William said to the mother. As a physician, William was used to being the bearer of bad news. *Your father is dead*, or *your mother. Your son has not survived his affliction. The child will not live. I have done all that I can.* All that any man can, his learning notwithstanding.

Yet he never got used to it. Who could, seeing the stricken faces, hearing the pounding hearts fail, the knees buckling under the burden of grief and, often, bitter regret at things done or left undone, the things said or unsaid?

The promise of heaven made it no easier.

"You were saying why your daughter...disowned you," William said, hesitant to press on but knowing that he must. Before he could ask the tailor why, the man answered.

"It was because we disapproved of her marriage choice," the tailor said bitterly, "and would not give her our blessing."

For a moment, William could not speak, prevented by an amazement that quickly turned to fear, as though he were standing at the edge of deep gulf and about to step into an abyss. He had not thought her parents were alive. She had admitted to having been abused by her employers, but said nothing of being married.

He thought he might have misunderstood what the tailor said. William looked to the wife, Elizabeth. Her grieved expression had not changed at her husband's words. He had not misunderstood.

"She was married?" William asked, struggling to speak, his mind clouded with confusion and dismay.

It was the wife who answered. "Oh yes, sir, and a poorer choice for a husband she could not have made. He was a dishonest man, a wicked man, a fraudster."

"What manner of fraudster?" William brought himself to ask.

"A manner of magician. He had a long staff with an iron head by which he claimed he could find treasure long buried. He would walk the fields, waving it about, pretending it were effective to that end. He talked many hereabouts into giving money to him in hope some hidden hoard might be found. There was no hoard, Saxon or Roman. There was only this miscreant with his staff, absconding with their money, money they had given him for shares in what was found. And there was worse."

"Worse, Master Sheldon?"

"After he married her, he corrupted her. She became a partner in his... devious practices. How did she die?"

William told him, glad that it was an illness that took her, an act of God and not man. Then he asked the question to which he already knew the answer.

"And her husband's name, Master Sheldon?"

"John, John Broderick. That was the vile fellow's name. Tell me, Doctor, you say my daughter is dead. What of Broderick? Does he still live? I pray God he does not, for he does not deserve life who so corrupted her."

William told him his son-in-law was dead, but he did not say that Johane had killed him, although the tailor might have found some satisfaction in that.

* * *

Johane Sheldon, or Broderick, her married name, was buried the next morning, next to the brother with whom she never got along. The parents did not come to the service. Their hearts were broken, not because of their daughter's death but because of the long and bitter estrangement. The priest from the church spoke words of consolation, the same ancient script he might have used over any Christian's body. He was a man nearly the sexton's age and read the service in a shrill, high-pitched voice and in a manner of English William had never heard.

It occurred to William that she might have been laid to rest beside her husband. That would have been the custom, what might have been expected. But his body had disappeared from the house in another vanishing act, although this was the final one. Doubtless he was at rest now in some obscure place or simply at the bottom of the Thames. More likely the latter. Besides, he thought, Johane had made a choice on that last day of her life. She had chosen William over John Broderick.

That's how he now understood what had happened in that wretched house in Southwark. She had chosen him because she loved him more than the wicked man who had bewitched her. William decided that was how he would see it. He could not bring himself to see it any other way.

Johane was not around to tell him otherwise.

Sixty-One

A man may think he knows the truth of things, only to find himself wrong from the start, that the foundation of his belief is an illusion, a chimera, a house built on the sand of his own imagination. Others may have drawn him into it, and he may blame them for deceiving him, but if he be honest he finds at last that he has deceived himself, shaping reality the way he wants it to be, needs it to be, all evidence to the contrary be damned.

He had seen it a thousand times in his science, in the writings of the ancients and the learned treatises of his contemporaries. Practices and theories unverifiable, illogical, with all the credibility of myth, but mindlessly avowed by wise men who should know better.

And occasionally he found the principle true in his personal experience. He had been duped before, but never so badly.

William thought a lot about this in days to come. He remembered the night on the island when he rescued Johane from Broderick, or supposed he did.

It had been no rescue. He saw that now. There had been no rape nor threat of one. It had been a lovers' tryst, by mutual consent because they were man and wife, doubtless hungry for each other, frustrated by the false roles that divided them and caused them to keep their true relationship a secret.

He remembered, painfully, the night Johane had disappeared. She had not been abducted, never really threatened. Riding off in the cart with the coffin full of treasure. Laughing at him, the poor, pitiful love-sick doctor. And he remembered most painfully the same night he asked Johane to marry him, her reservations expressed so eloquently and falsely, since she was already married—and to William's worst enemy, and sharing every secret of their plan with him.

He had returned to Livesey because she asked him to, but also because Broderick wanted him back, him and his magnets to bring up the treasure. He saw it all now, and he would have laughed out loud at his foolishness, had the pain in his heart not run so deep.

By letter he informed Lord Burghley that Johane was dead and the cause, which seemed innocent enough. The sweating sickness, *sudor anglicus,* a. common enough malady to require no further explanation. People died of it all the time. He also told him that John Broderick was dead—and that Johane had shot him to save William's life.

But of Johane's complicity with the man who was her husband and co-conspirator, he said nothing. Lord Burghley would not like learning that a woman he had also trusted was false, a schemer like her husband, worming her way into his affections and thereby making use of how many persons in this sordid business. Mildred Challoner, who loved her and whom she allowed to love her; the stable boy whose rabid attentiveness she made use of, probably to intercept his letters to Burghley; Lord Burghley himself; and finally William, besotted with love, blind to her treachery, eager to think the best of her and overlook the sins of her past.

No, Burghley didn't need to know all of that. William's misjudgment would not cause him to rise in his lordship's esteem. Burghley had his coveted golden tablet. The queen had the treasure to feed the royal coffers. Broderick was dead. Johane's death was unfortunate, but no result of criminal enterprise. No, Burghley knew all he needed to know.

But William's head was filled with questions. Was Johane really the granddaughter of Isaac Silva? Almost certainly not. Was she an accomplice in Silva's murder? Almost certainly, at the behest of her husband to say the least. Had she ever loved William?

She saved his life. Wasn't that an act of love?

Or perhaps only a deathbed repentance. One good deed to absolve a life of deception. Yet William lived because of it. There was something in that.

Sixty-Two

A month after Johane's death, William received a letter from Lady Challoner. She asked about Johane. Was she returning to the island? Johane had taken her horse. A jeweled pendant was missing from her jewelry box, and she hated to think that Johane had stolen it. Lady Challoner wanted to know if William knew where she was and when she would return.

It was the silver pendant she wore about her neck the night she died. The dolphin with the boy mounted upon it. William remembered now. He had seen it first on Mildred Challoner's neck. William still had it. It was all now that remained of her.

He had Thomas wrap it up in a heavy wool cloth and sent it by special messenger, along with a note saying that Johane had died and that he didn't know about the horse.

He imagined Mildred Challoner receiving the package and weeping at the news. He imagined her not caring that Johane had stolen the pendant or the horse, or even learning, if she should ever, that her beloved companion was not the person she seemed. Or coming to know, should she ever, that she was as much a victim of betrayal as William was, as the great Lord Burghley was, as truth was.

Johane's name meant *God is gracious*. And she was loved by many, despite herself.

THE END